# A LITTLE HELP FROM YOUR FRIENDS

"Down! Down! Take cover!"

Something whizzed past my head. Flu_____ smashed into my open door as I took a k____ ____ he obsidian creatures we'd seen o_ ____ eared in the ruins of the pyr___ __ ___ ___ ear them before while ___ ___ ___ oof windows up, but t_ ___ ___ ___ here was a high-pitched hooti_ ___ ___ ed. Little rocks were coming in strai_ ___ ger ones were being lobbed on high traje___ ___ ke mortar shells. There were so many impacts it was like being in a hailstorm.

I knew time compressed whenever I experienced a vision like that. Only a second or two had passed in the real world, but even zoning out that long had nearly gotten my head taken off. "Listen, whoever you are, I know you're trying to help here, but put the Chosen One magic bullshit on hold until I'm behind cover next time!"

Milo was lying prone on the driver's side. He shouted at me under the truck, "What?"

"I'm not talking to you," I said as I leaned around the door and shouldered Cazador. Two hundred yards away, one of the little baboon-looking bastards was scurrying across the open toward us. The scope was so clear it was like I could reach out and touch him. I put the crosshairs on its chest and pulled the trigger. With the suppressor attached the rifle made nothing but a *whump* noise. The creature fell on its face, skidding through the gravel. Immediately, I had to pull back as half a dozen rocks bounced off my armored door. I waited a second, rolled out again, spotted a pair of glowing jade eyes, and snapped off another shot. One of the lights went out and the thing dropped.

*That's what you get for bringing rocks to a gunfight.*

## BAEN BOOKS by LARRY CORREIA

*Target Rich Environment, Volume 1*
*Target Rich Environment, Volume 2*

### Saga of the Forgotten Warrior
*Son of the Black Sword*
*House of Assassins*
*Destroyer of Worlds*

### The Grimnoir Chronicles
*Hard Magic*
*Spellbound*
*Warbound*

### Monster Hunter International
*Monster Hunter International*
*Monster Hunter Vendetta*
*Monster Hunter Alpha*
*Monster Hunter Legion*
*Monster Hunter Nemesis*
*Monster Hunter Siege*
*Monster Hunter Bloodlines*
*Monster Hunter Memoirs: Grunge* (with John Ringo)
*Monster Hunter Memoirs: Sinners* (with John Ringo)
*Monster Hunter Memoirs: Saints* (with John Ringo)
*Monster Hunter Guardian* (with Sarah A. Hoyt)

### Dead Six (with Mike Kupari)
*Dead Six*
*Swords of Exodus*
*Alliance of Shadows*
*Invisible Wars: The Collected Dead Six* (omnibus)

To purchase any of these titles in e-book form, please go to
www.baen.com.

# MONSTER HUNTER
## SIEGE

## Larry Correia

MONSTER HUNTER SIEGE

A Baen Books Original

Baen Publishing Enterprises
P.O. Box 1403
Riverdale, NY 10471
www.baen.com

ISBN: 978-1-4814-8327-8

Cover art by Alan Pollack

First Baen paperback printing, May 2018
Third Baen paperback printing, November 2021

Library of Congress Control Number: 2017023382

Distributed by Simon & Schuster
1230 Avenue of the Americas
New York, NY 10020

Pages by Joy Freeman (www.pagesbyjoy.com)
Printed in the United States of America

To Larry L.

I would like to thank Reader Force Alpha for all of their feedback. Special thanks to Nicki Kenyon for helping out with all the Russian culture and language parts, and to Mike Massa for information about ships and amphibious landings. And as always, I couldn't do this without Toni Weisskopf and the crew at Baen Books.

# MONSTER HUNTER
# SIEGE

# PROLOGUE

Thirty years ago Auhangamea Pitt invaded the Soviet Union. It wasn't his first time, and even though he ended up getting shot through the brain, this trip wouldn't be his last.

His team had been sent by an agency with no name, snuck there in a submarine that had traveled beneath the Arctic ice. They were all pros, collected from various elite units, and given this temporary additional duty. Pitt was the senior NCO, but when you got loaned to Special Task Force Unicorn you no longer held a rank. Everybody was Mister whatever their assigned fake name was for the duration of the operation.

Only Auhangamea Pitt had been loaned to STFU so many times now, the full-timers just called him the Destroyer. He had developed a reputation over the years. He'd get the job done with minimal drama and could be trusted to never speak of it again. There were plenty of men who were just as good at covert operations as he was, but many of those would be tempted to ask questions afterwards, like how did that guy with the scales breathe fire? Not the Destroyer. Monday morning he'd be back at his day job preparing to fight normal Communists, and he wouldn't give Unicorn another thought until the next time they needed some regular human soldiers to babysit one of their special snowflakes.

They carried no identification, their clothing had no tags, and they were armed with subguns manufactured without serial numbers. They were *sanitized*. If captured, their existence would be denied, and the rest of their miserable lives would be spent being interrogated by the KGB. There would be no international incident, just a shallow grave . . . if they were lucky.

The mission was comparatively straightforward this time. A Task Force asset had been spying on a secure military testing area on an island. The team would take a raft to shore, go inland, and retrieve him. They weren't told why he was there, or why it was important enough to risk sending an attack sub into the Barents Sea to pick him up. Frankly, the Destroyer didn't want to know. Nothing good ever came from asking too many questions about Task Force business. He had seen some weird things while assigned to Unicorn, and didn't like to dwell on it afterwards.

The team had been briefed aboard the sub, given a pickup location, and the code phrases to make sure they had the right man. The Destroyer had violated his personal rule against asking too many questions, because he needed to make sure this particular asset wasn't too *special*. Not that he minded, but if the asset turned out to be a five-hundred-pound monstrosity with a bull's head again, it'd swamp the raft. Plus, the horns might poke holes in the rubber.

However, they were told that this particular asset would appear and act like a normal man *for the duration*. Whatever the hell that was supposed to mean.

It turned out that none of those details mattered anyway, because they walked right into an ambush.

Two minutes into the hopelessly outnumbered and lopsided fight, a rifle bullet struck Auhangamea Pitt through the base of the skull. The 7.62x54R round was fired from a Dragunov rifle approximately two hundred yards away, but it still retained enough destructive energy to easily shatter the bone and fling blood and brain tissue ten feet. His spinal column was severed, and the medulla oblongata—the part of the brain which regulated unconscious functions like respiration and heartbeat—was completely pulverized.

He had been running. Moving target and poor light. It was either a really lucky shot or the Russian sniper was damned good. Either way, it didn't matter; the base of the brain was the best target in the human body. Hitting it with a bullet was like flipping a kill switch. He'd made that shot several times over the years and knew that it meant instantaneous death. Lights out.

Only somehow the lights stayed on as he'd toppled over the edge of an icy cliff. The sixty-foot fall would be more than sufficient to break most of the bones in his body. Going down, he knew he was double fucked, but it wasn't like you could be extra dead. He hit the rocks like a trash bag full of stew.

So when Auhangamea Pitt found himself lying broken in a puddle of blood, paralyzed, but still somehow conscious of the world around him, his first thought was *Well, this is bullshit.*

He lay there for a while, listening helplessly as the rest of his team perished. Once the gunfire tapered off, the Russians walked to the edge of the cliff and shined a light down on him, but it was obvious that he was dead, so they didn't even bother to climb down. Once the flashlights weren't pointed at his eyes, he was able to watch the northern lights. The aurora borealis was so beautiful, this wasn't the worst place to die. There had been plenty of close calls in stinking jungles and third world back alleys that would have been worse, so he watched the pretty lights and waited for death, more mystified than frightened.

He was a warrior and warriors die in war. There was no reason to be a big baby about it. Or maybe the bullet had torn out the part of his brain that processed fear? There was either going to be something next—or nothing. All he knew was that he should have gotten on with it by now.

The being that appeared above him was made of light. At first he thought his brain had finally run out of oxygen, and this was that light-at-the-end-of-the-tunnel thing that the near death experience people always talked about. He'd always thought that sounded like bullshit. Only this wasn't a tunnel; this light was walking toward him. It was a man made of light, so logically the Destroyer figured it was an angel...Considering the life he had led it was a little surprising it wasn't a devil. Most of the people he'd offed must have had it coming after all.

*You are trapped between the world of the living and the world of the dead,* the blob of light said. *Fate has brought you here before us because your bloodline is the key. We will postpone death until the cycle is complete. In exchange you will prepare the God Slayer for the final confrontation between good and evil.*

Which all sounded like hippie nonsense to the Destroyer, but it wasn't like he was in any position to argue semantics. More of the beings had gathered around him. It was a glowing angel beach party.

Then a light touched his head and filled the bullet wound with dreams.

He saw so much, so fast. It wasn't a glimpse into the future so much as a mission packet, and a demonstration of the serious repercussions of failure. He would have a son. That son would die saving the world or he would die trying and the world would fall. It was all or nothing. He was shown the signs which foretold the end, and then he was given a glimpse of the end.

That little peek into the future demonstrated that the part of his brain that processed fear was working just fine. What he saw scared the hell out of him.

*War is coming. The demon beneath the mountain will rise. The Chosen must not be given the truth until then. Once you reveal the truth, we will no longer stave off your death, and death is a jealous thing. The Chosen must find the truth of things on his own. You will prepare him so that he may survive the crucible, but you must not ever fight his battles for him. Can you do this?*

What did they expect him to do with a shattered spine and collapsed lungs? Nod? *Sure.* And then he hoped the light got the message. *I got this.*

*We can only hope so. It is a terrible burden, sending your son to die so that others may live.*

❖     ❖     ❖

"So then I woke up covered in blood and otherwise fine. I got back to the raft, signaled my ride, and went home. Before that mission I used to say there wasn't a godless heathen Communist born who could kill Auhangamea Pitt. Turns out there was, but even then it took the jackass a few decades to get it to stick. So that's it, boys." Dad sighed as he leaned back in his chair. "That's how we got to this. Now you know."

My father, my brother Mosh, and I were sitting around Dad's kitchen table. We had been there listening to him talk for an hour. I had absorbed the story better than my brother—who was looking incredulous and bewildered—but to be fair, I'd seen a lot more supernatural stuff than he had.

"That's it?" Mosh asked. "Holy shit, Dad, you just told us a story about you coming back from the dead, war angels versus mountain demons, prophecies about the apocalypse, and *that's it?*"

Dad shrugged. "I don't think they picked me because I'm inclined to be flighty."

Mosh just sat there, mouth open, trying to come to terms with what he'd just heard. "Okay... That is so *metal.*" Then Mosh asked the question I lacked the courage to. "So the story is told. Do you really think you're going to kick the bucket now?"

"Maybe... Beats me."

"Aren't you scared?" Mosh asked.

The tough old bastard actually laughed. "More like relieved. I've been carrying this secret a long damned time. Those things haunted my dreams off and on your whole lives. Little glimpses of the world dying if I dropped the ball. I guess they thought I needed the reminder to stay on task. Look, dying don't scare me. I've been retired for years. It's basically the same thing. By the way, don't you dare tell your mom I said that." Dad turned and looked me square in the eyes. "Better question, are you?"

"Scared?" I asked.

"Sure." He'd figured out that I was the son this all fell on. If his supposed angels were telling the truth, I would be the one giving up my life to save the world. "Are you scared?"

"I'd be a fool not to be."

"Good answer. It's on you now. I did what I could. Was it perfect? Hell no. But I look at you two and how you turned out and all I can do is hope it'll be good enough. I didn't know exactly what was coming, and I didn't just want to raise killers. That's easy. I tried to raise *good men*. Owen, from what I've heard, you've seen some shit. You'll be ready to face whatever comes. Remember, you've got the training, the skills, and a hell of a good crew at your side. You've got enough stubbornness to never back down, but try to have enough humility to learn from your screwups." Then he looked toward Mosh and scowled. "David... Well, you've still got a lot to learn."

If he had said that to the old Mosh, it would have turned into a protest, and then a fight against the man who never thought anything was good enough. Maybe my little brother would storm off for a few years and become a rock superstar just to spite him or something... Only a few days ago my brother had watched a casino get sucked into another dimension, so right now he conceded the point. "Fair enough."

"So what happens next?"

"They didn't exactly brief me on the timeline. There

are signs. Some have happened." He began ticking off on his fingers. "Time got broken. That demon's symbol began appearing. More bad things are coming. You're going to make them right. It is time you take the fight to him."

"Anything in particular I should be watching out for?"

"I've got a general sense of dread and a suspicion a whole lot of bad things are involved, but it's fuzzy after the demon starts putting his mark on things. Destiny only gets you so far. My gut feeling is that what happens next is still up in the air, but this son of a bitch is so evil, nothing is off the table. He'll hide in plain sight. Come at you sideways. There's nothing he won't do against you. You'll figure out the rest as you go ... Anybody else want a beer?" Dad got up and walked to the fridge.

"No thanks, Dad." Mosh had been steadily drinking himself to death since the Condition had cut off his fingers, but I think he'd gone cold turkey since we'd escaped Las Vegas, so hopefully he was getting his life in order. To be fair I had to remember I had a head start in the apocalypse business; my poor brother was still playing catch up.

Dad opened the refrigerator door, stared at the contents for a moment, and then collapsed.

# CHAPTER 1

*One Week Later*

I was carrying a bucket full of severed limbs and human organs to the incinerator. Say what you will about Agent Franks, but whenever he visited MHI, it was never boring.

It had been a busy night. The Body Shack was trashed. As I dumped the contents of the bucket into the fire, Gretchen the Orc was still collecting bloody towels and surgical implements, while Milo sprayed down the floor with a hose. Red blood mingled with the glowing blue of the legendary Elixir of Life, and it all went swirling down the drain.

"This is why we need to hire another janitor," Milo said.

This was where we'd put Franks back together. The real mess was where Earl Harbinger and Agent Franks had decided to reenact Frankenstein versus the Wolfman. In *my house*. It had been an epic battle, which I had abruptly cut short by driving a truck through the wall and running over them both. My wife—the lovely Julie Shackleford—had gone back to examine the extensive damage those two had inflicted on her beloved ancestral family mansion. I'm glad she had left while Gretchen and Milo were trying to save Franks, because after all the work she'd personally put into restoring that old place by hand, she might have shot Franks in his big smug face when he woke up. She wasn't particularly happy with Earl either.

Using a secret recipe found in Franks's possession, Trip Jones had cooked up a vat full of the Elixir of Life, which Gretchen had then used to bring Franks back to life. Right after we had gotten Franks put back together with spare parts, a mysterious stranger had arrived, but Earl said that he was from a secret order of Catholic warrior monks, and they were *all right*. Then our uninvited guest had borrowed a demon tracking relic we had just had lying around, and gone off to do whatever it was mystical holy warriors do.

Like I said...Franks? Never dull.

Not that regular Monster Hunters were slouches. I was still on crutches from fighting a nightmare dragon in Las Vegas. It had been one hell of a month.

"You said Franks wanted to trade information for our old broken demon tracker thingy." Milo looked up from spraying down the stainless steel operating table and saw me reading. "So what did you get? He used up all my best cadavers so I hope it's good."

Now that we were done saving Franks and he'd gone on his merry way, we could get to the important stuff. I slammed the door on the incinerator and pulled the piece of paper out of my pocket. There was an address written on it in Franks's oddly small handwriting.

"He said this was for a *multidimensional research facility* that worked with the MCB."

"'Multi,' like they research other dimensions, or 'multi' like it exists simultaneously in other planes of existence?"

That was a fair question. In this business it really could go either way. "Well, the address is in Albuquerque, so I'm assuming study. You know how sensitive MCB gets about portals."

"For once I can't blame the Feds for being jumpy." Milo was our resident mad scientist, but even he didn't like messing with black magic. "So what are we supposed to do? Take a tour?"

"Supposedly they can tell us what happened to the Hunters we left behind at the Last Dragon."

"Whoa..." MHI had two Hunters missing in action. Between the other companies there were a dozen more whose bodies had never been found. "Good trade."

"We'll see. Franks is a dick, but he's honest about it. If he says there's a way, there's a way. I'm going to go find out what's at this address." I started hobbling for the door. I had one forearm casted and one foot in a big plastic booty, but I'd left my crutch leaning in the corner. Gretchen made a grumbling noise beneath her mask. She had been giving me vile tasting orcish healing potions for the last week so the bones would knit faster, but she'd warned me to take it easy. I had a hunch that was going to be a challenge. "Yeah, I know, Doc. Working on it."

Gretchen just clucked disapprovingly and went back to picking up entrails.

A little while ago I'd had to make a tough call. Abandon some good men to certain death in order to dust off and try to get a monster to chase us, or stick around to evacuate them and possibly get everyone killed. It hadn't been an easy decision, but it had been the right one. I'd sacrificed a few to try and save many. Luckily the gamble had paid off and hundreds of us had made it back alive.

But it haunted me.

Everyone assumed VanZant and Lococo were dead. The Hunters assembled at the first annual International Conference of Monster Hunting Professionals had been some of the toughest, hardest, most experienced monster-killing badasses ever assembled, yet when the Last Dragon casino got sucked into the nightmare realm, many of us had bought it, and the rest had barely escaped with our lives. We'd only been stuck there for a few *hours*. How in the world could a handful of Hunters survive a land of shifting nightmare fog that made your worst nightmares come to life, for nearly two *weeks*?

Even if by some miracle they were still alive, they were beyond our reach. Creating portals to the other side was the sort of thing done by necromancers and insane wannabe wizards. It never ended well. So even if they'd survived somehow, we couldn't help them. And that was almost worse.

But logic didn't matter. These were my people, so I had to know.

Originally I was just going to look the address up myself, but you don't make it very long as a Monster Hunter without a healthy amount of paranoia. The most wanted fugitive in the world had given this to me. And he was being pursued by Stricken, who was some kind of superspy with a stable full of monster assassins, who'd already screwed my company over multiple times, with the full weight and authority of the US government behind him. The last thing I wanted to do was draw Stricken's malevolent gaze again. I think he only spared my life in Las Vegas on a lark.

My computer knowledge extended to Excel spreadsheets and that was about it, but hidden in the basement of the MHI compound's main building was our IT department. Since it consisted of a single internet troll, it probably shouldn't be called a department, but when he wasn't distracted being a completely awful contrarian douchebag to random strangers on Facebook, Melvin actually did pretty good work.

This section was off-limits to newbies and anyone else who might flip out if they knew we employed an eight-foot-tall monster to keep our network running. I used my crutch to bang on the door. It was almost four in the morning, but as far as I could tell, Melvin didn't actually sleep. Sleep would cut into his *Call of Duty* time.

"Hey, troll! I need you to do something."

"Go away!" Melvin shouted through the door. I could hear explosions and gunfire. "Melvin is on epic kill streak! *Epic!*"

After Trip had cut a deal with this thing, we'd learned pretty fast that you couldn't interact with a troll like a regular employee. There was no reasoning with internet trolls. You had to establish dominance. I pounded on the door again. "Listen, you PUFF-applicable pile of garden hoses, get off your lazy ass."

"Bite me, accounting department. Talk to Melvin's supervisor."

"Fine. I'll go get Holly."

Originally we'd tried using Trip as Melvin's supervisor, since he'd been the one to give Melvin a job offer—under duress—but Trip was just too damned nice. Now Holly, on the other hand, she scared the crap out of Melvin. The video game was suddenly silent. Two seconds later the door creaked open. The hideous green monster loomed over me. His snaggly teeth were coated in so much old sugar that they'd begun growing moss. His eyes were blinking and twitchy, fueled by dozens of Red Bulls.

"How may Melvin serve you today, Mr. Monster Hunter?" He shuffled aside so I could enter.

"Research."

When we had first hired Melvin, our *network* was one box under Dorcas's desk and this had been a storage room. Now the place was filled with server racks and blinking lights. His desk was an old door on top of a stack of cinder blocks, but there were six monitors on top of it. We'd spent a lot of money on hardware for him, but when he wasn't being useless he could actually be kind of handy. It all worked out financially because we didn't actually pay Melvin in anything other than snack foods and bandwidth.

"It smells like troll in here."

"Odor of excellence," he wheezed. "Should bottle and sell as Axe body spray. Make *millions*."

"Focus, Melvin. I've got an address. I want to know everything about it. What's there, who owns it, who works there, what they're doing, and every possible way to get in."

"Is your Google broke, scrub? This insults Melvin's leet skillz."

"The hard part is you have to do it without raising any red flags. Nobody can know we're interested in this."

"Who you worried spying? NSA? CIA?"

"Special Task Force Unicorn."

"Oh..." The troll let out a long hissing noise. I think that indicated fear. *Good.* "Melvin no like Unicorn."

"Nobody likes them, for good reasons." Stricken had kidnapped Earl's girlfriend, used us all as pawns in Las Vegas, and if what Franks was telling us tonight was accurate, even had Agent Myers killed. I still didn't know how I felt about that. "So don't get caught."

A couple of hours later I went upstairs armed with fresh intel. The sun wasn't up yet, but there were a handful of Hunters hanging out around Dorcas's desk. Somebody had brewed a pot of coffee. They were all too excited talking about the events of the night and the potential ramifications to go back to bed. Trip and Holly were there. So was my brother.

"Hey, man. Where you been? I thought you'd gone back to help Julie. Your place is *trashed.*" Mosh offered me a cup of a coffee, but distracted, I brushed past and went to the memorial wall instead.

Every Hunter who had ever been killed or gone missing in action since the founding of MHI had a spot on this wall. There had been a lot of silver plaques when I'd started, and we had added too damned many since.

"What are you doing, Z?" Holly asked.

The shiniest, newest plaques were from Las Vegas. We were so used to losing people that we were obnoxiously efficient about getting these made quickly. I found the two I was looking for. *John VanZant. Jason Lococo.* Everybody gave me a curious look as I pulled those off the wall.

"Not yet."

And then I limped off. I had a flight to catch.

An hour later I was at the Montgomery Regional Airport, sitting on a bench, waiting. I had hired a private jet and was waiting for the pilot to arrive. MHI owned its own cargo plane, but since this might be a wild goose chase, I didn't feel comfortable taking advantage of company assets. I was doing this on my own dime. What Melvin had turned up made me suspicious that either Franks had been yanking my chain, or this was some sort of clever secret squirrel cover-up. It just didn't seem like the sort of place they'd hide some weirdo paranormal research facility. Regardless, I'd grabbed a go-bag, sent Julie a text that I needed to take a quick trip, and then driven straight to Montgomery's little airport.

While I was killing time, I checked my emails. There was another one from Mom about Dad. It wasn't good. I put my phone away. It was all secondhand bad medical reports. I couldn't look at that now. Damn, I was tired.

"Bad news?"

Surprised, I looked up to see Julie standing there, glasses perched on the end of her nose, big green duffel bag over one shoulder, cleaned up from earlier—though she'd missed a spot and had some dried blood under one ear, yet still gorgeous as usual. Her long dark hair was tied up haphazardly for once, so I could see the black line on her neck. That meant she must have been really weary, because she usually tried to hide the Guardian's mark.

I blinked stupidly. "What're you doing here?"

"Taking a trip apparently." My wife gave me a tired smile. "I got your text." She dropped her bag on the floor and then flopped down in the seat next to me. "Cryptic."

The waiting room was nearly deserted at this hour. Nobody was close enough to eavesdrop. "I figured if Stricken suspected public enemy number one was going to try and make contact with us, all our communications are being monitored."

"More than likely. From the look on your face though, whatever you were reading's not good. Your dad?"

"Yeah. He's not doing any better." His condition had been degrading steadily ever since he'd spoken to me and Mosh. His borrowed time was up, his purpose fulfilled. At least that awful, shitty part of his prophecy had proven to be true. "I don't know what to do."

Julie put her hand on mine. "I'm so sorry."

I changed the subject. "What are you doing here?"

"If I sat around any longer looking at what's left of our place, I was going to lose it, so I might as well do something useful. I was finally getting the old house looking half decent. Damn Earl."

"Where is he, anyway?"

"I think he's tailing Franks to see if he can find Heather."

That was ballsy, but sounded about right for Earl. "We should go help."

"I asked. Earl very specifically said we're not supposed to. He made a deal; MHI sits this one out."

"You say so." I hoped our boss knew what he was doing.

"Trying to avenge the love of his life, I can forgive him jumping the gun and wrecking the house, but Earl's paying for the repairs. *All* the repairs. Franks's blood is everywhere. I'm hiring contractors for that mess. So in the meantime, I'm going with you."

"But you're—"

"A couple months pregnant, not a fragile porcelain doll. I come from a long line of hardy Southern gunslinger moms who squeezed out babies and then got right back to work, so don't try and coddle me. You're the one that's supposed to be taking it easy, not me."

"Okay." We'd had this discussion before. I had finally gotten her to agree to avoid active monster hunting for the safety of our kid. "This shouldn't be anything dangerous."

"Honestly, I think I should at least be able to provide sniper fire until I can't buckle my armor anymore."

"You promised," I reminded her. And of course, minutes after I'd finally gotten her to make that promise, we'd had Frankenstein versus the Wolfman in our living room.

"I'm kidding. Look, I'm still coming to terms with the idea. Being a mom doesn't seem real yet. I wasn't exactly expecting this. Having a family? With all of the weirdness in our lives?"

She was mostly worried about the Guardian's curse. We still didn't have a clue what that was doing to her, let alone our baby. "Your folks were Monster Hunters and you turned out great."

"Just as long as the two of us don't end up like my parents."

"That's not going to happen." At minimum, my Chosen thing and her Guardian thing meant we couldn't be turned into vampires, but I was pretty sure she was speaking *in general*. There are plenty of ways to go out badly that didn't involve becoming one of the undead.

Julie changed the subject. Between me not wanting to dwell on my dad and her not wanting to worry about impending parenthood, pretty soon we would be talking about the weather. "Melvin told me what you're looking for. I just hope you aren't getting your hopes up."

"Realistically, I know they're gone. But Lococo had a daughter. It would be nice to tell her I know for sure what happened to her dad."

"I've known VanZant for years. He's one of our best. We owe it to them. But these people actually knowing anything useful is a long shot. This trip will probably end up as begging academics or arguing with government employees. Negotiation is my job. You, on the other hand, have a spotty track record for diplomacy."

She handled all of MHI's contracts and could charm or schmooze just about anybody. I was good with spreadsheets. "That's a diplomatic way of putting it."

"Exactly." She laid her head on my shoulder and snuggled up against me. "I didn't get a lick of sleep because of stupid Franks. Wake me up when it's time to waddle to the plane."

"Whatever. You don't even look pregnant yet. But I bet in a couple months you'll have the sexiest waddle ever."

"Damned right I will."

I was glad she was here.


Julie rang the doorbell.

The way Franks had made it sound I'd been expecting something fancy. Like a brutalist concrete building that could serve as a bunker, or something high tech with lots of black glass and swoopy architecture, that sort of thing. Multidimensional research sounded impressive.

I hadn't been expecting a house in a middle-class suburb of Albuquerque, New Mexico. It wasn't even that big a house. According to Melvin it was twenty-five hundred square feet of brick, stucco, and lame. It was owned by a real estate company that was more than likely a shell corporation for the MCB and had been for a few years. There was zero indication that there was a secret-tunnel network beneath it hiding anything interesting, like a supercollider, or a star gate, or something. This was the kind of street that had minivans parked on it. Instead of lawns everybody had sand, gravel, or cactus. Across the street and two houses down a little girl was peddling Girl Scout cookies.

"It's not exactly Cheyenne Mountain," Julie stated as she rang the doorbell again.

"I don't know. Check out cookie girl."

"She's adorable."

"*Too* adorable. She's eyeballing us. I bet she's an undercover MCB sharpshooter."

"The pigtails are a dead giveaway," she agreed sarcastically.

"You've got to admit that's a pretty high-speed, low-drag haircut."

"I rocked that look when I was that age." Julie gave up on the bell and gave the door a firm knock. It wasn't even a metal security door or anything. Just regular soft wood. If I hadn't had one foot in a plastic booty, I could have kicked it open in one try.

We had an MHI team in New Mexico already. Julie had rightfully pointed out that there was no reason we couldn't have asked them to do this and saved us a trip. Of course, she'd said that, but she hadn't tried to talk me out of it either. I think we both needed to feel like we were doing something proactive.

The blinds in the nearest window shook as somebody peeked through at us. They quickly snapped shut.

"I hope this isn't Agent Franks's idea of a joke and something horrible lives here," Julie muttered.

"If we're about to get eaten, I'm glad my last act of defiance was getting Mosh to tattoo our smiley face logo on him."

There was the sound of locks being undone, and then the door creaked open. It was dark inside. All I could make out was part of a face and one eye. There was a security chain latched on the inside, but that was a laughable safety feature to a three-hundred-pounder like me. The door must have been even thinner than I thought, because he had heard what I'd said. "You know Agent Franks?"

"We're passingly familiar," Julie said, not wanting to commit to having just seen the thing with the quarter billion dollar PUFF bounty on his head. "Is this—"

"He's not here, is he?" The guy inside sounded young, but breathy, like he was chunky and needed an inhaler. He tried craning his head around to see past me through the crack. "Agent Franks scares me. I don't want any trouble."

"You've not been watching the news lately, have you? Franks is indisposed. Listen, sir, we were told you might be able to help us with something."

He stopped his futile scanning for Franks long

enough to take a good look at my wife. "Hang on...
Are you Julie Shackleford?"

"I am."

"*The* Julie Shackleford?"

As opposed to all the other Julie Shacklefords?
"That's me."

"No way!" He quickly closed the door, there was a
rattle as he undid the chain, and then he flung the
door wide open. "I'm a huge fan!"

I about fell off the porch. He had one eye. Not
like one eye, missing the other, sort of thing, but
one great big eye right in the middle of his lumpy,
misshapen face.

"You're a cyclops," Julie stated calmly.

But despite being a fearsome monster of myth and
legend, he was just kind of standing there, grinning
stupidly. The cyclops was a big fellow, portly, but only
about as tall as I was. In a typical illustration they'd
be wearing a fur loincloth and carrying a tree for a
club. This one was wearing a fuzzy blue bathrobe,
sweat pants, and bright green Crocs.

"And your biggest fan! Oh man, I can't believe
this!" He actually clapped his hands together with
glee. "Yay!"

Across the street, cookie girl had caught up with
us. She'd rightly figured I had the look of a mark who
would purchase my body weight in Samoas if given the
opportunity. When she saw the cyclops she screamed,
dropped her Thin Mints, and ran for her life.

"Whoops! I'm not supposed to be seen by the
neighbors without my disguise. I could lose my exemption." The cyclops had great big buck teeth. "Oh well.
Come in. Come in!"

Julie and I exchanged glances. Cyclops were supposed to be these rare, badass giants, carrying off heroes to dark caves to be devoured. He was just so goofy-looking that I hadn't even been tempted to reach for my gun. I had no idea how long ago it had been since a cyclops had caused trouble, nor did I know the last time a Hunter had collected PUFF on one. Decades? The scholarly types had figured them for extinct.

Julie shrugged. *What the hell? Why not?* She entered the home. I sighed, then followed.

Other than the large number of comic book posters stuck on the walls, the interior of his house was utterly normal. He had a scraggly beard, but it only seemed to be growing out of his neck. Judging by the orange dust all over him, and the bag on the couch, he'd been eating Cheetos. The TV was paused on some anime.

Once we were inside he closed the door and locked it behind him.

"This is such an honor. I'm Poly. Welcome to Albuquerque."

"It is a pleasure to meet you, Pauly."

"No, Poly. It's short for Polyphemus. Sorry. I'm totally geeking out. Julie Shackleford is in my house."

"I've never met a cyclops before," Julie said with the utmost politeness.

"Aren't you supposed to be gigantic?" I asked, but Julie immediately gave me a look like *don't mess this up*. Don't blame me. I was just wondering if maybe we'd found a midget cyclops.

"Us being giants is a hateful inaccurate stereotype that exists because the ancient Greeks were racist.

And super short. It's all relative." He turned back to Julie. I swear the cyclops was going full-on fan boy. He was damned near giddy. "I've never met anyone from MHI before, let alone a legend. Do you know Milo Anderson? Oh my gosh . . . You totally know Milo Anderson!" He looked me over with his huge gelatinous eyeball. "And you're Owen Pitt."

"That's me."

He shrugged. "That's cool I guess."

*Ouch.*

"If you don't mind me asking, how do you know about us, Poly?"

"Remote viewing and MCB reports mostly, but you're way prettier in person." The cyclops gulped. He began to blush. "I'm sorry. That probably sounded rude."

"That's fine," Julie said quickly. I was about to interject *No, it isn't*, but she continued. "Remote viewing, you do that for the MCB?"

"Mostly. I like when they ask me to look at stuff you were involved in. It's better than Netflix. You're the best."

Julie nodded. That was awkward. "Thanks."

"They captured me, but Agent Myers got me a provisional PUFF exemption because I can see some things humans can't. They pay me to look at pictures and tell them stuff. It's a sweet deal. It sure beats living in a cave and stealing goats. And I get to help the heroes!" He sounded really proud as he began to lumber down the hallway. "Come on. I'll show you."

One side of the hall was filled with movie posters. The other side was action figures, still in the packaging. I'd have to introduce this guy to Trip. They'd get along great. Probably start a weekly game night.

"What do you mean by 'help the heroes'?" Julie asked.

"Agent Myers and his guys. They're super nice. Well, except for Franks. Obviously. He's kind of a dick. I was locked up in this prison with all sorts of awful monsters and these other guys were doing experiments on my brain. They weren't nice at all. Even threatened to pluck my eye out. Can you believe it? But after that big rift in Alabama a couple years ago, Agent Myers thought I could help, so he snuck me out of the prison in the middle of the night. I've been here ever since."

"Why did he do that?"

"Because us cyclops can see things humans can't. That's why there aren't many of us left. Once humans figured that out they started stealing us. Most of us aren't helpful and nice like me, so humans just suck their eyeball out to make into drugs to give other humans to try and get our powers. It never works good. When they try to see far away, human eyes are too wimpy and start squirting blood."

"Gross." And here I'd always thought all those supposed Cold War remote-viewing conspiracy theories were nonsense. We stopped, closed door on one side, bathroom on the other. The sink was covered in tubes of acne cream. "What kind of things can you see?"

"Like they'll tell me there's a rift, and I can see into the other side a little. Or something will happen, and they'll take pictures of it from a satellite, and then Agent Myers will have me look at the pictures and tell them all the things they can't see. Like spirits and ghosts, or what the people in the picture were saying at the time."

"You can *see* conversations. In the past?"

"Sometimes. He gets super happy when I do that. Agent Myers or one of his friends check in on me once in a while, but I'm not allowed to talk to anybody else from the government. Agent Myers said I could get in a lot of trouble if I do that."

This all sounded like it wasn't the government hiding him, but he was being hidden from the government. Had Myers stolen Poly from STFU? Judging by our humble surroundings, I had a sneaky feeling this was one of Myers's off-the-books operations. The poor cyclops didn't even know that his benefactor was dead.

"Are you allowed to leave?" I asked.

"Nope." Poly pulled up one leg of his sweat pants to display an ankle monitor. "I can go in the backyard or as far as the mailbox, but only if I wear my disguise. No outside world past the mail box for me... But I can talk to you guys, right? I mean, you're Julie Friggin' Shackleford, for Zeus's sake!"

"Absolutely," Julie agreed, and she was so nice she probably felt guilty for taking advantage of Myers's captive cyclops nerd.

Poly opened the door. There was a drawing table in the middle of the room. Every wall was covered in maps, from floor to ceiling, most of them the regular, printed folding kind, but then there were others that appeared to have been drawn by hand. Those maps were almost childlike in their simplicity, with cartoon terrain features, and place names with rough letters that looked drawn rather than written.

"Sorry. I don't draw good." Poly held up his fingers and wiggled them. They looked like fat sausages. "I can't see everything that comes through the holes

in the world, but I see some, and when I see them
early enough, that makes Myers really happy. Humans
think two eyes is good, but your eyes suck. Depth
perception isn't all that. Two eyes, but only one world.
Cyclops have one eye, but we can see two worlds at
the same time. It's flipped. You can only see what's
in front of you. It gets blurry but us cyclops can see
things far away, through walls, on the other side of
the world—even sometimes through time if we look
hard enough." Poly turned to me and grinned. His
front teeth were way too big, like a beaver. "I can
tell you know what seeing through time is like, huh,
Owen Pitt?"

"Yeah, a little."

Julie took out her phone and started taking pictures
of the maps. Poly didn't seem to mind. I spotted a
map of Las Vegas on top of the nearest pile and
walked over to it. A circle had been drawn around
the Last Dragon.

"Agent Myers asked me to focus extra hard there,
to make sure nothing else bad was sneaking through."

Next to it was one of the hand-drawn maps. "Last
Dragon" had been scribbled on that page next to a
big black X. It took me a moment to realize that map
wasn't of any place on Earth. The terrain features
were meaningless scribbles. The place names were
gibberish. "Julie, check this out."

"That's when it went into the bad place where
nightmares come from," Poly said. "It's one of the
between worlds. You've both been there, so you know.
I don't like looking there at all. It is sad and scary
and everything that lives there is mean and hungry.
You were lucky to get away."

This was what we'd come for. "Not all of us got out. We left some friends behind. Can you tell what happened to them?"

The cyclops nodded vigorously. It made his double chins jiggle. "Some got stuck but some died. That left seven."

"Seven are still alive?" Julie gave me an incredulous look.

"They sure are, Julie Shackleford. The door is closed, so I can't see clear no more. But human lives glow. 'Embers,' Agent Myers called them. Humans in a bad place are sparks in the dark. So I know seven good guys remain."

I believed him. It was like a punch to the gut. There were survivors. But we couldn't help them. That was almost worse. "Can you see how they're doing? Did they find a place to hide? Are they safe?"

"Sorry." The cyclops shrugged his meaty shoulders. "It's like windows. Open I can see fine. When the blinds are closed I can see the light coming through, but I can't see what they're doing. Next time they open up, I'll be able to see probably."

Julie was staring at the map of the Nightmare Realm. "What the hell do we do now?"

Myers had sprung this cyclops to keep an eye on rifts. It was worth a shot. "Next time they open... Poly, do you know any other ways into the Nightmare Realm?"

He shook his head in the negative. That made the jelly of his great big eye slosh. It made me a little nauseous to look at. "I can't watch the whole world at once. That would be silly. I can only see places when I look at them hard, and Agent Myers calls and tells me where to look. I guess there's tiny ones all the time, where the little nightmare thingies pop out, but nothing you could squeeze a human through. Though come to think of it, there's . . . No. Never mind."

"What is it, Poly?" Julie gently coaxed.

"There's one place that opens every year when the stars line up right, but it is too scary, even for Julie Shackleford and MHI. If you go there you would all die. And that would be super sad."

I started to say something, but Julie shook her head. *Right. Diplomacy.* I was too impatient and pushy, but I wasn't too proud to admit it. I had a sneaky feeling that if I was the one interrogating Poly, we wouldn't have even made it this far.

"It's fine, Poly. We'll be careful."

"I don't have many friends. All the other cyclops have gone away. Agent Myers is my friend but he's so busy he doesn't visit much. You could be my friend, Julie Shackleford. But if you go there, you'll die, and we can't be friends if you're dead."

He was wrong there. I had a bunch of friends who were dead.

"Just because you tell us about it doesn't mean we'll do anything dangerous with that knowledge. We just want to understand." Julie was very patient. She was going to be a great mom. "It's very important to us. Please?"

"Okay." Poly was clearly agitated. "Come on. I'll show you Agent Myers's *Big Secret Project.*" He wandered from the office back into the hall. "He said if I did a good enough job watching for this one special bad guy he'd put me in a cosplay disguise and take me to DragonCon. I want to be in the parade."

The other bedroom was set up similar to the first, only even more cluttered if that was possible. One entire wall was taken up by a big map of the world. Maybe it was because there were a bunch of pushpins stuck all over it that it reminded me of the map we had started putting together in a casino hotel room, based upon odd cases and rumors from the world's Monster Hunters, all involving an unknown underground menace.

Julie realized the same thing. "It's like Earl's mobilization map for all the underground anomalies... All the ones we know about are flagged here. Only there's a lot more locations on this one than on ours."

"Things come crawling out of the dirt. They've been getting busier. Every week Agent Myers calls and gives me a new place to watch and I tell him if I saw anything. There are so many now I can't hardly keep up looking at them. Agent Myers tries not to act scared when he visits, but I can tell he's afraid."

It was color coded. The yellow pins seemed to correspond with the various sinkholes and tunnels that had opened up, leaving out of the way rural villages entirely depopulated. There was a yellow pin in the ocean where the Chinese navy had blown up an underwater city. There was a black pin at DeSoya Caverns and another one in New Zealand where we'd fought the Arbmunep. There were also green and white pins all over, and one big red thumbtack near the top.

"Green is for Fey. They're weird and tricky. Black is for Old Ones. They hurt my eye. Agent Myers says for me never to look at their side because I'll go crazy. White is for stuff Agent Myers wasn't sure about."

"Yellow?"

"Agent Myers doesn't know much about them, just

that the same symbol shows up. Wherever it is, I can't see around it very good. They belong to a very bad thing that got woke up when time got broken."

"Crap."

"Don't blame yourself," Julie told me. "If you hadn't used the artifact, then Lord Machado would have won and we'd all be doomed anyway."

"Still . . ."

"The different color pins don't like each other," Poly said. "They fight the good guys, but they fight each other too."

I knew our fate was intertwined with the various warring cosmic factions, I'd just never seen it so laid out and color coded for my convenience before. "What makes these places special?"

"These are where worlds rub against each other and the borders get fuzzy. Sometimes monsters come through there."

"There's that many?" Julie was a little taken aback. "I mean, we know it happens, but still . . . That's insane."

There were a cluster of different color pins stuck in Natchy Bottom. That I could believe.

"Humans call them places of power," Poly offered helpfully. "Black magic is stronger there."

"We're passingly familiar with the concept," I muttered. "What about this big red guy?"

"That's the one that made Agent Myers the most scared. I'm supposed to look at it every single day to see if stuff is happening there. Sometimes there are things on top. But I think the scary part is what's beneath."

"What's beneath there, Poly?" Julie asked as she took a picture of the big map.

"The end of the world I think." Water began pouring

out of his big squishy eye. I realized Poly had started crying. He sniffed. "A city of monsters. A very bad thing lives there, maybe the baddest thing of all, come to ruin everything. Agent Myers thinks the bad thing is there for now, but if he leaves I'm supposed to call right away. He's the one that's been making the yellow pins show up, to test the good guys, so he can learn how to beat the heroes. Agent Myers is very afraid of him, and he's the bravest human I know."

Julie touched him gently on the shoulder. "It's going to be okay." That seemed to calm him down. "What can you tell us about the bad thing?"

"Not much. He's hard to look at. It's like he's in more than one place at a time, and more than one time in one place. Though I think he's mostly stayed there since he woke up. But he has lots of almost as bad things working for him, and they come and go all over the place, spying or making trouble."

Either the cyclops really was a childlike innocent, or he was the best actor ever, but if Myers had taken the risk of stealing and hiding him from Unicorn, that meant his remote viewing thing was legit.

"This scary place that opens to the nightmare world, it's there, isn't it?"

Hesitant, Poly lifted one sausage finger to point, but then paused. "Promise you won't go there?"

"I won't lie to you. I can't make that promise, Poly," Julie said. "But we'll do our best, and we'll try to be safe. Heroes have to do dangerous things sometimes to help others. That's what makes us the good guys."

"I knew you would be as brave as Agent Myers." And then, sure enough, Poly the Cyclops pointed at the big red pin. "It's in the City of Monsters."

It was way up north, on a large island off the coast of Russia. I read the name. "Son of a bitch." My hands closed into fists. My lips twisted into an unconscious snarl. My reaction must have startled Poly, because he took a nervous step back.

"What's wrong, Owen?"

"That's where they killed my dad."

Something big happened while Julie and I were on our way to the airport. I'd not checked the news recently, but I could tell by the way all of the other travelers had gathered around the TV screens in hushed silence that it was bad news, unfolding live.

I limped to the back of the crowd, not close enough to hear the announcer, but I could read the scroll along the bottom of the screen. India. Death toll unknown, but it was in the hundreds.

"What happened?" I asked the nearest waiting passenger.

"They think a chemical plant caught fire," she said. "The poison gas burned a whole town. That's so sad."

The video showed terrified crowds of people running for their lives. Fires raged out of control in the background as buildings collapsed.

"It's probably just an accident," Julie whispered.

"I hope so." Which was a terrible thing to say, but there it was. When you worked in this business it was really easy to get paranoid that every single tragedy you saw on the news was just a cover story to explain away the existence of monsters. In reality plenty of regular, normal-bad things happened every day. We could have gotten hit by a truck on the way here. Or our plane could crash on takeoff, and that was just rotten luck. No monsters necessary. And sometimes towns just catch on fire and rapidly burn to the ground without the forces of evil holding the match.

But then the live camera angle changed, away from the refugees and toward a nearby hillside, where a giant symbol had been freshly burned into the stone. The camera only lingered on it for a moment. Most people wouldn't recognize it as anything other than random char. We knew it was a calling card.

Julie sighed. "Damn it. Not again."

Somebody at CNN must have been read in, because the live feed was cut. They switched to the studio, where they began introducing a *chemical expert*, who I was certain would be paid off by the MCB to regurgitate whatever the Indian government's official cover story for the incident was.

I was seeing red. How many more people had to die because I'd woken this thing up?

"Are you okay?" Julie tried to take my hand, but it had unconsciously clenched into a fist.

"I won't be until we stop this son of a bitch."

# CHAPTER 2

I had my ducks in a row. Now it was time to make my pitch.

"Earl, you got a minute?"

"Maybe later, Z. I'm still catching up with all the team leads' reports, and we've got an active Newbie class I'm supposed to be evaluating."

My boss had been having one hell of a morning. Since he had gotten back, Earl had been absolutely slammed catching up with various pieces of business, and Dorcas had been sending him calls nonstop. That's what happens when you drop off the face of the Earth for several days to spring your girlfriend from a secret government monster death squad. They'd gotten that sorted out without getting MHI further involved in the Franks versus Unicorn debacle. Stricken was on the run. Heather Kerkonen had a new boss—who actually sounded like she wasn't an evil plotting megalomaniac like her predecessor—and now Earl was trying to get our company back to normal.

I was about to ruin any chance of normal. At least rescuing Heather had put him in a halfway decent mood, so I hoped he wouldn't shoot down my pitch.

I'd caught Earl in the hall near the front door, trying to escape toward the shooting range. He glanced toward Dorcas's desk. She was on the phone, and he was probably annoyed that me delaying him meant she had time to send him another phone call. "Talk fast."

"I know you're swamped, but this is important."

"Yo, Earl." Dorcas lifted her phone. "Mayorga's team is down one medical retirement, and another for a knee surgery. She wants to know when she's going to get a replacement shooter sent her way."

"Her and everybody else in this company." Earl just shook his head, and pulled out a cigarette. Then he realized he was still indoors, sighed, and put it away. "That goat rope in Vegas screwed us over. Tell her I'll call her back."

"Seriously, I need a minute, Earl. This is important," I said.

"We talking accounting—I need to sign off on something important, because I truly could not care less about the books right now—or are we talking monsters important?"

"Monsters. Though it wouldn't kill you to look at a P&L once in a while."

"Aw," Earl waved one hand dismissively. "That's what I've got you kids for. What do you need?"

"Not here. My office."

"This had better not be some accountant trick to make me look at a spreadsheet."

The truth of the matter was that I'd been planning, following leads, and doing research for a week. And if I was right, the entity I wanted to pick a fight with had invisible eyes everywhere. MHI was notorious for our distrust of magic, but we used it when we had to. I'd gotten Tanya to put some elven charms on my office which would supposedly ward off eavesdropping spirits. She promised they were powerful and would last for a few days. I didn't really know if our token trailer park elf was full of crap or not, but it was worth a shot. But I wasn't going to explain that to Earl here with Newbies of unknown character wandering around. I'd learned my lesson about that the hard way.

Earl followed me upstairs. I'd ditched my crutch for a cane, and I'd doubled up on Gretchen's foul tasting *alternative medicine*. I was healing fast. Orc potions were made out of things like ground-up teeth, pine cones, and raccoon bones, with no logical explanation for why they helped, but damn if they didn't work great.

My office wasn't very big, and most of it was filled with shelves and filing cabinets. Earl had let me hire an outside CPA firm—read in on PUFF obviously—to do our taxes, and a retired Hunter as a bookkeeper for the boring data entry bits, so that was nice. Since I squeezed in my company number-crunching in between monster killing, there were guns, gear, and boxes of ammo stacked on top of all the cabinets.

Back when I'd been a regular accountant, I'd had a dummy hand grenade on my desk with a tag with the numeral one attached to the pin and a plaque beneath that read TAKE A NUMBER. I couldn't use that here because it might get mixed up with the regular hand grenades, and that could be disastrous. I closed the door behind Earl and locked it. Elf magic would keep out our enemy's ghosts, and the door would keep out curious Hunters. Hopefully there weren't any invisible gnomes hiding in any drawers or anything.

As usual, Earl didn't miss much. "There's elf runes chalked on your wall. Why the secrecy?"

I flopped into my chair. Earl sat on the other side of my desk. He wasn't too grumpy yet, so I had to strike while the iron is hot. "You know about the trip Julie and I took to Albuquerque."

"A little. She mentioned it when I got back, in between bouts of yelling at me for redecorating her house with Franks's guts."

"It's hell on the carpets."

"She's already given me an itemized bill indicating that fact. I didn't even know there were cyclops still around. I know what you're thinking, Z. Based on this monster's word, you want to put together a rescue mission. I feel your pain, I really do. Losing men is a hell of a thing. John was a good friend of mine. Lococo saved my life in Copper Lake. But going back in there after them will be dangerous."

Earl had no idea. I was thinking way bigger than just a simple rescue mission. "We can't just leave those Hunters there. That's not how we do things."

"I know that. I didn't say we weren't going to do anything. Assuming this one-eyed fat kid Myers has on house arrest is providing actionable intel, isn't lying or nuts, and by some miracle seven Hunters are still alive, *and* they're still alive months from now when this supposed gate opens, sure. But truthfully, I don't know what to do about it."

"Way ahead of you." I unlocked my top drawer and pulled out a stack of paper. The two silver plaques I'd pulled off the wall were in there for safekeeping. "I've been doing some poking around—"

"Hang on." Earl held up one hand. "Before you get

all spun up, I just want you to know I've seen this before. I know what you're thinking."

"I'm fine."

"Bull. You're holding yourself personally accountable for those missing Hunters and it's eating at you. That's good."

"What's good about that?"

"When you get to the point that life-and-death command decisions come easy for you, then it's time to hang it up. It's a hell of a responsibility. Every time you make a call, a Hunter's life is in your hands. Leaders make mistakes, people die. Hell, sometimes we do everything right and they still die anyway. You think you're the first Hunter who has had to leave a man behind? You're not."

I exhaled. Logically, I knew he was right, but it still sucked. "I know I did what I had to, but I keep second-guessing it."

"Been there. Dwell on it long enough and you'll come up with some imaginary solution where everything would've come up roses and sunshine. But that's bullshit. This hesitation business costs lives. So you make a decision, you see it through the best you can. Try not to screw up. When you do, afterwards you pick up the pieces and try to make things right. I'll do everything I can to bring them back, but I don't want you trying anything stupid just because you're chasing a white whale. You get me?"

"I got a B on my eighth-grade book report about *Moby Dick*. So maybe?"

"Smartass. I don't need to lose any more Hunters trying to get back our two."

That was assuming VanZant and Lococo were among the living, and the seven survivors weren't all members of rival companies. "Earl, I give you my word. I'm calm and rational as I can be. Everything I'm about to propose I've thought through. I'm not flying by the seat of my pants here, and I'm not going to do anything stupid."

"At least not stupider than what we do any other given day. Good. Because with that whole Chosen One thing you've got going on, when you go off half-cocked, things gets weird."

"Fair enough. Here's the deal. You know this big, evil bastard who has been messing with us?"

"Yeah, Z, it's been kind of hard to miss. What about him?"

"All of these recent events, he's been provoking us, testing our resolve. He's been screwing around on our turf just to see how we react. It's time we hit back. Action beats reaction. I want to go on the offensive."

"You and me both. And how do you intend to do that?"

"I'm not talking about just a rescue mission. I'm proposing an *invasion*."

Earl's smile faded. "You're serious?"

"As a heart attack." I spread out the papers on my desk. "I don't think the location Myers had the cyclops watching is just some regular Place of Power with a gate hidden inside, like DeSoya Caverns. It's a significant target where our bad guy was sleeping away the eons until I accidentally woke him up. At minimum it's an important staging area. At most, it's still his home base."

"Hold on now. I looked at the map after I talked to Julie. There's nothing of note there. It never came up on MHI's radar before. As far as what I heard this morning, your cyclops buddy didn't know jack about it except it made Myers clutch his pearls. What makes you so sure?"

"Because about thirty years ago, that's the same spot my dad got his brains blown out on a secret recon mission working for Unicorn, before being brought back to life by angels, so that his son could save the world."

Earl groaned. "Aw, damn it. Not this mystical prophecy stuff again."

"Mystical or not, you know it works."

"Sure. I've seen you be right too many times with the whole Dreamer, talking to ghosts, reading memories thing for it not to be. Flexible minds and whatnot, but that doesn't mean I have to enjoy relying on it to plan an op. I like facts and logic in my mysticism."

"Says the werewolf!"

"Now that's just hurtful. All right. I knew your dad long before that. The Destroyer's as sharp a man as there's ever been. He's the living embodiment of *no bullshit*. He says this is a legit target?"

"Sort of." I spent the next few minutes catching Earl up on my father's—hopefully not deathbed—confession. The hard part was next, when I had to talk about the aftermath.

"The thing is, Earl, when they said that was the only reason he got to stay alive, they weren't messing around. A few minutes after he got done talking to me and Mosh, he got dizzy. Fell down. His nose started to bleed." I trailed off. It had been all over his shirt, all over the kitchen floor. Mosh had laid there on the linoleum, cradling Dad's head, while I'd called 911. It had been awful. "He passed out. The bleeding wouldn't stop. I thought he was going to choke on it. It's like getting that story off his chest pulled a plug or flipped a switch. I swear, I saw him shrink right before our eyes. I thought he was going to die on us right there."

My boss was stone-faced. "How come you didn't tell me about this before?"

The truth was that I was nervous Earl might be worried about my state of mind and temporarily pull me off the roster. "It was family business."

"The minute you married my great-granddaughter we became family. How's Destroyer now?"

"Weak. Good days, bad days, in and out of the hospital, but mostly in lately. Mom's been giving me updates. Doctors don't understand what's wrong with him. He's deteriorating physically. Mentally, he's fine. They see the place where the Others healed him and think it's an inoperable tumor. There's no diagnosis for 'Sorry, the angels are done with you, time's up on your borrowed life.'"

"So that's why your brother took sick leave to get out of the Newbie class he'd just volunteered for." Earl nodded slowly as he pulled out a smoke. "Command decision, Mosh has got enough extracurricular experience lately that I'll make sure he doesn't get held back. Seeing the real world damn near wrecked him. That boy needs to be a Hunter."

"Pitts don't do good without a purpose. So about this invasion . . ."

"Trust me on this one, Z. Take some time and spend it with your dad. In the end, your kin—by blood or by choice—they're all we've got. You should be there too."

"I will. Soon. Only this was what he was kept alive for. Let me make his sacrifice mean something. Please."

Earl lit a cigarette. I wasn't about to complain about him violating his no smoking in other people's office self-imposed rule. He was quiet for a long time, smoking and leaning back in his chair, deep in thought. He began drumming his fingers on the arm of the chair as he pondered on it, a habit that Julie had inherited.

"Okay, Z. Let's talk invasion, then. What do we know about this particular monster?"

"Almost nothing."

"What do we know about the location?"

"Even less."

"That's a whole lot of nothing."

"We've got to start somewhere. He's older than dirt, the scary ass Great Old Ones see him as a competitor. He's powerful enough to freak out Management, turn Myers into an insomniac, and even the Nachtmar tried to use him to frighten me into teaming up. He's controlled or manipulated some dangerous creatures, and judging by the symbols left behind, his reach is global. I've made a list of all the specifics we do know about him, and I've come up with a plan of how we can learn more. I can walk you through it."

"Hell, I bet this plan of yours has got bullet points." Earl muttered as he took the papers, "You're such an accountant."

"Bullet points are awesome." It was a good thing I'd held off on showing him the Excel file I'd built detailing the resources I'd need. That might have been a touch much. "Just check it out. When we go in, we'll be loaded for bear, ready for anything and everything. I want this son of a bitch to regret crawling out of his hole."

Earl read my notes...and nodded slowly. I could tell he was seriously thinking about it. Our unknown enemy was powerful, malicious, and had hit us repeatedly *and* gotten away with it. I was hoping he wouldn't be able to resist his natural inclination to hit back.

"What day is this gate supposed to open?"

I flipped around my desk calendar. I had already counted. "One hundred and forty-seven days from today. We get in there, wreck his place, blast his minions, seize that gate, and get our guys back."

"And kill him."

"If he's there, obviously."

Earl passed the papers back to me. "I want to know *everything* about what we're facing, with accent on the parts about how we put him in the grave. You hearing me? We do this, it can't be half-ass. If we're dealing with something that makes Old Ones skittish, that means a potential world ender, and that means he's gonna be tough. Things that think they've got what it takes to conquer everything usually are. If that's the case, we're talking about one hell of an operation, all hands on deck. We made some friends in Vegas, so we can reach out to them too. I ain't too proud to ask for help."

"Absolutely, Boss. So does that mean the mission is a go?"

"Draft who you need from my team. Anybody else is need-to-know basis only. We play this close to the vest. We don't know how far this monster's reach goes, so take no chances. For the time being this is now your only job. I'll give you a few weeks to convince me it's doable."

I'd take it. "I'll put it down on my calendar as *tentative.*"

"But go see your dad first." Earl stood up. "That's an order."

"I will." It was going to be hard to see somebody that strong, rendered weak. My dad had raised us to be tough, but Pitts sucked at the emotional side of things.

"Trust me. You'll regret it the rest of your life if you don't." He began walking to the door.

"Hey, Earl."

"Yeah, Z?" He paused in the doorway.

"You ever done an op this big before?"

"Hell, kid," he called out as he left. "I invaded Normandy."

Dad was back in the hospital. I'd heard Mom and Mosh were taking turns at his bedside. Since my flight got in so late I didn't want to inconvenience them, so I just caught a cab from the airport. Of course, that meant I surprised my mom, who immediately got upset that I'd paid for a taxi when she could have picked me up. My good intentions or relative wealth didn't matter, because Mom is *frugal*. Which was our family's nice way of saying she was incredibly cheap.

To be fair, she'd grown up in a Communist country where things like fresh fruit and splinter-free toilet paper were luxuries reserved for the connected. If you spent a buck unnecessarily around Mom, you were going to get a lecture about it. The only thing the Pitts spent ludicrous amounts of guilt-free money on was for stockpiling ammunition and canned food. Both of my parents had agreed that was cool. Anything beyond that, Mom didn't like it. She still buried coffee cans full of cash in the yard and didn't trust banks.

All of that meant I never told her the reason Dad was getting care from the best doctors in the best hospital in the state, instead of taking a number at the VA, was because I'd written the administrator here a big honking donation check.

Since Dad was asleep, Mom and I hung out in the waiting room and talked for a bit. It was obvious she hadn't been sleeping and was strung out on hospital cafeteria coffee. Mom had been an athlete in her youth, and she'd aged gracefully, so I think this was one of the first times that I saw her actually look old. Like old-lady *old*.

But tired or not, she was still a nonstop rambling chatterbox of motherliness. To pass the time she'd brought in a shoe box of old photographs and was organizing them into albums. She called it *scrapbooking*. I sat next to her on the couch and let the interrogation begin.

"How is Julie doing? I don't want her working too hard. I need a healthy grandbaby. She'd better take it easy, because Pitt children are very large. Both of you were ten-pounders. You were like carrying a bowling ball."

"She's doing okay, but not working too hard doesn't come easy for Julie. She likes to stay busy."

"She says that now, but *bowling ball*."

Mom had already given me the latest update on Dad's condition—declining—and his outlook—grumpy, though the second one was normal. "How're you doing?"

"Oh, me?" She waved one hand dismissively. "I'm fine."

She always said she was fine. "No, really. How are you holding up?"

"Great."

"Mom . . ."

Her forced smile died. "I'm tired. I've known this day was coming for a long time, but that doesn't change it being hard. But I'm glad my boys are here . . . and yet from the guilty look on your face, you're about to say not for long."

"I'm really sorry, but I'm working on something important."

"Related to your father's dream?"

"Yeah."

"The part where one of his sons has to die to save the world?" She shook her head. "Don't act surprised that I know things. I've been hearing about that from him since the doctor told us you were a boy and your father looked so distraught and guilty that I knew something was wrong. I dragged the truth out of him then and I've put up with his nonsense ever since."

"That must have been tough."

"Eh." She shrugged. "I married a Green Beret. If I'd wanted easy I would have done like my mother always told me and married a politician."

That made me grin. "Dad was a real catch."

"I thought so. When my family defected, your father was one of the soldiers who got us out. I fell in love with him the day we met. Of course, your grandfather was an important man, and he didn't approve of me falling for an American, especially one who wasn't white."

"Did Grandpa ever get over it?"

"We didn't give him much of a choice. Eventually he came around. Your father is impossible to argue with when he sets his mind to something. You are so much like him it is funny."

"I inherited his ugly mug."

"Not that. And neither of you are ugly!" Of course, moms and wives are delusional and biased. "I'll show you. I'll find one of him young." She began flipping through the old photos. "Here. Look at this one."

It was a picture of Dad in Vietnam. He had never been the pose-for-a-picture kind of guy, so somebody had caught him slogging through a swamp. He was wearing tiger-stripe camo, a boonie hat, carrying an old CAR, and covered in mud. He was just a kid, but even then he was squat and muscle-bound. He even had that same squinty-eyed scowl I'd know my whole life. Even twenty-year-old Dad had been a total hard-ass.

"You can see why I fell in love with him."

"Yeah. He was quite the catch."

Mom snorted. "Frivolous women want a pretty man, but a smart woman wants a man who is a man. Julie understands. But I wasn't talking about how you look alike, I mean you both always thought you could save everybody. He never could tolerate a bully either. It's why you got into so many fights when you were a boy. And I guess, as you got older you stayed the same, and your fights just got bigger and bigger."

"You've got no idea."

"Oh, I understand more than you think. You used your fists then and now you use Abominator."

I had given up on trying to correct her on that one.

"All those years when he was in the Army, you boys would ask him about how come he had to go away again, and he'd tell you something about duty, and honor, and loyalty, and fighting for freedom, but that isn't why he did it. He said those things because they seemed like the right thing to say. Men he respected talked like that, and he was never good at putting words to things himself."

"No kidding." English was Mom's third language and she was still the far better communicator of the two.

"He went and fought because some people can't help but stand up to evil. They're born to fight. They're smart enough to know what will happen if they lose, but they're brave anyway. They see a wrong, and they'll bleed to fix it. They'll take any abuse, but won't let anyone harm their friends. They do the right thing even when it is hard. *That* is how you're just like him."

I didn't know what to say. "That means a lot."

"Keep this one." She handed me the old Vietnam picture. "And remember I lived happily with that kind of stubborn man all these years, and to do that you have to be just as stubborn as they are. So when I say I'll be fine, you'd better believe it, kiddo."

I sat there in silence for hours. Dad was sleeping. Always muscular and imposing, he seemed to have shrunk. Big guys look funny when they suddenly lose a bunch of weight.

Mom had gone home for a bit. Mosh had taken over the waiting room couch and gone to sleep, and I'd gone into Dad's room and pulled up a chair next to his bed.

Dad woke up an hour before dawn. Because of the constantly changing drug cocktails they had him on, his sleep schedule was wonky, but one nice thing about donating enough money to a hospital for them to buy a new MRI machine is that none of the staff give you crap about visiting hours.

Of course the first thing out of Dad's mouth when he saw me was, "What the hell are you doing here?"

"I came to check on you."

Dad scowled. His eyes were sunken and there were big dark circles around them, so even though scowling was his default expression, this one seemed particularly judgy. Surprisingly, his voice was stronger than expected from how he looked. "You shouldn't be screwing around when you've got a mission to complete."

"I'm working on it."

"No, you're here being a big crybaby because I'm sick. Dry those eyes, you pussy. My condition shouldn't come as a surprise. You moping around isn't going to fix anything."

That made me laugh. I don't know why I'd expected a terminal illness to make him less cantankerous. "I said I'm working on it, you grumpy old bastard." And I said that with love. "My boss ordered me to come and see you before he'd sign off on declaring war on your ancient superdemon."

Dad smiled. "Ah, of course he did. How is Mr. Wolf?"

"Worried I don't appreciate how good a man raised me."

"You're gonna make me blush."

"Mr. Wolf also ordered Gretchen, our orc healer, to mix up a thermos full of *medicine* for you. It should help keep you strong."

"Tell him thanks."

"You won't thank anybody after you taste it."

Dad reached out and grabbed my hand. There wasn't a lot of strength left in his grip. "It is really good to see you, son."

"You too, Dad."

That was about all we could say. Pitt men really

weren't good at the emotional stuff. We were both quiet for a long time.

"I'm going to tell you something difficult, Owen, and I need you to listen. You've got work to do, and we both know you're the only one who can do it. I should have died a long time ago, but I worked too hard to be a distraction now. When are you going to make your move?"

"We've got a window in about six months."

"Then here's the deal. You don't have time to grieve. I made them give me thirty extra years. I swear to you I can make it that much longer, just so I can watch my boy come home victorious. Six more months? That's nothing. They owe me that much."

I lost it then. I put my head down and began to sob uncontrollably. Dad reached out, put his hand on the side of my head and dragged me down, so we were forehead to forehead, and whispered. "Listen to me, Owen. Listen. I love you, son. Everything I did was for love. It's up to you to protect them now. Everybody. You understand?"

I couldn't speak, so I nodded. I was getting tears on his hospital gown.

"Okay. Good boy." He held me for a while. "Good boy."

"When we win, it'll be because you taught me how," I said. Then he let go, and I leaned back and wiped my eyes. "Thanks, Dad."

The moment passed, and Auhangamea Pitt got right back to being his gruff self. "Good. You'd better kick his ass. Now get back to work."

"Yes, sir."

❖    ❖    ❖

Mosh volunteered to drive me back to the airport. I had told him I was fine calling a cab, but he'd insisted. I got the feeling he just really needed to talk to someone right then. So we'd borrowed Mom's car, and then wound up spending most of the drive in awkward silence. We were both a little shell-shocked.

I was still worried about my brother. He had been messed up after the Condition had screwed up his hand and the MCB had ruined his career. A washed-up rock star drinking himself to death was a bad cliché way to go. Except after helping save the day in Las Vegas, he'd joined MHI, and that seemed to have given him a purpose again. I just didn't know if that was a solid foundation, or if it was a crack waiting to happen.

It wasn't until we were getting close to our destination that Mosh tried getting what was bugging him off his chest. "It's weird, man. Big revelation about his fate, and just like that, everything is different. Stupid little things don't matter anymore. Perspective changes." He sighed. "I spent a lot of years being angry."

"I never said you were wrong to be." Dad had been harder on him than me. We were both overachievers, but I had a natural talent for violence, while Mosh had always had to work at it. My relationship with Dad had been difficult, but my brother's had been impossible. "Besides, Pitts accomplish great things when motivated by spite."

"I know. I thought, I'll show him. But none of that mattered. I had nothing, then I had everything, then I had nothing, but Dad stayed exactly the same. He didn't care about that stuff. How much time did I waste, just because I couldn't see? I thought he was cruel, and now I know it was the opposite all along. He didn't think he could afford compassion. He pushed us hard because he loved us, so in a way, I hated his guts, because he did the best he could. How messed up is that? Now that I know Dad had reasons for being how he was—weird, crazy reasons, but still—things make more sense. I wish he could have just told us what was up."

Except the angel who'd brought him back to life had ordered him not to. Dad had been stuck, and now that Mosh understood that, he was feeling like an asshole for all of the stupid pointless fights between them. So rather than rub it in I just gave a noncommittal, "Uh-huh."

Mosh snorted. "I'm glad you're as good as he is about talking things out."

"Just don't get us in a wreck with all those salty tears of sadness in your eyes." It was a very *Dad* thing to say. Both of us had a laugh. "Naw, I'm with you, Mosh. I get it. I really do. Regret sucks."

We were nearing the drop-off lane. "From what you've said, I'm guessing there's no chance Harbinger is going to let any Newbies go on this big job of yours."

"Not a snowball's chance in hell."

"Figured...On the bright side, Mom is going to need somebody to stick around. It might actually be fun to spend some time with Dad for once, and actually... I don't know, get to know him, talk man to man."

"And if he starts yelling at you, at least it can't be for long because he'll need a hit on the oxygen mask."

Mosh snorted. "Always the optimist." There was an open spot at the drop-off and arrivals area. He pulled in. "Well, this is it."

"Take care of Mom and Dad." I started to get out. "And take care of yourself. I worry about you."

"Wait, Owen. Something else. You need to be careful—"

"We don't even know for sure there will be a mission yet, but if there is I'll do my best—"

My brother cut me off. "Dude, I was going to say careful you don't screw up your kid! Julie's having a baby. That's a big deal! Here we are talking about Dad and all our weird baggage. You've got a chance to do it right. Don't screw it up!"

*Great, no pressure or anything.*

# CHAPTER 3

I'd spent the last ten minutes dangling from a rope, in a pitch-black elevator shaft, descending far beneath the Earth's surface. The only light was from the little LED flashlight strapped to my forehead. I'd been trained, and Milo had rigged up the ropes, and there was nobody better at that sort of thing in the company than him, but that didn't mean I had to like the trip. By the time my boots hit solid ground, my heart was racing and my limbs were trembling. I hated stuff like this. There was a reason you didn't see very many big dudes climbing mountains.

Milo on the other hand seemed to be having a blast. "Looking good, Z!" He nearly blinded me with his headlamp when he came over to unhook me from the ropes. He'd gone down the shaft first and had made it look like a piece of cake, kicking off the walls and dropping twenty feet at a time. Milo climbed like he was part spider monkey. I had figured the power to the elevator would be cut; that was why I'd asked him to come along on this one. Trip I'd invited because he was the biggest geek I knew, and if I went to talk to a dragon without him, he'd probably never speak to me again.

"Wasn't that fun?" Milo asked.

"Yeah." I took a deep breath. "Fun."

"Just wait until we get to climb back up!" Milo slapped me on the shoulder. The rope swung free and the D-ring made a *clang* as it hit the side of the shaft. "Don't worry. It'll be a piece of cake."

Only if the cake was made out of acrophobia and nausea. Go toe-to-toe with a monster? No problem. But that whole random chance of snapping a rope and tumbling to my death part, I had a problem with. It had only been a few days since Gretchen had cut the cast off my forearm. This probably wasn't what our healer had in mind when she'd told me not to strain myself too much. Oh well. That's what fistfuls of Ibuprofen were for.

I got on my radio. "This is Pitt. I've safely reached the bottom."

"Bottom of what? Oh, that's right. You can't tell me that. Still all clear up here," Eddings radioed back. Our Las Vegas team lead and one of his men were ready to hoist our butts out in a hurry if security showed up. "Jones is on his way down now."

That was good news, because we really weren't supposed to be in here. The five of us had dressed as construction workers and snuck into the ruins of the Last Dragon at three in the morning. The section of the Strip in front was a massive around-the-clock construction project. There was a fence around the Last Dragon, but the MCB had finished their operation, and all they'd left behind was a small security team of rent-a-cops.

It had been a weird feeling going back inside this place. The casino had been completely trashed. Big swaths of it had been blown to pieces and there was a giant sinkhole right in the middle where the Nachtmar's nightmare dragon had crawled out.

The MCB had done a masterful job successfully covering up one of the biggest public monster events in US history. It had been the crowning achievement of Myers's career as a professional bullshit artist. And life in Las Vegas was returning to normal.

Since this was some of the most valuable commercial real estate in the world, demolition crews were scheduled to tear the place down soon. I assumed it was scrubbed, but just in case the MCB still had a presence here we didn't know about, two more of Eddings's Hunters were out front on lookout. None of the Las Vegas team knew what Milo and I were doing here, but Earl had told them we were on a special assignment for him, and that had to be good enough.

"It bugs me we can't tell these guys what we're up to," Milo said. "Eddings is solid. He wouldn't tell anybody."

"I'm sure he's great, but I made a promise to try and keep Management secret. He's probably going to be ticked off as it is that I told our team."

"I know. It still sucks though."

"True that." At least I'd never had the chance to sign that NDA, because I'm pretty sure Management hadn't been bluffing about the lawsuits. I could see the light bouncing above as Trip descended. He was faster at it than me, but not nearly as graceful as Milo. "Almost there, man!"

"I can't believe Milo does stuff like this for a hobby." Trip hit the floor a moment later, grinning. Of course, rappelling down a hole was rather exhilarating for him. "I must really want to meet a dragon."

The walls were rock, like we'd stepped into a mine shaft. We were armed, but only with concealable handguns we wouldn't mind ditching if we got rolled up by security. While Milo got Trip unhooked, I pointed my flashlight down the tunnel. "He was down that way."

Management's fate was a mystery. We didn't know if the Nachtmar had gotten him or not. And if the last dragon was dead, had the MCB found his secret lair? It wasn't like this cave was on any of the building plans. I only knew about it because the dragon had hijacked my elevator. The tunnel hadn't changed at all, so maybe we'd get lucky.

"If the treasure is still down here, I've got dibs on a moon rock," Milo said. "Whoa...I just had a thought. What would happen if I gave a moon rock to Earl?"

"I have no idea. But no looting. We're just here for information on our bad guy." I said that mostly because dragon hearing was way better than human's, and if he was still around I didn't want to offend him. In reality, if he was gone but his hoard was still here, that Terracotta Warrior would look badass in my freshly remodeled living room.

The dragon had been unfailingly polite, so if he was still alive I probably shouldn't barge in unannounced. It wasn't smart to startle things that could squish you like a bug. Super hearing or not, I raised my voice to be safe. "*Hello!* Management! Are you home?"

It echoed several times. We waited. There was no answer.

"Here goes."

A short walk later, we reached the cave. It was so big our powerful flashlights were barely sufficient to illuminate one corner, but even then I could tell we were too late. I shined the light back and forth, bouncing it off of crystal formations. I muttered something profane.

"Bummer," said Milo the master of understatement.

The cave wasn't just empty, it had been stripped. The last time I'd been here the vast space had been packed with stuff—everything from rare paintings to Greek statues. Now there wasn't so much as a coin on the ground. There was no sign of the dragon or any of his collection. The air tasted moist and stale. There were still electrical cables strung up, but everything they'd been powering was long gone.

"I'd really been hoping to meet the dragon. You made him sound awesome."

"I guess if you're into that sort of thing."

"Man, who isn't into giant thunder lizards?" Milo asked as he shined his light toward the ceiling. It didn't reach.

I kept walking along the walls, searching for some clue as to what had happened. The dragon had been my best hope, because in addition to collecting physical treasures, Management had collected information. He had been telling me about the real enemy when the Nachtmar had interrupted our conversation by dragging the whole casino into another dimension.

There were big cracks in the otherwise smooth walls. I didn't remember those from before, but I'd been on a bit of sensory overload at the time. Then I noticed the blackened scorch marks and deep gashes that must have been caused by claws.

Trip whistled. "It looks like they had one heck of a fight."

The back of the cave was partially collapsed. There

had been a freight elevator there, which was how Management had gotten fed, but now the whole area was covered in fallen rocks and dirt. I really didn't want to mess around back there for fear of causing any further collapse.

Milo joined me. "So what do you think happened to your big friend?"

"No idea." He could have gotten out the freight shaft, but he'd sounded pretty beat up by the Nachtmar when I'd last heard from him over the radio. "Maybe he died here and the MCB removed his body?"

"It's possible. The floors have been swept and hit with a dust vac. They've definitely had a cleanup crew down here. If he left anything for you, the MCB took it already."

"Are you getting anything else, Z?" Trip asked cautiously.

"You know . . ." Milo made a pair of finger guns and stuck them against his temples. Between the headlamp and the big red Viking beard, he looked really crazy doing that. "In your *brain?*"

I had never asked to be psychic. Frankly, it was a pain in the ass. "Not in the slightest."

But maybe they had a point. As a creature of magic, Management had recognized that I was one of the Chosen. It was possible that once he had realized how dire our circumstances were, he'd left something that only someone like me would be able to find. Sadly, it wasn't like this champion of a cosmic faction business came with instructions. I hadn't even known I'd been applying for the job.

"Look at Z's face. He's gonna go for it," Milo said.

Sometimes, I could watch other people's memories

from their perspective. With humans, it required physical contact and me *really* wanting to know about a specific memory. Though I'd pulled it off with a gnome and even a shoggoth—let me tell you, that was one weird-ass experience—but with something as ancient and powerful as Management? It beat the hell out of me. I'd have to go by instinct.

There was a blasted scorch mark on a nearby rock pillar. It had been so hot that it had melted half of it into slag. I don't know why I fixated on that. It felt... *energetic.* "Hang on." I laid my open hand on the rock.

It must have looked kind of dramatic, because Milo began to chant. "Chosen One. Chosen One," like this was a sporting event.

"Dude, please," Trip told him. "You're embarrassing him."

"Just trying to help motivate our psychic."

"If you bust out pom-poms I'm going back up that rope."

"Oh, I bet if it was Holly dressed up like a cheerleader, nobody would mind."

Trip started to give Milo a sarcastic response, but thought about it for a second. "Okay. That's true."

"Guys. Come on."

"Sorry, Z," they said simultaneously.

Despite my fellow Hunters being themselves, I could tell there was something lingering here. It's hard to explain, but it felt like a memory. As I focused, I could almost but not quite hear Management's voice talking to me. Only this wasn't like taking something from a human mind. Now that I had gotten quite a bit of practice, I could grab those in an instant, like reflexively snatching a ball tossed to me out of the air.

This felt *heavy*. This wasn't a ball. This was a pallet of bricks precariously balanced on top of a stick.

"Here goes."

I gave the stick a mental shove. The bricks fell on us.

"What the heck?" Trip muttered as blue flames appeared around my hand.

I jerked my arm away, but the flaming handprint remained. It began to spread across the rock, picking up speed at it went. Within seconds the pillar was engulfed, and the fire was rolling outward across the floor. Luckily, there was no heat accompanying it. It washed over my feet. Milo yelped and jumped as it flew past him.

"You seeing this too?" I asked. They didn't answer, but by the looks on their faces, staring at the imaginary glowing fire that was up to their knees, the answer was yes. Items grew from the fire: shelves, cases, caskets, thrones—even cars—all of the dragon's treasures. The glow climbed up the wall until it lit the distant ceiling. We were standing in a neon blue world. "I've never had anyth—"

There was a deafening roar followed by a sound like lightning. I put my hands over my ears. All of us instinctively ducked as something gigantic whooshed overhead. It was a dragon wing, stretching across half the cavern. The other wing materialized, beating, but there was no wind. The roar grew until I thought it was going to swallow us all.

The body formed, big as a train car stood on end. Powerful limbs formed out of thin air. It all became clear, and I gasped in awe as Management towered above me. His mighty, horned head turned on his long serpentine neck, as he opened jaws sufficient to chew a whole cow, and a cone of blue fire burst forth, snaking from side to side. It washed over us.

I couldn't help but flinch. If that had been real, we would have all been instantly consumed, but we weren't in the presence of this mighty force of nature. This was just an imprint left behind. The glowing version of Management was translucent. I could see rock on the opposite side of the cave through his shimmering scales and membranous wings. The collected treasures were blurry. There was a table full of jewels partially *through* Trip's leg. There was a flaming blue suit of armor next to me. I swiped my hand through it, and it rippled like water.

"What is this?" Milo shouted to be heard over the rushing wind. He was on his knees, covering his head, pistol in hand. "Is it like a hologram?"

Another shape was rising up through the floor, even bigger than Management. This one was pitch-black. It originated from an entirely different form of magic. The glowing blue dragon got ready to fight.

"It's a memory."

The nightmare dragon rose, dwarfing Management, absolutely filling the cavern. It had been the Nachtmar's ultimate form. It snarled something incomprehensible, probably in the ancient dragon tongue. But our pudgy old dragon wasn't going to back down from any challenge, no matter how unwinnable. Management flung himself across the space, claws spread, tail whipping.

Imaginary or not, it was still scary as hell.

Priceless treasures went flying. A super car was tossed, flipping end over end through the air, only to be struck by the Nachtmar's tail and launched back across the cave. The flame world shook as the real world stood still, a memory of an earthquake. The noise was inconceivable. Glowing boulders fell from the ceiling. One flashed right through Milo and exploded into gravel when it struck. He looked around, bewildered, but unharmed.

The dragons were crashing back and forth, claws sunk into each other. Glowing blood spilled. Their necks were intertwined, teeth snapping. But it was like watching a child fight a grown man. The Nachtmar got a mouthful of wing, and there was a horrific *crunch* as he bit through Management. My host screamed. The Nachtmar struck with unbelievable fury, hurling Management down, right through where we were standing, and for an instant I could see bones and internal organs. But Management slid right through us. He hit the wall and bright blue fire rolled up one of the cracks in the wall, demonstrating how it had been created.

Only Management was one tough old bugger; he rolled over and went right back to it. This was his house and he was going to defend it. But ten seconds later his head made another dent in the cave as the Nachtmar effortlessly threw him down.

Management was dragging himself away, crashing through his hoard. The nightmare followed, looming over him and speaking again in the dragon tongue. I didn't understand Dragon, but I knew the Nachtmar enough to know he was gloating. Then he turned in a flash and vanished through the real world's fallen rocks.

I knew exactly what happened next.

Sides heaving, it took a minute for the old dragon to catch his breath. Management's gigantic head, lacerated and torn, had stopped only a few feet away from where I was standing. One horn was splintered and broken. "Activate radio. MHI channel three." The dragon coughed. "I'm sorry, Mr. Pitt. It would appear that I have underestimated our foe."

I heard my own voice as if it was coming from speakers on the wall. "Management? Is that you?"

"Yes. I did my best, but I could not stop him. He ripped it from my mind. He combed through my treasures . . . He went back to the beginning when I was a hatchling and the great dragonfathers ruled the sky. Beware . . . He means to devour you."

That was when we had lost contact, and the terrifying creation had come after us.

"Mr. Pitt. You are our only hope to defeat the nightmare. Can you hear me, Mr. Pitt? Come in." Management's breathing was labored. "Drat."

I stared into those shining dinner-plate-sized eyes. It was like he was looking right through me. It was hard to read a dragon's expression, but I saw sadness. It quickly turned to realization. Management lifted one shaking claw, jabbed the tip into the stone, and made a mark. Those in particular hadn't been battle damage. The sign had to be some form of dragon magic and how he'd left me this message.

"I make a desperate gamble . . . You have been chosen. If you survive today, I know what you will do. If you can hear me now it is because you have defeated the Nachtmar, and returned because we were denied the opportunity to finish our conversation." He wheezed. "The cause . . . The being who released this nightmare upon us, I have prepared a dossier about him. I dared not transmit it for risk of interception. However, I was not so foolhardy to fail to prepare a backup. Go to the Law Offices of Rondeau, Katz and Smith. Ask for Benjamin Rondeau."

The dragon's eye flicked over to the side, where the suit of armor had been caught in a burst of dragon fire during the battle. The steel had gone all soft and bendy in the heat. "Oh, that belonged to Henry the Eighth. What a shame. Curse this dreadful Nachtmar. I hope you make the fiend suffer, Mr. Pitt."

"We killed the hell out of him," I answered. Not that he could actually hear me.

"The Nachtmar is just a symptom. There will be others until you tear this evil out by the roots." Management's voice had died off to a whisper. "My people called him . . . Asag."

When he said that name, the blue fire flared violently. By the time I could see again, the fires were shrinking and the glow fading. The treasures began to disintegrate around us. Bits of blue fire broke away, drifting upwards, until they blinked out of existence. It was like standing in a field made of static.

"Mr. Pitt, or whichever Chosen hears these words, may your God of light guide your way . . ." Management closed his eyes. "Now, I must rest . . ."

The dragon disappeared.

I blinked a few times. The cave had returned to normal.

My friends were staring at me, dumbfounded.

"You guys heard that too, right?"

Trip gave a vigorous nod. "Man, you're just full of surprises."

"The light show was the dragon's doing. The rest, I'm still getting the hang of."

"But did he survive?" Milo asked.

"No idea. I hope so." He had really been in bad shape. More than likely they'd butchered him into easily managed pieces, and those were being studied in some MCB facility. "I really like the old guy."

"I bet he made it." Trip was an optimist. Plus, he had always been a sucker for anything magical and not super evil. "Let's get out of here before Eddings gets arrested, they cut the ropes, and we're stuck."

"Let's go find this Rondeau . . . Ah hell, that was so distracting I almost forgot now we've got to climb up an elevator shaft."

"Worth it!" At least Milo was pumped. "Holographic dragon fight was way cooler than Laser Floyd. This trip has been great!"

# CHAPTER 4

The Law Offices of Rondeau, Katz and Smith were in a really nice building a few miles from the Last Dragon. According to Eddings it was one of those big corporate firms with a local rep for being a bunch of cutthroat mega-sharks. Since Management was so absurdly rich and secretly invested in everything, it made sense that he'd keep a fleet of high-powered lawyers on retainer.

After having breakfast at a greasy spoon, we said our goodbyes to the Las Vegas team, then stopped at our hotel and changed out of our construction worker outfits. Since our next stop was upscale, we needed to look the part. I hadn't brought a suit, but I could at least step it up to a shirt with buttons and pants without fifteen extra pockets. I'd been a corporate accountant, I could pull off business casual. Trip on the other hand actually managed to look comfortable in a tie, though I think that was only because that was how he dressed for church every Sunday. And Milo... well, considering the *stylish* blazer he'd brought along was bright green and purple—it made him look like the Riddler—we'd just leave him in the parking lot.

So the three of us left to pay a visit to Management's lawyer. Eddings hadn't been lying, it really was a fancy establishment. The cheapest car in the lot was a new Audi. There were lots of young, hard-charger, Harvard-grad-looking assholes heading into work, wearing expensive suits, expensive haircuts, and drinking overpriced coffees. My immediate dislike for them told me that maybe Mom's *frugal* nature had rubbed off on me. This was probably the sort of place that Grant Jefferson had done his lawyering.

As Trip and I walked up the steps to the entrance, the first clue that something had gone wrong recently was the work crew replacing a window on the top floor. The next was the police tape blocking off some of the landscaping beneath. There were still little shiny bits of glass in the flowerbed. Inside, the receptionists were all dressed in black and some of them looked like they'd been crying recently.

Trip gave me a nervous glance. *Uh-oh.*

I went up to the desk. She had a little nameplate in front of her that read Marcy. "Hi. I'd like to talk to Mr. Rondeau."

She tried to remain professional, but at the mention of the name she immediately got weepy. "I'm sorry, but he passed away recently."

"I'm so sorry to hear that." I gritted my teeth. Our target must have found out Management was keeping tabs on him. Outwardly, I remained calm, but inside I really wanted to swear and kick something. "I'm shocked."

Trip knew me well enough that he could tell I was pissed, so he stepped in. "Do you mind me asking what happened?"

"The police said he committed suicide." Now she was getting really teary eyed and even had to reach for a Kleenex. It must be nice having a receptionist who actually seemed to like people. We had Dorcas. "It was terrible. Ben was the nicest boss ever. He seemed fine. Then one day he just jumped out of his window."

"That's so tragic. I'm terribly sorry."

"He had a wife and an ex-wife with kids."

"The best thing you can do is reach out, let them know they're loved, and keep them in your prayers." And when somebody as genuinely good-natured and well-intentioned as Trip said stuff like that, it was obviously not just meant as a platitude. He actually seemed to cheer her up a little. "Was he all by himself?"

"What do you mean?"

"I mean were there any witnesses? I'm just thinking, if it was so unexpected, maybe it was an accident, and he just fell out the window."

"Oh no . . . Apparently he had some kind of breakdown. He called his secretary right before, ranting about how some creature appeared in his office and . . ." She sniffed and composed herself. "Never mind. I'd better not talk about it . . ."

*Well, shit.*

"I'm so sorry, did you gentlemen have an appointment?"

"We were just supposed to pick something up. Maybe he left it for us?"

"And what was your name, sir?" She began clicking away at her computer.

"Look under Last Dragon."

"The casino? We don't have any business with them

that I'm aware of. Oh, my gosh! Were you there during the terrorist attack?"

"Luckily, we were off-site." *Way off-site.* "See if it was filed under Management." As I said that she gave me an odd look. "It's like a stage name."

She looked to Trip. "Are you a rapper?"

"Gospel singer," I said before Trip could respond. "And magician. Gospel-singing magician. His performance is breathtaking."

"Oh." She went back to typing. Trip rolled his eyes at me. He was lucky; if I'd had longer to think of something better, I would have said he was in a Prince tribute band. "I'm sorry, sir, but there's nothing in Mr. Rondeau's schedule or notes under that name, but don't worry. None of the work he did for any of his clients is lost."

I had a sneaky suspicion that this particular work was long gone.

"I could call for another associate to assist if you would like."

And have Asag's minions toss some other poor bastard out the window for poking around in his business? "No, thanks. We've got to go."

"Again, my condolences for your loss," Trip said. Then we headed for the door.

Outside, the two of us stopped. I squinted at the passing lawyers. "That was a bust."

"Sure was," Trip said. "The guy holding Management's backup gets murdered right after MCB scrubs his cave? Our bad guy found out somehow. What now?"

"Fly home empty-handed, I guess."

Dejected and annoyed, we headed back to the rental car, only to find our red-bearded Riddler looking smug.

As I got into the passenger's seat I said, "We got shot down. What're you smiling about?"

"This." Milo held up a scrap of paper. "You got somebody's attention. One of the lawyers just walked by in a real hurry and dropped this next to the car. It was a little too ham-fisted for random littering, so I waited until he was gone, then picked it up."

I took the note. It read, "You want the dragon file? It'll cost you. Let's do lunch." Followed by an address.

"You shifty bastards," I muttered. Then I passed the note to Trip.

"I wonder what the cost is going to be," he said.

"That depends on whether the guy with the file realizes what he's involved with. How stupid did he look, Milo?"

He shrugged. "Average stupid?"

The address was a sleazy dive bar. It was the kind of establishment where Jon Taffer would throw the food on the floor and yell at the management for not caring hard enough. Our renegade lawyer had probably picked it because it was the kind of sketchy hole where clandestine parties conducted shady business in the movies. The problem was that in real life, this time of day, there were only a couple of alcoholics inside, so the one clean-cut, twenty-something white dude wearing khakis and a polo shirt kind of stuck out.

I walked in the door at noon on the dot. It took me all of two seconds to pick out the lawyer. And most of that was because I had to wait for my eyes to adjust from being out in the sunshine. He had a corner booth. Back to the wall, even. That was a nice touch. I walked straight over to him and sat down.

"How'd you know it was me?" he asked.

"You're kidding, right?"

"Okay, okay. You can call me Mr. Steele."

I snorted. "Your name is Kevin Maxwell and you're an associate at Rondeau, Katz and Smith."

"How'd you know that?"

"My buddy found your picture and bio on the company website."

"Oh . . . Fine." He actually hadn't expected that. *Don't quit your day job.* "What should I call you?"

"Yukon Cornelius. Now quit wasting my time. I want that file."

I wasn't even trying to be intimidating, but Kevin was looking a little cowed. "It's going to cost you."

"Yeah, you covered that in your note. How much?" A waitress came by. Dive or not, that was some pretty quick service. Or maybe when you got stuck working in the middle of the day you got desperate for tips. "Hang on, Kevin."

"What do you want, honey?"

"Coke." I was betting the soda gun in this place hadn't been cleaned since I'd graduated high school. It would be like drinking carbonated botulism. "In a can, please."

"Pretty boy here is having a Sprite. Bunch of hard party animals at this table."

I handed her a fifty. "Then how about some privacy?"

"Hey, thanks, hon." She stuck Ulysses S. Grant in her bra as she wandered off.

"Great." I turned back to Kevin. "Now where were we?"

He leaned in conspiratorially. "I overheard you asking about *Management*."

"Do you even have any idea who that is?"

"Everybody connected knows he's the organized crime lord that secretly runs a bunch of casinos in this town."

"Awesome." It was good Kevin thought this was some sort of criminal thing, because that was way less weird than what it actually was. "You run with that."

"I heard Ben Rondeau talking to Management on the phone. I knew how valuable this was, so when he died I snagged the thumb drive. And if Management wants it back, you're going to have to pay me for it."

"Well, duh." I was silent while the waitress brought me a Coke in a dusty glass bottle. Unfortunately, it was warm. That's what I got for not being specific. "Thanks."

Once she was gone, Kevin went back to trying to play the tough guy. "I've got it someplace safe."

"I sure hope so, because you have no clue what you're involved with." I tried not to be too threatening as I said that. I was afraid Kevin might try to run, and then I'd have to choke him out, and that would cause a scene. Some people are jittery like that. Kevin and I were probably about the same age, but I was guessing the two of us had taken very different life paths.

"Whatever Mr. Rondeau had, it was important enough to kill for. I know he didn't commit suicide. Somebody pushed him out that window." He said it like it was a big shocking revelation.

"Yeah, no shit. I'm actually an expert on the topic of defenestration. But since we're on the subject, the receptionist said he was talking weird before he died. Do you know what he said?"

"Sure, but it was weird. He said that this red devil had started following him. I'm talking horns and a tail, hooves, wings, third eye in the middle of its forehead, the works—that kind of devil. I think he was under so much pressure secretly working for you mafia types that he had a psychotic break or something."

"Yeah, because being stalked by a demon is *so* implausible. Before I buy back Don Management's property, you got anything else to share?"

"We'd just had a meeting. He was all agitated. Not two seconds after we close the door, I hear him screaming in his office about the devil coming from him. I don't know, the hit man must have been hiding in the closet or something. I heard the glass break, and then I heard this real creepy voice say something right before he tossed Ben out the window."

"What?"

Kevin was wide-eyed and a little freaked out. "How dare you share the master's name?"

That meant the red devil was another of Asag's minions. "Tough guy like you, I'm surprised you didn't kick the door in to go save your boss."

"I was, until Mr. Creepy Voice asks that, like he was really pissed off, like how dare you? Then *whoosh*, Ben takes a header right into the flowerbed."

Kevin's company bio said he'd gone to Stanford, but he was trying way too hard to sound like he was from New Jersey. It was kind of painful. "Okay. How much do you want?"

"A million dollars. In cash."

I laughed in his face. I think that hurt his feelings. "I'll give you twenty bucks."

"You gave the waitress a fifty!"

"Well, she's not the one drawing the wrath of an unholy terror down on her head. Trust me, Kevin. Taking that file off of your hands will be the biggest favor anyone has ever done for you. The second they find out you've got it, you're toast."

"If you don't pay me, then I'll leak this file to the press!"

"That would actually be hilarious if you did. Twenty bucks and I'll pay for your Sprite."

"Come on. I know Mr. Management is a billionaire," he whined. "I've got student loans to pay off."

Trip was watching the back exit. Milo was out front. Both of them were listening to all of this over the radio. "And this is why Julie handles the negotiations," Trip said in my earpiece.

"Seriously, you think I work for the *mafia*—"

"Well, just look at you!"

"And you're attempting to blackmail the *mafia*?" Monster Hunters ended up paying a lot of bribes, that was just the cost of doing business in our often legally nebulous world, but now I was just offended in principle. "How about I just punch you in the head until you tell me where it is?"

"But I don't want to get punched in the head!"

"Nobody wants to get punched in the head, Kevin. That's why people like me use it as a negotiating tool. You'd think they'd have covered that at Stanford Law. I got an accounting degree from a state college and I still figured that out pretty early on."

"Z, you've got company. Four tough guys pulling up on motorcycles," Milo warned over my earpiece. "Might just be normal customers. Three are stopping by the front door. Last one kept going."

"Please tell me you're not a trial lawyer."

"I do entertainment law."

"Good. For a second I was feeling really bad that you might end up representing some poor sucker in court." Maybe dealing with Shane "Ultimate Fighting Lawyer" Durant had spoiled me, but I'd come to expect more backbone from the legal profession. Now that asshole was focused like a laser beam, so I was betting he was a beast in court. "I've got about two hundred bucks in my wallet. How about you can have all of that *and* as a bonus I don't break your nose for annoying me?"

"Again with the punching. Can we table the punching for a bit? How about half a million?"

I could hear the distinctive noise of the Harleys up front. The engines stopped. I glanced over. The waitress was looking out the window, curious, which told me these weren't regulars. I watched the front door. "Hang on a minute."

"That last biker just pulled up around the back," Trip said.

Well, that was suspicious.

"A quarter million?"

"Dude, you suck at this. Just shut up for a second."

"He's just watching the back door, like he's expecting someone to make a run for it."

That meant whoever they were, they didn't know me very well.

Two bikers strutted in like they owned the place. The last one stayed outside. *Real suspicious.* They were wearing leather vests and jeans, and sporting as many tats as my brother, only Mosh's were classier. One was a skinhead and the other had a beard that was nearly as good as Milo's. Then I noticed the patch on the bikers' vests. The emblem was a black squid with red eyes. I hurried and turned around so they wouldn't see me through the booth.

"Oh, not these jokers again," I muttered, knowing that Milo and Trip would pick it up. "We've got Condition." The Sanctified Church of the Temporary Mortal Condition were my least favorite death cultists ever. They gave death cults a bad name, and that took effort.

"Condition what?" Kevin whispered back.

"Condition you're screwed."

"Say the word, Z. We'll come in guns blazing."

"Hold on, guys." I glared at Kevin. "Did you try to set up a meeting to sell that drive to anyone else?"

"There was this attractive British chick asking about Management yesterday. I dropped a note for her to find too."

That had probably been Lucinda Hood. "You're an idiot."

"How was I supposed to know she wasn't with you?"

I should have just shot the Old One–worshipping jackasses and gotten it over with while their eyes were adjusting to the dimness. But Hunters couldn't just go around shooting human beings with impunity. The cops arresting me weren't going to know what the Sanctified Church of the Temporary Mortal Condition was, or even care, because that whole Freedom of Religion thing still covered apocalyptic cults, at least until it was too late.

If they weren't PUFF-applicable, then I was supposed to behave like any other law-abiding citizen. The MCB hated the Condition, so I'd probably get off. *Eventually. Maybe.* But I didn't have time to sit in jail, and I didn't want the MCB asking questions about what we were up to and screwing up our mission.

The bikers spotted Kevin as easily as I had and started walking this way. The waitress/bartender spoke up. "Get you boys something?"

"Shut your whore mouth, bitch."

Still recruiting from the best and brightest, I see. *Stay classy, Condition. Stay classy.*

Even though I was going to try and solve this without committing a bunch of felonies, I pulled my compact .45 from inside my waistband holster and held it under the table. Kevin saw me do that, and his eyes went wide. "Play it cool," I warned him. "You don't know what they're talking about. You didn't leave any note. If anything happens, stay low and try not to get shot."

The bikers stopped at our booth. The bald one had his hands in fists at his side. *Amateur.* You wanted to keep your hands loose. Clenched muscles slowed you down. Beardly folded his arms, trying to do that thing where it puffs up your biceps to make them look bigger. Neat trick, but I've never needed to do that. They obviously knew who Kevin was, but apparently they didn't know me. "Who the hell are you?"

I almost told them my real name, but I refrained. "I'm his wingman. We're here to pick up chicks."

"Whatever..." Baldy turned to our hapless lawyer. "Where's the dragon file?"

Kevin looked terrified. *Come on. Tell these jokers to take a hike. You can do—*

"I want one million dollars in exchange for the drive!" Kevin blurted.

*Shit.*

The bikers started laughing. It was that sort of sadistic "we're about to kidnap and torture a dude" laugh which indicated the Condition's negotiation with Kevin was going to go even worse than mine had. "Hey, wingman, you're gonna want to beat it. We need to have a little talk with your friend out back."

"I'm afraid I can't do that. The buddy system is sacred." Since neither of them recognized me, they were probably newer recruits. I can't imagine I was super popular over there, having blown up their god and all. Since I'd killed her father, Lucinda was probably still holding a grudge too.

"Have it your way, tough guy." Baldy gave a sharp whistle, like he was calling a dog.

The front door opened and the last biker came in.

Now that one got my attention. He was dressed like the others, but under his leathers he was wearing a hoodie. It was pulled up tight, and he was keeping his head down. He walked toward us, half strut, half shuffle, like he was trying to mimic the others, but he wasn't used to walking like a human being.

I can't really claim monster detector as one of my gifts, but sometimes I just knew when something was wrong. Maybe it was related to the whole Chosen psychic thing, but when I came across something unnatural, I could just feel it in my gut. And the one in the hoodie was *off*. He didn't belong here. And by *here*, I don't mean this bar, I mean the mortal plane of existence.

"Hand over that file, or you're gonna have to deal with him," Beardly warned.

You didn't need to have any mystical monster sense to recognize that this thing was dangerous. The weird biker growled at the bartender/waitress as he went by. She quickly decided it was a good time to go check on something under the bar. The atmosphere in the room had changed. One of the two alcoholics got up and hurried out the front door, making him the smartest person here. The other one was too blitzed to know what was going on. So much for witnesses.

"What's he supposed to be?" I asked.

"He's bad news...Stop." Baldy held up one hand, and the creature obediently froze, head down, snorting aggressively. Those were not human noises. "Hold. Wait for instructions." It was obvious the thing was under Baldy's control, and the second he took it off the leash it would do something horrible to us. He turned back to me. "You should have left when you had the chance, wingman."

If Kevin hadn't wet his khakis yet, he was probably getting really close.

"Hold on," I told the bikers. "You guys can have him."

"Aw, man," Kevin moaned, probably realizing he was about to get his arms ripped off *and* still be stuck with student loans.

"But I've got one question first."

"What?" Beardly snapped.

"Is that thing PUFF-applicable?" I nodded toward the hoodie-wearing monstrosity.

"Huh?"

"Perpetual Unearthly Forces Fund. I'm thinking he's some kind of undead, and if that's the case, and you dipshits are running around with him, that means legally you count as necromancers. Now I figure you're too stupid to animate the dead yourself, but that's a technicality."

They exchanged a confused glance. I guess at this point, people were usually quaking at their scary pet monster and begging for mercy, not getting lippy over definitions.

"Lucinda Hood must really be hard up for muscle these days to recruit you brainiacs. Look. It's simple. If you're necromancers, it means legally I can do this—"

I opened fire.

The compact STI jumped in my hand. I couldn't aim from under the table, but at this range, it didn't matter much. I just pointed it in their general direction and started yanking the trigger. Baldy got hit in the thigh and twice in the pelvis. Beardly took one in the gut and another to the knee. As they went crashing down, I shifted and put four holes in Hoodie, but whatever it was, it didn't react. Apparently it took the command to *hold* very literally. I slid out of the booth, covering them with my pistol.

"If you're necromancers, the MCB can't give me any shit for shooting you!" I hoped Kevin was taking notes, because these mopes had just gotten *lawyered*.

One was screaming. The other swearing, but the command for their undead to activate must have been in there somewhere, because it whipped its head back and roared. The hood fell. You could mistake it for a living thing, if the light was really bad and you weren't that close, but at conversational distance it was obviously a mess of patchwork body parts. I had guessed right. It was a stitched-together zombified automaton, Hood family recipe. And Lucinda was getting pretty good if she was building undead with enough grace to ride a bike.

I shot it right between its sunken yellow eyes. It blinked. I fired my last .45 round damned near through the same hole. But it still didn't go down. *Crap.* With these things you had to absolutely wreck their brains.

Before one of the cultists could shout the command to attack, I grabbed my still unopened bottle of Coke, and stabbed it right into the monster's forehead, aiming for the bullet holes. Thankfully it didn't shatter in my hands. My aim was good. Skin split and skull cracked. I shoved until the bottle got stuck, then I grabbed the automaton by the back of the head and slammed it facedown into our table, hard as I could, driving the Coke deep into its brain cavity. The bottle shattered. The table broke. And the undead hit the ground in a twitching heap, spraying ooze and soda. Kevin screamed and climbed up onto his seat.

I turned back to the wounded bikers just as Baldy was reaching into his vest . . . only Milo got there before he could draw, and Baldy caught a Birkenstock to the face.

Trip rushed in the back, pistol in hand. He took in the mess, then shot the automaton in the base of the skull twice just to be sure. "I tossed the last one in the dumpster."

My ears were ringing. "Did you kill him?"

"Eh . . . Maybe?" Trip looked a little embarrassed. "That depends on how hard his head is. I wasn't trying to, but I was in a hurry."

Kevin was still screaming, and that was getting on my nerves. The guy I'd shot in the stomach was making less noise. "Shush already!"

The waitress/bartender, and I was realizing now probable owner, had stuck her head around the corner. She saw us pointing pistols at two men bleeding on her floor, and one really obviously dead body, and then she ducked back down. I hoped she was dialing 911, not preparing to hang a shotgun around the corner to blast us.

"Don't worry," I shouted in her direction. "You're safe. We're the good guys. Everything is under control." Even if she believed me, she probably wasn't thinking I was that good of a tipper anymore.

After Milo had disarmed the bikers, he had gotten his phone out. "Hey, Eddings...Yeah. It's Milo. Sorry to bug you again, but since we're not supposed to be here, would you mind coming down and collecting the PUFF on a..." He looked at the monster. "Huh. I'm not actually sure, but Owen killed it with a soda pop...No...Really."

The Las Vegas team had all the right contacts with the local PD to handle supernatural business, and they could get all this sorted out. The necromancers would get turned over to the MCB for questioning. As far as the government would be concerned, it would be from MHI Las Vegas, and my guys would have had nothing to do with this.

What was the Sanctified Church of the Temporary Mortal Condition doing here anyway? Baldy was passed out, so I squatted down next to Beardly. I checked his neck. Sure enough, he was wearing one of those necklaces with an amulet of their old—now blown to smithereens—squid god on it. I knew from one particularly awful near-death experience that the second he gave away too much about the Condition, it would choke him to death, and then he'd reanimate as a zombie.

"Listen carefully, asshole. I'm only going to ask this once. I know you work for Lucinda Hood. Who does the Condition worship now?"

"The Dread Overlord sees all!"

"Your Dread Overlord sees zip. He's dead."

"You're lying! He grants us power you can't even begin to—" I pistol-whipped him upside his stupid cultist head, hard enough to knock him cold. The *clunk* was extremely satisfying.

"What's that about?" Trip asked.

"Lucinda has her dad's idiot cult believing their Great Old One is still alive. She's got them doing Asag's bidding and they don't even know it."

"The Condition attracts power-hungry psychos. As long as their black magic keeps working, you think they're going to get too theologically picky about who is actually answering their prayers?" As an actual religious person, doing unto others as he'd have done unto him, Trip was offended as hell by these whackadoodle psychopaths. "That's a rhetorical question."

I went back over to the booth, stepped over the foaming zombie, grabbed Kevin by his polo shirt, and hoisted him up so we were eye to eye. He appeared to be going into shock. That was probably a lot of sudden violence for a regular boring person to process. "Hey!" I snapped my fingers a couple of times in front of his nose. That briefly got him to focus on something other than the monster. "Back to negotiations. I want to revise my previous offer."

"Up?" he asked hopefully.

I shook my head *no*.

He looked really dejected. "Okay, okay." He reached into his pocket, then held up a little thumb drive. "Here. Just take it."

"You had it *on* you?" I dropped him. "You are literally the worst blackmailer ever!"

# CHAPTER 5

I was sitting at the MHI compound's conference table, looking at Management's files. Earl Harbinger was reading over my shoulder. Again, the door was locked, and even though I had no idea if Tanya's elf squiggles actually kept away disembodied spirits or not, I'd gotten pretty good at making them myself.

"This is the mother lode," my boss muttered. We were so used to working in the dark against the forces of evil, having anything this solid was like a Christmas miracle. "Every recorded detail of every event related to this Asag since you woke him up. Every document and eyewitness report. The way most of this is written, I'm betting that dragon had a mole inside the MCB feeding him intel."

"Is this good enough to convince you to approve the mission?"

"Knowing about your adversary is a good start, but the key to a successful invasion means you need to know the terrain. All you've got on that island is that Myers stuck a pin in a map and told a cyclops to stare at it. And if we're going to rescue John and

86

Jason, we need to know how to cross over to the other side, and more importantly, how to come back in one piece."

My enthusiastic desire to kick some monster ass aside, Earl was right. "I've got some ideas on that stuff..."

"Don't forget what they say. Good generals study tactics, but great generals study logistics. The target is north of the Arctic Circle in a country that isn't big on letting foreign Hunters screw around on their turf."

I sighed. "Friggin' politics."

"If this job was all blowing shit up, it would be easy. It's one thing to say we want to conduct an op, but another to get all the pieces in place. All the firepower in the world is useless if we can't get it there. But this is good. You're learning, Z. I'm not going to be around to run this company forever, and I'd like to know that my great-granddaughter's right-hand man isn't an idiot."

"Come on, Earl. You're too ornery to die."

"Die? Hell, after reading that dragon file, I was talking about retiring." He clapped me on the shoulder and then headed for the exit. "Clock's ticking."

"I'm going to have to put a hurting on the travel budget," I warned him.

"You know I never look at those expense reports anyway."

"I'll go alone and try to keep it cheap."

"Bullshit. You'll take a partner to watch your back. You've got frequent flier miles, use them."

Jet lag is annoying and long flights screw me up. It was lunchtime in London, but felt like dinner. I knew from experience that when I tried to go to sleep tonight, I'd really want breakfast. I hated flying all over the place, but Earl had given me a month, so I was going to make the most of it.

I was sitting at an outdoor table at a little restaurant overlooking the Thames. I had a good view of the Tower Bridge. The weather was cloudy and a little too moist. I'd bought one of those floppy tweed hats and a big scarf. The excuse was to help serve as a disguise in case the Condition had people here. The reality was they were keeping me warm. Let's be honest. When you're six foot five, scary, and a very solid three-hundred-plus pounds, *disguise* is a nebulous concept at best.

A cab pulled up and a man got out. I checked my watch. As was expected, my guest had arrived exactly on time. He had a reputation for being precise. He paid the driver and walked over. I recognized him from the picture Julie had shown me from a hunt where MHI had teamed up with The Van Helsing Institute years ago. Only in that one he'd been much younger, and wearing body armor instead of a three-piece suit. What is it with British guys and those skinny suits?

A moment later the hostess showed my guest in. He was tall, in his thirties, thin but wiry. Nice suit or not, he still exuded that Hunter vibe, unconsciously scanning the room, looking for trouble, realizing we had the outdoor deck to ourselves, and then sizing me up when I stood to shake hands.

"Dr. Rigby?"

"No need for the 'doctor.' My friends simply call me Rigby, Mr. Pitt." I was twice his mass, but he had a strong handshake.

"It's just Owen then. Thanks for coming. Have a seat."

He did. "Thank you for the invitation. Your reputation precedes you."

"It's no big deal." Actually I got a little embarrassed talking about my exploits. Half the time what other Hunters had heard was exaggerated or flat-out wrong anyway. "You've got an impressive resume yourself."

"I have simply carried on the family business."

"Meaning after a stint in the SAS you became a traveling monster expert. So what color is the boathouse at Hereford?"

"I love that film, but I have no idea what color it is. I was captain of my rowing team at Oxford, though."

Julie had caught me up on the inside baseball. The Rigby family were the UK's closest equivalent to the Shacklefords. The Van Helsing Institute tended to be a little more gentlemanly, academic, and refined, and a whole lot less redneck, but before he'd gone on to become some sort of expert occult super scholar at Oxford, Ben Rigby's grandfather had been blowing up Nazi monsters for the Special Operations Executive during World War II. Earl said the Rigby family was *all right*.

"I hope business is good here."

"Monster attacks are nightmarishly frequent in London, so it has been lucrative."

We made small talk. He knew my wife, but hadn't seen her since she'd visited his mother's ancestral estate in Scotland one summer when Julie had been a teenager. Then we talked innocuous shop talk. The British treated monster hunting differently than we did in America, with the government and private sector working closely together. British Hunters weren't allowed nearly as much hardware as we were, so the government did most of the trigger pulling. The Van Helsing Institute was more like detectives than mercenaries.

The waitress came out and took our order. I asked for fish and chips, because that seemed *properly British*. Rigby ordered a hamburger and a pint of beer. After she left, he got back to work.

"So what really brings you to London, Owen? Your message indicated that you wanted to discuss a business opportunity. Yet you wished to meet in private rather than in our offices. In addition, you asked for me specifically, rather than Howard Isherwood, though MHI is fully aware that Howard administers all of our contractual dealings. I must admit that I am curious as to the nature of your visit."

"You guys really have the coolest accent."

"We merely consider it *talking*."

"I bet the chicks dig it."

"I'd assume so, but I would not know. However, my partner finds it appealing."

Julie hadn't told me *that* about Rigby. Not that I particularly cared. The dude was supposed to be good at hunting monsters. I didn't give a crap about what my colleagues did in their personal lives unless it messed with my job. "Okay then."

"Please, continue."

"Okay, here's the deal. I came to you because—no offense to your company—we don't know them. Earl Harbinger vouched for you and your family." In fact, the Rigbys were some of the few people outside of MHI who knew Earl was a werewolf, and that family knowledge went back a *long* time. "We're working a job involving a High-Value Target. The thing we're up against has a reputation for having spies everywhere."

Rigby nodded. "Both supernatural and earthly spies, I presume. Hence the elven runes designed to ward off ghosts chalked on the boards beneath our table, and your associate up on the bridge pretending to be a tourist with the binoculars, observing anyone who wanders by to make sure we are not being eavesdropped on."

"He's good." Holly Newcastle said in my earpiece. "Cute too. Too bad on the gay thing, because that accent really is a panty dropper."

"Never mind her. She just volunteered to come along because she wanted to go shopping and play tourist afterward."

"Seriously, I could listen to him read the phonebook."

I reached into my coat and turned down the volume on my radio. "We also swept the place for bugs because he has human cultists working for him. I'm here because I need a favor. I've got a source that said we could find more information about our HVT in Oxford's sealed collections. MHI has a pass, but nobody knows it as well as you guys. If my people go poking around in there about him, somebody is bound to notice."

"Everyone with access is sworn to secrecy, but the secret collection is rather vast. It would not surprise me to know the forces of evil keep an eye on it. Oxford has been collecting monster lore and occult volumes for centuries. Who is your source?"

"The individual who organized the first annual International Conference of Monster Hunting Professionals. Which was, unfortunately, also the last annual Conference of Monster Hunting Professionals."

"After that debacle I can understand your source's desire for anonymity. I'm sorry I missed Las Vegas. I was on a consultation in Iraq. Many of my associates were at that conference. Not all of them came home. I would have liked to help. Such a terrible business."

"Yeah, it pretty much sucked."

"Speaking of which, I was told you had broken your arm there. I must have been misinformed."

"Naw, I broke the shit out of it, but we have an orc witch doctor. She knocks months off of recuperation."

"That is nice. We have to make do with a leprechaun."

Now Rigby was just messing with me. "Since VHI has unlimited access to the collection, and you're a regular there, I was hoping you could do some research for us."

"If a creature has ever crossed the path of man, there will be a mention of it in there somewhere. The issue is folklore and legend are notoriously unreliable, and the collection is an unfortunate mingling of both fact and fiction. However, I also have sources within the Supernatural Service. That is our equivalent to your MCB. What would I be looking for?"

"Three things." I glanced around. It appeared to be all clear. "First, anything there is about a being known as Asag."

Rigby gave me a curious look. "Disorder." I must have appeared perplexed, because he immediately clarified. "I'm sorry. I'm something of an expert on ancient Mesopotamian mythology. Assuming we are speaking of the same creature—and he was once rather infamous—that is what Asag translates as ... Disorder."

"That actually seems really fitting. So far he's been

a behind-the-scenes string-puller more than an in-your-face, Hulk-smash kind of monster."

"Appropriate for a being who could best be described as a god of chaos. Asag was the demonic villain in a cuneiform poem that is several thousand years old, so hideous that his mere presence boiled the fish in the rivers. He is real then?"

"Oh yeah, and he's a dick. MCB has him flagged as a potential extinction-level threat, not that they ever tell us anything. He was behind the attack in Vegas, and a whole bunch of other things. Anything you could find could help."

I think the monster detective took that as a challenge. "Consider it done."

He was being a little too helpful. There were lots of altruistic heroic types in this business, but only suckers worked for free. "What could MHI do for you in return?"

"If this Asag of yours is a world ender, that means the PUFF bounty would be astronomical. I know what your Lord Machado payout was. Even if it is bagged outside of the United States, if the threat is sufficient your government will still pay PUFF, like they did on the Arbmunep. I'll help you, but in exchange the Institute gets a piece of the action."

"Standard consulting percentages off the total, and equal shares based upon any manpower provided to the actual operation." I was ready for this. I was the company's accountant after all.

"That sounds more than reasonable."

Rigby was sharp, but he probably didn't yet realize the sheer scope of what I was putting together. This was going to need to be a multi-company operation anyway, so by agreeing to that I wasn't giving up too much. "I'm fine with that. But you can't tell a soul what you're working on until we bring you in officially. Deal?"

"We have a deal. And the next item on your shopping list?"

This was worth a shot. "Anything you can get your hands on related to how travel works in the Nightmare Realm, and how to get back safely."

He stared at me, incredulous. "Are you mad?" He didn't need an answer. He just shook his head, as if to say *it's your funeral*. "Very well. And last?"

"Anything you can find about monster activity, current or historical, on Severny Island."

"I've heard of it. There has been quite an uptick of monster activity there in recent years. Wait..." He chuckled. "That's really where your target is?"

"Yeah. So?"

"You're pulling my leg." Rigby laughed harder this time. "You're serious? Bloody hell."

"What?"

"Then you've got a problem, mate. Severny is covered by a KMCG contract. Any monster problems there belong to Ivan Krasnov's company. You'd need to get the Russian government's permission to operate there, which means you need Krasnov's approval." When I showed no reaction to this apparently really bad news, he asked, "Do you even know Krasnov?"

"No. Should I?"

"Lucky you. Working mostly in America, I can understand why you haven't heard of him. Every European company knows that knob. MCB probably wouldn't let him within a hundred clicks of your border without calling in an airstrike."

"He's one of us?"

"Oh, no. No. *No.* I mean, he is dodgy as fuck but he's *technically* a Monster Hunter . . ." When the subject of Krasnov came up, the gentlemanly Oxford airs went out the window. "Well, it's complicated. I'd call him a rat bastard, but that would be an insult to rats. And bastards!" Rigby just shook his head, took out a notepad and began writing down contact information. He tore the page out and handed it to me. "Here. This is how you reach him. Good luck. You'll need it."

He hadn't even said that about going into the Nightmare Realm.

A couple of days later Holly and I met two men at the Sheremetyevo Airport in Moscow. Both of them were nearly my size and of similar build, wearing suits which looked expensive yet which still didn't conceal their shoulder holsters very well. Neither of them seemed to speak a word of English. I couldn't tell if these guys were supposed to be Hunters or just scary thug types, but they'd been the ones holding up a sign with MHI written on it after we'd gotten through customs. So, what the hell? Life is an adventure.

They led us out to a parked Mercedes limousine with dark tinted windows. One of them roughly tossed our bags in the trunk while the other lit a cigarette and got into the driver's seat. Baggage guy came around and opened the rear door for us. He nodded for us to get in.

"So, do we tip him?" Holly asked. The thug must have taken that as a compliment or thought she was flirting, because he gave her a smile. He had several gold teeth right in front. "Okay then," she said as she got in the car.

I ducked my head and followed. The Russian slammed the door behind me. We ended up sitting facing backwards. The interior of the limo was cheesy rather than classy. It had a very Big Eighties vibe, real plush red seats and purple lights. There was a bottle of champagne in a bucket of ice. The limo felt like a rolling disco. Sitting in the back, giving us a huge grin that was as cheesy as his car, was a gigantic, bald man with a bushy mustache. And when I say gigantic, I mean picture somebody who was once as big and muscular as me, but then drape another twenty years and fifty pounds of flab on him. He was a big dude. And *loud*. And *enthusiastic*.

"Welcome to Russia, Monster Hunters International! I hope the flight was most excellent. You will now enjoy my hospitality." He had a booming voice and an accent like a stereotype in a spy movie. "Owen Zastava Pitt and Holly Newcastle, I am your host, Krasnov!"

When I'd called and told Earl our next stop on our European research trip, he'd laughed at me like Rigby had. When it came to rival monster hunting organizations, Earl rated everyone on a scale of Asshole to All Right. Earl had never worked with the Hunters of KMCG personally, but by reputation alone, apparently Ivan Krasnov pegged Asshole so hard that he'd broken the meter. When I'd asked how bad this was going to be, Earl told me not to drink anything that might be drugged unless I wanted to wake up in a bathtub full of ice missing a kidney.

"It is an honor to meet you, Mr. Krasnov," Holly said.

"Ah, you are even more beautiful than I was warned, Miss Holly. I have enjoyed the company of many beautiful women, but you are both the sexy and the deadly. With body of movie star, and brain of doctor, and you have killed all the things!"

That took her a second to digest. She actually seemed charmed by such refreshing honesty. "How sweet."

"And Mr. Owen, who has exploded Old One, you as well are welcomed to the finest monster hunting company in all of Russia." He spread his thick arms wide. "Krasnov's Multinational Corporation of Greatness."

He wasn't joking either. That was actually what he'd named the thing.

We pulled out into traffic. Judging by the way it rode, the Mercedes must have been armored like a tank. Since I'd learned about how the monster hunting business worked in this country, that made a lot of sense. It was so cutthroat and territorial they often had as much to fear from their competitors as the actual monsters.

Russia had always had a monster problem. Nobody really knew why. Maybe it was because it was just such a vast area, with so many wild places with low population densities, monsters thought it was a good place to hide. According to the old myths, this part of the world had once been lousy with Fey, and lots of them had stuck around. More recently, the Soviets had dabbled in experiments which made Decision Week look like a Cub Scout Jamboree, and let a lot of nasty things loose into the world in the process. Hell, maybe they just liked the weather, but whatever the reason, Russia had a ton of monsters in it.

Before the Soviet Union fell, monsters were handled strictly by the government. They weren't fast or efficient about it, but they took care of outbreaks with an extra helping of overkill. Earl had described them as absolutely *brutal,* and that meant a lot coming from a man who'd once driven a snow cutter through a town full of zombie werewolves. When the Soviet Union went away, so did most of their secret monster eradication programs. For the decade following, monster hunting remained the government's job, but it wasn't getting done very well. The only thing they were still good at was silencing witnesses, and apparently they were far less merciful about it than our MCB. However, with very few people actively hunting them, the monster populations exploded.

But such is the glorious nature of capitalism, that if there is a service in need of doing, and a way to make a ruble at it, somebody will step up and do the job. Unfortunately, since monster hunting was illegal, and the population wasn't well armed enough to do it anyway, that meant the only people willing to do what needed to be done, who could get their hands on the hardware necessary, were the kind of people who simply did not give a crap about the rules. For example, a young Siberian Spetsnaz officer who looted his armory, deserted, and then got rich getting paid by oligarchs and the Russian mafia to blast any critter that was cutting into their profits.

I was told that criminals only thrive in Russia if the Kremlin allows them to, which means that when necessary they are at the government's disposal. Fast forward a generation, the Russians had their own contract-based version of PUFF, and men like Ivan Krasnov were *legitimate businessman.*

"I have heard much of legendary MHI. I always

hoped to meet. I wished to attend this conference in your Last Vegas but could not."

Since everything in Krasnov's orbit seemed to be simultaneously expensive yet tacky, he'd probably love Vegas. "You should have come. It was great. Until the part with all the horror and dying."

"Yes, yes. I was invited. But your Department of Homeland Security was upset at me so I could not go to your country. Eh. You misplace one truckload of missiles and they put you on terrorist watch list like common criminal. What are you gonna do?"

That was the other problem with hunters here. They were a little more diversified in their income streams than the rest of us. When you've got a perfectly good private army of heavily armed professional killers— who get bored easily—you might as well keep them busy somehow.

Krasnov reached for the limo's snack bin. "Caviar? It's very expensive."

"No, thanks."

"Ha! More for me!"

After a three-hour-long, ten-course dinner at a ridiculously nice restaurant, Krasnov's limo had dropped us off at our hotel. It seemed old, but nice. He'd pronounced it a dump unfit for such illustrious guests, and had offered to take us to a place which was *so much classier*, but I was keeping my word and trying not to spend too much. Tonight we had been wined and dined, and given a tour as we were driven around the city, being told a lot of loud and boisterous stories the whole time, but as far as actual business conducted... it wasn't going too well.

As we were dragging our suitcases down the hall, Holly was complaining. "That was a lot of flash, but not a lot of substance."

"Can't think. I'm in meat shock."

"Well, duh, you ate like a whole wild boar, Z. Did you actually have to eat its face?"

"Snout's the best part of the boar." Not that I was an expert, but that's what Krasnov had loudly declared to the entire restaurant. I switched to my bad impersonation of our host. "Honored guest must eat all the pig nose!"

"I'm pretty sure he was just messing with you to see if you'd actually do it, you freak."

"I had to eat all the snout, Holly. For America."

"Whatever. I mean we got a lot of platitudes about working together, building a bridge to a better tomorrow, and all that nonsense, but you can't pin him down. You'd think somebody that large wouldn't be that slippery."

We couldn't bring up the real reason for our visit until we trusted him not to leak it. And he wasn't going to trust us enough to tell us anything until he knew the real reason for why we were here. Plus there had been a dozen other people at dinner, half of whom I had no idea who they were, or why they were there, and none of them spoke English. Not counting the two bodyguards, some guests seemed to be other Hunters, a couple I think were expensive prostitutes, and one guy was apparently a famous hockey player. So it had been more of a dinner party for Krasnov to shout *look at my new American friends* than a clandestine meeting to discuss going to war with a demon.

"Yeah, and then it got really awkward when the hockey jock assumed since you were on vacation without your wife I must be your mistress," Holly said, grimacing. "As if. No offense, Z."

"None taken." Holly was like my sister. We both knew I was utterly devoted to Julie, and that was before taking into account that my wife could snipe me from a mile away if I ever cheated on her. "On the bright side, them thinking I was your date kept the number of drunk dudes hitting on you to a minimum. We'll figure out our next step in the morning."

"Krasnov thinks of himself as a lady's man. I bet I could get him to trust us."

"That's really taking one for the team."

"Not like that. I mean I can charm him. You've just got to make eye contact, smile a lot, and pretend to listen. Trust me, there's a science to flirting. I made bank as a dancer. I've known a lot of Krasnovs...I bet he owns a closet full of tracksuits."

"Not that I doubt your skills, but let's not underestimate him. You don't end up top dog in a system like this by being stupid or easily manipulated." I found my room number. Holly's room was across the hall.

"Night, Z. I really need a shower."

Once I had some privacy I called home. Eleven at night here was like two in the afternoon there if I remembered right. Julie picked up immediately.

"How's Moscow?"

"Prettier than I expected, but the trip's not exactly been fruitful." Stricken's replacement was supposedly not evil, so I didn't know if our calls were still being monitored or not, but we were still going to play it safe and keep everything nice and vague. As far as the rest of the world knew, this was just MHI on a goodwill visit looking for new business opportunities with other companies. "We had a nice dinner party. I ate the whole wild boar."

"That's nice, hon. Listen, I did some more checking with some of the central European Hunters. Tadeusz at White Eagle and Libor at Phantom have both worked with Krasnov before." Those companies were from Poland and the Czech Republic respectively. After their performance in Vegas, Earl rated both of those companies as All Right. "The verdict's not good."

"Let me guess. He's basically a mob boss."

"Pretty much. They don't think he's insane or anything like that, just criminal."

"He's actually kind of jolly in person."

"He'll lie, cheat, steal, and probably worse. He's fundamentally dishonest but really gleeful about it. White Eagle got ripped off so badly on a bounty once that if Krasnov ever shows his face in Poland they'll probably just murder him. But that doesn't stop his guys from poaching on other Hunters' turf."

"Lovely."

"He's supposedly devout Russian Orthodox, but I was told a lot of mobsters there are, so I don't know if he's devout or that's just politically expedient. Be careful. Anything you tell him might just get sold to the highest bidder."

"I was afraid of that." That meant we were going to have to find another way to learn about the island without alerting Asag.

We spoke for a while, about how she was feeling—tired and nauseous—if there was anything new with my dad—there wasn't—and the general innocuous stuff married couples talk about when one of us is far away so we could pretend they were near. When I got tired enough to maybe sleep, I told her I loved her and said my goodbyes.

After we hung up, I shut off the light and got into bed. Normally I'd have a gun on the nightstand, but I had no legal way of bringing a firearm into this country. I'm sure I could have gotten some easy enough. Heck, I could have just asked Krasnov for one. I'd thought about it, but he was the type of man I wouldn't put it past to sic the cops on me, so I could get a weapons charge, so he could bail me out and I'd have to owe him a *favor*. No thanks.

Sure, a gun is just a tool, my mind is the weapon, and all that, but not having a gun made me nervous. So after a few minutes of staring at the darkened ceiling, I got up, dragged a couch in front of the door, and then went back to bed.

Just after two in the morning somebody knocked on my door.

I must not have been sleeping well, because I leapt out of bed, ready to fight to the death, in my underwear. I went to the door and rudely shouted, "Who is it!" In my defense, random late-night hotel-room knocks were how I'd first met Martin Hood, and he'd ended up throwing a toilet at me.

"It is I, Krasnov."

I had to climb over the couch to look through the peephole. Sure enough, there was his enormous round face looking back. Because of the fish-eye effect of the glass, I realized he had a mustache that would have made Stalin proud. He'd probably gotten bored and wanted to hit a strip club or something. I pushed the couch out of the way and opened the door.

He'd ditched his flashy suit and was wearing some extra-extra-large camouflage fatigues and a blue beret. He had a pistol in a flap holster on his belt and was even wearing a *sword.* Unless Moscow strip clubs were surprisingly rowdy, there went my initial theory as to the nature of his visit. "What're you doing here?" I asked, still unsure if this was all a bad dream brought on by an overdose of boar snout. "What's going on?"

It was weird, but he actually looked a little bashful. "I could not sleep. I got thinking. The two of us must get to know each other better before we can conduct proper business. Are we friends?"

"Yeah?"

"Some, but I think not yet really. There is not real trust between us. I can tell you do not speak freely about why you have come here."

"To be fair—"

"Yes! Yes! I as well hesitate to speak truth. You do not trust me. Do not worry. My feelings are not hurt...much. So I think to myself, what is best way for Monster Hunters to become like family? It is to hunt monsters, of course!"

"Okay, I get what you're saying but—"

"Wait." It was hard to tell, but I think he was trying to be sincere. "To get the measure of a Hunter, you must hunt together. Then, my company received tip of monster here in town. This is fate! So now we hunt monster. I have left my men home. You will leave Miss Holly. Only the two of us will do this. We will fight evil together, Krasnov and Pitt! And then we will know if we wish to conduct real business or not. No more wasting time."

Holly had heard the commotion and opened her door a crack. She'd thrown on a bathrobe, and I wasn't surprised to see that she'd unscrewed a table leg to use as an improvised club. I wasn't the only one who had a hard time sleeping without weapons. Krasnov turned to her and theatrically tipped his beret. "Good morning, Miss Holly."

"Morning?" she grumbled. "It's kick-you-in-the-face o'clock."

"I did not mean to wake you, Miss Holly. I am taking Owen out for a rampage."

"Rampage?"

"This is the right word, no?"

"You're not going on a rampage without me," Holly said.

"*Nyet.* I insist. Do not worry for your friend. It is only small monster. Not too dangerous. This is man business only. Do not offend your host. Come, Comrade! Why are you still in your underpants? There are monsters to be killed!" He hurried down the hall. It wasn't particularly graceful. "We will meet downstairs!"

Holly watched him go, then turned to me. "Did he just call you 'comrade'? Is that still a thing?"

# CHAPTER 6

Krasnov drove us across the city to a part of town that was darker and more run-down than what we'd seen so far. This time he'd ditched the gaudy limo for a plain sedan and, true to his word, he'd left his entourage behind. The neighborhood we were in now was mostly concrete apartment buildings with a lot of graffiti sprayed on them.

"So what's the monster?"

"It is surprise. I do not think you have these in America."

Great. I loved surprises, especially the kind that could murder you. I still wasn't sure if this was a monster hunt, or if I was about to be kidnapped and held for ransom. "Can you at least tell me where we're going?"

"It is old public pool. Broken down, not used for years. We got tip he is hiding there tonight. We have looked for this monster for many weeks." He pulled the sedan into a parking lot in front of a squat, square, really ugly building. Judging by the broken windows and weeds growing around it, this place had been abandoned for years. The only other car in the lot was a police car. Krasnov drove up so the driver-side windows were right next to each other.

The nervous-looking cop didn't seem surprised to see him. Krasnov began asking him questions and giving orders. I understood most of it, all pretty straightforward stuff, witnesses saw one creature, there might be some gunfire noise, keep out meddlers, if we're not out in an hour we're probably dead, that sort of thing. My mom had gone to school in Russia and was fairly fluent, and as a kid I'd loved playing language games with her. Lots of that had stuck. Krasnov, however, didn't know I understood any of his language because I'd played stupid at dinner, waiting to see how much he lied, though his translating had been fairly accurate so far.

When he was done grilling the cop, Krasnov passed over an envelope full of cash. The cop shoved it into his vest and then drove off to block the street. My biggest takeaway from that conversation was the thing we were hunting was called a *Vodyanoy*.

Krasnov drove right up to the front door, parked, and killed the engine. "Here we go!" He got out.

I followed. "Am I supposed to just use harsh language?"

"What kind of terrible host do you take me for?" He walked around to the back of the car and popped the trunk. "Help yourself."

There were several weapons in the trunk, just kind of dumped there in a haphazard pile. Krasnov pulled out a load-bearing vest, covered in magazine pouches, and put it on. Only when he tried to buckle it around his belly, the straps were an inch too short. "Eh . . . It must have shrunk."

"Yeah, ballistic nylon will do that." I had a sneaky feeling that my host had been enjoying the good life a bit much and hadn't gotten out in the field for a while.

He finally gave up on getting the vest closed and pulled out a Bizon submachine gun for himself. I couldn't tell what all was in there, it was such a mess, so I pulled out a matching one. At least that way if Krasnov got killed I knew I could use the extra weird helical magazines on his vest.

I hated borrowing equipment. That required me to have faith in someone else's weapon maintenance. I worked the charging handle to clear it. Everything felt right. Then I dry-fired it at the trunk to hear the snap of the trigger. Everything felt okay. I checked to make sure the weapon-mounted light worked by shining it on the pavement. There was a clunky red dot sight mounted on it, and I made sure that worked too.

"You are familiar with Kalashnikov style, yes?"

It took me a second to figure out the hinge to rock a mag into place, then I chambered a round, and flipped the safety back up. "Remind me afterwards and I'll tell you about Abomination."

There was a pouch with some extra mags. I threw the strap over my shoulder like a camouflage purse. *Very fashionable.* I had my own flashlight in my pocket that I could count on. I missed my knives. But there was a nasty-looking camp hatchet, so I took that and shoved the handle through my belt. "You got a secondary? Handguns I mean?" Krasnov reached into the back of the trunk and pulled out—I kid you not—a plastic grocery sack filled with pistols. "Nice."

"Only the finest for you."

I pulled out one of the Grachs and checked the

chamber. The Russian pistol was ugly as sin and ergo-
nomic as a brick, but it would have to do. I loaded it,
then I felt really ghetto as I shoved it into the back
of my waistband. Professionals used holsters for a reason. If I did anything more strenuous than walk in a
straight line, that pistol would probably slide down my
pant leg and end up on the ground. I stuck an extra
magazine into the pocket of my jeans just in case.

My host ditched his silly hat and pulled on a balaclava. He offered me one. I looked at it funny. "What?
You do not cover faces when you work in America?"

"Not usually."

"Eh . . . It makes it harder for people to seek retribu-
tion after you accidentally break their things."

*When in Rome* . . . I put the mask on. Whoever had
worn it last had been a heavy smoker.

The last thing Krasnov pulled out of the trunk
was a sledgehammer. Then he walked straight up to
the double doors and smashed the lock. Three big
hits with the hammer and the heavy door was toast.

The interior was extremely dark. The streetlamps
from outside didn't help much when all the unbro-
ken windows were covered in dust and cobwebs. I
shouldered the gun and squeezed the pressure pad
to turn on the light. I swept into the first room. The
only thing inside was trash and some broken furniture.

Krasnov was humming. I'm pretty sure it was one
of the songs from Tetris. He pointed his subgun's
muzzle at a faded sign on the wall. "The pool is that
way. Our *Vodnik* friend will be in water."

Nobody had been in here for years. "You'd think
it would be drained."

"He is smart. He would turn the faucet on. They

like water. My mother always said after they rip out your spirit, they have to keep it in a little bubble under the water, or it will float away."

I stopped. "Hold on. What the hell are we dealing with?"

"It is called *Vodyanoy*. A water monster from Fey age. This one has drowned many little childrens." He went back to humming as he walked down the hall, kicking cans and bottles out of the way with his boots. Stealth and subtlety weren't exactly his thing.

"How tough are they?"

"They are like men. Some tough. Some not so tough. This *Vodyanoy* is from the river, eh, should be medium-tough at most."

"That sounds like a pretty scientific measurement."

"What we do is more art than science, my friend!" There was another door at the end of the hall. It was locked, too, so Krasnov smashed it with the sledge-hammer. Being a softer interior door, it flew right open. That made a bang that must have surely been heard through the entire building. "Like men, some Fey are nice, some are not so nice. This *Vodyanoy* is very not nice."

"I take it we're not trying to sneak up on it."

"Of course not. There are only two of us. He will think two men are not so many to kill. He will attack, but we will show him who is getting killed! This way we will not have to search."

The air in this corridor was warm and moist. It smelled swampy. We were getting closer to the pool. I was moving forward, crouched a bit, metal stock pressed against my shoulder, ready to fire in an instant. Krasnov was just blundering along, stubby Bizon casually in hand.

Our guns were only 9mms, which by MHI's standards was a round reserved for pixies. They worked fine on people, but monsters tended to be more resilient, which was why we made the big bucks. "And what if he's more than medium-tough?"

"We run away and blow up building with bomb. But then the city pays less on contract. So bullets are more profitable." Then he went back to humming.

There were locker rooms on one side, and saunas on the other. There was a slimy, black trail leading to one of them. That door was open just a bit, so I shoved it the rest of the way with the muzzle, then pied the corner. The floor was covered in bones, white, glistening, and licked clean. Most of them were from dogs and cats, but there were a few that were obviously human.

"Told you he liked to eat the childrens." Krasnov leaned around and took in the whole sauna. "Looks like some grown-ups too! Quite the appetite this one has! This will be a fine bounty."

Next was a set of double doors. The slime trail led right through them. Before Krasnov could gleefully hit them with his sledgehammer, I shook my head, then pushed on one of the doors with my boot. It swung freely. Looking a little disappointed, Krasnov set the hammer down and got his Bizon ready.

We entered, and the air was so moist, foul, and unnaturally warm that it was like getting smacked in the face with the Everglades. It was a big room. There was a large swimming pool taking up the center. The water had turned thick, green, and was covered in scum. It really stunk in here. A kind of fetid, humid, rotting stench. The only reason we could breathe at all was that there had been glass panels in the ceiling and some of those had shattered so the stench could waft into the night.

Clouds of little flies buzzed in front of my face and got in my eyes. Okay, one nice thing about wearing the ridiculous, stinky balaclava was that the insects couldn't fly up my nose.

"Come out, watery asshole!" Krasnov shouted. "We know you are here!"

The only response was when several large bubbles rose through the murk and burst open at the top. That made it smell even worse.

"He probably doesn't speak English," I suggested.

"Of course!" And then Krasnov launched into a giant tirade of profanity-laced insults in Russian. I only understood about half of them, but they were mostly about the *Vodyanoy's* mother and her promiscuous nature.

I nodded to the side, warning him that I was going to go right. Since he'd told me nothing about what this thing could do, I didn't want to be standing right next to him in case it turned out it could breathe fire, or spit acid, or who knew what. Things that got filed under Fey get *weird*. I had to step carefully. The tile was slick with mold.

Krasnov kept up the insults for a couple of minutes, and I'm fairly sure he never repeated himself. I couldn't speak for the aquatic monster, but I know I would've been insulted. But after that initial gurgle of bubbles, there'd been no sign of the thing.

The fat man stopped his tirade. He looked over at me. "Eh. Maybe he is not hom—"

The pool exploded.

Disgusting filth sprayed the walls as the monster launched itself from the bottom of the pool. A green bolt of enraged muscle hit Krasnov like a truck.

It was hard to tell what was happening because sludge had gotten all over my weapon light. Blinking slime out of my eyes, I swung my gun over, but the monster was on him, and the two were rolling across the floor. I didn't have a shot. Slipping and sliding, I tried to get closer.

Krasnov was shouting and trying to lever his subgun around, but the beast was shaking him back and forth like a terrier with a rat. It was actually a little smaller than the Hunter, but it must have been really *strong*. I timed it, and the instant it raised one misshapen arm to rip his face off, I popped off two quick shots into the back of its head.

It turned around and hissed.

The *Vodyanoy* was part man, part frog. It had two great big glassy eyes far out on the top of its lumpy head, and a mouth that had to be a foot across. It was jowly and had a green beard made of algae. The creature was fat, squat, and sitting on top of Krasnov's massive gut, with one webbed hand wrapped around the straps of his load-bearing vest. A pink tongue popped out of its mouth, way too long, and rubbed the spots where I had shot it, glaring at me the whole time, as if to say *I can't believe you did that*.

I had like fifty-something more where that came from so I opened up on it.

The monster leapt off, bounding halfway across the room to stick to the wall, and then it instantaneously rebounded and launched itself at me. It was lightning fast. I tried to dodge to the side, but the floor was slicker than snot, and I slipped, crashing against the tile and sliding through the mold. The *Vodyanoy* flew past, landed behind me, flipped over, and started waddling back toward me.

I rolled over, lifted the gun, aimed, and *snap*. In an instant, that pink tongue shot out like a whip, struck the receiver, suction-cupped on, and then ripped it right out of my hands. The tongue detached from the gun somewhere on the way back, and the Bizon went spinning end over end, to disappear into the pool with a *plop*.

It started waddling toward me again, the weird googly eyes seeming to point in different directions. I tried to get up, to make distance, but it was like the floor was greased, and all I succeeded in doing was sliding around and embarrassing myself. I reached for the Grach in my waistband, but of course, it wasn't there. Because we use holsters for a *reason*.

But then one of its big eyes compressed violently as Krasnov put a bullet in it. The eyeball didn't burst, but the way the *Vodyanoy* started blinking its massive eyelids, it had certainly felt that one. It tilted its head violently, then bounded right over me, nearly reaching the tall ceiling, and headed straight for the Russian. It seemed to want to kill him more. Maybe Krasnov really had hurt its feelings when he'd made fun of its mother.

Krasnov kept on shooting. I found a rusty metal towel rack on the wall and used that for stability as I got back to my feet.

"I do not think this is medium-tough!" Krasnov shouted as his bullets did basically nothing against the rubbery beast.

With one gun in the drink and the other bouncing around, the light in here was awful. I pulled the Streamlight out of my pocket and turned it on. I spotted the Grach where it had fallen out of my waistband, and picked it up. I liked my flashlights actually mounted on the gun, but if you hold a little light through your fingers like a cigar in your off hand, you can still get a pretty good two-handed shooting grip. I shot the *Vodyanoy* repeatedly in the back. It turned, the tongue flashed out again, and wrapped itself around the muzzle of the pistol. It was warm, slimy, and really, really gross on my hands. I barely got my finger out of the trigger guard before the pistol was sucked away.

This time it simply swallowed the smaller gun. The creature actually looked smug about it.

Krasnov bashed the monster over the head with the metal folding stock of his Bizon. It retaliated by grabbing him by the shoulders, swinging him around, and tossing him through a glass partition into the showers. Krasnov hit the wall hard. From the way he struggled back to his hands and knees, he was obviously dazed.

I pulled the little camp axe from my belt and followed. I had to use the wall to keep from falling over. It was like going to the roller rink as a kid and wearing skates for the first time.

One googly eye looked at Krasnov while the other looked at me, like *now I'm gonna eat your friend, what are you going to do about it, human?* Then it toddled over to finish him off.

Except I managed to get there just as it was picking Krasnov up, and planted my hatchet into the back of its fleshy head. The blade hit with a very solid *thunk*.

It dropped him. The weird Fey made a noise that sounded like *mrrrrrpp?* It spun, but I planted one boot onto its slimy back and wouldn't let go of that axe handle. We began to spin around the room. I dropped my flashlight and held onto the axe with both hands. It kept twirling, trying to reach me. It was like a dog chasing its tail. I was getting dizzy. It was a *Vodyanoy* rodeo. Pink blood started squirting out of the hole in its head. It almost looked like shampoo.

As we spun by, I saw the Russian was trying to get up. "A little help here, Krasnov!"

Since it couldn't flail around with its arms enough to dislodge me, the monster decided to head back to the pool. If I wouldn't let go, it would just drown me. My flashlight got kicked by a webbed foot, but at least it ended up being pointed at a tile wall, so the bounce back made it so I could clearly see my approaching doom. It waddled for the edge. If I went in that muck I probably wasn't coming back out, but I didn't want to let this jerk get away either.

Only I didn't have to make that call, because with a roar, Krasnov ran over and bodychecked all of us back to the floor.

This was a real mess. I ended up on the bottom of the dog pile. The frog man was rolling and thrashing. Krasnov got up and kicked it in the chest. I wrenched the axe out, and hacked the hell out of it again, but I didn't have as good an angle. It was spraying bubbly pink blood slime in every direction. It kept hitting me with its squishy elbows.

It rolled off, flipped back to feet, and crouched, like it was going to launch itself back to the safety of the pool.

I slammed the little axe through its knee. The leap turned into a sprawl.

Krasnov apparently remembered that he'd been lugging a sword around this whole time, quit giving it the boot, and drew his blade. It was a long saber of some kind. He swung it hard. When he hit the Fey in the back, the flesh parted and gave us a pink shampoo lawn sprinkler effect.

At that point the two of us just went to hacking at the Fey. It was hardly what I would call professional. I would have given anything for my kukri right then instead of this dull little hunk of thrift store garbage. Luckily, the monster didn't have claws, but it could still knock the hell out of you. It clocked me in the side of the head and sent me sliding into the wall.

Krasnov retaliated by running it completely through with his sword. He speared it through its back so hard that steel pierced out its chest. The *Vodyanoy* seemed really perturbed at that, spun around, and threw him back into the showers again. But since it had to turn around to do that, it presented me a perfectly good sword handle, which I grabbed, twisted hard, and ripped back out.

*"Mrrrrrrrp?"* the annoyed *Vodyanoy* asked, as it turned around to beat me to death.

Somehow I'd wound up with a sword, so I lifted it, and kept it pointed between us. I didn't know a damned thing about sword fighting, but that part seemed pretty self-explanatory.

Krasnov struggled back up, but rather than getting back to the fight, he headed for the door.

"Where are you going?" I shouted after him.

"Do not worry, you have got him!" Krasnov said as he fled.

"Son of a bitch!" That's what I got for trusting a gangster. But then I had to concentrate on the slimy frog man that was flailing away at me with its ridiculous gorilla arms. The sword's grip was only long enough to get one hand on it, but it was light enough that I could swing it really fast. I wasn't going to get any points for style, but I just kept hacking at the rubbery thing. Most of the hits bounced off, but a few parted flesh and more pink blood spilled.

Only the *Vodyanoy* didn't seem to notice the cuts or care. If this was medium-tough I'd hate to see what they considered difficult around here. It was backing me into a corner. Because of how slick the floor was, I couldn't even do much about that except try not to lose my footing. I should have been scared, but I was too busy being angry. For several tense seconds the two of us kept trying to murder each other.

*THUD.*

The *Vodyanoy* froze. Both of its great googly eyes turned inward to study the sledgehammer that was embedded deep in the top of its head. Krasnov had not only come back, he'd come back with his hammer, and he hit it so damned hard that its skull seemed to deflate. He lifted the sledgehammer to strike again, and the Fey just stood there quivering on its stumpy legs, probably because Krasnov had given it brain damage.

That gave me enough time to get up and slash the monster hard across the abdomen. It was such a solid hit that I felt the jolt clear up to my elbow. The rubbery meat opened and all sorts of disgusting, stinky, pink awfulness fell out. The inside of the *Vodyanoy* smelled a lot worse than the outside. *Hey, there's my pistol.*

Krasnov hit it in the skull again with an awful *crunch.* I took a wild guess at where its heart would be and stabbed it there. One of those must have worked because the *Vodyanoy* toppled into a smelly, disgusting, slime-covered heap. But neither of us was feeling confident that it was actually dead, so we spent the next few minutes bludgeoning and hacking it by the light of our discarded flashlights, until we were out of breath, but we were absolutely sure it was finished.

"Apologies." Krasnov was panting and sounded like he was about to have a heart attack. It was a good reminder to keep up on my cardio so I wouldn't end up looking like him in a couple decades. "That was little bit more aggressive *Vodyanoy* than I was expecting."

"No shit?" I gasped. "I just thought you really knew how to throw a rampage."

A little while later I was back in the parking lot, watching the sunrise over the concrete apartment buildings. I'd found a working hose around back and rinsed most of the *Vodyanoy's* slime blood off of my clothing, so now I was soaked in cold water and freezing my ass off. But that stuff had been so foul that the shivering was worth it.

"I have vodka in the car," Krasnov offered.

"No thanks."

"I do not understand turning down good vodka." Krasnov was leaning on the trunk of his car, also soaked to the bone, but the advantage of being fat was all that insulation. Plus he was a Siberian, so this wasn't cold by his standards. He had, however, gotten the living crap kicked out of him by the *Vodyanoy*, had two black eyes, a split lip, and was generally beat to hell. He was smoking a Cuban cigar and had put his ridiculous beret back on so he'd look respectable when the government authorities who were on their way arrived to tag the body and pronounce the contract filled.

"You seem grumpy. I must admit I was not the most honest with you, Owen."

"This is my shocked face."

"Not about the *Vodyanoy*. That was surprise. He was supposed to be little fellow. But you saved my life, and a Krasnov never forgets such a thing. We have killed a monster together, and that makes us like brothers! Brothers should not keep secrets one from the other. I suspect I know why you have not told me what brings you to Russia."

He wasn't currently blustering, posturing, or yelling, so I was tempted to believe him. However, I wasn't going to commit to anything until I was certain he wasn't going to immediately sell our mission out to Asag. "Let's hear your theory."

Krasnov sighed at my obvious evasion. "I know that my reputation is not so good among Western Hunters. Things are done different here. I do what I must. I do not have luxury to be picky about how business gets done. But you must know that there is one thing that a Krasnov will *never* lie about."

"Yeah? What's that?"

He looked me square in the eyes. "I *hate* monsters."

"Welcome to the club."

"No, no." He shook his head. "You do not understand. There is a game with people. You play, you
try to win. You can stretch the truth for business. It
is only money. But when it comes to monsters, it is
*us* against *them*. It is *war!* Monsters must be beaten,
no matter what. My worst enemy becomes best friend
when beasts attack us. Men put aside our differences
to defeat monster evil...It is said that you killed a
god, yes? I think you intend to do it again, no?"

"Something like that."

"Then you would not have come seeking my help
if it was not needed. I tell you this with all the
sincerity of my heart: if it is a big monster you have
come here to destroy, then I will help. I *must* help.
It is my duty."

He *sounded* sincere. "I am here about a particular
monster, one that endangers us all. But secrecy is of
the essence. I'd need assurances that you'd not talk
about my mission—*our* mission—to anyone."

"I am very good at keeping secrets." Krasnov stroked
his magnificent mustache thoughtfully. "I will do better
than make promises. Promises are just words." He'd
taken off his sword and sheath to clean the slime off,
and left them sitting on the trunk of the car. Krasnov
picked the sword up, studied it for a moment, and
then stood up with a grunt and a pained grimace.
The *Vodyanoy* had really done a number on him. He
hobbled over to face me. "This is a Cossack blade.
It belonged to my grandfather who carried it in the
Great Patriotic War, and his grandfather, and maybe
his grandfather before him. For generations Krasnovs
have defended this land against demons and Fey, and

when I learned of this, I left the army to do what I must to carry on such legacy. And whole time I used this!" He presented the sword to me. "Here!"

"I can't take—"

"Not to keep, but you take it until our work is done. It is symbol of trust! When battle is joined, and I have proven a true and faithful friend, you can give it back. This way you know that I only speak the truth!"

*Damn.* That really was something. I took hold of the sword. "Thank you."

Only he didn't let go yet. He squinted at me. "*And* my company keeps *all* Russian government contract funds for any monsters killed in my territory."

"You shifty, conniving dirtbag."

"Thank you, Owen."

"We're putting up the muscle...half."

"Ninety percent. You Americans can't claim it without me anyway."

"Sixty, forty."

"Ha! For such a pittance I would not even be able to guarantee the safe passage of your equipment. At eighty percent I would be able to take care of customs and bribery. There are many thieves in Russia."

"You don't say..." He was way better at negotiation than Kevin the junior lawyer. "Seventy, thirty."

"Excellent." Krasnov grinned, thinking I was a sucker. "MHI gets thirty percent of Russian contract monies. We have deal, yes?"

Normally PUFF could only be collected if it was killed in the US or its territorial interests, unless the MCB categorized the monster as a potential extinction-level threat or minion of a potential extinction-level threat, and then they didn't care where you killed it, as long as it got dead. Asag would certainly count. That took care of the US. Because of their byzantine laws, I hadn't thought we'd be able to collect *any* of the Russian government's version of PUFF, but there was nothing better than getting paid multiple times for the same work. "You're on."

"Then it is settled." He let go of the sword. "Please, take good care of that."

"I will." Then he engulfed me in a ridiculous, rib-crushing bear hug. He actually lifted my boots off the ground. My back popped. "Ooof."

He dropped me. "Now that we are officially associates, what can I really do for you?"

This was as much as I could hope for. I had to go for it. "We need to conduct a large-scale operation on Severny Island."

"I know this place." Krasnov scowled. "Do not tell me you wish to visit the anomaly at Sukhoy Nos Cape."

"That's it."

"That is a very bad place, my friend. There is great evil there."

"I certainly hope so."

While Krasnov spoke with the government officials from their shadowy MCB equivalent, I wandered over to where Holly had been spying on us the whole time. Of course she'd followed us. I'd carried a tracking device on me. I hadn't trusted Krasnov as far as I could throw him, and since he outweighed me, that wasn't very far at all.

She was leaning against a light pole down the street. "You look like shit." Holly said as I approached. "Want me to call a taxi?"

"Naw, I'll ride back with Krasnov. We're business partners now...or something."

"Sweet. You're a made man." She opened her coat to show me she had an old Stechkin machine pistol tucked in her pants. "I stole this from your buddy's car after you went inside, so you'll probably want to put it back in the glove box before he notices."

"Were you going to bust in and rescue us eventually?"

"When I realized it was an actual legit monster in there and they weren't just abducting you to harvest your corneas to sell them on the internet, I hung back. I didn't want to break up the male bonding moment. I figured two big strapping studs like you should be able to handle whatever that was. The way you smell, I'm assuming some sort of sewer squid."

"I wish." I handed her the Krasnov family ancestral sword. "Check out my awesome new sword. It is a symbol of our trust and enduring friendship, and him getting seventy percent of any Russian bounty money for basically nothing."

Holly half drew it and studied the shiny blade. She ran her thumb down the edge. "You do realize this is probably a fake and he bought it at a gas station, right?"

"Very possibly, but I figure with Krasnov, it's the sentiment that counts."

# CHAPTER 7

One thing about gallivanting around the world, you get really behind in your paperwork. MHI had a lot of revenue, but a corresponding ton of expenses. As the Finance Department, it was my job to make sure everything got tracked and every account balanced. Even when I was traveling I would still check in whenever I could and work remotely. Not that any of our employees were stupid enough to risk embezzling from Earl Harbinger, but mistakes happen. A good accountant caught those fast. You had to keep up with this stuff.

Which was why I found myself staring at my phone, confused as hell, and wondering why tens of millions of dollars had suddenly materialized in one of MHI's bank accounts.

Holly and I were standing in line to go back through customs with hundreds of other tired, cranky, jet-lagged travelers. She must have heard me make a strange noise, because she asked. "What's wrong? Please tell me Krasnov didn't hook you up with some souvenirs of questionable legality and you just now realized you'll need to declare them."

"We're rich."

"Well, yeah. I don't do this job strictly for the entertainment value."

"No." I held up my phone and whispered. "I mean unexpectedly rich. As in a whole bunch of money just got wired into MHI's accounts."

She leaned in, saw the number, and whistled. "Maybe Julie scored some awesome new contract while we were away."

"She didn't tell me about any, and besides, those take months to process all the paperwork. Something else is going on."

"Santa?" Holly put her hands to her cheeks and faked glee.

"I have been super good this year."

"Not me. Naughty list is where it's at."

"You are such a tease." It wasn't from the Treasury Department, so none of it was PUFF. There had been several big wire transfers, but I didn't recognize any of the company names. They were all generic corpo-speak names: global, omni, mega whatevers. I would have to delve more into this later, but that would have to wait until I was someplace with a more secure connection.

I made it through customs. Holly had a few issues. That was because you could import some alcohol without paying the federal excise tax, however, that was in liters, not gallons. And Krasnov's going-away gift baskets had been basically a suitcase full of expensive liquor bottles. I had to admit, it was fun to hear a Hunter argue with a federal agency other than the MCB.

While I waited for her to get through, another traveler bumped into me. He'd been head down, in a hurry, with a big roller bag. We both said "Excuse me." No big deal.

And a few seconds later a phone rang in my coat pocket. It was a different ringtone than I was used to. When I fished it out, I was surprised to discover a phone I'd never seen before. I looked around, but the traveler who had just bumped me was already gone.

The screen on the new phone just said *Management.*

"Hello?"

"Greetings, Mr. Pitt. Welcome back to your native land. I hope that you had a most pleasant journey."

I recognized the voice of Management the Dragon immediately. I had to laugh. "You're alive."

"Rumors of my death have been greatly exaggerated."

"I saw your place. That was a hell of a fight."

"Indeed, a most unfortunate loss of real estate. Many irreplaceable treasures were ruined. Arranging such a sudden move was both a terrible logistical burden, and a dreadful inconvenience. I intended to live the rest of my days there, so I was exceedingly cross. Do not worry. This line is encrypted so we may converse freely."

"I got the spell you left for me, and the file from your lawyer."

"You are a regular Sherlock Holmes, Mr. Pitt. I am afraid that my alerting you about our mutual opponent has greatly complicated my lifestyle. However, I prefer to always look on the bright side. In this case, I would prefer for certain individuals—such as ancient chaos demons or Machiavellian albinos—to retain the belief that I have perished . . . So please, walk while we speak, Mr. Pitt. The line may be secure, but our foes have spies everywhere and it is best not to underestimate them. The lovely maiden Miss Newcastle will catch up. And though it is difficult for a mammal of your stature, do try to look casual."

Management didn't really have room to talk about stature since he was the size of a train. I started walking. "I bet you're watching me through the security cameras now."

"Of course. Which companies do you think sold all of this equipment to the TSA?" The dragon seemed pleased with himself. "I am also aware that you have seen the status of your accounts this morning. I too check my portfolio promptly first thing every morning. Yes, yes. Those transfers are from some of my various shell companies. In fact, I also own a controlling interest in your bank. There will be several more substantial transfers over the next few days. They will each be followed with an imaginary services contract which will provide cover for tax purposes. No need to thank me, Mr. Pitt."

"I wasn't going to thank you just yet. MHI isn't a charity, and that kind of generosity always comes with a catch."

"No catch. I consider this an investment. My expected return on this investment is merely the due and dispassionate revenge against the being that unleashed a nightmare beast into my casino. Through analyzing your recent actions, I have come to understand your goals, and I fully support them. However, I do not think you have realized the financial magnitude of the endeavor you intend to undertake. Invasions are costly. Thus, I wish to bankroll this punitive expedition of yours. My greatest sadness is that I will not be able to participate in the glorious shopping spree which will surely ensue."

I could only imagine his vast bulk hiding in another gold-plated cave somewhere, plotting, but piles of money never hurt. "That sounds reasonable."

"It is your destiny to defeat him, so I have taken upon myself the destiny of paying for it all." Management chuckled. "I knew you were a man of discernment. All I would ask is that, as you humans would say, 'wreck his shit.' I want his plans thwarted. I want him to feel as frustrated as I have been."

"That's the general idea."

"Excellent, Mr. Pitt! Now this is a good place to stop your stroll."

I was walking past a food court. It smelled like too strong coffee and too expensive cinnamon buns. I stopped. "Do you happen to have any more information about our mutual friend?"

"Nay. Nothing beyond the file you have already retrieved. He has cloaked his dealings in deceit. He utilizes minions ignorant of their master's mission. It is difficult to separate the truth from the myth. Alas, I cannot even vouch for the accuracy of what I've already provided. Tread carefully, for this is an opponent we understand very little about. He is vile and cunning, yet his ultimate motives remain a mystery."

I was afraid of that. "How can I reach you?"

"You cannot. That would defeat the purpose of going into hiding. I did not ever intend to move from my last cave. I would be greatly saddened to ever be forced to do so again. If necessary, I will reach you. Now, if you will look to your left, there is a trash can. When we terminate this call, please place this phone into the receptacle."

"I've got to say it was good to hear your voice.

I'm really glad you made it out of there alive, Mr. Management."

"As am I, Mr. Pitt. As am I. Farewell and Godspeed."

After the dragon hung up on me, I put the phone into the trash. About ten seconds later a janitor conveniently came over and removed the bag. I had no doubt that bag was about to get tossed right into an evidence-scrubbing fire.

I bought a giant, expensive, airport cinnamon bun and waited for Holly to catch up. Earl might not want me to break too many expense accounts, but I figured this one was on Management.


It was Go/No-Go day.

That meant I got to give a briefing, present a plan, and then all the clever Hunters would try to poke holes in it. Nobody would hold back. Hunters don't get points for nice, and better to get the stupid ideas out of the way now than later, when they'd cost lives. After everybody had their say, Earl would make his final call. Since he'd been keeping up on all my findings so far, I was pretty sure he had already made his decision, but I also suspected Earl liked watching us argue just in case somebody brought up a point he hadn't thought of. Or maybe he just enjoyed a good fight.

The conference room was packed. Boss Shackleford sat at the head of the table, because even though Earl was the Director of Operations—and his dad— Raymond Shackleford the Third was still a big freaking deal and his opinion mattered more than the rest of the non-Shacklefords put together. Julie's grandpa had aged a lot over the years since I'd met him, but his mind was almost as sharp as the point on the hook he had for a hand. His health had gotten degraded enough that he was all but retired, but on paper he was still the official head of MHI, and had forgotten more about this life than most of us would ever know.

Julie was sitting to her grandpa's right. That was appropriate, and everybody knew she'd be taking the Boss Shackleford seat when he was gone. I knew she had my back, but when we were in this room talking company business, she was going to be the hard-ass businesswoman. She loved me and was carrying my child, but that didn't mean she was going to cut me any slack when her company's future and the lives of its employees were at stake.

Earl was up front telling everybody that this was important enough that they needed to shut up and pay attention to what I had to say. Julie and her grandpa were watching me. Those three were the votes that actually mattered, because when Earl made a call, his son and great-granddaughter were the only ones who had any hope of persuading him otherwise. Julie gave me a confident wink. With all the scars and the eye patch, the Boss's expression was too hard to read. I think he tolerated me, maybe even liked me a little bit, but had probably been hoping Julie would marry somebody better.

The rest of my team was there, too: Milo Anderson, Trip Jones, and Holly Newcastle. Plus Albert Lee was there as our chief researcher. All of them had been helping me gather information. They knew what was up.

Everybody else Earl had invited was still in the dark about my proposal, but each of them was here because they had some form of expertise that might prove useful. Several team leads and other experienced Hunters had been flown in and sworn to secrecy. Trying to read my audience, I could tell their moods ranged from curious to grumpy, but that was pretty normal for this crowd.

I had requested an elf and an orc representative. They were probably the only elf and orc in existence who could stand to be in the same room without murdering each other, but I'd learned that when you were dealing with ancient monsters, it helped to have some nonhuman perspectives. Edward was masked and hiding in the back corner. Since Tanya was a Newbie, I'd made her promise to keep her big elf mouth shut unless spoken to, so she was in back making flirty eyes at Ed. I never could tell if poor Ed was even aware of that or not.

While I mentally prepared, Earl was explaining that this proposed mission was my bright idea, specified that if we went ahead with it, participation would be voluntary, wrapped up his intro, and then turned it over to me. I took a breath. *Here goes.* All eyes were on me as I got up and walked to the front of the room. Earl sat down next to Julie, obviously enjoying my discomfort. The lights were turned down so we could use the projector.

"Thanks for coming all this way." I'd bribed Dorcas to pick up several boxes of doughnuts from a really good bakery in Montgomery. It's hard to get angry at a bad briefing when you're full of quality bear claws. "Everybody get a doughnut? There's plenty."

"You know, the last time you briefed the whole company was right before DeSoya Caverns." Ben Cody looked like a graying Grizzly Adams, but he was our big brain science genius, all-around badass, and was in charge of our team that handled our Department of Energy contracts. "How screwed are we this time?"

There was some general laughter at my expense. Which was good. When you've got a job this bloody you've got to have a sense of humor about yourself, and besides, when you're the guy who blows up time, you kind of deserve it. I waited for the laughter to taper off. "Yeah, there's a big threat, but this time we can get out in front of it. Rather than giving it a chance to get set, we're going to go kick its ass in its own house. I want to launch a surprise attack on the most dangerous monster currently active on Earth."

That sure got their attention.

"During Vegas we found out there was a mastermind behind the recent monster attacks around the world. His minions always leave his symbol behind. Trip?"

Trip was handling the AV portion, and on cue he hit the button. The now-familiar symbol of Asag swooshed onto the screen. This one was a photo from Yemen, finger-painted in blood. Yes, believe it or not, our war against an evil supernatural being was getting kicked off with a PowerPoint presentation, complete with animation.

"When we started our investigation into this threat, none of us realized how widespread his reach was." While I kept talking, Trip kept clicking through the pictures, and there were a lot. Symbol after symbol, usually surrounded by torn bodies and burning wreckage. "This is the signature of our high-value target. We now know of at least *two hundred* incidents, in thirty different countries, where people have died or vanished, and this sign was left behind to taunt us. From the evidence and the few times when Hunters have responded in time, we know we're dealing with at least a dozen different kinds of monsters, all working off the same general set of orders."

All the carnage shots out of the way, Trip paused at the picture Julie had taken of the map on Poly the Cyclops's wall.

"When Earl saw an early version of this map in Las Vegas he called it a mobilization. Our high-value target is pushing, testing us. Getting ready for something big. We don't know what his end game is, but it's obvious that it is bad."

"HVT is nice and all but this asshole got a name?" Jay Boone asked. He was the Atlanta team lead. I suspected Earl had picked him because, as one of the first boots on the ground in the war in Afghanistan, Boone knew a thing or two about the logistics of a big operation.

"Bunches of names. That's what happens when you've been a bad guy in myths for thousands of years. The Nachtmar called him He Who Ends All Things. But the most common name used is Asag or Azag, and though he's been mostly dormant over recent centuries, he has been around for a *really* long time."

"If he's that long-lived, are his origins Old One, Fey, or something else?" Priest asked. He'd been a South African soldier, then a man of the cloth—which was how he'd gotten the nickname—before becoming a Hunter. He was Boone's former second-in-command, and had been our Colorado team lead since Sam Haven had died.

"The MCB has Asag filed under *other*, as in I don't think they have a clue. As far as we can tell, he's got his own gang. We've got evidence that those factions fight against him, which tells us he's powerful, because otherwise they'd ignore or steamroll him. Asag shows up in the legends of several cultures, always as a demon, and always as a force of chaos. That name literally means Disorder. I've got a packet for each of you with everything we've dredged up on him so far, but the short version is that he's some kind of demonic force that exists to cause trouble, and hates mankind's guts."

Priest was already flipping through his packet. "Good work, Albert," he told our researcher.

"Thanks, but I had help." Lee stopped there, because out of respect for Management's privacy and safety, we needed to keep the dragon's involvement on the down low.

"What does Asag want?" Cody asked.

"What do any of these wannabe world conquerors ever want, Ben?" Earl responded.

"Fair point."

"I've got people working on that still. I owe the Van Helsing Institute detectives some hefty bonuses if they come up with anything good. We do know that various different kinds of monsters are flocking to his banner and causing trouble on his behalf. Even the Condition answers to him now."

That caused some murmurs. The Sanctified Church of the Temporary Mortal Condition held a special place in MHI's heart for being the dickheads who'd been bold enough to attack the MHI compound directly. Many of the assembled leads had been here for that event.

"I really don't like those guys." Milo stated the obvious. "It's been a long time and I still occasionally catch a whiff of zombie elephant in my workshop. You've got no idea how hard that was to clean up."

"Try some Febreze," Paxton suggested. "Works wonders on undead stink."

"Does Asag have a body, and can it be killed?" Priest asked, and that was a very good question.

"Not sure, but the legends say yes. He's been defeated here before." I signaled for Trip to change the picture, but he was way ahead of me. This one was of an ancient stone sculpture of a bull with a man's head. "According to an ancient poem called the Lugale, Ninurta defeated Asag with Sharur. I promise none of those words are made up."

"Hold on. Back up." Esmeralda Paxton was a petite lady who ran our Seattle team, and she kept up on folklore far better than the rest of us. "First off, all words are made-up. Second, Ninurta was a legendary hero, and if I recall correctly Sharur was his magical talking mace. Does Milo have one of those lying around I don't know about?"

"No," Milo said after a moment of mental inventory. "But that would be super cool!"

I held up my hands apologetically. "I'm still working out the details."

"Ninurta was the Akkadian god of war," Paxton continued.

"*And* hunting," I pointed out. "So basically the same as us...theoretically."

"It's commonly believed that Ninurta is based upon the same historical figure as Nimrod, the mighty hunter." Priest wasn't as up on that stuff as Paxton, but he was no slouch, especially when things took a biblical turn. "Only he grew so prideful in his might he challenged God by building the Tower of Babel."

Boone chuckled. "Hunters are a cocky bunch."

"Okay. However it actually went down, Asag was terrorizing Earth before, and some great hunter came along and knocked him out for a few thousand years. Now he's awake." I left off *because of me*. "If he didn't win then, it means there's a way to beat him now."

"Are we sure this being has actually returned?" That was asked by Maria Mayorga, who ran our New York City team. She was a solid, no-nonsense woman, who to me always looked really *angry*, but Earl liked her. New York City was practically a supernatural zoo and she still managed to keep a lid on it. "Maybe all that monster graffiti is something else."

"What, like a gang sign, and all of these nasty critters that are usually fighting each other have suddenly teamed up for shits and giggles?" Boone asked. "Come on, May."

"I've compiled the evidence for you to go over yourselves, but trust me, this is no coincidence. Asag is back. He's the one who released the Nachtmar, so he knows all about us. We either hit first, or we wait around until he's ready to hit us again."

Judging by the expressions I could read, it felt like most of them were with me. We were a territorial, protective bunch, and Asag had messed with us too many times. Give a Hunter a target, and the wheels were going to begin turning. *Good*. I kept pushing.

"Trip, show them the map." The picture changed to an image of the northern coast of Russia. "This is where we believe Asag's home base to be."

Cody recognized it immediately. "That's Severny Island."

"We got us a geography wizard," Holly said.

"I handle all our mad science contracts. It pays to know everywhere they did nuclear testing."

"Correct. That's Severny Island off the north coast

of Russia. They set off a *fifty*-megaton detonation there back in 1961. The Tsar Bomba they called it, the biggest explosion ever made by man."

Cody sighed. "Let me guess . . . Not actually a test."

"According to our sources, threatening America was great propaganda and all, but their real goal was to destroy an active supernatural site that they considered a danger to their national security. They'd already sent in an expedition to clear it out, but it failed. When that didn't work, they bombed it."

"They went to the Dwayne Myers school of conflict resolution," Lee said. That got a few chuckles. Special Agent Myers hadn't exactly been the most popular guy with this crowd, and to be fair, he had tried to nuke Alabama, but he sure knew how to get shit done.

Earl was scowling. "Let me cut in for a minute. According to the rumors Z has dug up recently, the man the Soviets originally sent in to handle that place was a KGB assassin by the name of Nikolai Petrov. Now, I knew Nikolai personally. If any of you are doubting the severity of the situation, let me just say that Nikolai was the absolute hardest motherfucker I've ever had the displeasure of meeting. He was my equal in capability, only he never got slowed down by little things like mercy or avoiding collateral damage. He was the best of the best, and I do not say that lightly. If a man like Nikolai threw in the towel and said it's easier to just drop the world's biggest bomb on the place rather than fight, it's *bad*."

The smiles died. If a place could outmatch somebody Earl rated that badass, it was grim.

"They call it Gorod Chudovish," I told them. "The City of Monsters."

Ed grumbled something. Holly asked him to repeat it. "Known to *urks*. Most . . . evil." Ed was an orc of so few words, that really had a chance to sink in. *"Evil."*

"Sounds lovely," Paxton said. "What level of activity are you expecting?"

"They didn't call it the suburb of monsters for a reason. Local intel makes this place sound like their version of Natchy Bottom on steroids. Three quarters of the island are permanently covered in a glacier, but there is one region, not too rugged and free of ice, and it just happens to have an old pyramid on it."

"How old are we talking?" Boone asked.

"Best guess? It was *under* the last ice age."

Boone groaned. "Old shit's the worst."

"The local people are the Nenets, the Russians called them Samoyeds. Their god of death, Nga, lived beneath the earth, and you get one convenient guess where they say the gateway was. A few explorers went there over the centuries, but all the expeditions turned out badly. Stories about the pyramid even showed up in turn-of-the-century American occult books, mostly nonsense about the pyramid being built by Atlanteans or it was a gateway to Mu, or the Hollow Earth, and crap like that. The big bomb quieted the place down for generations, but the ruins of the city are still there, and according to the Russian Hunters, they're teeming with monsters again. They built a military base on the island to keep an eye on things, but as long as the evil doesn't wander too far out, they leave it alone."

"Any chance you can get the report from the Petrov expedition?" Priest was leaning forward, intensely focused. He had been messing around earlier, but it was like he'd shifted gears, and now he was deadly serious. "That could be vital intel."

"We're working on it." Meaning Krasnov was trying to bribe some FSB employees. "I guarantee it is bad though, both in quality and quantity. We're talking every otherworldly creature you can think of, black magic, evil spirits, the works. I've already secured permission for us to conduct a large operation there, and by large, I mean an army of Hunters. We're going to need them."

"Napoleon and Hitler took armies into Russia too," Boone said. "Refresh my memory how that worked out?"

"Only this time the Russians are on our side. Sort of." There were a lot of groans and sighs at that. "I'll cover the details later, but we've come to an agreement with the local contract holder that will let us stage out of that military base. There's a harbor, an airstrip, and it is a straight shot up the coast to the ruins."

"I've heard how those Russian Hunting companies work. I'd rather go into business with the Yakuza," Paxton said.

Priest shook his head. "I respect the audacity, Owen, and I love the idea of striking first for once rather than just responding, but that is one of most inhospitable places on Earth. A million things could go wrong."

"Okay, if the Russians agree with us, how come we can't just get them to go all Tsar Bomba on the place again and save us the trip?" Cody asked. "They keep invading their neighbors anyway. A little saber-rattling nuclear testing would be easy enough to explain it to the world."

"Good point," Mayorga said. "I'm all in favor of letting other people blow shit up in their own territory rather than freezing my tits off at the ass end of the globe."

"We need to be there in person, in force, because there's another catch."

"We couldn't *get paid*," Holly stated.

"Worse." I could tell I was losing the leads. My only hope of swaying them was to let them know what was at stake, what had started it all. "You need to know what brought this place to our attention to begin with. Julie?"

The crowd turned toward my wife, who was happy to oblige. She'd field this part because Poly had talked her ear off. They had stayed in contact ever since we'd met. The MCB still didn't know we were on a first-name basis with their remote viewer, but Poly was such a Julie fanboy that he told her everything. I was pretty sure Poly had even friended her on Facebook.

"There is supposedly a gateway inside the City of Monsters. It opens to various other dimensions on different days of the years depending on how the stars align. In one hundred and thirty-seven days it will allow travel into the same Nightmare Realm the Last Dragon got sucked into."

"I don't get it," Mayorga said. "So?"

"We've got it on good authority that as of yesterday, seven of the Hunters who went missing from the Last Dragon are still alive."

You could have heard a pin drop.

"How could anyone possibly have survived that long in there?" Cody demanded. "You saw that place."

"We don't know how they've done it, but they have. They're stuck. We don't know their identities. They could be ours, or they could be from the other teams, but they all entered the Nightmare Realm from the Last Dragon." There were a lot of pained glances exchanged between the leaders. Very few of them knew Lococo because he was a Newbie, but all of them were friends with VanZant. "This portal is the only way we know of to reach them."

Hunters were a loyal bunch. We didn't like leaving anyone behind. The idea of spending months trapped in that horrific place was too awful to contemplate, but Julie had just hit them over the head with the thought. Whatever they had been contemplating before, Julie's revelation changed things.

"You're sure?" Paxton asked.

Julie nodded. "I believe our source is trustworthy and his methods are reliable."

"Well, we can't just leave them there." Paxton sighed. "If roles were reversed, and it was any of us left behind and VanZant here instead, we all know what he would do."

"Come hell or high water," Boss Shackleford spoke for the first time, "John would try to get us back."

The room was dead silent. That had done it. I could tell they were all in. The unquestionable character of a man who wasn't even here had just sealed the deal.

"So that's the overview." All eyes turned back to me. "This mission has two goals: rescue our guys; destroy Asag."

Trip closed his laptop. Somebody else turned the lights back on. The Hunters were silent for a long time, but there wouldn't be any objections over *should* we do the mission, but now we got to the tough part of *how?*

"You're certain this gate aligns in a hundred and thirty-something days?" Boone asked. "That's not that much time to put together an operation of this magnitude."

"You're right. It's complex. It'll be a challenge. We've still got a lot to learn. This requires planning and preparation, but it *is* doable."

"I hate to be the ugly fact lady," Mayorga interjected, "but it's overseas. How do we collect PUFF? This isn't going to be cheap."

Only a few of us knew about Management and his *donations*, and we couldn't let word of a mysterious benefactor get out. Julie was ready to field that one for me. "I had the lawyers double-check. If the MCB classifies a particular threat high enough, like world-threatening, then it doesn't matter which jurisdiction you bag it in. And same thing goes for any minions in its service."

"Just don't leave the planet to do it. That's how they got out of paying me for the Dread Overlord on a technicality," I said.

The experienced Hunters exchanged glances with each other across the table, and then they looked to Earl, who in turn looked to his son. "What do you think, Boss?"

"We're talking about laying *siege* to the City of Monsters with a whole army of Hunters . . ." The Boss pondered that for a moment. "This could possibly be the largest single mission this company has ever taken on."

"Yep," Earl said simply. "There's a lot of risk."

The Boss nodded. "It sure would be something to see though, wouldn't it?"

Earl Harbinger grinned. "Damned right it would."

And just like that, Operation Siege got the green light.

✦      ✦      ✦

When the meeting was over hours later, I had gone out in the hall to think. Julie found me out there alone.

"You okay, Hon?"

Earl had given assignments and put everybody to work. Most of them made sense with who would be overseeing what. Cody on defenses, both mundane and magical; Paxton on research; Boone, Priest, and Mayorga on logistics, tactics, and transportation; Julie handling the teaming arrangements with other companies, that sort of thing . . . But one assignment in particular didn't make a lick of sense.

"What the hell did Earl mean I'm *XO*?"

She patted me on the shoulder and gave me a very patient smile. "He's in charge, but you are his right hand. For the actual combat he's putting the team leads in charge. Before that, all the little stuff is going to go through you. You take responsibility for whatever he thinks needs doing. Something comes up, you handle it."

"Yeah, I know what executive officer means in context here, but *why?*" I was feeling a little overwhelmed. My chest felt like I needed to take a hit off an inhaler, and I hadn't used one of those in years. "There are Hunters in there with way more experience. I'm not—"

"Oh, bullshit." My wife said that in the kindest way possible. "This was your idea. You've seen it through this far, Earl wants you to see it through to the end."

"But on a mission, you're always his second-in-command."

"Normally, sure." Julie gave me a look like I was stupid. "On D-Day I'll be almost eight months pregnant. How's that supposed to work? And if we're up there for long, 'Hang on, Mister Horrifying Ancient

Monster from Hell, my water just broke. I'll get back to killing you in a minute after I deliver this giant super baby.'"

"Aw hell." I'd known that. We'd avoided talking about it much, but ever since we'd gotten the dates from Poly, we'd known there was no way Julie could be anywhere near the line of fire. Somebody had to keep the day-to-day operations of this company running while the rest of us were off on our big Arctic adventure. "You're right. And our giant super baby is going to be adorable...I hate that I'm not going to be here for you."

Julie just shook her head. "I'm a Monster Hunter, who married a Monster Hunter. I don't think either of us were under any romantic delusions about how life consuming our jobs are."

It wasn't just Julie and the baby, but my dad was on his death bed and I wasn't there for him. That sick feeling in my stomach was because I knew that I was going to do what I had to do. "Regardless, I should be here for the birth of our child."

"Sure you should. Only we're in danger and that comes first. You want to be there for important life-changing events? Great. But you know how many deployed soldiers have said that exact same thing throughout history? All of them. But they couldn't be there, because they had a job to do first. They're absent then, because they've got to defend their homes, so those kids they weren't there to see born can have a chance to grow up safe."

She had me there. "You're a tough chick."

"Not really. Right now I'm an emotional basket case of warring hormones. I've just had more time to think about this while you've been jet-setting around the world putting together your invasion." She laughed. "You want to feel guilty, fine. You can make it up to me later. But now, get your head on straight. Earl's got faith in you. Don't let him down."

"I won't."

"I love you." Julie engulfed me in a hug. "Get the mission done and then *come back*. That's the important thing. Bring everybody home safe."

I held her for a long time.

# CHAPTER 8

Being Earl's XO meant that I got every oddball assignment he didn't feel like dealing with himself, which was how I'd wound up arranging a peace summit. This mission needed all the help it could get. MHI's adopted orc tribe had already pledged their support, which was fantastic. A single orc healer was worth three trauma surgeons, orc warriors were badasses, and Skippy was fantastic air support.

However, we would be facing a creature that used black magic, in a place that absolutely oozed the stuff. We needed to be able to defend ourselves from dark powers, disembodied spirits, and curses beyond human understanding. Since mankind sucked at that sort of thing, that meant calling upon beings more *enlightened* than we were for such endeavors.

Which—sadly—meant we needed elves. Social issues aside, everyone agreed they were good at all that magic crap. The Queen talked a big game about being on disability, but she had no problem hiring her people out for odd jobs, all under the table of course.

Unless there was an orc involved, then no deal.

Elves and orcs despised each other. Our tribe didn't even like living in the same time zone as the Queen of the Elves. Working together was out of the question. It went back a long time. The animosity was older than man, and both sides agreed it started when they were both enslaved by the Fey. Nobody alive knew how the feud began, but they were both sure it was the other side's fault.

MHI had one single elven employee, Tanya, and Chief Skippy had raised hell about us hiring her. Only the intervention of his brother Edward had prevented a...strike? Riot? Beats me. But I didn't want to see what happened when an orc tribe got pissed off and hoisted the black flag.

But the main reason the orcs didn't strike was because Tanya was all into Ed, and Ed was *fond* of Tanya...I think. It was hard to tell with that whole interspecies romance thing, and frankly, it was none of my business. The situation might have gone all Romeo and Juliet on us, except Ed was the tribe's best warrior, and Tanya was just so damned chipper that even Skippy seemed to be gradually softening to her presence. Plus I don't think metal heads or rednecks were big on poisoning or suicide, so we had that going for us.

But accepting more elves? Hell no. And there was no way the Queen was going to entrust any of her valuable trackers on a mission with a bunch of orcs.

Not wanting to die, cursed and insane, on an arctic rock, I'd asked Ed and Tanya to arrange this meeting. Ed had annoyed his brother into it, and Tanya had called home to the Enchanted Forest to beg her mother to attend. She was still kind of on the outs there for abandoning her birthright, but Queen Ilrondelia, or "Mama" as Tanya called her, still wanted Tanya to send a cut of her PUFF earnings back to the trailer park, so had agreed to meet and parley. We had to pick neutral ground, which in this case was a barbeque place north of Tuscaloosa.

This made for the weirdest damned peace talks ever.

The brisket was good, the pulled pork was the best I'd ever had, and the décor was NASCAR-themed. The owner was a retired Hunter doing us a favor. He had given his employees the day off, put up the CLOSED sign, and cooked us a feast. When the Queen heard the food would be free—and afterwards there would be an open bar should they come to terms—she had brought her whole entourage all the way from the Enchanted Forest Trailer Park. So not to be outdone, Skippy had brought an equal number of his people. The parking lot was full of dilapidated pickup trucks and other clunkers.

The mood inside wasn't particularly festive. There were ten surly elves on one side of the room and ten grumpy orcs on the other, mutually stained with barbeque sauce, but glaring at each other. I'd thought ahead and unplugged the jukebox to keep a fight from breaking out over metal versus country music. At least we'd gotten both sides to check their weapons at the door. Trip was minding a gigantic pile of guns, knives, totem sticks, billy clubs, saps, axe handles, a single stick of dynamite, and even some cheap Chinese throwing stars. I'd even specified plastic cups, so nobody would be tempted to smash a beer bottle and then stab somebody with it.

We'd stuck one table in the dead center of the

room. As moderator, I was in the middle. On one side of me was Skippy and Ed. On the other was Tanya and the Queen. We'd brought in a special, reinforced comfy chair for her, because the Queen was one *big* lady. Because this was such a historical diplomatic occasion, she didn't even have any curlers in her hair. Skippy had worn his favorite Black Sabbath world tour shirt. We had gotten through the introductions, my proposal, and dinner with a minimal number of threats, insults, and walkouts.

"Y'all hunters ain't gonna last in no monster city." The Queen had put a hurting on a few plates of brisket, and practically drank a bottle of ranch dressing, so now it was time for business. She wiped her greasy face with a wet wipe and tossed it on the floor. "Y'all need elves, keeping the forces of e-ville off your backs."

"Yes, your majesty. That's exactly why we're here."

"Y'all need elves, but don't nobody need no filthy orc trash."

"Mama!"

*Uh-oh.* The orc side of the room began grumbling.

"*Urks* better," Skippy stated. "Pointy ear cow dumb."

Several orcs laughed. Like most sounds that came out of an orc, it was a guttural, deep, gravelly—yet surprisingly cheerful—noise. That caused the elf side of the room to stand up and start shouting.

Well, the Queen didn't stand up. Obviously. She filled her seat so thoroughly that I was worried we'd need a livestock hoist to get her out. "Who you calling cow, pig face?"

Skippy showed his tusks proudly, and then gave her a rude gesture that he'd probably learned from his adopted human brethren. Elves began throwing plastic cups. I needed to do something before the orcs started throwing chairs.

*"Enough!"* I bellowed at the top of my lungs. Julie had prepped me well beforehand how to avoid a rumble. I was all culturally educated and stuff. "Sit your hillbilly asses down!" That stopped the elves. Then I turned down the volume and looked Skippy square in his yellow eyes. "Insults at this table bring shame to the brother of the Great War Chief."

Skippy slowly nodded. Mosh wasn't even here, but I wasn't above using my brother's cred to my own advantage. Orc culture respected rock stars above all else, so making me look bad wasn't very *metal* of them.

"Bunch of tuskers hootin' and hollerin'," the Queen exclaimed. Which was funny since it wasn't like orcs were a particularly noisy people, but she seemed genuinely upset. "They wouldn't be so uppity if my princess hadn't been runnin' 'round wit one of 'em. She's my precious baby. I'm pained thinkin' 'bout this green skin puttin' his grimy paws all over her!"

Tanya was a young *lady* by elf standards, and right then she just looked embarrassed by her mother's behavior. "But, Mama, I love Ed!"

That caused most of the assembled orcs and elves to groan. At least they had something they could agree on.

"Meh . . . Skippy bet . . . Edward not first one there."

"Hey!" Tanya hurled her empty plastic cup at Skip's head, but I blocked it in midflight.

"Tanya, stand down. Skippy, please."

"No insult . . . Fact. Ed great warrior. Could do better."

"You just gonna sit there and let your brother talk

trash about your girlfriend?" Tanya demanded. By
trailer park elf standards, Tanya was hot and she knew
it. She was rocking the big hair, tank top, cut-offs,
and tramp stamp. "I'm royalty!"

Luckily, Ed seemed as content and mellow as usual.
Which was good, because realistically Ed could probably kill everybody in the room with just his fork.
All orcs were supernaturally blessed with one gift,
and Ed's was stabbing things. He just leaned back
in his chair and grunted something unintelligible.
The two orcs argued back and forth for a minute;
in English or Orcish, Ed was an orc of few words.
Finally, frustrated, Skippy just threw his hands up in
the air, like *whatever*.

I wasn't renting an entire barbeque joint just to
participate in their little soap opera. It was time to
cut to the chase. "Okay, listen up. I'm not a relationship counselor. You guys can settle your personal
drama later."

"But Skippy's being a dick! I understand Orcish.
He was saying Ed ain't ever gonna get a bunch of
other wives if his first wife's an elf! News flash, chief,
with me, he don't need no more other wives. I take
care of my man!"

"Tanya . . ." I used my stern voice. She was actually an MHI employee, had potential as a Hunter,
and really wanted to keep her job, so she was one
of the only ones here I had any actual leverage on.
"Remember what we're here for."

"Fine." Tanya folded her arms and sulked. Mama
seemed offended on her behalf.

Theoretically, I'd been given this assignment because
from the first time we'd met, Queen Ilrondelia had

recognized that I had a cosmic destiny and all that jazz. Supposedly that gave me some kind of clout in the Elven Court. Or that was all bullshit, and Earl just didn't want to have to deal with trailer park diplomacy that he knew would probably end up looking like a domestic disturbance on an episode of *Cops*.

*Here's hoping.* I addressed her as politely as possible. "Your majesty, I assure you that I would not have troubled your valuable time if this mission wasn't of the utmost importance."

"Well, you is the Dreamer. You'd know."

"I am. I know what's coming. The world is in terrible danger, only this time we have a chance to stop it early. MHI needs your help. We need your powerful magic. I'm pleading with you. Please. The world needs the infinite wisdom of your people."

"Suck-up," Skippy muttered under his breath.

"Now more than ever, MHI needs the help of the elves."

Oh, she liked that. The only thing worse than an elf was a smug elf. "Damned right y'all do."

"*And*...we need the help of the orcs."

Skippy threw the horns.

A scowl caused her multiple chins to flex, revealing that the last wet wipe had missed a whole lot of ranch and barbeque sauce, like a sticky, off-color zebra. The Queen was shifty, way smarter than she looked, and searching for an angle. "An if'n we don't?"

I started with an appeal to her pride. "Then you're going to have to live with the knowledge that a bunch of orcs helped save the world, and even though the elves had the chance to rise to the occasion, you didn't."

"Sure would be nice, for my kin to go over there

wit' y'all. Show up them snooty Yur-upeen elves.
Thinkin' they's better than us."

"I know how you feel." Actually, no, I didn't. European elves were supposed to be more traditional, but
they had a rep for being aloof and snooty, and wouldn't
work for humans. Her wanting American elves to look
tough to their cousins was great and all, but as Earl
liked to say, money talks while bullshit walks. It was
time to seal the deal. I reached under the table and
pulled out a fat, rubber-banded stack of hundred dollar
bills, put the money on the table, and slid it toward
her. "And you'd miss out on the signing bonus."

Her beady little eyes darted toward the cash. Skippy
looked at it too, but he yawned. We paid the orcs, but
they didn't really have much use for money beyond
downloading music and buying Warg Shampoo.

"What's in it for the tuskers?" she asked suspiciously.

"MHI our tribe," Skip said simply, like that was
the most blatantly obvious truth in the universe ever,
you greedy elf. "Duh."

But that wasn't entirely true. Skippy had already
specified their reward. Trip and I owed the orc village
another classic movie marathon, where we provided
helpful live commentary explaining all the confusing
human stuff, and snacks. The last one had been a big
hit. Skippy had hated *Red Dawn* because the helicopters weren't correct, Ed was disappointed the Predator
wasn't real because he wanted to fight one, but the
whole tribe had really loved *Conan the Barbarian*.

"I gots demands."

"And we are happy to hear them, your highness."

"Each of mine gets paid by the hour like normal,
cash, no IRS."

Now I was the one being insulted. "Obviously."

"My trackers never got to answer to no orc."

It wasn't like they were big on giving orders anyway. Before battle our orcs just kind of hung out, and during, they sort of did their own thing. "I think we can all agree that sounds fair."

"Now Skippy demands!" He thumped the table for emphasis. "Elfs no steal *urk* souls!"

"That's jus' ignorant! What'd anybody do with orc souls anyway?"

"Speak it!"

"Fine. We won't take nobody's soul."

Skippy seemed really proud to get that concession from her. He and Ed fist-bumped.

"Fine, but orcs can't go eatin' no elf babies or cuttin' off our ears to put on necklaces!"

The orcs snorted in unison, like that was the stupidest thing they'd ever heard. Why would the elves even bring a baby on the mission to begin with?

"I told ya' they don't make ear necklaces no more, Mama."

That was true. Earl had even added that stipulation to the MHI employee handbook after we had adopted the tribe.

"Shush, Tanya. We's negotiatin'."

An hour of intense debate later, the rulers shook on it. We had a deal. Elves and orcs would be working together. It was a truly historic moment. Then the elves pretty much cleaned out the bar.

# CHAPTER 9

I'd never been to the Holy Land before. Most people on their first trip to Israel, they'd probably see the sights, take a tour, that sort of thing. Trip was a devout kind of guy, and he really wanted to visit a bunch of the important biblical spots. Holly had heard the nightclub scene in Tel Aviv was great. I wouldn't know, I'm not a club kind of guy. I'd just be content to take care of business quietly, and then go back home.

But being Monster Hunters, and being here to talk to a professor who'd gone off the deep end, I wasn't going to hold my breath.

This trip was a result of the Van Helsing Institute's detective work. One of the things I'd asked Rigby to check on was traveling through the Nightmare Realm. He'd discovered that one of the Hunters who'd gone MIA from the Last Dragon was from an Israeli company called Maccabeus Security & Investigations, and that Hunter's father was an archeologist, who wasn't just read in on Unearthly Forces, he was one of the Israeli government's chief consultants on the subject. According to Rigby's friend at Maccabeus, the professor

had been consumed with finding out how to get his
son back ever since the incident. That included desperately digging into old forbidden tomes of esoteric
and occult knowledge, poking around ancient places
of power, and generally scaring the hell out of all
his coworkers.

Now, I didn't need to look very far from home to
see how that kind of fanatical dedication to cracking
the supernatural usually worked out. What happened
to Julie's dad was a perfect example. That kind of dark
knowledge had a way of getting into your head and
twisting things. You want to learn about the other side?
No problem. Because there is probably something there,
waiting, that would love to help you open the door. You
start poking around in that stuff, and down that road
lies nothing but a sad death or a padded cell.

However, since we were stupid enough to actually
*want* to go to the other side, we'd come all the way
here because the professor was following a lead that
might actually help us make it back.

The Hunter from Maccabeus who picked us up
was a solid-looking fellow in plain work clothes, who
still gave off a military vibe. He was nearly a foot
shorter than me, but he had a strong handshake and
introduced himself as David Gerecht. Surprisingly,
he had a British accent. Which I guessed explained
how he knew the VHI. He led us through a bunch
of security to the parking garage, where we loaded
all our bags into a Land Rover.

"Shotgun!" Holly exclaimed, which was totally not
fair, because I was eight inches taller. I went for the
door handle anyway, but she blocked me. "Snooze,
you lose, big guy."

I gave up and got in back. She was at least nice enough to pull her seat forward.

"I'll be taking you to see Professor Rothman directly," Gerecht explained as he got in the driver's side and put his seat belt on. He had a photograph of a woman and two kids stuck to his dash, and a well-read Bernard Cornwell novel on the center console. "When he found out MHI was interested in his latest project, he demanded to see you right away."

"That's good." Though honestly, after being squished into an airplane for that long I'd really wanted to shower, stretch out on an actual bed, and get in a nap first. The three of us had hit four countries in the last seven days—research and recruiting—so the travel was catching up to me.

"Since Ari disappeared, the professor has been killing himself, working around the clock. No sleep, no food, just work, and then running off to some other dig site. He's been very excited about an old fort out in the Judean Desert. That's where we'll be meeting him," Gerecht said as he drove us out of the garage.

Even though logically I knew what time it was here, and I could see out the windows at landing, it was still a little weird to see that it was dark out. I'd been flying around the world so much putting this mission together that it was like my internal clock had just given up. For me now, life was a perpetual four A.M.

"You want to tell me now why this is so important to MHI?"

"We're not at liberty to say yet," Trip explained. "No offense."

"I'm not that easy to offend, but you didn't just fly a few thousand kilometers on a whim." He waited a moment, but none of us fessed up. "That's fine. You don't have to tell us. My boss says that she looks forward to the legendary Earl Harbinger owing her a favor."

Earl had warned me about the head of Maccabeus in case we met. Aiya Trebitsch may have looked like a kindly little grandma, but she was an old-school Monster Hunter, who'd gotten her start ridding a kibbutz of a devil bat infestation with nothing but a Mauser K98 and a lot of attitude. She was still tough as nails, and her company followed her example.

"You don't sound like you're from here," Holly said.

"It's a land of immigrants. We speak a hundred languages in this country. Anyone you meet will probably know English, as well as Hebrew and Arabic. But yes, I immigrated here a long time ago. If anything, I still sound this way because I'm the one who always has to deal with foreigners, or handle the damned tourists who get in trouble. I grew up in London."

"So that's how you know the Rigbys?" I asked.

"Oh no. Wrong side of town for that. I'm from East London. The Van Helsing management are upper crust. I met them while they were consulting on a case in Jerusalem back when I was a police officer there. They were following a serial killer that was actually a doppelganger. Long story, but that was my first monster experience, Maccabeus made me an offer, and I've been there ever since."

It was hard to do much sightseeing at one in the morning. Even then, Trip was glued to his window just in case. The lights along the highway were nice, I guess.

"So where are we going again?" Holly asked.

"The Judean Desert. It is a long enough drive, you can get some sleep if you want, or I've got a cooler with sandwiches in it if you're hungry. The fortification Rothman is digging up was used by everyone from Romans to Crusaders. Don't worry about what hour we'll arrive. He'll still be up. Aiya is worried about him, so a couple of my team members are pulling security for the site."

"Why? Is it dangerous there?"

"Not particularly by our standards. That area hasn't been rocketed in months." Gerecht said that so deadpan that I wasn't sure if he was messing with us or not. "Mostly I think Aiya is worried the professor is going to pass out from exhaustion or forget to eat. We want to keep him healthy. He's a bit odd, but he's sort of a national treasure."

I woke up because the Land Rover slamming on the brakes caused me to bounce my chin off my chest. "Huh?"

"Car accident!" Holly exclaimed.

I didn't speak Hebrew, but I'm pretty sure Gerecht was swearing. I cracked open my eyes. Dust from our sudden stop wafted through the headlights. We were on a gravel road. Ahead of us was another vehicle, but its front end was down in a ditch. Beyond our lights the desert was pitch-black. I scanned around for threats. The red brake lights revealed nothing but sand and rocks behind us. Gerecht threw it in park and hopped out. He didn't bother to turn off the engine or even close the door, but immediately sprinted to the wreck.

Trip and Holly must have stayed awake, because both of them bolted from the car faster than I did. I started getting out too, but I'd been so deeply asleep that I'd drooled on my shirt, so it took me a second.

By the time I got there, Gerecht had gotten out a flashlight, slid down the ditch, and was reaching through the driver's side window. The vehicle must have been going fast, because its front end had completely crumpled against the rocks. I was still a little befuddled, but I realized that it was another Land Rover, matching ours down to the paint color, and that suggested company car.

"Help me. Gil is unconscious," our guide said.

"Don't move him. He could have a spinal injury. Get out of my way," Holly ordered as she climbed down. "I'm a medic."

Gerecht complied and Holly took his place in the window. She'd even brought her carry-on, in which I knew she always kept an emergency trauma kit. Holly had been going to nursing school when she had been recruited by MHI, and had gotten plenty of training and practical application ever since, especially for punctures, lacerations, and impact injuries.

"Who is it?" Trip shouted down at them.

"It's Gil. He's one of the two men I left guarding the professor."

"Get your light in here. He's breathing," Holly said. Gerecht stuck his flashlight through the window. "I've got a pulse. Air bag deployed. Looks like it knocked the shit out of him. Hang on . . . I've got blood. He's got a cut to the abdomen, and there's a stab wound on his leg."

He didn't get those from driving into a ditch. "How far are we from the site?"

"It's just over that next rise, less than a kilometer,"

Gerecht shouted back. "Something must have happened. Maybe he was going for help."

"Or running from something," Trip said. He'd pulled his own flashlight out and aimed it at the back of the crashed Land Rover. "Z, check this out."

I walked over to see what Trip was pointing at. It took my sleep-addled brain a second to process what I was looking at. The back window had been shattered. A pole was sticking out, and it had been poked into the rear of the back seat. *No. Wait. That's not a pole.* "Trip, is that a spear?"

"Yeah, man. I think it's a spear."

Gerecht shone his light in the back seat, swore again, then drew a handgun from a holster on his belt. *Yep. That was a spear.* He looked up at me. "There are weapons in the boot."

"On it."

I ran back to our Land Rover, opened the back gate and started shoving our luggage out of the way. There were several gun cases. I grabbed the top two. By the time I ran back, Trip had wrenched the spear free and climbed out.

"I'm no expert, but I'm pretty sure that's a friggin' spear." I said as I dumped the cases in the dirt and started unzipping one.

"It's a pilum. The Roman legions used them."

If anybody would know that, it was Trip. "Okay. Who is out in the desert throwing pilums at passing cars?" The first case contained a short-barreled, folding-stock micro Galil. The Velcro side pouches held loaded mags. *Score.*

"This isn't some replica. I think it's ancient." Trip shoved it toward me.

It wasn't a blade so much as a long metal shank, which had apparently bent on impact. The metal was dark, pitted, and flaking rust, like something you'd see in a museum. The wood looked old, and I bet I could twist it into pulp with my bare hands. But regardless of its age, something had just hurled it with a great deal of force. "What the hell, man?"

"It was stuck all the way through the back seat."

I rocked a mag into the Galil and worked the charging handle. Whatever it was out there in the desert throwing spears at people, I was more than happy to shoot the hell out of it.

Holly must have decided the wounded Hunter was safe to move, because she and Gerecht were dragging his unconscious body up the hill. Trip rushed over to help while I kept watch. They got him laid down in the headlights and Holly went back to work on him, while Gerecht and Trip armed up.

"What did Rothman set free?" I asked.

"It might not be supernatural. Could have just been an asshole with a big knife. Whatever it was, Gil was torqued," Holly stated. "I don't think it pierced his stomach, just muscle and fat, but that's a lot of little blood vessels cut. I'm going to have to tourniquet this leg." She pulled a black nylon bag out of her carry-on and took her tourniquet out. It was basically a strap, a buckle, and a lever. The hole was above his knee. It wasn't squirting, but it was a whole lot faster than a trickle. She cinched the strap around his thigh and grabbed the lever. "Hold him down. This will probably wake him up."

Trip and Gerecht got their hand on his shoulders. Holly cranked it tight. Gil woke up screaming and thrashing, but they kept him from hurting himself further.

"You'll be fine. You'll be fine," Gerecht kept telling his friend, while Holly went to work plugging the holes. "What happened?"

The wounded Hunter mumbled something I couldn't understand, but having lost too much blood, he was already nodding back off. His head dipped, and he was out.

"Stay with me, Gil! Gil? Damn it," Gerecht said.

"What did he say?" Trip asked.

"Centurion, I think."

"He's got a concussion." Holly ripped open a package with her teeth and spit out a chunk of wrapper. "So take that with a grain of salt."

Trip and I exchanged a nervous glance. She'd been too busy to see the Roman spear. *Centurion* was probably accurate. "Gerecht, you get revenants up here?"

"This dig wasn't listed as a danger site. There wasn't anything supernatural cataloged here. Unless..." he trailed off, scowling. "Rothman was mumbling about this tomb because it belonged to a mighty warrior, who had supposedly ventured into another world to rescue someone, but made it back because he'd found this artifact that would always show the way home. He thought this might be where the artifact is buried. But Aiya suspected he was desperate enough that if he found the remains he might attempt to commune with the dead, to ask the warrior how he'd done it. Our orders were not to let him try anything so stupid."

"You were babysitting. You think he would try anyway?"

"Desperation makes haste, and haste makes stupidity.

Rothman has read many of the old incantations; he could have tried something while my men weren't looking. Gil's phone was on the floor. He was trying to call me when he passed out and crashed."

"Right now we've got to assume Rothman woke up something nasty."

"Maybe, but all kinds of pain-in-the-ass undead collect in these old tombs." Gerecht looked toward the rise. "I've got another man in there, and there were some workers too. We have to save them."

"Your buddy here isn't crashing, but he's not got all night. I've got the bleeding slowed, but I can't tell if he's got any internal injuries. He needs a hospital bad." Holly had blood up to her elbows. Totally calm, she wiped her hands on her ruined shirt. She had seen a whole lot worse than this. "Was that little clinic we drove by on the way in the closest medical care?"

"Yes. Can you find your way back there?"

"No problem. I can evac him."

"You need a hand?" Trip asked.

"Just get him into the passenger seat. There's not much else you guys can do."

I jerked my head in the direction I thought the dig was supposed to be. "Then we'll head that way and look for the others."

Trip and I carried Gil to the still-running Land Rover and got him buckled in. While we did so, Gerecht was on his phone, speaking in rapid-fire Hebrew to someone I assumed was his boss. He hung up. "Help is on the way."

"How far out?" I asked.

"Too long to wait for them."

Holly flipped the vehicle around and went tearing

back toward civilization with the wounded man, while the three of us set out up the desert road. We ran as fast as we could, flashlights bouncing. The night was cool. The air was dry, probably the driest, cleanest air that had ever filled my lungs. My ankle still hadn't had a chance to fully heal, and it was burning. Gretchen was probably going to grumble at me again.

By the time we reached the top of the hill, I was breathing hard and sweating. The other two were fine. In my defense, Gerecht was close to half my mass, and Trip was a college athlete; I had about eighty pounds on him, and I hated running. I was just proud to keep up.

"There." Gerecht pointed his light. Like us, he was carrying an eyeball-melting flashlight that carried for a long ways. Monster Hunters wanted *all* the lumens.

At first it looked like a campsite more than anything. There were several big tents set up. If I'd not known what it had once been, I would have just thought the ancient fort was a bunch of rocks piled up to make a few walls. Caution tape had been strung up to keep anyone from falling into the black holes that were excavation pits. There were a few big construction lights, but they were off. The biggest tent had a generator next to it, but the engine wasn't running. There was a car and a truck parked there as well. Other than the yellow tape flapping in the desert wind, there was no movement.

"It could be dangerous. You two don't need to go in there with me. These aren't your people. This isn't your fight."

"Bull crap. We're going." Trip was very matter-of-fact about it. Most Hunters paused to figure out if there was an angle where we could get paid, but Trip was the sort who would do the hero thing for free.

Good thing he had me to look out for him. "Shared PUFF, or whatever you guys have here."

"Deal," Gerecht said without hesitation. "I was hoping you wouldn't want to mind your own business."

I snorted. "Mind our own business? You must not know any Americans."

"I appreciate it." Gerecht gave us a solemn nod as we started down the hill. "But for the record, my wife is from Illinois."

We shouldered our rifles and slowed to a fast walk, partially so we could be ready to engage any threats as soon as they popped up, and also because running down a rocky hill in the dark was a great way to break something. There wasn't any plant life to hide behind, but I tried to angle our approach so we could use big rocks for cover in case anything else started chucking spears at us. Gerecht had grabbed a black tactical vest out of his vehicle, so was the only one with all his gear in the right place. Trip and I had mags sticking out of our pockets. It was haphazard, but it would have to do.

"The largest tent was Rothman's base," Gerecht whispered.

"If he summoned something, it might not leave until he's dead," I warned. I'd been taught that was common with this sort of thing. Pacts sealed in blood and whatnot. What went unsaid was we might be the ones having to do the sealing-in-blood part.

"I know. We do what we have to."

"Let's play it smart and hopefully nobody has to die at all," Trip said.

I'd worked with Trip for years. He was my brother in battle. You train and fight with someone at your side long enough, you know exactly where they're going to be and what they're going to be doing. He would be solid, no matter what. Gerecht, I didn't know, but he seemed determined and carried himself like a pro.

So we headed into the unknown.

The camp was too quiet. No birds. No insects. Everything was so dry and hard here the wind didn't even seem to make much noise.

I was tense, but ready. I was rarely what I would describe as scared when doing this sort of thing anymore. Nervous and extremely aware of my mortality, yes, but you focus on the task at hand so much that stuff just becomes background noise. The more you fight, the more confident you get. Confident, but not cocky, because with experience comes a certain knowledge of just how fast things can go sideways, and how easily the human body can be destroyed in the process.

Not having any idea what had caused this mess to begin with, we cut the chatter. Despite cultural differences, hand signals for this sort of thing were pretty universal. You cover that side, you go that way, shoot anything that looks scary, etc. We spread out. Trip veered left. Gerecht took the middle. I flanked right. I was fifty yards from the big tent when I raised my fist in the universal sign for *Stop, there's an undead Roman up ahead.*

Okay. I added that last part, but they got the picture when they looked over and saw the eerily glowing skeleton dressed in rotting armor float around the side of the tent.

The hair on my arms stood up. The sight of the thing caused an involuntary shudder. It was unnatural. The bones were gleaming pale green; the armor was blackened from time and rotting apart. An unnatural green substance, part liquid, part fire, dripped from the eye sockets and every joint and between the ribs. I think that substance was what the big brains called ectoplasm. It seemed like the something was wearing the bones and armor as an ill-fitting suit. But clutched in one set of bone fingers was another decaying pilum. In the other was what was left of a gladius, and something about its manner told me this thing was really *pissed off*.

I took a knee behind a boulder. The skull swiveled over, two flaming holes aimed right at me. The jaw hinged open, and it began bellowing.

*"Vis mihi nummum. Age, me pugnare meretrix!"*

I didn't speak Latin, but I got the message when the pilum clanged off the rock next to my head and went spinning off into the desert.

*"Pugnare mihi!"* It waved the gladius around, like *come at me, bro.*

Apparently the old ghost wanted to fight. We were happy to oblige.

"Open fire!" I shouted. Trip had another borrowed micro Galil, Gerecht had a Tavor. Dust flew as bullets pierced the old armor. Bits of ancient leather and rust went flying. The skeleton shook back and forth as it was pelted. I leaned out and aimed. Shooting at night was easier when your target glows in the dark.

I stuck with rapid, aimed, semi-auto. This wasn't a person, and I didn't think it had any vital organs. So I put a bullet into everything, hoping there was some sort of weak spot. Eyes. Mouth. Where the heart would be. Nothing. The little gun kept bouncing against my shoulder. I didn't have my hearing protection, so my eardrums were taking a beating. Out of a barrel this short, 5.56 was really *loud*. The thing just stood there, seemingly annoyed at getting popped. Somebody nailed the gladius; it was in such rotten shape that the antique blade snapped.

The monster glanced down at its broken sword. It didn't have lips left to snarl, but I bet it would have if it could. It tossed the hilt into the sand and began floating my way, still uttering what I assumed were threats and insults in Latin. The Roman had an attitude.

I kept shooting, and when I ran dry, I yanked another magazine out of my jeans and reloaded. In that brief lull I saw the dead Roman's skeletal feet were hovering a few inches off the ground in a swirling circle of blown sand and green energy.

Okay, I admit, now I was getting a little scared.

"Fall back, Z," Trip shouted.

I moved out from behind cover, heading their way while the other two Hunters kept up the assault. That was when the Roman got its first real look at me.

*"Prohibere."*

That had sounded confused. Its tone had changed so drastically that I actually slowed down long enough to look back. The thing waved its skeletal arms, gesturing for me to come back, but I didn't stop until I was crouched behind some crates next to Trip.

When I stuck my head over the side, it still wasn't moving. Rather, it had stalled, floating in the open. It showed me its hands, not threatening this time, but rather to demonstrate that it was unarmed. I think it wanted to talk. "Cease fire! Cease fire!"

The gunfire stopped. There were dozens of new flaming .22 caliber holes in the armor, but none of them seemed to have had any effect anyway. There was a long awkward silence between us and the dead guy.

"What's going on?" Gerecht shouted.

"I think it wants to talk."

"I've got a man down. We don't have time for this."

"You got a better idea?"

The fiery Roman kept tilting its head, like we were talking gibberish. It asked something else. Trip looked up from his rifle, over at me, and shrugged. We had us a bit of an impasse.

"You speak Latin, Gerecht?"

"Not at all."

"Try Hebrew."

He did. *Nothing.* When he tried Arabic, the monster threw its hands up in the air in frustration, like *what is wrong with you idiots?* Because of getting inside Lord Machado's head, I could sort of speak archaic Portuguese, and even though it was five hundred years closer and a Romance language, I tried a formal greeting, and still got nothing, except for feeling silly saying it.

"Hang on," Trip said. He pulled out his phone. "Since we've been traveling so much I downloaded a translation app on my phone"—he tapped the screen a few times—"*and* . . . I can't access the internet from here."

"That's useless."

"You can download languages in advance and use it offline."

"That's handy."

"Except I didn't think I'd need Latin, Z!"

So the three of us spent a minute shouting various things in different languages at the monster, while it floated back and forth. It seemed to grow increasingly frustrated, but it was that or go back to shooting it. We had a diplomatic standoff. The monster even took off its helmet and ran its finger bones through where its now nonexistent hair had once been. It was a very human mannerism.

The monster floated a little closer. Put flesh on those bones and he probably wouldn't have come up to my shoulder. I guess they hadn't been big people back then.

It touched its breastplate. *"Sextus Bassus."*

That had to be its—rather *his*—name. I shifted the Galil to my off hand and moved out from behind cover. I pointed at myself. "Owen Pitt."

He said something else. I shrugged. Bassus shook his skull. *"Stulte."*

"I know that one," Trip said. "He's calling you a moron."

But the monster was already pointing at a freshly dug hole and complaining again. I was pretty sure he was angry that he'd been woken up. At least he was calmed down enough now that he'd temporarily stopped throwing spears at people. Then Bassus seemed to have a bright idea, dropped his helmet back on his glowing head, turned, and began hovering back toward the main tent.

"Hey, Trip. Since he's not watching us, how about you take the high ground and see if you can spot the others."

"Got it." He took off running for the ruins.

"Be careful." For all I knew, Rothman had animated an entire Roman legion. "If you see any other monsters, fall back."

Bassus disappeared beneath the canvas, though I could still see the glow through the seams as he puttered about. I moved back behind the crates and knelt. A moment later Bassus floated back out, now carrying somebody by the back of their collar. I put my light on him so I could get a better look. It was hard to tell when being dragged through the sand by a short ghost, but he was a thin man, with angular features, salt-and-pepper hair, probably around fifty, and he looked like he'd just been on the receiving end of a severe beating.

"That's Rothman," Gerecht called out.

The Roman dropped the professor on the ground, then pointed one bony finger at him and began shouting again. I didn't need to speak Latin to get the message of *this is the asshole who disturbed my grave!* Bassus may have been floating, but that didn't stop him from giving Rothman a swift kick to the stomach.

"Hey!" Gerecht shouted.

But that woke him, and he came to, coughing. An archeology professor had to be able to speak Latin, so before Bassus could go back to kicking his ass, I shouted, "Rothman! Speak to him in Latin!"

He must have heard me, because he quickly said something, and whatever it was caused the monster to pause his beating. Bassus asked him an angry question. Rothman was terrified, but he answered. The centurion lifted one hand, as if to backhand him, but Rothman gave what sounded like a very sincere apology and plea for mercy, and the hand slowly lowered.

"Awesome. Now let's all make friends," I shouted.

Rothman turned toward our lights. His face was covered in bruises and scratches. "Are you here to rescue us?"

"It's me—David. Don't worry, Doctor. We'll get you out."

"I read the incantation. I know you warned me not to, but I had to! There was a flash of lightning, and then this, this . . . *thing* burst from the ground and attacked us."

"You should have tried talking to him," I suggested.

"He wasn't in a talking mood then!"

"Well, he is now, so don't screw it up, Doc!"

I was betting that when he was alive, Bassus was one impatient son of a bitch, because he kicked Rothman again. Not as hard as the first time, but definitely letting him know who was in charge here. Bassus demanded something.

"He's ordering me to translate for him."

"Fantastic."

Only what an otherworldly being had in mind for *translate* was drastically different from what I'd been expecting. Because Bassus reached down, put his fingers on the professor's head, and the man screamed. The green glow engulfed Rothman's head.

Gerecht shouldered his rifle. "No!"

"Hold your fire!" I bellowed. I could still see his face beneath, and it seemed to be in one piece. My gut was telling me that action wasn't malevolent. "He's just trying to communicate."

"You'd better know what you're doing, Pitt."

*Occasionally.*

Rothman began to speak, only it wasn't his voice.

It was Bassus's. "That is better. I will use this one to speak through." The green liquid fire came dribbling out of Rothman's mouth as his eyes rolled up in his head.

"Can you understand us now?"

"Yes. This one has a ridiculous number of words."

"Don't hurt him."

The skull looked down. "The criminal scum is lucky I do not cut his hands and feet off and feed them to hounds. He cast spells in my tomb. He ripped me from my fields and put me back in this!"

"Remain calm, Bassus."

"You remain calm, Owen Pitt! Charon is toying with me. Look at me. I am a skeleton! I do not even have a dick!"

I could see how that would be upsetting. "Take it easy." I had no idea what Bassus's frame of reference was. I'd dealt with dead people before, and sometimes they weren't even aware of it. "A long time has passed since you were here. I hate to tell you this, but you are dead."

"This is obvious. I said it was my tomb. Do you think I am stupid?"

"Well, I don't know what you know. You're the one throwing a fit here."

"Come and fight me then. Is everyone stupid now? Or was I just unlucky enough to be violated by a gang of fools?"

Bassus was kind of an ass. "We don't want any trouble."

"I do not wish trouble either. You woke me!"

"And we're really sorry about that."

The skull swiveled back and forth. "Is this a trick? Where has the Nubian gone?"

I assumed that meant Trip. "He's looking for the

other people who were here, to see if they are still alive. Did you hurt them?"

"I educated them for their impudence, but I did not take their lives."

"Thank you for that."

"They are lucky. I was very annoyed when I arrived here."

"You stabbed one of them."

"I warned him not to run off. What kind of idiot does not listen to orders?"

The kind that didn't speak Latin, especially when it was being shouted by an angry flaming ghost. "You have my sincere apologies."

"Your mongrel garbage tongue hurts my ears."

"You don't even have ears."

"Scum!" Bassus laughed. "I like you. I saw that you are like me. Or like I once was. That is why I spared you."

"Spared me?" I snorted. "I don't know about that."

"You are a Chosen. As was I. You wear the mantle."

Now we were getting somewhere. That just meant that like me, some cosmic faction had picked him to fight for its interests. "I am."

"Then we are brothers in the eternal war. Seeing another brother gave me clarity. I remembered. My final orders warned me I might someday be dragged back to this world should another Chosen have need of my treasure. From the spell this fool used, I know what he was looking for, but he is unworthy. Do you seek the Ring of Bassus as well?"

"Maybe. I don't know what it does. In truth, I have to go into the Realm of Nightmares and I'm looking for any tools that can help me."

"I know that place. I have been there. It is a terrible land of swirling fog, murderous beasts, and treacherous criminal shit bags. Why would you willingly venture there?"

"An evil creature has taken some of my friends. I want to get them back."

"Ah...I did that once. The Legate of Judea's beautiful daughter was stolen away there. Having destroyed more monsters than anyone else in the empire, it was my appointed duty to save her."

"Did you?"

"Of course. Because I am amazing. And afterwards I bedded her repeatedly!"

He may have been dead for a couple thousand years, but Sextus Bassus would have fit in just fine with modern Hunters. "Well, good for you."

"Yes. Good times. We returned, because of this." The skeleton held up his other hand. I'd not noticed before, but there was a ring around one of the finger bones. "It will always lead the bearer toward that which he loves the most. It will show you the path home."

"That would be very useful."

"Of course it is. I just said so. I must know, in this day, who is your enemy? Who do you go to fight?"

"The demon called Asag."

"Jupiter's cock!" Bassus obviously recognized that name. "Asag Shedu is a terrifying foe. Then you will need all the help you can get. My ring is yours."

He swung his hand toward me, like an underhand pitch. With no flesh to hold it, the ring sailed smoothly off. It was still burning green on the flight over. I reached up and caught it. It was so freezing cold it stung. I held it in my palm and watched as the glow slowly died. The ectoplasm turned to water. When the light show was over, all that remained was a very plain silver ring.

"Thank you."

"It accomplishes no good buried. Use it well... Ah, I can feel it. You are why I was allowed here. It is good to know the gods still meddle when their champions are concerned." The glow around the bones began to dim. "Now I can I go back across the Styx."

"First, can you tell me about Asag?"

"He is sly. A creature of lies and trickery, not because he needs them, or because he is weak, but because deceptions please him. The lion is power-ful, yet he still hides in the weeds until it is time to strike. That is his way. When the time comes, Asag will strike, and your world will burn. I fought his minions once, you know."

"How did you beat them?"

"I did not. How do you think I ended up buried here?" The fire was dying, the ectoplasm turning to mist. "If Asag kills you too—which is very likely—come and visit me in the Fields of Elysium. We will... I search this one's mind for the proper words...*hang out.* Farewell, Owen Pitt."

He let go of Rothman's head. The glow immediately left him. The professor fell over, gasping for air. The now unanimated bones collapsed. The armor dropped lifelessly into the sand.

"So long, Bassus."


I got in another jet lag power nap, this time in a medical clinic's waiting room. Between airplanes, car rides, and weird situations, I was getting really good at getting all my necessary sleep in chairs. It was hell on your back though.

Holly woke me up by tossing a magazine at me from across the room.

Reaching for my gun that wasn't there, I snorted awake and recognized where I was. "Hey!"

"Don't get offended. Like I'm going to go over and shake the giant buff guy who once sucker punched a Navy SEAL for surprising him awake."

I stretched. We were the only ones in the waiting room. "The time I hit Sam was because I was in some mystical prophecy coma battling the Cursed One."

"Oh, like I can tell the difference."

"I was having a seizure that time!"

"That's what you normally look like: twitchy." Holly shrugged. "I don't know how Julie sleeps in the same bed as you."

"She does complain I'm a compulsive blanket stealer."

"I'll bet. Anyways, Rothman can talk now."

It was a small-town clinic. It didn't feel particularly foreign. Nobody even looked at us funny as we walked down the hall. Thankfully since Holly had her luggage, she'd been able to change out of the clothing that had been soaked with blood. "How're the others?"

"They'll all be fine. Your Roman dude kicked the living crap out of them. Broken bones, head injuries, and lots of bruises, but only the one was serious. Blood loss would have gotten him if we hadn't found him when we did, but he'll be okay. Though he's going to have to stay off that leg for a while."

"Man, everybody should have an orc on call."

"I'll suggest franchising to Gretchen when we get back." Holly stopped in front of one of the doorways.

There was a patient in the bed, but I couldn't see him because a nurse was in the way. "He's in here. Oh, that thing you were telling me about where the Roman grabbed him by the head?"

"Like a ventriloquist's dummy."

"You know that's not how ventriloquism works, right? No, I mean that rattled him good. He's pretty freaked out. And where the bone fingers touched, severe frostbite."

"Nasty." That made me glad Bassus had decided to slow down and wave the peace flag. The nurse gave us a smile as she walked past.

I hardly recognized him with all the bandages on his head now, but I was pretty certain it was the same man we'd rescued earlier. "Dr. Rothman. I'm Owen Pitt. This is Holly Newcastle. We're with MHI."

He gave us a very tired nod. "Please, come in." We walked up to the bed. "First of all, thank you for helping save us."

"No problem. How're you feeling?"

"Scrambled. In addition to the knock on the head, I've never been possessed before. My associate, David, went to get coffee. I think he's still very mad at me."

I couldn't blame Gerecht for being torqued. "Well, you did kind of raise the dead."

"That was a mistake. I did not mean to..." He must have noticed that we both thought he was full of shit, and gave a resigned sigh. "Perhaps a little, but I only wanted to speak with him. I only wanted information. I thought I could control it. The old scrolls gave no indication that he would physically manifest in our world. That was most unexpected."

"That's the thing about magic," Holly said. "It never

works the way we think it will, and it always has a cost. I've got a friend, her dad was about the smartest guy ever, and he thought he could figure it out like any other kind of technology. He nearly let the Old Ones invade Alabama."

"Ray Shackleford." Rothman sounded tired and resigned. "Yes. I'm aware. A cautionary tale, but this wasn't like that at all."

"Of course not." I put one hand on Holly's wrist to cut her off. I wasn't about to get self-righteous over the topic. Since I had a supposedly magic ring in my pocket, that would make me a bit of a hypocrite. "We came all this way because Rigby at the VHI said you've been working on something we're very interested in."

"Yes, of course. The Nightmare Realm. There could only be one reason you want to know about that awful place. You've found a way in." He waited for me to nod. "Good. You know about my son?"

"He was one of the MIA after the Last Dragon."

"Everyone tells me he's certainly dead, but Ari is a survivor. He's found a way."

"We've both been into the Nightmare Realm. It lives up to the name," Holly said. "I don't want you to get any false hopes."

"No. You don't understand. I would know if he was gone. I would feel it. Years ago, when Ari was just a boy, I was working in America, and my family was here. There was a suicide bombing on a bus. Many were killed. I was notified that my son was among them. Only I knew he had made it somehow. I felt it. It wasn't denial, I just *knew*. Sure enough, he survived; barely, but survive he did. And I feel the same thing now. I would know if he's gone. I would *know!* And until I *do* know, I will do everything in my power to bring him home!"

Holly and I shared a glance. She looked as uncertain as I felt. It was one thing to get your hopes up, but this man was going to kill himself trying regardless. I turned back to him. "Listen, we've got a good source of information who is telling us seven of the missing are still alive."

"We don't know their identities though," Holly cautioned. "Your son might be one of them, or he might not. We just don't know."

"He is," Rothman stated. "He is!" That was probably the first positive reinforcement he'd gotten since the incident. Tears began rolling from his eyes. "Any help I can give, it is yours. I remember what Sextus Bassus said: You're going there. I searched everywhere, but you've found a way, haven't you? I must know, is it a fixed Place of Power or have you found a way to tear a temporary rift?"

"Fixed. I'm pretty sure that if we found a way to tear another crazy hole like that alp did in Las Vegas, the MCB would exterminate us all."

"Excellent. Fixed is predictable. There are rules for fixed. Do you still have the ring?"

"I do."

"Keep it safe. The gate Bassus used was destroyed thousands of years ago, but I knew that when I did find another one, I'd still need a way to get back. All the tales say it is a treacherous land, constantly shifting. Time and space function differently there. Men have entered, been inside for what felt like a day, and have come out years later. Or they've spent months inside and returned to Earth where only a few hours had passed. It will do everything it can to confuse you, to keep you forever."

"We made it out before."

"You only dipped a toe into the water, and then snatched it back out. You could do that because you still existed in both worlds simultaneously. That is how a rift works. If they've been swept deeper inside the realm, you will have to leave the safety of the anchor point and venture after them. Bassus faced the same problem, so the empire's greatest mystics created that ring for him. It is like a compass with two points, one toward the hero's goal, and the other back toward what he loves the most. If I couldn't find it, I hoped to re-create their methods and make my own. In those days cosmic powers were more likely to take an interest and provide assistance. But like so many of the ancient things, their ways are lost to us now."

"Considering the opening portals and raising-the-dead bits when we start screwing around in that stuff, I'm not entirely convinced that's such a loss," Holly said.

"You don't understand, Ms. Newcastle. I'm one of the world's premier experts on the subject, and I only have a child's knowledge. We are dilettantes. Hobbyists. The odds of me being able to re-create that ring are a million to one, and I would likely die in the process. However, I was still willing to try. What I'm getting at is that we are not good at this, *unless* we receive help from an outside force. The little incantation I did in the tomb of Bassus was a desperate plea, nothing more. It shouldn't have worked at all, but it did." He stared right at me with thankful tear-filled eyes. "Because *you* were near. I did not just speak

Bassus's words, I had his thoughts. This meeting was the will of a higher power. This was *destined*."

He said that like it was a big revelation, and seemed a little deflated when I seemed unmoved. "Okay."

"No, really."

"This isn't my first rodeo with the Chosen One bit, Doc."

"It's like his hobby," Holly said.

"Regardless, you alone are the only man who can bring my son back, and for that I am so thankful."

That took a second to click. "Hang on. What do you mean...*alone*?"

# CHAPTER 10

I had a couple of days after getting back from Israel before I had to leave for the training camp. This mission would be a long one, so this would my last chance to see Julie for several months. I loved my job, but this time I was dreading leaving. I'll be honest, it was tough. Forty-eight hours isn't a whole lot of time when you know that's potentially all you've got left with the woman you love.

Much of the house was still trashed—thanks a lot, stupid Franks—but Julie had sent the contractors away so we could have some privacy. With most of MHI's senior leadership working on the upcoming big job, Julie was pretty much running the corporate office by herself, so she was still on call. However, she had left explicit instructions at the office that if anything happened while she was gone, they should handle it without her. If her phone rang, there had better at least be a Godzilla-equivalent monster rampaging through a major city or there would be hell to pay.

The job was turning out to be even bigger than I'd first thought, and now I knew about potential complications I was scared to even mention to Julie because I didn't want to worry her needlessly. Troubles were piling up, from crazy things like evil demigods to relatively normal things like an ailing parent. But for two days we just forgot about the business, upcoming challenges, and all the other crap we had to worry about, and instead just enjoyed each other's company.

It was awesome.

On the last night, we were lying in bed together in the dark and quiet. The window was open, the curtains moving in the breeze. It was a nice night just beneath a sheet. We'd stayed up way too late. Julie was still snuggled up against me, her head resting on my chest while I absently ran my fingers down her naked back.

This was more than I ever hoped for, more than I deserved. I was in love, but not just that...I *liked* Julie. I'd been lucky enough to marry the person I would have wanted to hang out with anyway. She was my partner. We were in it to win it, together. Team Us. Life was good, and worth fighting for.

"What's on your mind?" she asked.

"It's nothing. Go back to sleep."

"You might as well tell me. I can tell when something's bugging you. You breathe differently when you're being thoughtful."

I couldn't hide much from her. "I was thinking: this moment, right here. It's perfect. This is why I've got to make it back."

"You made it almost the whole weekend before you got all pensive and philosophical on me. That's pretty good for you. Are you worried?"

"Not really," I lied. "Are you?"

"Not at all." She was lying too. We both had a little laugh at that. "Oooh. Hang on." She rolled onto her back, grabbed my hand, and placed it flat on her abdomen. "Feel."

I waited several seconds. "I can't feel—" Then it *moved.* There was just this little flutter against my palm. It was *tiny.* "Whoa."

"We *made* that." I could see Julie's smile in the dark. "Pretty badass, huh?"

Somehow that little kick brightened my whole world. I don't think I've ever been happier. "Our little dude is going to be super strong."

"Just like his father."

Now it was my turn to grin like an idiot. "When I said it was perfect a minute ago, I didn't realize it could still get better. I love you more than anything. You're brilliant and beautiful, and I'm going to miss you so much."

"You get so cheesy sometimes. Owen, honey, you're going to win and you're going to come back to me so you can be a good dad to this kickass super baby. Nothing, whether it's man or monster, is going to stand in our way."

We kissed for a long time.

It probably shouldn't have come as a surprise that Earl Harbinger already owned several thousand acres of Alaskan wilderness. As much as Earl didn't like to talk finances, that man certainly understood how compound interest worked, had been alive long enough to take advantage of it, and had been around when land was *cheap.* I'd learned over the years that he'd accumulated property all over the place, under quite a few different names. I had asked Earl about all his real estate once. He'd said that the reason he liked buying land was that they weren't making any more of it.

Holly leaned past me to see out the window. "This place is *desolate*."

I thought it was kind of pretty in a rugged sort of way. There were mountains, ocean, trees, and snow. And ice. And then more snow. Which was funny, since it was spring everywhere else.

Trip—who was not by nature a cold weather kind of guy to begin with—shuddered.

The little cargo plane rolled to a stop. There was an actually decent asphalt runway, and there were even a few prefab buildings that didn't look too crappy, though I'd been told that most of us would be sleeping in what were basically shipping containers. The pilot killed the engines. I opened the door. Earl and Milo were already waiting for us.

"Welcome to the Monster Hunter International Cold Weather Training Facility," Earl said proudly as we climbed out of the cargo plane. "Or Camp Frostbite, as some of us with more delicate ladylike constitutions have taken to calling it."

"Earl wouldn't let Boone name it Camp Numb Nuts," Milo explained.

There was a strong wind coming in off the ocean. The air was *crisp*, which was a nice way of saying it felt like getting punched in the testicles by Frosty the Snowman. I could see why Boone had wanted to name the new training center that way.

"How was Israel?" Earl asked.

"Warm," answered Trip.

"Successful." I had a magic ring, the help of another

expert, and I think I was best buds with a dead Roman. "I'll catch you up as soon as we're somewhere safe to talk."

Earl gave an exaggerated look around the miles of wilderness. "I think we're okay."

"I mean—"

"I know what you mean, Z. Don't worry about ghosts. I've got that covered. I took care of a Chenoo outbreak in this neck of the woods fifty years ago. Hell of a thing, but my daddy taught me how to deal with Stone Coats when I was young. After that, me and the local Stone Coat came to an arrangement."

"I don't know what any of those things are."

"Indian earth spirits," Trip said, "that turn people into cannibal monsters."

There really were a lot of nasty things to keep up with in our line of work. "Oh . . . They sound like great neighbors."

"Ah, they ain't so bad once you get to know them. They're basically grumpy old bastards who just want these damned kids to stay off their lawn. So I blocked off access to their sacred valley, and bought up all the land around it. I just left an offering and told them we'd be moving up here for a spell so they won't curse us. They were appreciative of the gesture. If any of Asag's minions come poking around, ghostly or not, the local spirits will chase them off for us. Now grab your crap and follow me."

We were all bundled up in cold weather gear. Trip was from sunny Florida. Holly grew up in Las Vegas, and neither had my insulating bulk. They both looked absolutely miserable already, which was funny since Trip was usually the team's optimist.

"Don't look so glum. You kids should be glad winter lasts eight months up here. We'll be on our way to Russia by the time the mosquitos get really bad."

Our target was covered in ice year-round. D-Day was scheduled for the warmest time of the year, but we didn't know how long our operation was going to end up staying. If we were still there when it got cold, resupply would be a bitch. Just surviving in those conditions was tough, let alone remaining in fighting shape. Severny Island was a long way from Alabama. Plus, many of the other company's Hunters had never operated in an environment that cold. So Earl had decided to move most of our force to the new training center until D-Day. We needed the space and it would give us a chance to acclimatize to a similar environment for a few months and learn new survival skills.

I heard the other Hunters before I saw them because there was a constant stream of gunfire coming from the nearby hills. I'd seen Milo's invoices. We were shipping practice ammo up here by the pallet. We walked/crunched around the corner of a prefab, and I was surprised to see how busy the place was. There were Hunters everywhere.

Other than the aforementioned shooters, there were a few other groups, including a bunch of folks doing PT and pumping iron. It actually looked like a prison yard with all the outdoor weight benches. A giant tent served as the kitchen. A couple of the shipping containers were being used as classrooms. Men were moving supplies by pickup and four-wheeler. There had to be a few hundred people living here already.

"Impressive, huh? Julie's been shaking the trees,

which is tough considering she can't come right out and tell them over the phone what's going on."

Getting the face-to-face meetings was one reason I'd been spending so much time traveling lately. Just one of the perks to being the mission's XO. Julie got us in the door with her name and the family rep, shared hatred of the demon who was massacring people all over the world motivated them, and a shot at a percentage of a world-ending PUFF sealed the deal.

"As of this morning we're at four hundred and fifty Hunters from nine different companies." Earl pointed to where a bulldozer and a backhoe were working. "As soon as that crew gets the next set of facilities in, we'll have another three hundred volunteers on the way up. Flights and boats have been coming in nonstop. They're kicking in men, matériel, and money. I've been impressed by how much support we're getting for this mission."

"Look at us being all businessy. It fills my little black accountant heart with joy." I noticed there were different country and company flags flying from the various huts, hovels, and shipping containers. "This has got to be like herding cats."

"Actually, it ain't bad so far. We said no Newbies. Everybody is only sending experienced hands. They're all focused on revenge enough not to fight with each other. So far Julie's only been contacting folks I think are *all right*. All the companies that lost somebody at the Last Dragon were quick to jump in."

"Put Maccabeus Security down for twenty," Holly told him.

Milo sighed. "I'm going to need more porta potties."

Camp Frostbite was an impressive sight, but I had

to shake my head. "The more companies we draw from, the more likely it is for Asag to find out we're coming."

"And any group small enough to ensure secrecy wouldn't last ten minutes," Trip said through chattering teeth.

Sadly, he was correct. It was a trade-off we would just have to deal with. He might know we were gunning for him, but we could still try and minimize the details of *how* we were gunning for him.

"I'm impressed. How'd you get so much built so fast?"

Milo was happy I'd noticed all his hard work. "There was already an old gold-mining camp here; but for the new things, you'd be amazed how motivated oil company guys are when you promise epic bonuses for speedy work."

"Especially after one of the roughnecks got mauled by a bear," Earl said.

"Yeah . . . That kind of sucked. I had to shoot him. I'm going to make an awesome fur coat out of him though."

"The bear or the worker?" Holly asked.

"The bear, obviously," Milo said, missing the sarcasm. "The oil company guy would make a terrible coat."

Earl continued the tour. I could tell he was enjoying this. "Way over there is the arms room. Since everybody in this crowd is walking around armed—"

"Bears *everywhere*," Milo supplied helpfully. "And they wake up hungry."

"That building is for collecting the bigger stuff we're training on: rockets, missiles, mortars, crew served. That kind of thing. Our logistics team is working on shipping most of the heavy stuff directly to the island."

"How heavy are we talking here?" I asked.

"Terrain and weather allowing, light armored vehicles at least. Right now I'm trying to decide between tracked or wheeled. They've both got their pros and cons. The hard part is transport and offload, but if our logistics team can figure it out, I'm bringing a tank."

"I've always wanted some tanks," Milo said.

The accountant part of me recoiled in terror, but the Hunter side of me said "Awesome." It was a good thing we had Management's cash to get this rolling. Asag and his high-dollar minions had better be there to recover some costs, or this was going to be a huge loss.

"We've got the space and a lot of privacy out here. The locals think we're some paramilitary mercenary company. They don't want to snoop around because they figure they'll get shot trespassing."

"When I flew into the next town over on a supply run, I heard some folks whispering we're the CIA, and we're moving the space aliens from Roswell here," Milo said.

"That works too. Reporters are too lazy to hike." Earl paused to light up a cigarette. "I've been breaking the Hunters into teams based on their specialties. Working around the language barriers has been a pain in the ass, but Vegas gave them a bond. I put Nate on public relations because everybody likes him. Lots of grudges between some of these groups, but he's soothing hurt feelings. The companies are actually working together. This is shaping up to be a force to be reckoned with. If our intel isn't complete bullshit, if the PUFF-applicable bad guy is actually home, and if the Russians don't screw us over, this mission should go great."

"And I want a pony for Christmas," Holly said.

"You find a way to mitigate any of those ifs, and I'll make sure Santa brings you a whole horse farm."

"What did you tell the MCB, Earl?" Trip asked.

"Nothing yet. I assume they've seen all this on spy satellites by now, but a new training center's not violating any of their rules."

MCB oversaw monster hunting, and their rules tended to be arbitrary and capricious. Since I'd been with MHI, our governmental overlords had changed leadership three times, and the way those rules were enforced always changed with them. "They just got a new interim director, and I hear he's former Strike Force. They tend to be the shoot first and forget the questions department. What're you going to say if they come and inspect us, and demand to know what we're all doing up here?"

Earl shrugged. "Corporate team-building exercises."

"With *tanks?*"

"If they don't like it, they can fuck right off."

It was like Earl Harbinger's Day Camp for Wayward Youth.

Being supreme commander of whatever this was shaping up to be, Earl got first pick for where to bunk, so he'd claimed an old miner's shack on the outskirts of the camp. It was partially buried in the ground and looked like it had been there for a hundred years. There was only room inside for a cot and a potbellied stove.

"Cold don't bother me like it does the rest of you," Earl explained when I saw the dump. Even if we were in a blizzard he could be counted on to have nothing but that beat-up old leather bomber jacket he always wore. I didn't know about the insulating qualities of minotaur, but I suppose Earl could always grow fur if he needed to.

"Nice digs."

"I like the privacy."

I had told Earl we needed to talk. "Speaking of privacy," I looked around, but the nearest other Hunter was over a hundred yards away. "What are you going to do about the full moon?"

"Already dealt with." The stub where his finger had been was noticeable as he held his lighter up to his mouth to start another cigarette. "I catch a ride on a bush plane, they drop me off in the middle of nowhere with a radio and some supplies, and then come back a few days later."

That sounded . . . *lonely*. "That kind of sucks, Earl. Anything I can do to help?"

"I'm used to it, and I've had worse accommodations. You keep things running while I'm gone. Just if anybody already not in the know asks, you tell them I'm off on business. The whole Hunting world doesn't need to know what I am."

"I don't think I've ever asked, but that has to be tough for you."

"Some folks immediately hate me for it. Can't blame them, considering what the werewolves they deal with are like. But the ones who pity me are annoying as hell." The evergreens were so dense it was actually kind of quiet over here. Earl glanced around the forest, then sighed. "Truthfully, I don't mind going off by myself so much. It gives me time to ponder on things . . . You know, before Stricken hauled Heather off, the place we were hiding out wasn't so far from here. Those were probably some of the happiest days of my life."

"You heard from her lately? Is she doing okay?"

He shook his head, then stared off into the distance, distracted at the thought. "Not since after the Franks thing. We were together for a little bit after that, but STFU came looking for her. She liked the lady who replaced Stricken, and actually believed in their mission enough to go back willingly. They put her on some black op. Absolutely no communication. Whatever she's doing, she must think it's worth it . . ." he trailed off. "God, I miss her."

It was a remarkably human show of weakness from my boss. If he was a regular person, I probably would have patted him on the shoulder and told him it would be okay, but this was Earl Harbinger we were talking about here. Pat Earl you might lose a hand. He was kind of prickly about the emotional stuff. "She'll be back."

"I know she will. Red is a badass."

Sometimes Earl was hard to figure. He was a complicated guy. Hard as nails, but he'd gone so long not having anyone like him . . . to get that and then to have it taken away? That had to be a hell of a thing.

Earl's cigarette had burned down to the filter. He tossed it in the dirt and smashed it with his boot. "And Z?"

"Yeah, Earl?"

"Thanks for asking."

I nodded.

"Enough of the moping. Back to work." It was like he flipped a switch and the melancholy was gone. As long as he could focus on monster killing, Earl was good to go. "What'd you want to talk about?"

"We took the Israel trip because Rigby found us an expert who has been studying up on the Nightmare Realm. You know I picked his brain, and got some other good stuff, but there's a potential glitch with that part of our plan."

"An additional *glitch* in the part of our plan that's already the biggest crap shoot? The plan is take the city, kill the bad guy, send a rescue team through the gate, hold that position until they return, and then get the hell out. Glitch must be accountant code for FUBAR. Hit me."

A lot of what Rothman had talked about flew right past me. He'd worked for Microtel R&D back in the days when the MCB had been stupid enough to grant private companies permission to experiment with rifts. Rothman was tuned into that stuff like nobody else I'd ever spoken with. But his explanation was the kind of thing that would leave a guy with a bunch of science PhDs like Ben Cody scratching his head, let alone me. "Good news first: from what we know the Nightmare Realm isn't a fixed piece of geography. So if we go through a portal in Russia, we're not going to have to walk to their equivalent of Nevada to find where we left our guys."

"Good. I didn't feel like walking a few thousand miles."

"Yeah. It isn't an actual world, it's more like the space between worlds. It's a buffer zone. Some things live there, like the alp we fought, but it isn't a *place* as we understand the concept. It's a state of being."

Earl snorted. "I've been there and to the weird-ass

place the Old Ones live and still none of that metaphysical shit makes a lick of sense to me."

"Me either, and keep in mind that most of this is
guesswork, but it's guesswork by people a whole lot
smarter than me."

"Don't sell yourself short, Z. I wouldn't let any of
those assholes touch my taxes."

That was actually a pretty cool compliment. "Okay.
When the casino got sucked in, that part of the realm
was still stuck to Earth temporarily. It got closed
before things could get too strange, and most of the
things tethered to our world made it back."

"Most, but not all, like our boys."

"Exactly. They're out there somewhere, but the
longer they've been lost, the harder they're going to
be to find. It's like they are floating."

"Hopefully together, and not in separate directions."

"Uh . . . Maybe?" The analogy Rothman had used
was of a ship sinking in the ocean. Survivors on a raft
would be more affected by winds, and blown one way,
while survivors treading water with a life vest would be
at the mercy of the current, and carried another way.
Depending on the time and forces involved, survivors of
the same incident could end up a world apart. And yet,
fingers crossed, sometimes they all clung together. "Well,
Rothman's not sure. The only stories he's found where
somebody has gone there looking for someone, the search
was for one lone individual. But in each of those stories,
it was the hero's iron will that brought them together."

"Hero's *iron will*? He actually said that?" Earl asked
incredulously. I nodded. "Damned frilly academics,
thinking old poetry matches up with punch-you-in-
the-face reality."

"In this case though, it's probably accurate, in that it's literally man versus the realm. The only way you can find something is if you want it bad enough. Remember, it isn't like we can map this place. The only fixed points are where another reality is temporarily attached, and everything else is swirling around it. You know how planes and boats and people sometimes just disappear into nothing? He thinks a lot of those go through the random holes. They're temporary, unpredictable, but you're unlucky enough to hit one and *poof!* Gone. You turn around to go home, and the door is gone. You're stuck."

"If this buffer zone does that to us, then it does it to other worlds too. I bet nasty critters from all those different places crawl through those points." Earl took out another cigarette. "At least there won't be any lack of things for us to shoot at."

"The area just inside the gate will still be touching Earth. Things will work like we're used to, only our missing aren't going to be right there for us to grab. They're going to be out there floating in monster land, hopefully not getting munched on by monsters from other dimensions. I'm going to have to go looking for them. At that point it becomes me versus the realm. I don't know how it works, but the only way I'm going to find anything is if I bend the realm to my will and make it show me the way."

I could tell Earl knew where I was going with this while I spoke. Fire leapt from the end of his Zippo. He took his time getting the cigarette lit, then inhaled, held it, and let out a long stream of smoke. One nice thing about an outdoor meeting with Earl was less secondhand smoke.

"I'm sensing a troublesome emphasis on you being the one doing all this shit."

"That's the glitch. For this to work, it's got to be one man, one mind. More than one, they're going to get pulled in different directions. And once we're separated..." Trip had already given a report about our encounter with Sextus Bassus. I pulled out the ring and showed it to him. "We've only got one lifeline to find our way back. Without this, it would be really hard to find an exit. Not impossible, there's random holes, but unlikely because they're chaotic and unpredictable. That's why a fixed gate like the City of Monsters is so valuable."

"Assuming your new friend is right, and assuming that ghost wasn't yanking your chain and he got that out of the Roman equivalent of a Cracker Jack box, what makes you think you're the one man for this job?"

"I just know I am." I wasn't going to budge on this one.

"Rate we're going, I'm gonna have a thousand Hunters to choose from. We ain't exactly lacking for qualified specialists."

This was hard enough as it was already. I couldn't help it, but I was getting frustrated. "It's supposed to be me, Earl."

Earl didn't like his men pushing back against his decisions. "You think that Chosen One thing means you're the poor sap who always has to be at the tip of the spear. Thinking like that is gonna get you killed."

My frustration turned to anger. "I told you some about my dad's vision, but all those years he was getting us ready, it was because he'd been told one of his sons has to die saving the world. He died on

Severny Island. Asag is the reason he was sent back. Now we need one man to do this? It has to be me."

"Certain death is your selling point? All the better reason for me not to send you through that gate." I wasn't the only one getting mad. Earl raised his voice. "Why didn't you tell—never mind, I already know. That's a good argument to just send you home!"

"The hell you are."

"And you think I'm gonna toss you through a portal by yourself so Julie can be mad at me for the rest of her life, and my great-great-grandkid can grow up without a daddy? I don't think so."

I took a deep breath. "If it's about will, I'm the best one for the job, Earl."

"So what? Being stubborn don't get a trophy in this crowd. I've spent decades controlling the uncontrollable."

"So you're going to go through instead? Being so damned old is also why you've got more experience than anybody you'd leave in charge while you were out of pocket on the other side. The expedition needs you in charge. You know I'm right."

He knew I had him there. "Don't get high and mighty with me about what you think you can do."

"Remember that time I destroyed linear time?"

"Well..." Nobody would ever forget that.

"I didn't even have a *body* and I took the Cursed One's artifact from him. I'm the only man in history who walked off a zombie bite because I refused to turn. Great Old Ones couldn't break this." I stabbed two fingers into the side of my head. "This metaphysical bullshit you call it, yeah, I hate it too, but I'm the one who keeps making it through awful mind-blowing shit that seems to leave everybody else with scrambled brains. They—whoever they are—drafted me. Mordechai said I drew the short straw. I don't know if my dad's vision is real or a delusion or what, but I'm here for a reason. I don't know if I'm going to die there, none of us here know if we're going home or not, but damn it, if I am going to die, then it should be doing something important. I was born for this kind of thing, and you know it."

"Send you on a suicide mission because it's your destiny." Earl scowled at me for a long time, like he wanted to yell at me some more, but then he shook his head and began walking back to camp. "I'll think about it. We're done talking."

"That's bullshit, Earl!"

He didn't bother to turn around. "We're done, because if I made my decision right now, your ass would be on the next plane back to Alabama."

This time of year, nights up here were short. I had built a campfire in front of my luxurious new shipping container apartment, just far enough away that it wouldn't catch the straw bales we were using for insulation on fire. A bunch of the MHI regulars had gathered around, as well as some of our new friends. Milo was happy for the opportunity to make s'mores. There were a lot of these little bonfires going on around the camp. And being Hunters, somebody had flown in large quantities of alcohol. At one of the nearby fires they had started singing loudly in Spanish. Of course that meant the next barracks over had responded with a competing song in Polish, which got the Germans going, which set off my people, so on and so forth. At least the racket had probably scared the bears away.

Not being a drinker and having a terrible singing voice, I had skipped the festivities and used a sat phone to call my wife. I was sitting on a log in the dark. Julie was tired and grumpy that her back hurt, everything felt puffy, and our baby seemed to be practicing martial arts by kicking her bladder. There was nothing new about my dad. Apparently he was keeping his promise to be there to welcome me home. He was too stubborn to die. When I'd talked to Earl about having the will necessary for the job, I'd inherited that from him.

Julie was still venting to me. "I'm doing the best I can. Only we're as busy as ever but half of our employees are up there having fun."

I looked back at the hay-covered metal box I would be living in. "Super fun."

"You know what I mean. I'm shuffling resources, but we can't keep up. We're meeting our contracts, but our competitors are picking up PUFFs before we can get to them. PT Consulting has grabbed at least three gigs that should have been ours. They don't know where we are, but they're loving this. Armstrong even called me the other day to gloat about how either they're getting faster or we're getting slower. He is such a douche."

"The douchiest. Friggin' Parakeet Testicles."

Julie giggled. "You know, you could always bring Particle Toast in on the mission."

Getting her to laugh always made my day. "I would rather eat Gretchen's cooking than invite those polo-shirted dickweeds along for the ride. The only way they'd be useful is if our high-value target's weak-spot vulnerability was the overwhelming power of smug."

"Sure, but then they'd be shorthanded too. Plus, I think Holly has a thing for their lawyer. Did you know he dropped that lawsuit against her because she agreed to have dinner with him?"

"No way! She didn't tell me anything."

"Girl talk, hon. You don't get to participate. Come to think of it, you did not hear that rumor from me."

A figure appeared in the darkness practically right next to me. I jumped. "Got a minute, Z?" Earl moved like a ghost.

"You scared the shit out of me! Damn, man. Don't do that. Milo's giving out those bells hikers wear to keep the bears from eating them." Obviously, none of the Hunters—other than Milo—would use them. "You should put some on so you don't give people heart attacks."

"I'm not big on *tinkling* when I walk. And I wasn't even trying to be sneaky."

"Hey, Earl!" Julie shouted in my ear.

Of course, he heard her. "Hey, kiddo. I've got to borrow your husband."

She was a trained Monster Hunter, and she didn't even bother to question the man who'd practically raised her. When there was work to be done, you did it. "Love you, hon. 'Night." And she hung up before I could say anything else.

"Sorry about that. If I'd known who you were talking to I would have waited. That girl really misses you. I know it's hard not to be there right now. I was off on a hunt when my son was born too. It is what it is."

I was still kind of mad at him from earlier. Where did he get off threatening to boot me from the mission that I had come up with? "What's up?"

Normally, this would be where Earl would rattle off a series of commands, and I'd go do them, but instead he sat on the log next to me. He didn't talk for a long time. When he did, he sounded tired. "You think losing a few men because of a decision you made is tough? Try *hundreds*."

I didn't say anything.

"We do this job, men die. You go to war, men die. But we still do it because it's got to get done. If you're good at it, eventually you end up in charge, and then it's *your* men dying. It's awful. It's a shit deal. Every one of them will haunt your dreams even after so much time has passed you forgot their faces. I've lost Hunters, soldiers, friends . . . family. You want to get those men back. I know. Damn, I know."

Earl was blinking too much, like this was hard to say. I'd never seen that from him before.

"Julie is like my daughter. I love that girl so much. This is a family business but it kills me every time she goes out. Losing anyone is hard. Losing a brother, a *son*. That's harder."

I was moved. "Are you saying you think of me like a son?"

"Oh, hell no. You know my son. Even with one eye and a hook for a hand, he'd make you look like a pussy on your best day." Then he laughed. "You're all right, kid. But don't get a big head. I was thinking favorite son-in-law. Tops."

I grinned and shook my head.

We sat there for a bit, not boss and employee, nor mentor and student, but just two men who'd ended up in one hell of an unforgiving career . . . listening to some really awful, drunken, singing competitions.

"This business, with the factions picking champions and destinies . . . I've never told you what all I saw in Copper Lake. Me and Heather are like that too, I think. Whole lot of effort over a whole lot of centuries, all comes down to picking a few folks who can do what needs doing. At first, the idea of things out there testing us, picking the best . . . Where do they get off, using us like that? But the more I think about it, the more I realize the bad shit is coming anyway. At least this means somebody out there still cares what happens."

After a while I said, "I'm still the best man for this job, Earl."

"I know." He reached over and rested one hand on my shoulder. "All right, Z. Iron-will the hell out of that bitch."

# CHAPTER 11

I hate running. Hate, hate, *hate* it. Running is something that skinny people do so they can brag about it to those of us who come in adult sizes. I'm actually an okay sprinter. I've got long legs, and I'm surprisingly nimble for a big dude, but distance running is for masochists and crazy people who want to collect foot problems and repetitive stress injuries. My insane runner friends kept trying to tell me that at some point you were supposed to get this euphoric feeling during a run, but as far as I could tell that was propaganda they told themselves to feel better about having such a ridiculous pastime. The closest I ever came to *euphoria* was when the aches got numb. Running sucks.

*Hate it.*

But here I was, panting and sweating my way up a rugged mountain trail, into my sixth eight-minute mile, and still running my ass off. Because I'd decided that by D-Day I was going to be in the best shape of my life, or I was going to die trying.

Right about now though, with everything hurting and my lungs on fire, death seemed way more likely. But screw that. If there was one thing I did have in excess, it was stubbornness. I was used to my team counting on me, but this time I had a whole army. If Rothman's hypothesis about the gate was right, I couldn't let those missing Hunters down. The longer it took me to get out, the longer the guys on the outside had to hold the gate for us. I was doing this for all of them.

Thanks to Gretchen, my injuries from the Last Dragon were fully healed. I'd drank so much of her foul, magical, healing swill that I'd probably permanently damaged my sense of taste, but just five months ago I'd had a bone sticking out of my arm, so it was worth it. I'd started lifting hard again, hitting the heavy bag, even doing wind sprints and rope work.

When I wasn't managing things for Earl, I was working out, or I was being trained in something. Small unit tactics, land navigation, demolitions, you name it. With the talent pool we were recruiting from, it was pretty much guaranteed that for any military skillset there was, we probably had here one of the best in the world at it. Earl had immediately roped our most expert into educating the rest of us.

For me personally, that meant teaching people how to shoot better. I'd lost track, but I was burning through a case of practice ammo a day. My fingertips were nothing but unfeeling calluses from loading mags. With this many Type A show-offs present, we'd started the Camp Frostbite Four-Gun—rifle, pistol, shotgun, and grenade launcher—Weekly Shoot-Off and Barbeque Appreciation Society to see who was really the best. I was currently third overall, because though I dominated the close and fast stuff, there were some damned good precision riflemen here.

That was guns, but my fists were getting plenty of use too.

There was no shortage of other Hunters here who wanted to fight, and all of the tough guys wanted a shot at Owen Zastava Pitt. Legends of the Great Buffet Fight had grown in the telling. Milo had shipped in rubber mats so we wouldn't break anything getting tossed on the ground. We had to keep it friendly, because any Hunter injured doing stupid crap was one less Hunter capable of taking the island. We got as violent as we could short of anybody breaking a limb or dying. So it was all in good fun.

But all of that meant there wasn't any part of me that wasn't already sore before my daily run even began.

*Lococo and VanZant, you'd better still be alive when I get there.*

I didn't even know John VanZant that well. I liked the guy. I respected him. Julie had been friends with him for years, but it wasn't like we were buddies or anything. Since he was short, his guys called him the Hobbit. He'd been the company's mortar expert, because that's what he'd done in the Army, was one hell of a boxer, and had been one of our most popular team leads. He struck me as a modern warrior scholar: sharp, diplomatic, good sense of humor, but give him a challenge and VanZant would never back down.

Jason Lococo, on the other hand, I knew even less about personally, but our lives had collided long before either of us were Hunters. He had been an ex-con trying to make a living, and I had been a young punk with a chip on my shoulder trying to prove something. We'd met in an illegal underground fight, where I'd lost my mind and he'd lost his eye.

He was big—bigger than me. Like Franks big. And *tough*. Fists of stone and head like a brick. He seemed to have the personality of a brick too, though Earl told me to give him a chance, because he'd been a hero in Copper Lake, and he had a little girl he loved more than the whole world. But I never really did get that chance, because Lococo had been one of the lucky Newbies to get to visit the Last Dragon, yet unlucky enough for me to have to leave him behind. First, I'd ruined his life, and then a decision I made had taken it.

You don't realize how little you actually know someone until they're gone. Maybe if I'd done something different, they wouldn't have gotten stuck on that roof. There were too many ifs and maybes. Hunters have to make split-second decisions, and none of us bat a thousand.

There was nothing like a long run to give you time to dwell on every call you've ever had to make.

As I crested a rise, movement ahead caused me to break out of my funk and focus on the now. I slowed to a walk and put my hand on my pistol. With all the bears up here, of course I was running with a gun. There were enough of us constantly using the trail that there was always noise to warn off the wildlife, and help was always near. Milo had blazed a path that avoided most of the heavy cover, to keep us from getting inadvertently eaten by a grizzly. Only there were still a few spots where you could round a bend and surprise something, like this one.

There was a giant moose blocking the path, and it turned out moose were really big damned animals in person. The thing was magnificent and awkward at the same time. It was like a shaggy, lurpy cow on stilts, with antlers you could use for umbrellas.

It was amazing that something that big could be that stealthy. Twenty feet away from each other, we both stopped, watching. Those big black eyes were nonchalantly locked on me. Milo said that the moose up here actually killed more people than the bears. In case it was feeling frisky, I drew my .45, and then felt like an idiot because this bull moose was the size of a compact car and probably weighed a ton. A 230-grain bullet at 850 feet per second would probably *tickle*. I made a mental note to hit the armory before my next run and see what handguns they had in .454 Casull or .500 Magnum.

I admit, the moose was making me nervous.

"Hey," I said, hoping human noises would scare it off. "Beat it!"

The moose just stood there blocking the trail, with an attitude that said *Fuck you, I'm a moose*.

I could respect that.

"Fine. Be that way." My chest was heaving as I looked around. It was truly a beautiful, cloudy day. From up here the vista was cold ocean one way, craggy mountains the other, and the greatest army of Monster Hunters the world had ever seen below me. Sweat stung my eyes as I watched them getting ready to go kick evil's ass and save the world. It filled me with pride. There was something about a view this epic that made me feel like I could accomplish anything. We were going to complete this mission, defeat Asag, and I was going to bring my people home.

After that I would love my wife and raise my kid in a way that would make my father proud.

It was strange, but stopping for that one stark moment gave me hope.

Maybe this moose in the road was God's way of telling me to stop and reflect on life. Also that running was stupid, and it was time to turn around and go back down.

"Okay, I'm done," I gasped, "but me not doing this last mile is on you, not me."

The moose blinked stupidly. Then it suddenly turned and trotted off.

Still breathing hard, I watched it go. Within thirty seconds the giant had disappeared. I looked up the now-clear trail. I had no excuse not to keep going. "Shit."

Even nature was conspiring against me.

When I got back to camp, Milo was waiting, and he had that manic gleam in his eye that told me he'd been up to something awesome.

"I just finished something. Follow me, hurry!" He began walking away with purpose, the multiple bear bells on his belt jingling. He also had a can of pepper spray that was about the size of a fire extinguisher. Milo must have still felt bad about that grizzly he'd had to shoot.

"Okay. Hang on." I was soaked in sweat and everything was sore, but when Milo got in one of these moods, you dropped everything and went with him, because it was either going to be like Christmas, or you were at least going to get to see an awe-inspiring explosion. "What did you do? Taping cameras to bats again?"

Milo hurried toward the depot, and I obediently

fell in line behind him. "Hey, I only did that once; it was a legitimate science experiment. We're attacking an underground city, we could use a whole flock of spy drones! How was I supposed to know the little guy would escape, the battery pack would catch on fire, and it would be nesting in the roof of Earl's shack at the time?"

"PETA would have thrown a fit."

"Poor little dude, but I'm suspicious he sabotaged my camera. That bat did seem kind of depressed... Naw, what I need you for is pretty straightforward. I've got a new gun for you."

I was intrigued, but also a little offended. "I've got Abomination." My full-auto shotgun was something of a trademark for me. We'd been through hell together. Literally. When you find a piece of kit that never lets you down, you get really loyal to it. Telling me to get a new gun was like telling me to get a new wife. Thanks, but I like things the way they are. "You already built me a gun."

"I sure did, and it's great. But Earl told me about your harebrained universe-hopping idea, thinking you're going to have to go off by yourself in that crappy nightmare world. That's stupid, by the way, because I'm coming with you."

"Hey, I would love company, but I don't make the rules. If we get there and it turns out Rothman's wrong and we can have a whole MHI company picnic on the other side of the gate and still get back, I'm down with that. But when was the last time you were on a hunt and something worked out *more* conveniently than expected?"

"Hmmm..." Milo stopped to think, because that was

a hard question. I threw on the brakes and nearly collided with him. Good thing his bear bells made a handy warning device. "Fair point." He started walking again.

"Exactly. Murphy is like the patron saint of monster hunting."

"It's actually Saint Hubert. I know that because the Vatican guys get super sensitive if you make fun of their name. But okay, worst-case scenario then, if you have to go over there by yourself, and what if—" Milo stopped suddenly again. This time I did bump into him, playing a bad solo of "Jingle Bells." Milo was searching the nearby hillside. He pointed. "See that black rock? The one that looks kind of like a hippo taking a nap."

"An oddly specific description." I found the one he was talking about. It was about six hundred yards away. "Okay. Got it."

"Imagine you're all by yourself in awful swirling fog murder monster land, when uh-oh! There's a death hippo! Coming right at you!" Milo shouted. "What do you do?"

"First, I'd wonder if there's such a thing as a death hippo."

"It's the Nightmare Realm, anything can happen!" Milo shouted and waved his arms. "Quick! What do you do?"

"You said it was taking a nap."

"It was, but they're light sleepers known for their crankiness and now it's *coming right at you!*"

He was being loud enough that all of the nearby Hunters were looking at us. But then they saw the jingling red-bearded maniac was just Milo being Milo, and they went back to whatever they were doing. Even the foreign guys knew of his rep by now.

"Shoot it, I guess."

"With your twelve-gauge? All the way over there?"

He had me. Abomination was a short-range weapon. I'd killed things at thirty-five yards with buckshot, but by that range I'd lost a lot of velocity and most of the pellets had spread too far to keep them on target. "You said it was coming right at me. I'll switch mags and wait until Mr. Hippo gets to about a hundred yards in to hit him with slugs."

Milo shook his head sadly. "Too late. It already melted you with its heat vision. A very tragic way to end up on the memorial wall."

"Death hippos have eye lasers?"

He dragged out each syllable of his answer. "Probably . . ."

Silly as that example was, Milo was right. Having a gun optimized for hyperspeed face-wrecking at shouting distance was great when most of our engagements were indoors. I could walk back to the truck for a different weapon if I needed to, or I had teammates armed with all sorts of different weapons suitable for whatever popped up. If I was by myself, it would be just whatever I could carry. The last time we'd been there, the Nightmare Realm had seemed wide open, and Julie had been dropping demons like crazy with precision shots from far away.

Abomination also had a grenade launcher I could lob out to three hundred, but Milo would probably tell me the death hippo had taken hostages or something. I saw where this was going. "Okay, I'm assuming your wildly convoluted object lesson is to try and tell me that my regular gun doesn't have enough range for this mission. You could have just said that."

Milo stared at me blankly through his small round glasses. "But wildly convoluted is my teaching style." He turned around and started jingle-walking away. "Come on. We're wasting valuable range time."

"You probably only need one bell, not a whole symphony."

"Everybody else here thinks they're *too cool* to wear them, so I had the whole case left for myself. We'll see who's laughing when they get eaten by bears—completely flavorless because they're unseasoned by pepper spray—while I remain musically magnificent."

Milo stopped at the armory long enough to pick up a soft case and a range bag, then he had me grab a case of .308 and a sack full of magazines. The caliber made sense, since that was MHI's standard rifle round. It wasn't the flattest shooting cartridge ever, but it was common, and had a decent amount of thump to it. I started loading mags while we walked to the range.

One nice thing about Earl owning a mountain is that you don't have to skimp on a rifle range. It went basically forever. The guys had set dozens of steel targets out to a thousand yards. Milo dumped all his stuff on a picnic table and started unzipping the case, but then he paused for dramatic effect.

"Originally I ordered this for me, but odds are I'm not the one who's going to be wandering through a nightmare hellscape by myself. I figured you need something that could be precise at long range, but still handy and quick handling for anything up close, and it has to run no matter what. People think I'm the company's mechanical genius, but a machine without art has no soul. It's true for cars, guns, bicycles, watches, net cannons, whatever. My philosophy is

there are two ways to properly customize a machine.
A Perazzi shotgun is like a Bentley, classy and elegant,
pretty. On the other hand, this is more like a super
car; the art comes from the performance."

"Enough with the philosophical rambling. You're
killing me, dude." It was like being a little kid taunted
by birthday presents you couldn't unwrap. "Show me
already."

Milo finished unzipping the case.

It was an AR-10-style rifle with a suppressor and a big
honking scope on it, and it was finished in a distressed
bronze color, which was unique. "Ooooooh. Pretty."

"I know, right? It started as a JP Enterprises LRP-07.
They invited me to Minnesota to check out their fac-
tory. Cool guys. They make the best of the best. *I*
couldn't make a rifle nicer than this."

I picked it up. It was one solid chunk of gun, built
like a tank.

"Eighteen-inch supermatch, air-gauged, button-rifled,
cryo-treated barrel." When Milo began listing off
weapon stats he was the only person in the company
who could go more hard-core *riot nerd weaponspeak*
than me. "Low-mass operating system, high-pressure
bolt, silent-capture spring. MHI logo, obviously. See
that thing inside the handguard wrapped around the
barrel? That's a thermal dissipator . . . It has a radiator,
Owen. A *radiator.*"

"I see that. How does it shoot?"

"I've tested it. If you can see it, you can put a bullet
through it. This baby shoots better than you are capable
of shooting it. You're good, but you're not that good."

"Ouch . . ." But I wasn't the precision shooter in the
family. "Could Julie live up to it?"

"Probably." Milo shrugged. "Which is why I ordered her one just like it, only in 6.5 Creedmoor so it shoots flatter. My wife has that one. Shawna is going to give it to her at the baby shower."

Monster Hunter families tended to give useful baby shower gifts. What mom wants diapers when she could have a new sniper rifle? Regular people are so lame in comparison.

"The can is a SilencerCo Omega. It is silly quiet and less than a pound."

"Those death hippos will never hear me coming."

"Never underestimate my hypothetical death hippos, but no flash, no blast, you'll be a lot harder to spot. Side-charging, since it's going to have a silencer on it; you won't get carbon gas squirting up your nose."

"I hate that," I agreed. Shoot a thousand rounds through suppressed AR-10 rifles in an afternoon, when you blow your nose the Kleenex turns black. I worked the bolt. It was so smooth it was like somebody had stuck a warm stick of butter between two sheets of glass. I shouldered the rifle and pointed it downrange. The trigger had a roller around it so that your trigger finger always moved to the same consistent position. Milo had thought of everything. When I pulled it, the trigger broke so light and clean that it was damned near telepathic.

"Now look through the scope. It's a US Optics."

I did. The thousand-yard target suddenly seemed a *whole lot* closer. "This isn't a scope. This is the Hubble on a gun."

"Twenty-five power. You ever have one of those moments where you found yourself thinking I wish I had a little more magnification? Not anymore you won't. It's adjustable all the way down to five power. Horus reticle, I'll have to teach you how to use that, but it's a really nifty system. This scope is so tough that even Sam Haven wouldn't have been able to break one easily."

"He'd take that as a challenge, you know." But Milo was right. I could probably take this scope out of the Warne one-piece mount and hammer nails with it. Milo had also mounted angled iron sights too, so all I had to do was tilt it at a slight angle and I could aim down them instead, three-gun-competition style. "And these are for if I do go all gorilla luggage commercial and break my scope?"

"Or if the death hippo sneaks up on you."

"Those treacherous bastards." I was grinning. I loved this. It was even making me a little nostalgic because me and Milo geeking out over guns was one of my fondest memories from when I'd been a Newbie. Some people don't get appreciating your weapons, but those people have probably lived really sheltered lives. "So why is it bronze?"

"Cerakote actually, but even a Ferrari needs a nice paint job."

"Groovy. So what did you name it?"

"The *Cazador*."

That was pretty badass. *Oh yeah* . . . I was gonna kill me some monsters with this.

People don't call in the middle of the night unless something bad has happened. I've learned to dread calls like that. The sat phone started beeping around two in the morning. By the time I woke up and found it in the dark, I knew something had gone horribly wrong.

"It's Pitt."

"Owen," it was Julie. From that one word I could tell she was upset, and she was the kind of woman who rarely got emotionally dramatic. Something terrible must have happened back home.

I sat up. A sick knot formed in my stomach. "Are you and the baby okay?"

"We're fine. It's—"

"My dad?"

"No. He's hanging on..."

*Okay.* I took a deep breath. Anything else I could handle.

"Listen, I just heard from Poly again. He was really freaked out."

"What's wrong?"

"One of the sparks went out."

That terrible realization took a moment to sink in. "Oh no...No, no."

By this point the other Hunters bunking in my shipping container were waking up too. It was pitch-black, but I could hear the cots creaking and the rustle of sleeping bags. Normally they'd be telling me to shut up, to go back to sleep, but it must have been clear in my voice this was serious.

"Last time Poly looked, there were seven lives, now there are only six left."

"Have him look again."

"I did. I'm sorry, hon. We've lost one. Whoever it was, they're gone."

We talked for a few more seconds. There were no other details. Numb, I ended the call.

# CHAPTER 12

Though Krasnov was a loudmouth who was exceedingly likely to screw us over at the first opportunity, he seemed to be feeding us reliable intel. We had up-to-date reports from the Russian military base on Severny Island, and all of KMCG's case files for every monster encounter they'd ever had there.

Everything we got painted an interesting picture. The further south you were on the island, the safer it was. The closer you got to the ruins, the more likely you were to never be seen again. Bodies were rarely found. Usually when someone went missing, the official story was simple: blame it on the weather or say they slipped and fell down a hole or into the ocean. As rugged and unforgiving as the terrain was, that was entirely plausible.

The army was supposed to regularly patrol the region around the ruins. When they found a monster aboveground, they were supposed to pop it if they could or file a report and call in the contracted specialists, meaning Krasnov and Comrades. There were monitoring stations around the island, and if the supernatural activity got too hot, they were supposed to sound the alarm.

However, the truth of the matter was that outpost was an ass-end-of-nowhere-type assignment. The current government considered the region a blight, and messing with it was a resource suck, so they ignored it. Really motivated types didn't get those kinds of assignments. Watching ice melt and refreeze was an assignment best left to your bums, malcontents, and soldiers generally too incompetent to trust around other humans. The reports were always the same, there's nothing to see here, and some villagers fell down a hole.

When the army did accidentally send a go-getter, sometimes they'd get uppity, think they could actually handle their official mission, and take out a patrol to tackle the ruins themselves. If that officer didn't get fragged by his nonsuicidal men on the way, those patrols into the ruins inevitably ended badly. Krasnov had found us four reports like that over the last twenty years. Two patrols had disappeared entirely: half of one had come back delirious and gibbering mad, and the last had a few soldiers return, but they had either committed suicide or drank themselves to death soon afterward.

*Lovely.*

The weird part was the types of monster they'd found there, which was basically everything. It was a mishmash, and it made no geographical sense. There were the usual suspects, and things you'd expect from regional folklore, but sometimes they'd find oddballs that had no business being in that part of the world. Most of these were sightings we couldn't confirm, but over the years KMCG had identified creatures that were supposedly only found in Africa, like an asanbosam, or a South American ewaipanoma.

And even odder, the observation posts occasionally told stories of monsters fighting each other. Not that they wanted to get close enough to confirm, but there seemed to be a turf war going on around the ruins. Black blob creatures that sounded like shoggoths throwing down with ghostly riders in the sky, that kind of thing. So it was either like Poly had said, and the factions were warring against each other, or a lot of vodka had been consumed before those reports had been made.

What we had really been hoping for was the report about Nikolai Petrov's expedition to the City of Monsters. We still didn't know what actually lived in there. Petrov's was the last time human beings had ventured deep into the city and lived to tell about, but it had been a long time ago. It had been an old-school KGB operation, so secret that the top levels of their current government thought it was a myth. Krasnov had tried his sources for us but had gotten shot down. The report existed only as legend.

The day we got the Petrov Report changed everything at Camp Frostbite.

It was early in the afternoon, and we were in a planning meeting. There were a handful of us sitting on tree trunks and lawn chairs in front of a shipping container. Everyone except for me represented a different company's contingent, so I mostly kept my mouth shut and took notes. Less than half of the companies kicking in volunteers were represented, but that was because the rest of the leaders were off running errands. The operation had kind of snowballed. Shortly we would be moving a thousand men, hundreds of tons of equipment, a tribe of orcs, a handful of trailer park elves, and a partridge in a pear tree.

Not a moment too soon, because as it had warmed up, the mosquitos had started coming out in force. Camp Frostbite had turned into Camp Blood Cloud.

There had been a lot to talk about. Cooper had left MHI and taken a freelance gig where he'd run across another underground city. Earl had hired him back, and we had reviewed his report to see if there were any similarities with our city. Then the leaders had taken a call from Boone about the shoreline near the target. KMCG had gotten a contract—one of the soldiers at an observation post had turned into a vampire—so it had been a good excuse for us to send some of our scouts along with them to get a firsthand view ourselves. Boone had taken everybody we had with military training in amphibious landings. We needed a base camp on the island anyway, so Earl's idea had been to just park one on the beach.

"I know that Royal Marine from Van Helsing thinks it's doable, and Boone says the beach is perfect, but it's kind of nuts." Mayorga's face was on the laptop screen. The laptop had been set on a stump. She had bloodshot eyes, a cigarette dangling from her lip, and a big cup of coffee and a full ashtray in front of her. She was in an office, but the view out the window behind her revealed a shipyard. "This might not work."

"You were Navy. Figure it out," Earl ordered.

"I spent most of my time on aircraft carriers. We don't routinely drive those up the beach, Earl. Admirals get bitchy about that." She sighed as somebody behind her began yelling. "Hold your horses, dickhead!" she shouted at whoever was offscreen, then she turned back. "They're putting a rush job on the mods. This isn't going to be cheap."

"We know. Do your best."

"Is Pitt there?"

"Hey, May."

"One damned word about me going over my budget and I'll cram that spreadsheet up your ass. Mayorga out." The picture went black.

"She seems professional," Klaus Lindemann suggested politely.

"Maria is a perpetually angry woman, but she's persistent and remarkably good at what she does," Earl told him.

"Ah." Klaus nodded noncommittally. "That is nice."

I could tell the leader of Grimm Berlin thought MHI were cowboys. I was still glad they'd decided to join the mission, especially since they had gotten their asses kicked when they'd gone after the Franks bounty. There was no shame in losing to Franks. I'd argued against us taking that job offer, and not out of any love for the giant sullen mutant. The Germans were still damned good at what they did. Depending on who you asked, many would say they were the best in the business. Of course, we here at MHI disagreed, but we were polite about it . . . mostly.

"Trust me, Klaus. Americans know a thing or two about taking a beach. You can ask your grandpa."

Lindemann just smiled and shook his head. But since everyone else had a laugh at his expense, Klaus turned to Pierre Darne, leader of our French contingent. "Or we could ask Pierre's grandmother. I'm sure she warmly greeted many American men upon their arrival."

"I doubt that. Mamie was even less friendly than our lady who is boat shopping." Darne was one of those perpetually charming types, who greeted everything— from mom jokes to monsters—with a smile. He was the youngest of the leaders, but his company was like MHI—a family business—and he'd taken over when his father had been lost on the *Antoine-Henri*. Earl had been the one who had taken him out, but there were no hard feelings. Darne counted that as a mercy killing. The real death had come when his father had been turned into a vampire. He and Julie had talked it over once. They had a lot in common that way. "A minute with her and they would have swum back across the channel."

Well, at least our leadership was getting along. As they went back to ribbing each other, I noticed there was another call coming in over the satellite. It was an unknown contact. "Hey, Earl, mystery call. We got anybody else scheduled to check in?"

"Not that I can think of. Maybe something's happening back home."

I flipped the laptop around and played with it for a moment, trying to figure out how the program worked. Melvin said it was supposed to be encrypted, but it was a pain in the ass to get it to work right. Another window opened. I recognized the man on the other side of the camera instantly, with that smug skeletal albino face smiling at me from beneath his creepy orange sunglasses.

"Owen Z. Pitt," Stricken said. "I figured you would be there. I hope you're enjoying Alaska. How's Hakuna Matata, or however you pronounce your pop's name?"

"You son of a bitch."

That was about the nicest thing I could say about Stricken. Pond scum looked down on the former leader of Special Task Force Unicorn. He was an all-around conniving, evil, manipulative dirtbag.

"How'd you know where we are?"

"It must be stupid question time. That's insulting. Put your boss on already, Pitt."

The others had been talking and hadn't heard his voice, but Earl had. "It better not be . . ."

I turned the laptop around on the stump so they could all see. Without exception, every one of them said something insulting or profane when they saw him.

"Well, if it isn't the model UN of monster hunting. Look at you guys holding hands. It's precious."

"Go to hell and die!" Tadeusz Byreika shouted. The leader of White Eagle Military Contracting was a big, ripped, boisterous kind of guy, nothing at all like his grandfather. "And screw yourself, Stricken!"

"Get your order of operations straight, meathead," Stricken replied. "Bunch of rocket surgeons you've collected here, Earl."

Earl Harbinger didn't say a word to the man who'd practically enslaved his girlfriend, but I swear he was growling. If Stricken had actually been here, he'd be decapitated by now.

Everybody was ticked, but Klaus remained cool. "I'm surprised to see you show your face, Stricken. Rumor has it you have been replaced. You are a wanted man."

"Shit happens." Stricken shrugged his narrow shoulders. I'd only ever seen him in a suit, but oddly enough, today he was wearing a colorful Hawaiian shirt. It really didn't match his cavefish skin. "Come to think of it, I'd still have my cushy government job if that fossil Franks hadn't beat Grimm Berlin like a rented mule. How does it feel to screw the pooch on a two-hundred-fifty-million-dollar bounty?"

"You set us up," Klaus spat.

"The only thing I set you up to be was filthy rich . . . Hey, Yoshi," Stricken called out to the president of Strike Team Kiratowa. "Do you Japs still do that ritual seppuku thing to atone for epic fuck-ups? Because if you do, you should walk Klaus here through the process . . . A quarter *billion*, Klaus. I mean, holy shit, that has to keep you up at nights. That'll buy a lot of bratwurst."

"Pitt, mute it." Klaus said. I hit the button, then put my thumb over the camera so Stricken couldn't see us. The German stood up and pointed at Earl. "If STFU is involved in this mission in any way, we are out." There was a chorus of agreement from the others.

"Hold on. He's not. He also ain't Unicorn anymore. I know for a fact they want his scalp. I don't know what this asshole wants from us. The last time I saw him, I shot him in the back. Sadly, that Stricken turned out to be a decoy."

"Bummer," Byreika muttered.

"Tell me about it," Earl said.

"He did not call simply to goad us. He must want something. So what do we do?" Kiratowa asked.

"Assume any words that come out of his mouth are a filthy lie." Apparently Darne's perpetual good nature disappeared as soon as Stricken was involved.

"That's a good start," I said. "Is there a way to trace this, maybe see if there are any clues to his whereabouts?"

"So we can murder him?" Byreika asked hopefully.

"I was just going to pass the info on to Franks, kick back, and enjoy the show."

"Stricken is too clever to slip up that easy, and even if we had Melvin here, there's no way he'd let himself be tracked. We've got history. Let me do the talking." Earl was used to just being in charge, but he realized he was talking to peers and partners, and none of these men got to where they were in this business by being slouches, so he rephrased it. "Let me do the talking with this evil bastard, *please.*"

There were nods of agreement. Byreika spit on the ground.

Earl stood up and placed himself in front of the screen. "Go."

I pulled my thumb off the camera and turned the sound back on.

"Nice shirt, asshole," Earl said.

"You like it? I'm taking some vacation time. Use it or lose it, you know how government jobs are."

"The government wants you dead."

"Today." Stricken waved one hand dismissively. He had long, spindly fingers. "And when they see what tomorrow holds, they'll piss themselves in fear, and put me back in charge. You accidently create some demonic supersoldiers one time and everybody gets all butt hurt. They'll get over it. My outfit employs things that eat souls, and you think they're going to stay angry at me? I'm too good at what I do, and I'm the only one who knows where all the bodies are buried. In the meantime, I'll keep on enjoying this island living."

"With that skin, you should soak up some rays."

"Good one. Hey, did you tell Klaus that right after Franks crippled a bunch of his men, MHI stitched Franks back together? Oh, from that pained expression, I'm guessing not. Yeah, Klaus, MHI screwed you over. That's not very nice, patching up the thing who just kicked your ass, and not even having the decency to fess up about it."

Earl apologetically turned to Klaus. "There was a reason for the patching."

The German gave him a stiff nod, but he didn't look pleased at the revelation.

Stricken laughed. "I love sowing hate and discontent."

"Go to hell, Stricken," Klaus stated.

"I'm sensing a consensus about where all of you think I should go, but let me get to the point because I've got shit to do. I've got something you want."

Earl folded his arms. "Doubtful."

"Really? Because that fat Russian has been trying to swindle it out of every decrepit, old, retirement-home KGB agent he can find, and Rigby has been flouncing around Moscow trying to find the file, like some sort of big gay James Bond...so basically Roger Moore."

"Connery was the best."

"*Finally!* I knew we could find common ground, Earl. Thank you! It's all nonsense though. Back in my spying days I never got to wear a tux and I was never once issued a watch with a laser in it. Regardless, you obviously want the Petrov Report. I've got a copy of the Petrov Report. What do you say we do some business?"

I could tell Earl was thinking it over. Stricken was a puppet master, who'd been involved in every shady, crooked, shifty international intelligence deal there was. If anybody could get their hands on that report, it was Stricken. Except he was also a liar, who had previously nonchalantly condemned us all to death.

"If it's coming from you, it's probably fake. And even if it ain't, whatever you want in exchange is too much."

"You Hunters are so paranoid. You need to let it go, Earl. All that anger is going to prematurely age you . . . Oh, wait. That's right. It won't. Yeah, by the way, junior UN, Earl's a werewolf. A no kidding, for real, actual alpha boss werewolf. He probably didn't tell you that either."

All of the other company leaders stared at Earl, who gritted his teeth, and looked like he was about to punt-kick the laptop into the tree line. "I served my time. I earned my exemption. You've got no right—"

"Whoops. You must have forgot I'm a free agent the same way I forgot you being a werewolf was classified. Feel free to file an official complaint after I get a pardon and my job back."

I moved to close the program. Earl held up a hand. "Wait."

"Ah, so you are really interested. Good, because Nikolai saw some interesting things in there. It's special. Depending on how the stars align, that gate can get you anywhere from the Fey Lands to Jigoku. Here's the deal, Earl. I've already emailed Pitt the entire original file. You're so old I didn't know if you knew how to use a computer. You might not believe me, but the file is legit. You knew Nikolai, so you can verify the authenticity. Believe it or not, I don't care. It's all yours. Do with it as you will."

"What's in it for you?"

"I'm doing this for the good of all mankind. Contrary

to what you may think about me, I'm on the side of the angels."

I snorted.

The camera wasn't pointed at me now but Stricken still knew that was me. "Up yours, Pitt. I'd love for you Hunters to succeed. Asag Shedu is currently threat *numero uno* and he's no friend of mine. Anything that hurts him brings a smile to my face. You'll more than likely fail and die on that godforsaken rock, but at least it should be amusing." Stricken reached out for something and the call ended.

Everybody was quiet for a few seconds, and then the shouting started.

"We can trust nothing from Stricken!" Darne exclaimed.

Which was simultaneous with "MHI *helped* Franks?" from the offended Klaus.

And "You are a werewolf?" by the incredulous Byreika.

Everybody was yelling at Earl. He asked them to calm down, but Earl wasn't exactly the diplomatic sort, so it was more like telling them to shut their fool mouths. Kiratowa was the only leader not flipping out, so I just looked at him and shrugged. He returned the gesture. Normally I was the hothead, but these were all company owners so it was way over my pay grade.

"If MHI was working with Franks in secret, then Grimm Berlin can safely assume you would work with Stricken behind our backs."

"Yes, Harbinger. Is this some sort of trick?"

"Y'all need to zip it before I get angry."

"Werewolves are evil scum!" And even knowing

he was a werewolf, Byreika had the balls to actually *shove* Earl, who promptly shoved back, and the much larger man landed on his ass right in the dirt.

The only commander who wasn't fighting seemed to be growing impatient. Kiratowa was one of those men so lean and weathered it was impossible to guess his age, so I'm talking a range like somewhere between forty and an extremely fit senior citizen. He was normally unassuming, didn't seem to talk much, but had this sort of confident air that suggested he wasn't somebody you wanted to mess with. Still sitting on his lawn chair, he took two orange foam plugs out of his pocket, stuck them in his ears, then drew his handgun, pointed it in the air and fired. I barely had the time to put my hands over my ears. The rest didn't see it coming. To a man they all grabbed for a weapon.

"Enough bickering!"

That sure shut them right up. I didn't approve of the bad gun safety, but I had to admit it did the trick.

"Hey!" Darne shouted.

"We agreed upon no new recruits for this mission, only experienced warriors, in order to avoid pointless conflict. Why bother when instead, their leaders behave like children?"

Earl looked to the sky. "You know, that bullet is gonna land somewhere."

Kiratowa holstered his pistol and calmly removed the earplugs. "It is a big country. Now, let us resume acting like businessmen rather than barbarians."

"The ringing is worse when you don't see it coming." Darne stuck a finger in one ear and wiggled it around.

"Have my orc look at it." Earl extended one hand toward the fallen Byreika. "You guys should try super werewolf hearing. It regenerates in no time...Actually, don't. Because there's some significant downsides."

"It's true then?" Byreika looked at the offered hand for a moment like it might suddenly sprout claws. But then he realized he was being stupid, shook his head, and took the hand anyway.

"Yeah." Earl hoisted Byreika to his feet. "But I'd appreciate you keeping that to yourselves."

The Polish leader seemed a little embarrassed. Because frankly, if you take the time to think it over, it was pretty damned obvious that Earl had to be an atypical werewolf. "Now I understand how you earned your reputation, Harbinger."

"It does make it tougher for things to kill you. This also explains why I felt obligated to put Franks back together." Earl looked to Klaus. "Stricken left out the part where I'm the one who ripped Franks to pieces to begin with. It's a long story."

"We will make the time." Klaus was still ticked, but he seemed willing to listen.

"Please, gentlemen." Kiratowa gestured for them to sit. The leaders grudgingly did so. "Stricken wishes for us to fight. Are we his puppets? No. We are Earl Harbinger's guests here, and we must allow him the opportunity to respond to these allegations. We have much to discuss."

The leaders had much to discuss. I was busy opening Stricken's email.

The Petrov Report was forty pages long. Our copy consisted of photos of paper sheets obviously typed on a typewriter, now yellowed with age, and the accompanying hand-drawn maps. Sometimes the photographer had rushed; the page wasn't perfectly framed, and I could see that the papers had been hastily set on top of a green metal filing cabinet. The lighting was crap. Whoever had snapped these pictures had probably been in a hurry.

I could understand a lot of the language, but I couldn't read it worth a damn. For my first pass I'd downloaded that app Trip had recommended, so my phone could take the words in a picture and change them into English. It worked okay for individual words, but like most translation software, the narrative turned to unreadable nonsense. So I had drafted a few Hunters in the camp who could read Cyrillic to translate and put them to work.

It turned out there had actually been two Petrov expeditions into the City of Monsters. The first was in 1957, to assess the situation. What they discovered was that whatever ancient treasures might be in there weren't worth the cost. The second expedition was in the aftermath of the nuclear "tests," to see if anything could be salvaged from the wreckage. What Petrov discovered in the radioactive ruin led to the authorities leaving it alone ever since.

Even though it was in a rugged, difficult to get to, barely explored part of the world, people had known about the city forever. The natives considered it cursed and avoided it like the plague. Before the bomb, there had been several imposing obelisks, approximately four stories tall, surrounding a large central pyramid. The structures reflected the sun from miles away, so treasure hunters and fools had logically decided they must be coated in silver, or better, constructed of pure silver bars, so why not go get some? Everyone who tried disappeared. The first official expedition there had been sent by Peter the Great. It hadn't come back. The last scientific expedition had been sent by Tsar Nicholas, had been five hundred men strong, and of course, it hadn't come back either. I was sensing a trend.

We already knew about those lost attempts from Oxford, but we hadn't known that the early 1900s group had sent back a carrier pigeon with a brief report and a charcoal rubbing of what we now recognized as the symbol of Asag. The Tsar's men had made it inside the pyramid before vanishing. Their ominous final message was that they'd been spied upon by some odd subterranean creatures, but all was well.

The Russians left the cursed, frozen city alone for six decades after that, until an arms race persuaded them to take another crack at it. It was assumed to have been built by Elder Things or one of the ancient factions. Who knew what kind of knowledge or artifacts they could find there? They'd picked one of their deadliest agents and backed him with a thousand hardened troops, armed with every alchemical device and trinket that was supposed to work against the Old Ones. They'd been supported by MiGs, and even had a warship for fire support.

They had lasted a week.

*To: Committee for State Security – 17th Directorate Chairman*

*Summary of Inspection Expedition to State Anomaly 168. August 1, 1957 – Special Purpose Military Commissar N. Petrov, 1st Detachment, Zenith Group reporting.*

SA168, also known as *Gorod Chudovish*, is on Sukhoy Nos cape, Severny Island, of the Novaya Zemlya archipelago. At 1200 on July 20th, 1st ZGD made landfall at SA168. We were immediately set upon by a wide variety of supernatural creatures (see section A).

The attacks came in successive waves. With naval gun support 1st ZGD was able to clear the beachhead and approach SA168. We met heavy resistance at every step. Upon securing the upper levels of the pyramid, the attacks increased in frequency and intensity over the following days. Scout spotters were unable to ascertain where these waves originated from. It is my belief that they generated spontaneously from the city itself. The deeper we traveled, the worse it became.

The caverns beneath the pyramid seem to be a perpetual war zone. There exists a kilometer beneath the surface a terrible gate, which continually vomits forth horrors. My scientific advisors determined that these beings originate from a variety of rival dimensions (see section B). My own scouting ascertained that many of these creatures then take up residence beneath the city, continually making war against the other refugees.

I personally witnessed multiple clashes between rival groups of monsters. They seemed to look upon 1st ZGD as simply another group competing for supremacy (see Appendix 1 for maps and detailed engagement reports).

Note: I would caution you not to have too much faith in our maps. The city's structures seem to be constantly evolving. Paths appear. Doors disappear. It is geometric chaos and a cause for attrition as men are continually lost.

On July 26th we discovered what the rival factions were fighting over. While solo scouting, I came across a giant chamber holding an alien structure. We believe it to be the tomb of an elder god. The symbol upon the tomb matches that discovered by the Tsar's expedition.

The tomb itself was protected by an army of subterranean creatures. The vile, degenerate creatures were designated the Asakku by Dr. Koroborov (see Appendix 2). They were unable or unwilling to communicate. It is unknown if they are descended from the original inhabitants who built Gorod Chudovish, or are simply the dominant faction which has come through the gate since then. All of our attempts to breach this structure ended in death or insanity.

Having taken severe casualties, and unable to travel deeper into the catacombs, on July 27th at 1500 I declared a retreat.

The Chairman of the 17th Directorate is familiar with my record and achievements, so I trust you will not take this report lightly. I have never seen such depraved tortures inflicted upon man as that which the Asakku did to the captured solders of 1st ZGD. Nothing we could possibly find within SA168 could be worth the risk of releasing such darkness into our world.

I recommend scrubbing this abomination with atomic fire.

# CHAPTER 13

Most of us would be traveling by air, staging off the mainland, and landing at the little airstrip on Severny Island. Others would travel in multiple ships with our heavy equipment. Most of those ships would offload at the Russian base, which had a harbor and a dock. Those Hunters would then travel over land to the site. Earl had volun-told me that I would be on the ship that would eventually get beached right off our target site to serve as our base of operations. When I'd had no problem with that assignment, he had asked me if I had ever ridden on the ocean in a flat-bottomed, low-draft boat before. I had not. He'd told me I was in for a treat.

In other words, it was *awful*.

I didn't know a damned thing about sailing. I'd been on a handful of waterborne jobs since I'd joined MHI, but that was about it. Over the last few miserable days I'd learned a few things. A regular ship was relatively stable. It swayed, you got used to the movement, no big deal. The V-shaped hull cut through the waves like a knife, usually pretty smoothly.

Not this ridiculous pig. It smacked each wave like the wide side of a two by four. Which sucks when you're riding the two by four.

And the waves here were sometimes gigantic. It was frankly terrifying. Mayorga had explained to me—in very simple words because she thought I was a stupid landlubber—that a regular boat could be steered to take the big waves at the best possible angle, but our stupid boat had the responsive steering of a bus with square tires. So we hit everything head on in the most jarring way possible.

It wasn't just the smacking, but then there was the rolling side to side action. I spent a lot of my first few days on board barfing. It didn't help that everything inside our ship smelled like diesel fumes, mildew, and of course, puke.

Technically, this wasn't even a *ship*. In naval terms it was a Landing Ship Tank, which didn't make any sense to me, since it was big enough to park actual tanks inside. LST was apparently sailor-speak for *ship that sucks to drive*. Technically I think it was because it had a leaky garage door and a ramp for a front end. Our modified *Ropucha*-class had been built in Gdansk, Poland, back before I'd been born, and it was just over three hundred sixty feet of ugly and slow. It had started out as a military vessel, but we'd bought it from a civilian company that had modified it to lease out for cargo hauling jobs. Judging by the smell, I assumed that company's specialty had been transporting garbage trucks and toxic waste barrels. All the poor Hunters who had the words "Navy" or "Coast Guard" show up anywhere on their resume had been drafted as its crew.

Today the waves were relatively calm, so our crew had kept the vomiting to a minimum, and many of us had gone abovedeck to enjoy the fresh—albeit freezing—air. The sky here went forever, with the tallest, most magnificent clouds I'd ever seen. They looked like castles up there.

"Reports show clear sailing the rest of the way," Mayorga said. Our self-appointed captain was leaning on the rail next to me, drinking coffee and being her usual grumpy self. "Krasnov hired a couple of icebreakers to go ahead of us just in case, but we should be good to the island."

"It is summer," I pointed out.

"You think that particularly matters at this latitude? Before this part of the world was fully mapped, the ice routinely devoured ships. Forcing a northwest passage took guts and brains. And now we're doing it in a glorified garbage scow." She loudly cleared her sinuses and spit over the side. Mayorga might have been an attractive woman if she put her mind to it, but she really played up the hardened New Yorker shtick way too much for that. "Thank God for global warming."

We had someone monitoring the weather nonstop. This thing wasn't designed to survive an arctic storm. The currents were worse near shore, and it added miles to our trip, but we never dared get too far from land. We tried to plan around the weather, but if necessary we'd find the best place to park, and hope. Worst-case scenario, Earl would lose his forward operating base, hospital, and gun platform, and the expedition would have to get by with tents. Now normally I was the one hell-bent on not throwing away expensive resources needlessly, but I also wasn't keen on drowning.

Mayorga was still thinking out loud. "I asked Cody about that one time if he thought it was legit or not. Global warming, I mean. He said he's a theoretical physicist, not a climatologist, but then he talked for like twenty minutes about computer modeling issues and ice ages and science nerd politics. It made my head hurt."

"That's nice," I said as I got ready for our next bone-jarring impact.

The most obnoxious part of our sea journey wasn't just that our boat sucked, but that its name rubbed that suckiness in our faces. As far as the Russian government cared, this was a regular Krasnov operation. He held the contract for monster problems on the island, so legally speaking, this was just a routine mission that happened to bring along some foreign *consultants*. The fact that there were a thousand of us converging on the place with enough armament to overthrow a small country was merely a paperwork oversight on his part.

Yet because of those legal issues, it meant that our base ship needed to be owned by KMCG. They could get approval to have a privately owned armed vessel in their waters for monster hunting, but there was no way to do that with a foreign one. So our ship had officially been registered as the *Pride of Krasnov*. And I'm pretty sure he did that just to screw with us. The crew, of course, had begun calling it the *Bride of Krasnov*.

"You know what I wish they had here?" Mayorga asked.

"Warmth?"

"Pirates. Just imagine somebody trying to board us. We're the ultimate Q-ship. The *Bride* looks like trash, but we've got so many heavily armed badasses on board the look on those pirates' faces would be hilarious . . . briefly. Hell, I'm out of coffee."

"Do you ever stop drinking that stuff?"

"When I sleep, but thankfully I don't do that much so it doesn't cut into my intake. Go figure."

"Maybe you could have Milo rig you up an IV drip bag you could just carry around with you."

"He's one of those Mormons, so he'd probably lecture me about how coffee's bad for me." She had a malicious grin. "Come on, Pitt, every Hunter I know is addicted to something. What's yours?"

I thought about it for a second. "Dispensing indiscriminate justice and the righteous smell of gunpowder."

Mayorga chuckled. "I was going to guess accurate spreadsheets. Anyways, I've got to get back to the bridge. Carry on."

"Aye aye, Captain."

For me, *carrying on* meant prepping our mobile base and doing miscellaneous odd jobs. The *Bride* truly was a run-down piece of junk, and the emergency repairs had been to get it seaworthy enough to make one final journey, and to mount *lots* of guns. The interior remained crap. The crew spent our days unpacking gear, installing equipment, and trying to turn this hulk into a serviceable base.

None of that was particularly difficult, so I had plenty of time to think of things that could go wrong. The hardest job on the *Bride* was keeping the pumps working so we wouldn't sink, but I was mechanically incompetent and not of much use unless one of our engineers really needed to put some torque on something. I spent a lot of time trading messages with the various other groups of Hunters who were also converging on Severny Island, but those were just updates. I couldn't do much to help them either.

I'd gone from insanely busy to bored overnight. I'd helped organize this whole thing, but since I was going through that gate, Earl didn't want me in charge of anything on the island. It wouldn't do any good to have people looking to me for direction when I would be on the other side for who knew how long. Well, hopefully not too long, because Poly said the gate only pointed toward a specific world for a month.

The hardest part was knowing that I had done everything I could, and now there was nothing left but to wait.

So I went back to my cabin and reread the Petrov Report. In a few days this room would be our ops center and packed with Hunters, but for now I had one corner to myself. I'd stuck the old Vietnam pic of my dad in a little frame and put it on the wall. He made a good motivator.

The Report—which included accounts of both expeditions—wasn't happy reading, but I hoped it would be a help. Earl had read it too, and he felt certain it had really been written by his old enemy, Nikolai. While it was possible some of it had been altered by Stricken—with that nefarious weasel, who could tell—if it was accurate, it painted an ominous picture.

*To: Committee for State Security – 17th Directorate Chairman*

*Summary of 2nd Inspection Expedition to State Anomaly 168. July 15, 1962 – Special Purpose Military Commissar N. Petrov reporting.*

*It was with great relief that I heard of the Directorate's decision to bomb Gorod Chudovish. I was saddened to learn that the bombs would not be dropped directly on the site, but rather many kilometers away. It was felt that the pressure wave would be sufficient to destroy the aboveground structures and collapse the entrances to the catacombs, yet leave the interior undamaged should the state ever wish to study the anomaly again. A direct impact would be a waste of potential state resources.*

*In public, I supported the Directorate's decision to not turn SA168 into a crater. However, since this report is for the Chairman's eyes only, I will be frank. I believe your half measure was a mistake.*

*It was with great trepidation that I returned to SA168. Due to the extreme radioactivity at the site, I chose to undertake this mission alone. My condition allows me to recover from exposure which would permanently sicken or kill other soldiers. Stealth and quickness would allow me to avoid any remaining creatures. On July 12th at 2300 I left new Observation Post 2 on foot. I was able to cross through the blast zone. There were no signs of life aboveground. All that remained were ashen skeletons. Species indeterminate.*

*The aboveground structures have been completely destroyed. However, in the ruins of the pyramid I was able to find an open passage belowground. The under city was damaged, but as was initially reported, the city continues to change. It gave the appearance of healing itself. I regret to inform the Chairman that the dimensional gate remains intact. It is now a sunken, festering pit, but I saw that various creatures continue to crawl forth. Many of the warring monsters we documented earlier were killed, but new ones are already replacing them.*

*The great crypt chamber was not disturbed by the blast. The Asakku remain on guard there.*

*It is with great sadness that I must report that I discovered the fate of your dear friend Dr. Koroborov, who was thought lost on the previous expedition. I ambushed an Asakku hunting party. During the battle, what I first took to be a deformed Asakku addressed me in Russian. Afterwards I discovered that it was our good doctor. He had been physically mutilated, and his skin had been painted white to match his captors. At first I believed they had done this to him, but he had inflicted this upon himself, and willingly fought for the creatures.*

*Koroborov's mind seemed shattered, yet he informed me they were not guarding a tomb, for their god was not dead, rather sleeping for thousands of years. Our atomic bombs had merely made him stir briefly before returning to his slumber. The Asakku were greatly saddened by this, because the "awake time" was when their underground armies would be set free to "harvest all the flesh beneath the sky." After that he descended into mad ramblings, so I put him out of his misery and returned to report my findings.*

*I will speak plainly. I understand the Directorate's desire to utilize all of our supernatural assets—otherwise I would never have been spared and given the opportunity to serve the Motherland—but the mysteries within SA168 are beyond us. We should not toy with them. We do not belong there.*

*I beg of you, leave that accursed place be.*

✦          ✦          ✦

I stood alone on the deck, satellite phone forgotten in my hand.

Dad had broken his promise.

Mosh had called from the hospital to tell me. My brother had started sobbing. I could barely understand him. I'd thought I would be ready for this. I wasn't.

There wasn't enough night here. My skin was burning but tears were frozen on my cheeks. I couldn't remember crying.

It wasn't right. It wasn't *just*.

But it was over. He was gone. It took a while to sink in before numb turned to angry. We'd been cheated.

"You saved his life. You couldn't give him a few more weeks?" I shouted at the heavens. "Why? Why now? I'm doing what you want! I'm fighting your war! I don't even know who I'm fighting for! I don't even know who it was who sent him back! You think you can use us like pawns and throw us away when you're done! My dad sacrificed everything. *Everything!* He spent his whole life tortured knowing you selfish bastards were going to pull the plug as soon as his job was done. *He did it anyway!* He raised me for this knowing I'd die in the process. *He did it anyway!*"

The ship was pummeled by the waves, but I was too furious to feel the impacts. I didn't even realize that I'd smashed the sat phone into pieces against the grating. I was seething. My chest felt like it would burst. My hands were shaking. I didn't want to be here. I wanted to see my dad one last time. I wanted to comfort my mom. I wanted to hold my wife in my arms and be there for the birth of my child.

Only a bunch of cosmic factions beyond human understanding were having a turf war over my planet, and my family had gotten drafted. It was bullshit. It was a rigged game with no way out.

It was also what my father had raised me to do.

When I spoke again, my voice was nothing but a broken whisper. "I'll still get the job done, but I'm not doing it for you . . . I'm doing it for him."

# CHAPTER 14

The island was in sight.

I was on the bridge of the *Bride,* scanning the approaching landmass through a pair of binoculars. All I could make out from here were dreary gray rocks. The rocks went on for a while before they turned into the island's glacial cap. The sea between us was clear of ice and relatively calm.

From here the island looked lifeless. It probably wasn't.

"I'm not seeing any movement yet," I reported.

"Want to take bets on how long that will last?" James Conason was our helmsman. He was from our Florida team, and his background was driving a Coast Guard cutter. He said in comparison to his old ship, *Pride of Krasnov* was like going from a sports car to a bulldozer.

"Let them come," Mayorga muttered. She was also scanning the horizon for threats. "I didn't pay all that money to weld all these guns onto this barge hoping those *pendejos* would stay hiding underground. Close to two thousand meters. Full speed ahead."

The engine got louder and the ship shook more, but we weren't going to be setting any records in this thing.

With four people in it, the *Bride*'s bridge was cramped. This was no warship. Most of its life had been spent hauling vehicles up and down rivers and coastal waterways. You didn't exactly need the bridge of the *Enterprise* to pull that off. All we had to work with was a narrow metal room with a bank of windows on the front. It was even more crowded now since we'd installed quality instruments—most of which I didn't understand—and screens displaying information I didn't know how to decipher. There was one Hunter giving orders, one driving, one running communications, and me standing in the doorway being the mostly useless non-nautical type.

"Overland vehicles are on their way. Everything is still on schedule." Terry Van Ausdall was running all our comms and monitoring all of the various displays I didn't particularly understand. Like May, he was former Navy, but he'd gotten picked for this job because Earl said he was to electronics what Milo was to mechanical stuff. He had been the one who had installed all of the *Bride*'s new high-tech gizmos. "Skippy will be in range in three."

Mayorga checked her watch. "Anything else?"

"The pumps are working. The engine hasn't caught on fire for two whole days. We're redlined at a blistering fifteen knots."

"I could get out and swim faster," Conason grumbled.

"Skies are clear. It's a sweltering twenty degrees above zero. Winds are five knots from the north. And the Russians must have believed their loud fat dude with the big mustache that we're not invading them, because there's no naval vessels on the radar coming to sink us."

"They'd send a sub. Torpedo us. We'd never see it coming and sink in seconds. Plausible deniability. No international incident. That's what I'd do." Mayorga's default expression was a scowl. Even her team lovingly said that she had *resting bitch face*, but right now she seemed extra grumpy. "But realistically, the Russkies will let us kill all their super monsters for them, *then* declare us border crossing criminals."

"Eh...hope not." I'm the one who negotiated the Krasnov deal, but I had to admit she had a point. However, to prove that everything was safe, Krasnov had sent some of his men to join our ship's crew as a sign of solidarity. They hadn't snuck off in a lifeboat yet, so that was a good sign.

"Nothing's gone sideways yet. Something always goes sideways," she muttered. "That worries me."

The *Bride* was crash-slapping its way toward the beach. If we timed this right we would be in position to provide fire support before the convoy rolled up from the base. They'd been unloading and staging at the harbor and airfield for the last few days. Despite the huge number of armed foreigners, the local garrison had been polite, were happy to stay out of the way, and nobody had freaked out yet. It appeared Krasnov had kept up his end of the bargain. Word from Earl was the garrison commander seemed happy to have somebody clean out this nest of vipers for him so his life could go back to boring irrelevance. The Russians were supposed to be pretty nonchalant about how their monster hunting companies conducted business, but this had to be pushing it. Krasnov was either way more diplomatic in his native tongue, or he'd paid a shit ton of bribes to some generals.

We were getting close. There was a nervous energy in the air.

"Movement," Mayorga said. "North end of the beach."

I swung my binoculars over. Something white was flickering across the rocks. "Is that smoke?"

"No idea. Steam maybe. There shouldn't be any volcanic activity." By the time she said that, the white cloud had spread further along the ground and was moving way too fast. "Fog doesn't spontaneously generate in the sunshine on a clear day."

"Unless it's magic," I replied as it spilled outward to obscure our whole landing zone. I lowered my glass. "They've seen us coming. I think you just got that sideways you wanted."

"About damned time. Terry, alert Earl." While he did so, she picked up the handset for the ship's intercom. "Attention. This is your captain speaking. You should already be manning your battle stations, so if you're not, quit dicking around and get there now. If you look to your east, you will see beautiful Severny Island, where some weird-ass magic fog is now obscuring my parking space. Gentlemen, I want my parking space. Gun crews prepare to fire on my order." She dropped the mic back into the cradle. "Okay, boys. This is it."

We'd done all that we could do. Now it was a roll of the dice. The next few minutes passed in nervous silence as we got closer and closer. The range on our main gun was much greater than this, but from here we could cover the entire area around the ruins, spot our own impacts—our gun crew would need all the help they could get for accuracy—and this put the shore within range of our secondary weapons. When we were two thousand meters from the beach, Mayorga ordered the engines cut.

While the *Bride* settled, the unnatural fog grew to fill the beachhead. I wondered if it was going to continue creeping out toward us, but it stopped at the water's edge, lingering there, unnatural and malevolent.

"Something really doesn't want to be seen."

"Well, Pitt, that tells me they're extra ugly."

"Helos are doing their flyby," Terry said.

I raised my binoculars and found the black dots speeding through the blue sky. MHI and three other companies had donated air power. In order to be flown here and armed, the vehicles had been temporarily leased to Krasnov. Skippy didn't really understand the concept, but Earl had made it clear to our host company that if anything shifty happened concerning the ownership of our Hind they'd have to deal with a very angry tribe of orcs. And I don't care how much of a mobster you are, nobody wants to piss off orcs.

"Spotters got movement on the eastern edge of the fog, looks like they're preparing to defend against our convoy," Terry said as he rapidly wrote numbers down on a notepad. Our handful of helicopters and prop planes wasn't as impressive as the squadron of MiGs Nikolai Petrov had been able to call on, but our fliers still made for great eyes. "Skippy says they are not human. They're, quote, giant spike bug apes."

"Whatever the hell that is, as long as we're sure they're not friendlies." Mayorga flipped channels on her radio. Terry was in contact with the convoy, but every individual Hunter had their own radio, and we were organized into channels and subchannels, by team, responsibilities, and language barriers. Organizing that had been a huge pain in the ass, but I'd made a spreadsheet for everybody so it wasn't too confusing. Mayorga had memorized every channel. "One-oh-five team, this is the captain. Fire mission." She snapped her fingers impatiently, and Terry handed her the notepad. She checked it against the laminated map on the wall to make sure the location made sense—we weren't about to blast our friends—and then began reading off the coordinates. She waited while they read them back to her. "Confirm. Give them hell."

We'd snuck in a few test firings of our 105mm howitzer on the voyage here. Since this wasn't the most stable firing platform, they'd have to time the waves, and an old artillery piece bolted to your deck wasn't exactly a technological marvel of modern computerized naval gunnery; this probably wasn't going to be super accurate. Except a 105mm high-explosive shell makes one hell of an impact, so *accuracy* was a relative concept. There's that old saying about horseshoes and hand grenades. In comparison this thing just needed to land in the same zip code.

I stepped out the door to get a better view of the gun crew on the deck ahead of me. They were on the prow, getting blasted with salt spray every time the *Bride* came back down. It took about half a minute for the five-man team to get the gigantic thing dialed in. I love all guns, but I'd never been trained for this sort of thing. These guys had all been artillery in various militaries, and they had been practicing together for the last couple months, so it was like watching a choreographed ballet, only if ballet wasn't boring and ended with a really awesome explosion. I made sure my hearing protection was in place. This friggin' thing was *loud*. I couldn't make out what he was saying, but their leader was shouting orders. One Hunter stepped away, pulling on a cord and—

*BOOM!*

Even fifty feet away the blast still compressed the jelly of my eyeballs. It made me grin. No wonder I'd never met an arty guy who didn't have hearing damage. I snapped my binoculars up and waited for the impact. It came a moment later on the far side of the fog, throwing up a massive plume of dust and smoke. *Nice.*

There were a bunch of other Hunters assembled up top, manning the secondary guns, waiting for a chance to do their jobs, and all of them cheered that explosion. Months of training and preparation came down to this. Asag had been working in the darkness, hurting us so many times, it felt *good* to hit back.

The howitzer had been mounted on what was basically a great big sled to absorb recoil. It bounced back, then slid back into place on hydraulics. Within seconds the gun crew had the breach open and was running what looked like a giant pool noodle up the howitzer's barrel to clear it, while the others prepped the next shell. They were rolling now. Mayorga must have given them the go-ahead to make it rain.

I stepped back into the bridge. The three Hunters in there were snapping short, terse sentences back and forth. Lots of stuff was happening, and none of it was my area of expertise. So I kept my big stupid mouth shut and let the professionals work. The choppers were calling in more targets. The convoy was tearing ass toward the objective, and the *Bride* was going to beat it like a meat tenderizer until they got too close.

The second howitzer blast rattled the windows and caused dust to rain from the ceiling.

"Skippy says that impact was one hundred meters south of target."

All things considered, that probably wasn't too bad, but Mayorga banged her fist against the console in front of her and shouted, "Unacceptable!" She got on the radio and started giving instructions to the gun crew. Her corrections were delivered in this calm, rational, clearly stated manner, but when she hung up it turned into, "I didn't drive this piece of shit across the top half of the world to *miss!*" Then she downed the rest of her coffee. "Terry, get me more targets! Pitt!" She stuck her stained mug toward me. It had the logo of the USS *Ronald Reagan* on it. "Reload."

"Yes, ma'am." I went over to the coffeepot, happy to feel useful.

The howitzer kept up an impressive rate of fire, getting off a shot about once every ten to twelve seconds. They were blasting the crap out of the landing zone. According to the radio chatter, as long as we landed shots anywhere in the fog, we were killing something. Keep in mind, the pilots could only see the creatures *big enough* to stick out of the fog, and there were still plenty of things moving. From up there, it must have looked like we'd kicked an anthill.

"Something is moving along the shore dead ahead." Through my binoculars I couldn't make out much through the mist, but whatever it was appeared to be *slithering* like a snake, only it had to be about the size of a killer whale. "There's a *hell if I know what* at twelve o'clock."

"What does that punk think he's looking at?" Mayorga said as she lifted the microphone. "We're getting eyeballed. Twenty mil batteries, light up that beach."

Our pair of twin 20mm autocannons let rip. There was one forward, and a second one directly above our roof. I'd never been in the bridge when these had fired before. It was like being inside a metal drum while it was rhythmically beaten with a hammer. Earl had *procured* these four Oerlikons off of a damaged frigate in the Pacific, shipped them home, and had them in storage since World War II. Free autocannons? I guess there were some perks to working for a secret organization like Special Task Force Unicorn, or whatever they'd called it back in those days.

Gigantic tracers flew into the fog as the slither whale beat a hasty retreat. The Oerlikons may have been antiques, but they still worked just fine.

"Engine room says they've got noise on the outside of the hull. Tapping. Like claws maybe. Possible intruders coming up portside."

"Pitt!" Mayorga shouted.

"Here."

"You heard the man, prepare to repel borders."

Now that was something I was good at. "Yes, ma'am."

With the way Gorod Chudovish seemed to act as some sort of monster magnet, drawing all sorts of nastiness here from across multiple worlds, it wasn't surprising that there'd be threats from under the water too. So we'd practiced for this.

"Yo, Ponchik! We've got company!" I shouted as I

ran down the catwalk. Ponchik was Krasnov's rep on board. "Port side."

I think he said "good" but it was hard to tell, because it was drowned out by our howitzer's muzzle blast. The four men Krasnov had sent to join the *Bride* took up their weapons and followed me. Since they'd gotten here too late to get put on any of the gun crews, they were my rapid response team for the front of the ship. Trip and four other Hunters were aft. I clicked over and radioed him too. "Trip, it's Z. Check the sides. Something's climbing aboard."

"Roger that."

The deck was slick with ice and slush as I ran toward the edge. Since going overboard in these waters meant quickly freezing to death, and there was the possibility something might breech us, or we might have to rope up and scrape something off the side, the response teams were all dressed in ridiculous, cumbersome, neoprene, cold-water immersion suits, with regular load-bearing vests on top. Normally Monster Hunters look kind of badass when we go to work, but you can't really look cool dressed in a bright orange condom.

I reached the safety rail and glanced over the edge. "Oh, shit!"

The side of the ship was *swarming* with bodies. They were ichthyoid, with weird fish features stretched over small, misshapen, humanoid forms. Their rubbery skin glistened with slime. Their webbed fingers ended in sharp points. They were climbing, slowly and clumsily, but steadily, like their nasty scaly bodies were suctioned onto the metal. The closest one was only a few feet below and it looked up at me with giant blank eyes, its mouth puckering open and closed like the world's evilest carp. The scene was nightmare fuel.

I backed up, flipped to the ship's main channel, and hit transmit. "This is the response team. We've got a ton of saughafin coming up. Hundreds. I repeat, hundreds of Deep Ones." I motioned with my hands for Ponchik and his men to spread out as they approached so we could cover as much area as possible. "We need backup."

Mayorga's voice came over the intercom. "Attention, crew. Deep Ones are crawling up the sides of our ship. All odd-numbered gun teams, go give our guests a warm welcome. Even-numbered teams stay on your guns."

As our howitzer fired again, I peered back over the side. There were so many green bodies churning the water directly beneath us, it was like we parked in a pile of thrashing, twitching fish monsters. It was really disgusting. As the *Bride* lifted on the waves, it revealed more creatures stuck to the side, like fleshy, nasty barnacles.

Everybody hated Deep Ones. Mankind had been dropping depth charges on them whenever they were discovered since the Twenties. With this many attacking, there had to be a huge settlement right beneath us. They were vile beings, smarter than they looked, with a language and customs, but as far as we could tell those mostly consisted of kidnapping people to sacrifice to their weird gods.

The others had caught up with me. Ponchik, a big, muscular, Dolph Lundgren–looking dude, spoke pretty good English. "Fish men." He turned to me, disgusted. "They will lay their eggs in us!"

"Screw that noise." I'd left Cazador back with my

armor. I figured for this kind of up-close-and-personal business, it was Abomination time. I swung my 12-gauge over the side. *"Open fire!"*

The closest fish man was right beneath my feet, mouth popping rhythmically. Its head exploded so violently that purple blood splattered on my survival suit. The four Russians hung their rifles over and let rip, all of us on full-auto. There were so friggin' many of these things that we couldn't miss.

Bodies ruptured. Limbs were blown off. The swarm kept climbing. Their slime had to be like glue; their bodies were so suctioned onto the metal sides, that even after you killed them, they didn't fall right away, they just kind of hung there flopping, until they peeled off, all while their fishy brethren kept climbing right over them.

The worst part was that they never made a sound.

I reloaded. "Keep it up!"

"This is aft response team," Trip said. "There's more here. The ship is completely surrounded."

The other Hunters who had left their battle stations reached the sides and joined in. Within seconds the entire ship was surrounded in a ring of continuous small arms fire. The waves crashing beneath us went from ice blue, to pink, to purple, and then into a horrific slime foam as the fish men's guts chummed the sea.

I went on the main channel. "Mayorga, this is Pitt. They must have a settlement right below us. We need to go."

"If we move, we can't provide fire support to the convoy. They've got some big shit in that fog. Hold them as long as you can."

I let go of my radio and went back to shooting.

"Did we interrupt a fish man orgy or something?" Ponchik shouted.

"That's really gross, man." The howitzer fired again. "The skipper says we hold them as long as we can. Pick a zone, cover it!"

Someone else came over the ship's general channel, but they neglected to identify themselves. I suppose they were a little distracted. "One o'clock high! Incoming!"

I was too busy slaughtering disgusting fish men to see what that meant, but it couldn't be good.

One of Krasnov's men had quit shooting to clear a malfunction, enabling a saughafin to get its claws over the safety rails. It turned out as soon as you gave them a proper handhold, they were way faster. The Russian was still wrestling with the charging handle as the monster got its webbed feet onto the deck. I stepped over as I flipped out Abomination's bayonet, and drove it right through the creature's brain. I twisted it out in a spray of purple and the thing dropped soundlessly.

"Get your shit together or transition to a different weapon!"

Ponchik berated him in Russian too. The Hunter seemed chastised. Good. It beat having eggs laid in you. He got the malfunction cleared and got back in the fight.

"*Tupitsa!* Forgive him, Mr. Owen. Sergei is inexperienced."

"Damn it, I told Krasnov no Newbies." I went back to killing, with blobs of purple brain flying off Abomination's bayonet with every muzzle blast.

"*Da.* But it is a party," Ponchik said as he reloaded. "Sergei is Mr. Krasnov's first cousin. He employs many relatives. The boss wanted no one to feel left out."

I don't know how we pulled it off, but we held them off. I'd fire off a mag, reflexively reload, dump that mag, repeat. I just kept working the muzzle back and forth, blasting everything. I'd fired so many magazines full of buckshot so fast I was getting sore, and since I practice so much that I have literal shoulder calluses, that was saying something. Abomination was getting so hot it was burning my neoprene gloves. It was like shooting fish men in a barrel. It was *disturbing.* I'd always been told these creatures were cowardly, only attacking when they had overwhelming force, and they'd bail if you put up sufficient resistance. Only these were downright suicidal. We must have parked on top of the most fanatical fish men in the world.

Suddenly I felt the *Bride* lurch beneath my feet. Either we'd just started moving again, or there were so damned many fish men underneath us they'd picked us up and were carrying us.

"Oh, my gosh. You should have seen what happened when the propellers came on!" Trip exclaimed. "That is the most blood I have ever seen!"

*Moving then . . .*

Mayorga came over the intercom again. "All AA gunners back to your stations. Unknown airborne targets closing. One-oh-five team cease fire and help clean up the fish men. We're driving for the island."

That was probably a good call. Our howitzer could only keep up that high rate of fire for a few minutes before it got dangerously hot. I really didn't want to cook off one of those shells. It would probably crack our ship in half.

The *Bride* slowly moved out of the awful chum

puddle. I hadn't heard the splash as Milo's special barrels had gotten rolled over the side, but I sure felt them when the depth charges went off. Vast plumes of water were hurled into the air behind us. Water doesn't really compress in an explosion, so any Deep Ones that had been swimming our way had just gotten mulched.

Luckily, the remaining creatures began detaching from the side of the ship and falling back into the discolored water to get away. We'd survived that wave. I could only imagine how bad it would have gone if they'd made it topside. In a matter of minutes we had killed hundreds of them. The sides of our ship had been painted purple. While Sergei started puking, I checked my chest rig. Most of the mag pouches were empty. I looked down. There were empty plastic magazines all over the deck, and so many shotgun hulls that it looked like a skeet range.

*Damn*... And we hadn't even reached the island yet.

"What's wrong, Owen?" Ponchik asked, obviously excited. "We beat them!"

"That's a lot of potential bounty money and no bodies to show for it." We were out of our jurisdiction, but a good argument could be made that these were in league with Asag and therefore PUFF-applicable. We had cameras all over the ship, so hopefully we could get a turn-in off of that evidence alone. Fanatic, banzai-charging saughafin might even be a special case, which would mean requesting a PUFF adjuster and a big payout. "Just business, you know."

"Oh..." He was breathing hard and probably just happy to not have fish eggs laid in him today. "I was not thinking of that."

"I'm an accountant. Can't help myself."

There was a new noise ahead as somebody opened up with a minigun. I couldn't see what they were shooting at from here, but a line of orange tracers leapt into the sky.

"Ponchik, watch for stragglers. I'm heading back to the bridge." I closed Abomination's bayonet so I wouldn't slice open my survival suit, slung it, and started climbing the nearest ladder.

There was a high-pitched wailing noise as something flew past overhead. By the time I reached the bridge, another minigun on the aft end of the ship was firing into the air, tracers chasing after whatever had buzzed us.

The bridge was nonstop back and forth, controlled chaos. The *Bride* was about to make its final landing. There were dots and arrows all over the monitors as the various parts of our operation moved into position. Terry was giving constant updates over the thunder of guns. Mayorga saw me enter out of the corner of her eye. I'm hard to miss at six foot five, especially in bright orange and covered in purple fish monster blood. "Status?"

"Boarders repelled. Response teams are watching for another wave."

"Hmmm..." Mayorga downed the last of her coffee. "Great. Now we deal with the sky squids." She handed me her mug. "Refill."

"What?"

"Refill."

"No. I mean about the *sky squids*."

"Kind of a misnomer it turns out. These look more like cucumbers with bat wings and tentacles, but the AA teams are driving them off. Keep that coffee coming."

Captain resupplied with caffeine, I unslung Abomination, shrugged out of my shotgun load-bearing vest, and buckled on the one filled with rifle magazines. Normally the coatrack in here would be used for mundane hats and jackets, but since it was all Hunters, now it was covered in guns and dangling pouches. I grabbed Cazador. The beach was coming up fast, so I might be able to get some potshots at monsters on the ground before we got there.

As I went back onto the catwalk, the scene was surreal. A gaseous blimp of a monster was ghosting past, being rapidly chewed into pieces by the miniguns. It corkscrewed into the ocean spewing slime from a thousand fresh bullet holes. Skippy blasted past in his MI-24, blaring heavy metal from the speakers and lancing rockets into the fog. The *Bride* was heading toward the beach at an angle, so every gun on our starboard side was in range and indiscriminately spraying the beach. That included the two twin Oerlikons, three belt-fed grenade launchers, and several fifty-cals. Every place Mayorga could have a pintle mount bolted onto this thing, there was one. There was noise, smoke, and pandemonium. We were cutting down the forces of evil with superior firepower.

I'd never seen a sky squid before, and I didn't get to see this one for long, because its ghastly mutilated corpse disappeared quickly beneath the waves. I really hoped that one had been caught on camera—not just because I wanted to get a better look at it, but because the PUFF on those things was ridiculous.

The fog was getting patchy. Every now and then

there were glimpses of dark stone through the white shroud. I didn't know if we'd hit whatever had summoned the fog, or maybe our elves were fighting back. All I knew was our improved view was giving us a target-rich environment. There wasn't much for me to do with a single precision rifle, because by the time I saw something, one of the crew-served weapons was dropping heavy hate on it. I braced Cazador over the rail anyway and started popping off rounds at anything that moved.

Whenever I caught sight of a beast in the fog, I let it have it. I'd turned the scope down to its lowest setting of 5x magnification so I could have a wider field of view. Even at that, the small glimpses I got told me there was all sorts of weirdness in there. I saw various shapes and colors, insects, men with no heads, glowing bloated slugs. Nikolai hadn't been kidding. Everything was fighting for a piece of this place. I put the reticle on whatever looked unnatural and start pulling the trigger until it disappeared again. Cazador barely moved as I fired. I made it through a whole mag that way, putting holes into several unknown creatures by the time Mayorga shouted, "Pitt!"

"You can't need another refill already."

"No. Check this out."

I rushed back into the bridge. Through the windows, the beach was right in front of us. I'd been so focused on shooting things that I hadn't realized how close we were to landing.

The captain was grinning, having the time of her life. "This was your bright idea. I thought you'd want to see it happen."

Ten knots is faster than it sounds when you're on a

big-ass ship about to crash into a big-ass island. The gravel beach did not look very inviting. Explosions were ripping through the rocks, hurling shrapnel and monster bits in every direction.

"That's kind of scary."

"Tell me about it. My old job I'd get court-martialed for this." Mayorga picked up her microphone. "Brace for impact. Brace for impact!"

Everybody on the bridge held their breath. Mayorga crossed herself. I hadn't known she was religious. I grabbed onto a rail. Several agonizing seconds passed.

*Crunch.*

"That wasn't so b—"

*CRUNCH!*

That took me right off my slick rubber booties. I hit the floor. All I could hear was the hellacious grinding noise as the *Pride of Krasnov* scraped its awful flat bottom across the rocks. Everything was shaking. It felt like the ship was about to rattle itself apart. Guns swung back and forth on the coatrack. A flat screen fell off the wall. The grinding went on and on. Something big and metal broke beneath us.

Then, we stopped. We'd landed.

"Docking complete," Conason announced.

Everybody else had been smart enough to be seated so they'd had better luck than I had. Mayorga hadn't even spilled her coffee.

I got back to my feet. "Congratulations, gentlemen. We are now a fort."

It was too quiet. Our gunfire had stopped so the crew could take the hit of landing. I looked out the window. At some point it had gotten cracked. It was as if our arrival had punched a hole. It was almost like the fog had recoiled in surprise and retreated. The area immediately around us was totally clear. A hundred yards away the fog was still a solid, pulsing mass. It felt *angry*.

The fog started creeping slowly back toward us.

Mayorga grabbed her microphone and activated the intercom. "Get back on your guns. We've got company. Everyone cover your sector. You know what to do."

I don't know what was seen moving in the fog, but somebody lit it up with a minigun. Tracers cut a swath through the mist. There was an unholy screech as the creature fled.

"*Bride* has landed. *Bride* has landed," Terry said into the radio. He listened as the others relayed something back. "The convoy can't cross directly to us through the fog. They're looping around and coming up the coast to our south. ETA ten minutes."

"Do not fire indiscriminately toward the south. Friendlies inbound from the south. Repeat, friendlies inbound from the south. You shoot our backup and I'll kill you myself." She let go of the button and took a deep breath. "If we can manage to link up without any blue on blue, this will have gone better than I expected."

Terry cut in. "Milo says the ramp is jammed."

"Damn it. I was worried that would happen. Tell him to get it unstuck as fast as he can."

My gear bag was in the corner. Nothing was coming to kill us for a minute, so I began getting out of my ridiculous survival suit. I started wrestling my way out of the stupid neoprene. It was so obnoxiously clingy it was tempting to just cut it off with my knife.

"If you don't need me, I'll head to the cargo bay."

"You really want a piece of this island, don't you, Pitt?"

She had a point. It had once killed my father. I didn't want to just take this place, I wanted to hurt everything on it. "I guess that's what I do best."

"I thought that was bitching about team leads going over budget."

"Love you too, Skipper." I threw my rifle pouch vest on over my coat and slung Cazador. I'd put the rest of my stuff on when I had the chance. "Good luck."

# CHAPTER 15

The *Bride* had come to rest at an angle. We were tilted about ten degrees to the right. It made walking a little weird, but it was a whole lot nicer than the endless crashing and swaying. I was definitely a land mammal.

As I ran down the deck, there was sporadic gunfire from my people, but most of the targets had pulled back. There were eerie noises coming from the fog: groans, moans, screeches, and a sound like hyenas laughing. There were also occasional crashes and roars, as the various things on the island blundered into each other. It sounded like they were fighting each other as much or more than they were fighting us.

I popped a hatch and slid down a ladder. The engines were still running, all the lights were on, and there were Hunters scrambling everywhere, getting ready to take the beach. By the time I got to the cargo bay our 105mm howitzer was firing again. It shook the walls down here. The gun crew would have to compensate for being parked at an angle, but we'd be a lot more accurate grounded than on the waves.

Jay Boone was in charge of securing the beachhead and was in front shouting orders. Milo Anderson was at the door controls. He had been appointed combat cargo officer, which basically meant that Milo had to figure out how to cram over a hundred Hunters and a bunch of assorted vehicles in here in the most efficient way possible, so we could get off fast enough to secure the beach long enough for the rest of the party to show up.

The vast ramp that made up the front of our ship was making a terrible hydraulic whine, but it wasn't moving much. There were a bunch of Hunters here, all dressed in winter clothing. Many of us weren't as armored up as we would be on a normal job, because armor gets heavy fast. We were going to be working mounted-to-dismounted in rugged, cold, unimproved terrain. Warm clothing is bulky. Winter gloves are a pain in the ass. Even though we would be riding in vehicles much of the time, everybody was carrying packs with supplies and survival equipment. Some of the Hunters looked excited, others nervous, some grim, more cracking jokes, and a few stone-faced and impossible to read, but however they got their heads right, every single one of them was ready to fight.

In a previous civilian life, the *Bride* had been used to haul vehicles up and down rivers and intercoastal waterways. If it could fit trucks, it could fit armored vehicles.

Or in this case, a T-72M tank.

When I'd been putting this operation together, the Czech Monster Hunters had been all in. They were a relatively small outfit, but they had a lot of pride, had lost a man in Vegas, and were eager to crack some heads in payback. When they'd heard Lindemann and Krasnov were both involved, they had refused to be outdone by their larger competitors to their west and east. I believe the actual quote from their company president—after being translated into English—was *Those assholes may have more men but will they donate a tank?*

That was hard to argue with, especially since Earl had really wanted to play with one.

The Ostrava One was forty-one tons of steel and badassitude. The 780 horsepower engine was deafening inside our metal box and the diesel fumes were threatening to choke us all. It had a bunch of exclamation points painted on the turret. I was too broad shouldered to even fit through the hatch to get inside that thing, but I was really jealous of the Hunters who were about to use it to go kick some monster's teeth in.

There were other vehicles in line behind *Ostrava One*, but we'd only brought the one tank. Mayorga had vetoed more. One was bad enough. That much extra weight and we'd have ground out far earlier and would be wading ashore. The rest were Oshkosh light tactical vehicles. An OLTV is basically an armored 4x4 pickup you could stick machine guns and grenade launchers on. Management must have owned stock in them or something, because he had hooked us up with a really good discount. It sure as hell beat walking.

With the help of some big Hunters with pry bars, the ramp opened a crack, enough to reveal there was a dead saughafin still stuck to it. It was opening, but *slowly*. Daylight flooded the bay. Freezing wind swept away the built-up fumes. Milo kept impatiently mashing the big red button, as if that would make the hydraulics go any faster.

Trip and Holly joined me, still wearing their survival suits. All of the designated response team people had, because there was a good chance one of us would end up overboard, but the suits hadn't been necessary. She had to shout to be heard over the noise of all the engines. "What's the holdup? Boone's landing party was supposed to roll out the minute we stopped moving."

"Ramp's stuck." Which turned out to be a pretty unnecessary explanation once they saw Milo jumping up and down on the end of a pry bar.

"Top's secure for now. Feints only," Trip reported. "It moves, it gets a twenty-millimeter to the face. Big stuff is holding back."

"You know that'll change the second we set foot on this beach."

"We're getting in the middle of a monster gang war, Z. They'll see us as a challenge."

"They should, because we are," Holly said. She dropped her gear bag and started stripping out of her suit: Holly really didn't care who was watching. Trip and I politely turned around, noticed one of the foreign Hunters ogling her, and we both shook our heads in warning, like *Dude, you do not know who you are messing with*. Holly might take the staring as a compliment, or she might hit him with a brick. Flip a coin. He wisely went back to doing whatever it was he'd been doing before the hot blonde had started wrestling her way out of skintight neoprene.

Trip hadn't had a chance to get out of his ridiculous survival suit yet either. His was yellow. "This new look might not be working for me, but at least it was warm." He began struggling out of the ridiculous getup and into something less clumsy and more bulletproof.

"You look like militant Sponge Bob."

Milo had started beating the ramp with a wrench. The Czech standing in the commander's hatch offered to just drive through it with their tank. It would have been comical if we weren't trying to launch an attack.

"I just heard about your dad. I'm sorry. I wish you would've told me," Trip said.

I knew I hadn't really processed it yet, but Auhangamea Pitt hadn't raised me to be the introspective, emotionally stable type anyway. I'd grieve when the fighting was done. "He'd want me focused on the job."

"God gave him a mission, just like us. He fought the good fight and now he's in a better place. You can't ask for much more than that."

And Trip was so damned sincere about it, that actually meant something. My eyes began to water. I blamed it on the diesel fumes. "Thanks."

He finished tying his boots and stood up. "You ready for this?"

"Hell yeah."

With a triumphant shout from Milo as the ramp went crashing down, it was time to hit the beach.

As predicted, the lull didn't last.

Ostrava One rumbled out first, clanking down the metal ramp and shaking the entire ship. It drove the ramp deep into the ground. The saughafin corpse that had been stuck beneath the ramp popped like a grape. The tank sank into the gravel as it moved slowly and carefully forward. The ground had more give than expected, but it wasn't soft enough to stop us. A Hunter was standing up in the hatch, manning the gigantic machine gun mounted on top and scanning for threats. The tank got far enough out that there was plenty of room for the OLTVs to pull out behind it, and stopped.

The Hunters moved out as the gun crews kept watch above us. I walked down the ramp, paralleling an armored truck. The *Bride* had traveled a surprising distance up the beach, but the surf was still licking the ramp. Hunters who were fanning to the side were splashing through shockingly cold water. Trip was probably regretting ditching his SpongeBob suit.

A Van Helsing Hunter who had been a Royal Marine was at the base of the ramp, directing traffic. Boone was ten feet past him, telling everyone where to go. Since we'd not been able to predict exactly where we'd land, he was having to improvise on the fly based on the terrain, which consisted of nothing but beach and a lot of rocks.

Something weird was going on. The temperature was already freezing cold, but it was dropping fast. An unnatural chill swept over us. I'd felt something similar before, usually around vampires, but this was different, and worse. The salt water tossed by the waves froze solid before it landed. I didn't have a thermometer handy, but the air on the beach had gone from twenty above to twenty below in the last two minutes.

"What the hell?" Holly managed to gasp through chattering teeth. "Freezing magic *bullshit*!"

There was a noise in the fog, a belligerent roar so loud it drowned out the tank's engine. The hair on my neck stood up. That awful sound flipped an ancient, primal switch in my brain, warning me to run or get eaten. Even the hardest Monster Hunters seized up when they heard it. Whatever made that sound was pure terror.

"Where were they hiding something that big?" Boone shouted. Then he went back to giving directions. "Screw it! Keep moving!" The Hunters snapped out of it and pushed on. Boone waved the truck I was next to toward the right. He saw us. "You three post up on that boulder pile."

"Got it." The Oshkosh was headed that direction anyway. If we were going somewhere, it might as well be in the shadow of an armored vehicle until we got there.

"Get up there and—" The roar came again, much closer this time. Boone grimaced as it shorted out his hearing protection.

The ground shook. Then it shook again. It was like a miniature earthquake every other second. Those were *footsteps*.

"Run!"

The fog was rolling back in. As painfully cold as it had gotten, it should have frozen solid, but instead it just clung to us. Visibility was a fuzzy fifty feet at best. It was all gray mist and slightly darker gray ground. The sun was shining above, but you wouldn't know it in here.

The truck drove forward. The three of us ran alongside, slipping across newly frozen puddles of seawater and sliding across loose stones. The gunners on the *Bride* saw something and opened fire. High-velocity shells ripped through the air over our heads to smack into distant meat with an audible *thwack*. The answering roar was really pissed off.

A belt-fed 40mm grenade launcher began firing rhythmically. Out in the mist I briefly caught a chain of explosions, three hundred yards away, and thirty feet *up*. The flashes briefly illuminated a massive, humanoid body.

"That's tall!" Trip exclaimed.

"This must be how gnomes feel all the time."

The earthquakes went from sporadic to a drum beat as the thing picked up its pace. The loose gravel was vibrating like it had been set on top of a subwoofer.

The truck hit the brakes as the fifty-cal on top let rip. We never even made it to the rock pile we were supposed to claim. I braced my rifle over the hood and got ready. Hopefully the OLTVs would give me a warning before they took off so they wouldn't drive over my feet.

"Is a rifle even going to scratch that thing?" Holly shouted next to my ear.

"Maybe it's got a weak spot." I peered through my scope and got my first good look at the approaching threat. It *filled* my scope. The thing had legs as big around as tree trunks and arms that hung nearly to its distant knees, was covered in blue skin and bony protuberances, and was big as a friggin' house. I don't think anything on it would count as a *weak spot*. "Giant! It's a giant!"

Trip got on his radio. "Target is a giant. I repeat, giant."

We'd gone over giants in Newbie training, mostly in hushed tones, but it wasn't like mankind ran into them much anymore. They were a nightmare left over from darker times. They were rare—thank God for that, because they were supposed to be ridiculously hard to kill. In the olden days, one of these things could eat a *town*. How a giant had wound up here, I'd never know, but in the island's never-ending turf war, this had to be the heavyweight champ.

"According to the square cube law, there's no way that thing can exist," Trip said fearfully.

"That's helpful right now!" Holly snapped back.

It was too close to safely shoot the 105 at it, and the *Bride*'s nose-upward angle probably meant they couldn't depress the muzzle enough to hit it anyway, but we nailed the giant with everything else on that beach. It was like a mad minute on a spectacular firing line. Skippy and another chopper had gotten the call too, and had swooped in, dropping rockets on the monster's shoulders.

But the giant was still getting closer.

It was hard to tell what it really looked like, so wreathed in shrapnel and shockwaves, but the giant was misshapen, like it had been pulled out of the oven too early. The fairytales lied. These things only looked human in the vaguest sense of the term. It looked kind of clumsy, but covering a quarter of a football field with each step, it was closing fast.

I realized it was heading right for us, or at least for the truck we were hiding behind. I stepped away and banged my fist on the hood. "Move! Move!"

The Hunter in the driver's seat put the hammer down. The wheels sprayed gravel. The fifty on top kept firing as it bounced away. The three of us started running back toward the ship, only the world was shaking so bad that it was hard to stay on our feet.

There was a world-shattering boom as the Ostrava One fired its 125mm main gun. The tank shell zipped right past me. I don't know if I threw myself down because of instinct or if the concussion took me off my feet. You don't really have time to think through the physics at a time like that. All I knew was that as I hit the ground the shell struck the giant's torso. The mighty beast lurched to the side as the explosion rocked the beach.

Holly was still running. Trip came back, grabbed me by the arm, and yanked me upright just as it began raining blood and meat all around us. Some of the pieces were the size of Thanksgiving turkeys. Not wanting to be killed by flying meat shrapnel, we took off. I looked back to see that the giant was not only still standing, he was pursuing the OLTV. One absent kick and the heavy armored truck was deformed and flipping end over end. By the time it crashed on its side, the giant had spun around and was heading toward the *Bride*. We were in its way.

Holly saw that it was going to catch me and Trip, and she slid to a halt and opened fire. It was a futile noble gesture.

"Shit!" I put my head down and sprinted as fast as I could. It made absolutely no difference. The giant caught up to Trip and me in a fraction of a second. It leaned over and swept its hand along the ground in a flash, tearing up a vast swath of earth.

I found myself sailing through the air, spinning around in a cloud of gravel.

The ocean was below me. Rocks peppered it like rain. Then it rushed up to hit me.

I crashed through the ice-cold surf. The shock was incredible. I struck the rocks beneath a second later. That hurt less than the water.

Getting dunked in ice water is a terrible sensation. The cold hit like an electric shock. It caused an uncontrollable gasp. Water filled my mouth. I thrashed, trying to get my bearings, got my knees on the bottom, and scrambled up. Skin burning, heart racing, I wretched, sucked in air, and tried to get my bearings. I forced myself up. It was only waist-deep. The air hit me in the face like a brick.

I was *forty feet* from shore. It hadn't so much as hit me—if it had I'd be dead—but more like I'd been swept up like a dust bunny in front of a broom.

The giant was heading for the ship. I didn't see Holly or Trip anywhere. Ostrava One fired again, the tank's autoloader capable of pumping out a round every six seconds. From the way this shell punched a football-sized hole clean through the giant's guts and out its back in a shower of gore, they'd switched from high-explosive to armor-piercing.

I was hyperventilating. It was so shockingly cold that I could barely think. All I could do was struggle toward land or die, so I did, clumsily, until I realized Trip was floating facedown a bit further out to sea. Arms wide, head down, motionless. I tried to shout his name, but the muscles of my jaw were reflexively clenched too tight. I waded toward him.

The tank's AP round must have done the trick, because the giant lurched and stumbled toward the ocean. The next shell punched through its chest and the giant toppled into the surf. It struck the water so hard that a wave came back and hit me and knocked me over again. I came up sputtering, grasping for Trip. My fingers didn't want to work. I caught hold of his vest and flipped him over. His eyes were closed. I couldn't tell if he was breathing. I started dragging him back toward the beach.

That meant going directly toward the monster. There was no way around. It had landed on its side, but was already struggling again to its hands and knees. It lifted its hideous, bumpy head, water drizzling down, blood pouring out of the massive hole in its abdomen, and it looked our way, lips parting in a snarl, revealing ivory teeth as big as my head.

Those huge eyes were focused directly on me, out splashing in the shallow end. There was intelligence in the giant's eyes, far more than expected. Then it spoke. Each word was deafening, its breath a foul, stinking wind. It was clearly language, and a complicated one at that. Unable to speak, I gave my answer by reaching for the rifle that was still slung across by body. I lifted Cazador with one shaking hand, raised it to hip level, and fired.

The side of the giant's head exploded. Pieces flew violently in every direction. There was a gaping exit wound where its ear had been. I was so dizzy and befuddled that I stared stupidly at Cazador for a moment, thinking, *Did I do that?* before I realized that had come from the tank.

*Boom. Head shot.*

The light in those eyes went out. The massive body crashed into the water again. This time my feet were planted and ready so I wasn't washed away by the impact wave. I let my rifle hang, and went back to dragging Trip through the pink surf. I was trying to tell him that everything was going to be okay, but I couldn't form words.

The rest remains an incoherent blur. I don't remember getting Trip back on the beach. I don't remember collapsing, curling into a ball, and shivering until other Hunters got there to help us. But as I lay there, world spinning, I did remember the giant's words, and somehow I could understand their meaning.

*We will never let you free Asag.*

# CHAPTER 16

I had helped set up the ship's hospital. I hadn't planned on being one of the first patients. Since Hunters tended to be pessimists, we had picked two of the bigger rooms on the ship to serve as the infirmary. I'd been stripped out of my clothes, dried off, and stuck under a heated blanket. Occasionally a deck gun would fire, which told me I needed to get back to work.

"They need me out there, Doc."

Boris Todorovic came from Hurley's team out of Florida, had grown up in the Yugoslavian civil war before immigrating to America and still had the accent, but had been an honest-to-goodness medical doctor before joining MHI. He had the reputation of being a beast in a fight but for this mission he was more valuable saving lives than taking them, so Earl had been put him in charge of our infirmary.

Boris was currently standing next to my bed, dressed in scrubs rather than body armor, but still keeping me from doing my job. It turned out a man who had earned a reputation for once dismembering a luska with a fire axe had a very no-nonsense bedside manner.

"Sorry, Pitt. Until the shivering stops and the heart rate comes down, you're staying here."

"I'm fine."

"Your words are slurred, a classic sign of hypothermia." Boris started walking away.

"That's just how I talk."

"You say so, Mumbles. Here ... catch." He tossed a wooden tongue depressor at me. I not only failed to catch it, but it hit me in the nose too. "The patient demonstrates obvious lack of coordination."

Trip was in the next bed over. "To be fair, he's always like that. Z can't catch a cold."

"You're not helping my case." I threw the little piece of wood back at Boris and missed.

"Throw one at me, Doc." Trip sounded kind of drunk. "I'd totally catch it."

"You're both lucky that giant did more of a scoop and toss than an outright hit. But you were in twenty-nine-degree salt water for a few minutes, and already chilled before. Being in wet clothing afterwards certainly didn't help matters. Your core temperatures dropped too much. Even mild hypothermia causes confusion and poor decision making. So you want to go play with guns and explosives? Not on my watch. I'll check back in an hour and see if you're doing better. Trip, in addition to being hypothermic, you've got a concussion, so you're not going anywhere for a while." Boris walked off to check on his patients on the other side of the room.

It took my normally quick-witted friend several seconds to think of a response. "I collect concussions like you collect Barbie dolls, Doc!"

"Barbies? Really, Trip?"

"I don't know, man." Trip closed his eyes and sank back into his pillow. "I've got the worst headache ever."

"Because even if he did actually collect dolls, which I doubt, because seriously, look at the guy, it isn't like he's going to get nerd-shamed by someone who paints tiny little metal dudes."

"They're miniatures. For wargaming. Now quit talking. Your words are hurting my brain."

But I had doctor's orders to not let Trip fall asleep. "Getting tossed across a beach by Frosty the Super Giant hurt your brain. I saved you from drowning."

Trip groaned. "I'll thank you after I'm done wishing for death's sweet embrace."

There were three other Hunters in the infirmary with us. Two had been in the flipped truck. Their driver—Cooper, it turned out—had crawled out of the wreck without so much as a bruise. The last Hunter was from the French contingent and had been on the convoy. They never even saw what threw it, but something had hurled a rock right into the turret hard enough to split his scalp wide open and nearly rip one ear off. It had been dangling by a strip of flesh when they'd carried him in. Boris had just kind of stuck the ear back on as best as he could, taped it down, and the French Hunter was getting flown out on the next chopper.

The lost ear was gross, but that was it so far, five stable in the infirmary, nobody in a bag. Considering the ridiculous quantity and quality of monsters we'd blasted on the way in, that was remarkably lucky. I figured it was our reward for doing our homework and hitting with overwhelming force. I figured now that the various monster groups knew we were here, and a force to be reckoned with, it was only going to get harder.

Which was another reason I needed to get back to work as soon as possible. If we were still on track, today we would secure and fortify the beachhead. Tonight we'd hold, because even though night was very short here, monsters usually loved to attack in the dark, and tomorrow we would hit the ruins. If Earl saw me like this, weak and brain-froze, I was worried he'd pull the plug on letting me go through the gate. I needed to get moving, to either avoid Earl entirely, or to at least look like I had my shit together when he saw me.

"Hey, Trip. I just remembered I need to do something. Try not to slip into a coma." I sat up and waited for the dizziness to pass. *Wow*. The room was spinning. I was a little nauseous. The weird angle we'd landed at certainly wasn't helping the effect.

"Where do you think you're going?"

"To get my gear bag from the cargo bay. I can recuperate while I put my armor on." I got out of bed before I remembered I was naked. It was true: even mild hypothermia makes you stupid. "Shit."

"Yo, you need pants, man."

"They're in the bag." I thought about streaking across the whole ship, but that was probably what Dr. Boris meant about *poor decision making*. The worst part would be the *cold* metal floors, so I began looking around to see if there were any slippers stashed in here, but my poor decision was postponed because Holly and Earl walked in. I hurried and covered myself with the electric blanket.

"Aw, cute. Z's acting like I've never seen one of those before," Holly said.

"Have some dignity, boy," Earl snapped. "There's a lady present."

Holly snorted.

"Hey, Boss." I nodded politely. "Holly."

She'd been right there with us, between a tank and a giant, and by some miracle there wasn't a scratch on her. Sometimes in the chaos of battle that was just the way things shook out. Holly smirked at me. "Considering that ice bath must've caused some shrinkage, still not bad, Z. No wonder Julie married you."

"Thanks?"

"Knock it off, kids." Earl stopped between our beds. "How're you two doing?"

"Awesome," I lied.

"That's why your skin is bright red and you're shaking like a leaf," Holly said.

"I'm not red," Trip declared.

"I helped haul your ass in here. It's the first time I've seen a black guy turn blue."

Trip waved one hand dismissively as if getting swatted like a bug was no big deal. "You worry too much, Holly."

"Spare me, Dreadlock Smurf."

"I'm ready to get back to it," I told Earl. "I'll be fine."

"Outstanding." I was pretty sure Earl knew I was lying, but he wasn't big on coddling his Hunters. Earl was a walk-it-off sort. Normally if one of his men said they were ready to fight, he'd take them at their word. However, I must have looked really bad, because instead he called out, "Hey, Boris, got a minute?"

The doctor wandered back over. "What is it?"

Earl was shaking a cigarette from a dwindling

pack before he realized this was technically a hospital room. "You mind?"

"Eh . . ." The doctor shrugged. "Nobody's on oxygen."

"Want one?"

"I smoked for two years so I could wear a nicotine patch for five. No thanks."

"Quitter." Earl snorted. "What's the status? I need all the Hunters I can get."

"As soon as it's safe for Skippy to land, Darne's man needs to go to the airfield and then back to the mainland. He's not going to die, but he needs reconstructive surgery, and there's nothing else I can do for him here. I want Jones and Neely here overnight because of head trauma. Brian Musgrave broke three fingers when the truck landed, but he says it's his off hand, so you should be able to put him doing something."

"And Pitt?"

"I'll be ready to hit the ruins, no problem," I asserted.

"You base this on your medical degree? Do I tell you how to make the spreadsheets? No? Shut up." He turned back to Earl. "Let him warm up and he should be fine in a bit."

*Groovy.* I didn't do all this work to end up sitting on the bench.

"Thanks, Boris. You need anything else, just ask. You get more patients, I can send you Gretchen and her healers, but until then I can use them as mobile field medics. What's your plan if anything sneaks in here?"

"I would hit it with an axe, as is the way of my people." The doctor said that so nonchalantly that none of us could tell if he was joking or not. "When you bring me wounded, make sure to bring their guns.

Anybody not sedated can still fight. Now, if you will excuse me, Neely still needs stitches."

After Boris moved off, Earl muttered. "That sumbitch is hard-core."

"So what's up, Earl? You've got to be too busy right now to be checking on mild injuries."

Earl looked around. The other Hunters were on the opposite side of the room and couldn't hear him over the generator. "Don't know about minor. Did you see that ear? Damn that must've hurt. But you're right. We're digging in and securing the perimeter. Cody's team is setting up instrumentation and the elves are drawing supposedly magical squiggles on everything. I made time because I heard something troubling about that giant the Czechs brained."

"I told Earl what you were mumbling while we dragged you in here," Holly said.

I honestly didn't remember saying anything. "First rule of polar bear club is you don't talk about polar bear club."

"Everybody on the beachhead heard that giant making noise, but it was all nonsense to us. You told me you understood what he had said, and that it was important."

"Okay, yeah." It was coming back. "I did. It was like he was talking to me directly."

"You learning ancient monster languages now?" Earl asked, incredulous. "Because I've only known one of us who had the gift of tongues to pull that off, and he's been gone since the Christmas Party."

"Nothing like that. I don't know if this is part of the whole Chosen thing, and no, there was no evil black lightning like when I see other people's memories, but I just knew. I heard him the same as everybody else, but it's like I could understand the meaning in my head. The giant told me they would never let us free Asag."

"Assuming this isn't the brain damage talking..." Holly said.

"Trip's the one with the concussion."

"I was thinking long-term brain damage, Captain Headbutt."

"So it's either telepathy or delusion." Earl scowled. "What's your gut tell you?"

I shrugged.

"How sure are you?"

I was an accountant at heart. When I gave an estimate I liked it to be accurate, but this magic Chosen One job didn't seem to work like that, so I pulled a guesstimate out of my ass. "Seventy percent?"

"The us must be us Hunters obviously, but who is *they*?" Holly asked. "Does the giant have friends or was he just talking the monster gangs in general?"

It made sense to me. "Nikolai said there are all sorts of factions fighting over this place. The ones down below worshiped Asag; maybe the giant didn't. If it turns out the giant's bunch is potential allies, it's too bad we shot him with a tank."

"Now that's what I'd call a failure to communicate," Trip muttered.

"That would be tragic, but we're collecting PUFF on that big fella either way." Our boss was a pragmatist.

"Don't worry, Earl. If the MCB asks on the paperwork, I'll tell them the giant's last words were 'Screw all humans. Asag the Category Five Extinction-Level Threat is my best friend.'"

"That's the spirit, Z."

"Hang on." Holly was being dead serious for once, and the rest of her team knew that when she quit being flippant or sarcastic, it was probably important. "What about the part about us freeing him? We've been working under the assumption that he was already awake since the time break in Natchy Bottom."

"Yeah, Asag's reign of terror is my fault. Rub it in, why don't you?"

"Don't feel bad, kid. Do this long enough, you're bound to wake up some superdemons."

"Really, Earl?"

"No . . . But what do you mean, Holly? We've seen plenty of evidence that this bastard is active."

"Sure, Earl, active. But if Z's right, the giant said *free*. For such a supposed badass elder god that he even intimidates Great Old Ones, we keep running into his minions, or his worshippers, or things he's set free, but in all the years since Z woke him up, he's never once shown his face."

"What are you getting at?"

Holly was grim. "I'm wondering if this thing beneath the island is actually a tomb, or is it a prison?"

As the sun went down for the brief and freezing night, the *Bride* was a hotbed of activity. It had gone from crappy boat to crowded fire base. We had spent a month moving vehicles to the island, and all of them were parked here, armed and ready. It was a lot of firepower. We were watching with flying drone cams, night-vision, thermal, and naked eyeballs. Hundreds of Hunters were dug in like ticks, using the buddy system, and sleeping in shifts.

While I stood in the command room, occasionally there would be a bunch of noise, muzzle flashes, and explosions from somewhere along the perimeter. Then a few seconds later somebody would get on the radio to explain what they had just vaporized. Lots of things tested us, but nothing was stupid enough to come at us head-on again since the giant had gotten capped. It must have been the cause of the fog too, because it had been clear ever since.

The command room was crowded. Earl was in the middle, and from the way he was processing everything and spitting out orders, if monster hunting hadn't worked out for him he probably would have made a pretty good general.

Not wanting to feel left out, Krasnov had arrived in a helicopter and joined us aboard his namesake. He had brought a Russian Orthodox priest with him to bless our weaponry. I was glad to see Krasnov here. Not for his pleasant company, but because if he was physically present, that meant he truly believed the Russian government was not going to suddenly get cold feet about the operation. So in a way, Krasnov was like a big, fat, heavily mustached canary in the coal mine. If he suddenly left, that told the rest of us we needed to haul ass to the airfield.

But as long as we kept killing off all their troublesome monsters, the local officials would probably stay happy. Between the frost giant and the greater sky squid we'd killed, the Russians should be loving us right now. In extra good news, the bullet-riddled corpse of that sky squid had washed ashore. Those things were Special Class, so we didn't even need to be in US jurisdiction to collect PUFF on them. *Cha-ching!*

When Krasnov saw me he came over and congratu-
lated me on planning "most successful and glorious
invasion," which obviously, he then reminded me, could
not have been accomplished without his brilliant politi-
cal and logistical help. And since he'd since proven
his unquestionable integrity, Krasnov had asked for
his symbolic sword back, which meant that it probably
was actually a family heirloom, and not just purchased
at a flea market, because he wouldn't have bothered.
Frankly, I was a little surprised.

Next to the command center was the room where
the smart people had set up. We didn't really have a
better name for them, but it was where all the brainy
Hunters with their Mensa cards were gathered trying to
figure out what was actually going on beneath Severny.
We had hard science guys like Cody, occult experts
like Dr. Rothman and Ben Rigby, and researchers
like Lee and Paxton. And of course, Tanya, Princess
of the Elves, self-declared expert on magic... which
was driving Cody a bit crazy.

When I came in to brief them about what I'd heard
the giant say, Tanya was helpfully telling Cody that he
was "book smart just like Bill Nye the Science Guy."
Cody, who had a pile of degrees, had responded that
No, he was an *actual scientist*, and if she continued
to bug him with *elven foolishness* he was going to say
to hell with it and retire.

None of the Academic Decathlon knew what to
make of the giant's words, and I figured roughly
half of them assumed I had just been punch-drunk
and imagined understanding the language. Academics
loved to argue. They were still debating if Rothman's interpretation was correct, and only a chosen

individual would be able to go through the gate, or if a whole team could pass, but when it came to the giant's cryptic warning, there was nothing in any record about Asag being imprisoned here, it was always that he was asleep or in some kind of demon stasis, just waiting for the end of the world. And they had searched everything.

Rigby thought it was just as likely that the giant was a disciple of Asag, and had been trying to trick us into not harming its master. It could just be an attempt to keep us away from his tomb . . . But you don't make it long in this business by being incautious, and if the demon was awake but stuck, the last thing we wanted to do was set him free, so they'd take the possible warning under advisement.

Regardless, in a few hours we would be leaving for the ruins.

# CHAPTER 17

*"'Cause we got a great big convoy, ain't it a beautiful sight! We're gonna roll this big old convoy, rockin' through the night!"* Milo Anderson had a terrible singing voice. *"Convoy!"*

"The sun's up. You can't really call it all through the night," I pointed out.

*"Convoy!"*

Milo was driving our truck. I was in the passenger seat. We had three more Hunters in back and another manning the turret. There were a dozen vehicles ahead of us and far more behind. There was no road between our base and the ruins, but the ground between wasn't too rugged. It was one of the main reasons we'd picked this landing site.

We had plotted a course that was a balance of speed and safety. Our planners had picked out every ravine and dangerous terrain feature on the way and marked them on the map. Depressions make great ambush spots. Narrow paths are easy to block. Our lead vehicle was being driven by a Hunter who had been a Finnish rally car champ. We could radio coordinates back to our howitzer for fire support. Every truck had a winch and a tow bar. If something broke down, we'd drag it out immediately. If a vehicle couldn't be unstuck in seconds, we'd abandon it, and every Hunter riding in it would pile into other vehicles. We weren't stopping for anything.

Monster Hunters take our convoying very seriously.

Two helicopters were overhead. Skippy was having the time of his life continually blowing stuff up. He was positively giddy by orc standards. There weren't any pesky human laws to hold him back here like there were in the US, and he really loved shooting rocket pods at every weird critter that looked at us funny.

The downside of this much hardware was the absurd fuel consumption. I'd run the numbers in advance. This operation was a massive resource suck, but as long as we had a clear shot back to the harbor and the airfield, we could keep up our siege of the City of Monsters. Our fort boat would be receiving gas, ammo, food, and drinking water daily. Until the Russian government became unhappy with our presence, we had a reliable supply line. The stuff coming into port was legitimate contract shipping funded by Management, but we also had backup supply chains from shady do-not-worry-is-good-deal Krasnov contacts if necessary. The day that lifeline was cut, it was time to get the hell out. Hopefully ahead of the army units they would surely be sending to arrest us.

Krasnov was feeling pretty optimistic that his government would be pleased with our results. I wasn't nearly as optimistic as our mob boss. Right now this was still a mutually beneficial business arrangement, but I had zero faith that would continue indefinitely. Too many times I had seen some bureaucrat from my own ham-fisted government suddenly change their mind and pull the rug out from under Hunters. I had even less faith in somebody else's government not being assholes. I'm patriotic like that.

"This is Harbinger. We are five minutes out. Keep your heads on a swivel."

I pretended to speak into an imaginary CB radio. "Breaker one nine, good buddy, this here is Rubber Duck. We're clean from here to Taco Town."

"Ten four, Pig Pen!" That made Milo's day. "I knew you appreciated classic movies, Z. Okay, everybody sing along! *Convoy!*"

The Hunters in the back of our vehicle shared confused looks. None of them were from the US and their English wasn't that good, so the odds of them being fans of obscure 1970s movies was pretty slim, but damn it, when Milo wants a sing-along, that enthusiasm is contagious. *"Que es 'Convoy'?"*

"Only the greatest trucking movie theme song ever. Okay. I'll teach you guys the words. I've had this thing memorized since I got a bootleg VHS tape when I was a little kid. Everybody now!" Milo immediately launched into song.

Things like Milo's goofy singing while heading into a radioactive war zone may seem unprofessional, but we were driving across a place that just oozed evil. You could feel the oppressive weight dragging down your soul. We spent our days dealing with dead victims and the things that mutilated them, so Hunters tended to be a flippant bunch. The darker your job, the better refined your sense of humor needed to be or you were destined to burn out, and Milo had been doing this job for a *long* time.

"This is Truck Four. Contact right. Rocky ridge at three o'clock. Lost visual."

"This is Truck Twelve. Contact left. Movement in the ravine we just passed."

Sadly, singing time was over. "Here we go."

Milo gave me a grim nod and gripped the wheel tight. We were going forty miles an hour in armored boxes. We should be safe. Monsters tended to lack in the ranged-weapon category, but you never know, things could surprise you. The trade-off was that the ride sucked; as a big dude I was cramped and getting tired of banging my knees and head with every bump.

I kept scanning for threats. The landscape here was black with white snow stripes. The wind and weather had long since scrubbed all the small stuff, so the vehicles ahead of us weren't kicking up any obscuring dust. The convoy was passing through a valley filled with shale, dirty snow, and icy streams. More calls came in. There was movement all around us.

Suddenly, the whole valley rose up.

I hadn't seen them because their bodies were as black as the rock they'd been lying on. Eyes glowing jade, each creature was only about the size of a baboon, but there were hundreds of them.

"What the—"

Long spindly arms flashed as they hurled rocks in rapid-fire succession. They had no problem hitting a moving target. Projectiles clanged off our armor with shocking force. They were putting dents in the plates. Against flesh, one of those would hit like a bullet.

"Light 'em up."

The convoy didn't even slow down as every turret fired. Miniguns cut a swath through the obsidian monkeys. Fifty-cals blew them into pieces. And then they all disappeared in expanding clouds of shrapnel produced by our belt-fed 40mm grenade launchers. A few seconds later, there was nothing but a field of mangled corpses and we were speeding away.

"What the hell were those?"

"I've got no idea. Never seen them before. This island is *weird*." Then, because Milo was a polite host, he tried to translate that for our guests. *"La isla es no bueno."* His Spanish was about as good as his singing.

If this was a regular mission, we would have stopped to make sure they were dead and collected the bodies for PUFF. The curious part of me wanted to examine one of those obsidian monkeys to see what they were. The accountant part of me was sad to leave perfectly good PUFF money on the ground. Only the practical part of me was glad we were focused on the big picture. I wanted to win, rescue our guys, and head home. Hey, who knows? Maybe after we murdered Asag, these little guys would still be here . . . Though realistically, knowing how evil this place was, something would have scavenged their bones or animated the corpses by then.

"This is Harbinger. The ruins are in sight. Air cover sees some hostiles on the ground. Skippy is clearing us a path."

From the background sound our orc pilot's musical selection today was provided by Sabaton. "Skippy charge!"

MHI's Hind roared past, too low for comfort, but Skippy didn't give a crap. The Hind raced to the head of the convoy and then bolted upwards at a steep angle. He climbed rapidly for several seconds, leveled out, and then dropped like a rock. Nose down, guns blazing.

Nikolai Petrov may have had a squadron of MiGs, but we had a *Skippy*.

There was a long chain of explosions ahead of us. Something the size of a yak caught on fire and tried to run across a field. I watched the six-legged fireball in morbid amusement until one of the orc door gunners walked a line of tracers across it. The mystery creature lay down and burned. If PETA saw that they would be pissed. The Hind kept turning and shooting. Skippy owned the sky and dispensed vengeance like a wrathful god.

"Savage."

The song "The Last Stand" came over all our radios again.

"What best in life, Harb Anger? Skippy crush. Drive enemy! Hear lame things from their womens!" Skippy had almost gotten the Conan quote right. I was so proud of him.

"Skip is going to be super sad when we get back home and the MCB won't allow him to use that kind of ordnance on every job," Milo said with a little bit of awe in his voice.

We were almost there.

I felt an involuntary shiver run down my spine. I looked to Milo. He'd felt it too and gone a little gray. I looked to the back. All of the Hunters had been jovial and charged up a minute ago, but that had been replaced with a creeping fear. We were all feeling it one way or another. It was almost as if we had just driven across an invisible line and our subconscious minds were trying to warn us that we really didn't belong here.

We had entered the borders of the ancient city.

Earl was a lead-from-the-front kind of commander, so was riding in the lead vehicle in order to have the best view. Once he confirmed that our aerial recon was accurate, Earl declared we would be sticking to the original plan. There was a flat area between the remains of the pyramid and the obelisks that was relatively free of debris. That spot would give us a good view of most of the ruins. It was time to circle the wagons.

"From convoy to wagon train. Come on, Milo, you've got to know the words to some wagon-train-related song."

Milo just grunted something in the negative and concentrated on driving. You know a place is really putting out the negative waves when it's enough to shake Milo off his game.

Our truck blasted past the ruined base of an obelisk. The silver had been scorched black by nuclear fire. The alien carvings were too ruined to discern. I was thankful for that small mercy. It was hard to tell now, weathered by time, then blown to pieces by man, but the city must have been impressive once. The base of the pyramid was a jumbled, jagged mess. The blocks that had made up the upper levels had been hurled hundreds of yards by Tsar Bomba. It was hard to even comprehend such a powerfully destructive force. The remainder of the structure had collapsed in on itself, leaving what appeared to be nothing but a misshapen hill.

The trucks were peeling off, forming a circle, nearly bumper to bumper, but angled so that none of us were blocked in. The mounted guns were turned outward. The interior of the circle would provide us cover and room to work.

"Button up. Keep those doors closed. From here on, make sure you're wearing your radiation badges. Keep the alpha detectors on at all times. Wait for the signal before getting out."

The delay was so our smart folks could check for radioactivity. Cody had been beating us over the head for months about how to avoid getting irradiated. When you open a room, don't go charging in. Try not to disturb something that's been sitting covered for years, and if you do, don't breath the dust. So on and so forth. Enough time had passed that we should be fine, but we weren't taking anything for granted. It was possible there could still be deadly pockets. We'd brought full environmental suits, but hoped we wouldn't need them. Same with our portable decontamination showers here, though we had much nicer ones ready back at the *Bride*.

I reached up and touched the dosimeter clipped to my vest to make sure it was still there. It had alarms preset for certain levels and cumulative exposure. This little thing was going to be my best friend. I really didn't want to survive wave after wave of awful monsters to go home and die of cancer.

We sat there for a moment, engines still running. I watched out the window. The only thing I could see moving was the tattered remains of something Skippy had bombed whipping in the wind. It looked like sackcloth over a cow-sized rib cage.

"Readings are clear. Move out."

I swung open my heavy door. "Welcome to the City of Monsters."

The instant my boots hit the rocks, black lightning flashed.

From high atop the gleaming silver pyramid, the Warlord looked down upon his army and was pleased. They were crowded between the great obelisks, awaiting the word of their god. When the command came, they would go forth and drown the world in the blood of men. The Children of the Mountain were eager.

The Warlord lifted his four arms and began a chant. *Great Asag had carved them from the mountain and given them life. They lived to kill. They killed to live.*

A hundred thousand voices took up the chant.

Their anger was growing. The Warlord fed on their rage. For too long the Children of the Mountain had hid in the depths. Their god had gone to defeat the champion of man once and for all, and once Nimrod fell, the blood would flow. There were seven other cities with seven other armies with seven other warlords, all like this one, beneath every corner of the land, ready. There waited five other cities beneath five oceans, their armies made of a different species, but united in purpose. At the killing time they would hunt the men in their fields and in their homes. They would dig beneath their castles and cause their walls to crumble. In the end there would be no place to hide. The Children of Adam would be slaughtered by the Children of the Mountain.

*They lived to kill. They killed to live.*

They would slaughter and take what was theirs.

They would consume all flesh and live beneath their sun. Once every man was gone, then the Children would destroy each other until none remained, because Great Asag willed it.

A mighty flash of lightning, black as the deep earth, tore across the top of the world.

It was over. A champion had fallen.

Rain began to fall. The Warlord raised his arms and watched as his white flesh was speckled with red. His four outstretched hands were quickly covered in blood.

It was a sign, but not the one they had been waiting for. Their god had been defeated. Man had won. The Warlord screamed. Furious, the Children of the Mountain clawed and rent their own skin, howling their rage up at the sky as the falling blood turned to fire.

In the distance there was a wall of smoke. *He returns.* Great Asag was not quite dead, but all his Children could feel his weakness, and the Children wept.

Their god had been crippled. Now was not their time. The world beneath the sun would not be theirs today. Great Asag would descend below until he was strong again. Yet it takes a long time for a god to heal. A multitude of threats would come to try and steal his mantle.

The Warlord knew what must be done. Many of the Children would go below, to wait, to breed, to guard the deeps and watch over their lord's slumber. But for the rest...

As the Warlord slashed his own throat, the Children turned on each other, and the army disintegrated into tearing flesh and breaking bones. If they could not slay man today, then they would slay each other instead, forever cursing this place, and sacrificing their lives to feed their god.

*They killed so Asag may live.*

Reality returned with a machine gun's roar.

My head cleared. I was still standing next to our truck. Except now Milo was shouting something, trying to be heard over the Browning M2 pounding away on the roof of our truck.

"Down! Down! Take cover!"

Something whizzed past my head. Flung rocks smashed into my open door as I took a knee. More of the obsidian creatures we'd seen on the way in had appeared in the ruins of the pyramid. I hadn't been able to hear them before while we were driving with the bulletproof windows up, but they were a screechy bunch. There was a high-pitched hooting noise as they attacked. Little rocks were coming in straight, while bigger ones were being lobbed on high trajectories like mortar shells. There were so many impacts it was like being in a hailstorm.

It took a second for the vision to fade. That memory had been so full of . . . It was hard to describe . . . malice, jealousy, fanaticism . . . and the feeling was lingering. I wanted to puke.

I knew time compressed whenever I experienced a vision like that. Only a second or two had passed in the real world, but even zoning out that long had nearly gotten my head taken off. "Listen, whoever you are, I know you're trying to help here, but put the Chosen One magic bullshit on hold until I'm behind cover next time!"

Milo was lying prone on the driver's side. He shouted at me under the truck, "What?"

"I'm not talking to you," I said as I leaned around the door and shouldered Cazador. Two hundred yards away, one of the little baboon-looking bastards was scurrying across the open toward us. The scope was so clear it was like I could reach out and touch him. I put the crosshairs on its chest and pulled the trigger. With the suppressor attached the rifle made nothing but a *whump* noise. The creature fell on its face, skidding through the gravel. Immediately, I had to pull back as half a dozen rocks bounced off my armored door. I waited a second, rolled out again, spotted a pair of glowing jade eyes, and snapped off another shot. One of the lights went out and the thing dropped.

*That's what you get for bringing rocks to a gunfight.*

But then I had to pull back again as a rock the size of my fist cracked my armored window. Another big one bounced off the open door behind me, hard enough to slam it on the Hunter who was trying to get out.

*Enough of this shit.* I got on my belly below the door and started picking off monkey monsters as fast as I could.

Only Earl was even more impatient than I was, because he straight up called for an artillery strike. The 105mm round made an eerie noise as it flew over us. I'd seen it fired, but I had never been near one of the impacts before. It turned out to be a far different experience.

The shell landed on the opposite side of the pyramid, right where a bunch of the creatures were rallying, and obliterated them. One instant they were there, the next they were gone. A plume of dust rose into the air as monster parts came spiraling out of the sky. This island had once seen Tsar Bomba, and this was nothing compared to that, but any mushroom-shaped cloud is still pretty damned impressive when you're right next to it.

A whole bunch of jade eyes turned fearfully toward the explosion. Whatever these things were, they weren't stupid. They knew when they were outgunned. The panicked hooting must have signaled a retreat, because they turned tail and fled. All of us kept shooting until they disappeared deeper into the ruins. I hit two more before they got away.

"That's right! There's a new sheriff in town!"

In the great monster turf war, mankind had just claimed another block.

Cody came over the radio. "Everybody back inside and button up! Now!"

The howitzer's explosion had looked neat, but we were downwind. That meant we needed to hide until Cody could make sure we weren't going to get irradiated by the dust cloud it had stirred up. I would have gotten back into Milo's truck, but I heard Earl shouting my name. He was gesturing for me to run over. I looked at the approaching cloud, then back at him. Harbinger was scarier. I sprinted over.

"What's up?"

"Climb in. Hurry."

I crammed into the back, shoulder to shoulder with some other Hunters. It was really tight. Earl was up front. He looked back as I got in and slammed the door behind me. "We closed? Good." He was in leader mode. Earl got intense at times like this. "I saw your blank slack-jawed expression when we came under attack. What did you see this time?"

He knew me too well. I glanced around to see

who else was in the truck. They were mostly strangers. "It can wait."

"No. It can't. Talk."

I tried to keep the Chosen thing to myself. I felt like it either made me a target or it would make some Hunters trust me less. Too many people at MHI knew already. I hated talking about it in front of anybody I didn't have to. You'd think a guy who'd been keeping his lycanthropy a secret for so long would understand that, but no, Earl had to put the safety of a thousand other Hunters first, and he was right to do so.

"I got a vision of what this place was like a long time ago. Couldn't tell you when. The things that lived here—from Nikolai's description it's the Asakku, or what they're descended from at least. Asag created them to be his soldiers, and they worshipped him like a god. This was his prepared fallback spot if he was ever defeated, where he could recover and wait for another chance to rise again. He got hurt badly and fled here."

"Any clue how Asag lost last time?"

"Rigby and Management were right. The Asakku blamed Nimrod the Hunter, and they just thought he was a mortal man. I didn't see how he did it, just the aftermath. It's hard to give too many specifics, because the mind the memory came from was really messed up, and it's not like it was thinking in clear English, but that's my take on it."

When I started talking about visions and alien memories, our Finnish rally car champ just looked at me in the rearview mirror and frowned. But come to think of it, that was the only facial expression I'd ever seen from him.

Earl thought about it as the potentially deadly dust

rolled across our windows. "Any actionable intel in your visions? Anything that can help us right now?"

"I can tell you why the island is cursed slash haunted as hell, though. It's because a hundred thousand of those assholes genocided themselves in a mass suicide orgy right where we're standing."

I didn't know the Hunter sitting next to me, but from the accent he was an Australian. "You're a psychic?"

"Something like that. Long story. Sometimes they give me visions from the past to be helpful."

"Who's *they?*"

"Longer story."

Earl stopped the perplexed Hunter before he could ask another question. "The Asakku are still down there. What about their capabilities, weaknesses?"

"This mind was so screwed up it was hard to tell. Brutal but smart. They always see red. I'm talking angry and superfanatical. They've got a perpetual desire to kill hardwired into them. They're way weirder to read than a gnome, but not nearly as alien as a shoggoth memory."

"Fuck me sideways," said the Australian. The Finn grunted in agreement.

Cody's voice came over the radio. "Checking for alpha particles... Radiation levels are elevated, but acceptable. Watch your damned badges."

"Go tell the elves about this vision in case it helps them tune in their mystical crap. They're big on the whole dreamer business," Earl told me. Then he keyed his radio, "This is Harbinger. Everyone move out and secure the perimeter."

I got out, thankfully without any crazy-magic-lightning brain strokes this time.

On the other side of the circle was the truck we had given the elves. It was easy to spot because it had been spray painted with logos to look like something off of NASCAR. I'm fairly certain they weren't actually being sponsored by Pizza Hut and Mountain Dew.

Nate Shackleford was their driver. If I thought I'd been screwed by getting stuck on the *Bride* for the awful trip over, at least I hadn't been made Speaker to the Elves. Trip was lucky he'd gotten that head injury, because otherwise he would have been part-nered with Nate today; Trip was actually pretty patient with elves. As a show of respect to the Queen, part of our deal was that MHI's liaison to the Elven Nation would be a Shackleford, because by Hunter standards, Shacklefords were royalty. And the Queen appreciated her some royalty.

Nate had matured a lot since I'd first met him. He had still been a kid when his father had gone off the deep end. As the youngest, he'd been in the shadow of his badass older brother, Ray, and after *his* death, when Julie had stepped up to fulfill Ray's duties, Nate had kind of just been swept along. He wasn't a natural born leader like his siblings were, but he had made such a heroic stand at the Last Dragon that it had restored a lot of the faith in the Shackleford family name with our allied companies. I really liked my brother-in-law.

He saw me coming. "Hey, Z. Julie told me about your dad. I'm really sorry."

"It's okay." As long as I focused on work, I didn't have time to be sad.

"She said that you wouldn't talk about it much with her either. She's worried about you. If you need somebody to talk to..." The Shackleford kids knew a thing or two about losing parents, only their story was far more tragic. "Or if there's anything I can do, just ask. We're family."

I changed the subject. "How's elf-sitting going?"

Nate grimaced. "They smoke more than Earl. And if I have to listen to any more banjo music, I swear I'm going to eat my Glock."

"Don't talk like that. This island is doom and gloom like Natchy Bottom. It'll get in your head and find a way to make bad things come true."

"Banjo music, Z. Bad things have already come true. Luckily, our elves will ward off curses and insanity, unless their music gets us first."

"It can't be that bad—" And then an elf got out of the back of the truck carrying an actual banjo. "Whoa...I thought you were just talking like on the radio or something."

"Oh, no. I could tune that out. The Elf Queen decided this much powerful magic means we needed a *bard* to chronicle our exploits."

"You're making that up."

"I wish." Nate turned around and pointed at the debarking elves. "You know Tanya. That's Eugene with the bow, Elmo's their senior tracker wizard whatever, and the *Deliverance*-looking one with the banjo is Gilroy. Gilroy Starfire. Again, not making that up." More elves were piling out of the truck. You could really cram them in there like a clown car. "That's Clete, Boomer, Hershel, and the slow one they just call Frog."

"No shit." Honestly I couldn't tell them apart. All of the humans around us were either in body armor or winter gear. The elves were in mismatched deer hunting camouflage. Except for Tanya, who had managed to score a pink camo parka and fur boots. The one I thought was Elmo was drinking a Bud Light. Two of the elves had bumped heads getting out; they exchanged insults, then began shoving each other. It quickly turned into a wrestling match. *This* was supposed to be our only defense against the island's invisible ghostly threats.

"We're so going to die," Nate muttered.

"Get your skinny asses off the ground!" Tanya shouted. "Rolling around like a bunch of morons! Y'all are embarrassing me in front of my fellow Monster Hunters." She went over and kicked the top elf in the butt with her fuzzy boot with remarkable force. That knocked him on his side. Elmo laughed at him, but then she smacked the beer out of his hand. "Get your shit together and look professional!"

"Maybe not," I whispered back to Nate. It was possible there was some steel left in the elven royal line after all.

Elmo looked down upon his spilled beer with great sadness. "Yes, your highness." But then he got into the spirit. "Y'all heard the princess. Start marking some spells! I don't wanna see no spirits or haints floating 'round these here round-ears!"

The elves moved out. They had guns too, but if this went according to plan, their best weapon would be in the form of chalk, paint, and Sharpies. We had lots of people who could shoot, but none of us humans could do what these elves could—supposedly—do.

"Sorry about that," Tanya said to us. "My kin get a little rambunctious. They don't get out of the Enchanted Forest."

"I can see that."

"Ed!" Tanya shrieked, as Edward the Orc walked past me. I hadn't even heard him coming, but Ed was basically a ninja, so that wasn't surprising. She ran over, jumped up, wrapped her arms around his neck, and her legs around his torso, and squealed, "My bodyguard has arrived!"

Poor Ed just stood there awkwardly with the elf girl on him. You couldn't read his expression with the mask and goggles, but his posture said, *Beats me, I just work here.* Orcs weren't huge on public displays of affection.

Tanya let go and dropped off of him. "Why ain't you wearing the good luck charm I gave you?"

Ed had once defiantly faced down a dragon solo, but he humored his girlfriend, reached into his parka, pulled out a badly crumpled cowboy hat, and put it on top of his ski mask—backwards.

"That look actually works for you, Ed," I told him. It was kind of odd. The cold, oppressive feeling of the island was dragging most of us down, but Tanya was positively glowing. "Are your people ready for this?"

"Better than okay!" The princess gave me an enthusiastic grin. She was having a blast. "You don't get it. My mama has kept us hid for a long time. For our own safety, looking out for us, I know, but my people need adventuring. It's in our blood. For y'all this is a job. For us, it's the future. We pull this off, all the elves in all the trailer parks in the world gonna be talking 'bout what we did here. No more sitting on their fat asses collecting welfare. Imagine elves getting out in the big world! Imagine more elves getting jobs at MHI!"

That was kind of terrifying, in a redneck apocalypse kind of way.

Nate groaned. "Fantastic. I'll go unload our gear," he said as he escaped.

But I saw where Tanya was coming from. Her once-great people had lost their pride, and she was looking for a way for them to start believing in themselves again. Her mother was content to exist. Tanya was young and naïve, but also energetic and ambitious. She really was the future of her people. May God have mercy on their souls.

"I knew we could count on the elves. Right now I've got to update you on—"

"Dreamer stuff. Oh, don't look surprised. I can tell they just showed you something. Their magic is still all over you. It's super strong too."

"You can actually see the connection?"

"I gotta remember human brains are all squishy for this stuff. You been touched. I can't see far enuf to tell who it comes from, but there's powerful magic on you, big medicine, hocus-pocus, call it what you want. You always had it. Born with it probably. Mama said you had it when she first met you, but you got it heavy on you now. Way heavy. You held up before, so now they're pilin' more hopes on hoping you don't break. Somebody up there is betting on you big time."

"Is that somebody *good?*"

"Uh . . ." Tanya bit her lip. That very basic question caught her off guard. "More 'n likely?"

"That's comforting."

"The big things out there don't really get good and evil like we do down here."

"I've found they tend to be more goal-oriented than morally motivated."

"That sounds 'bout right." Tanya popped a stick of gum in her mouth and began chewing loudly. "Mama says the factions pick champs and chumps, and humans are usually chumps. No offense."

"None taken." I'd gotten used to being a pawn in a cosmic chess game.

"Mr. Harbinger's the same way. Your wife is the same way too."

"Hold on." That had come out of nowhere. "What about Julie?"

Tanya was taken aback. "You don't know? Humans are even blinder than I thought. Yeah. From the marks. There's eyes on her too, different eyes than on you, but it's like y'all are horses in the same race. Some're betting on you, another big thing is betting on her. Mama says somebody even picked that scary bugger Franks. Don't know why they'd do that!"

"Have you said anything to Julie about this?"

"Nope. She tries to hide that she's been marked. I was trying to be polite! It ain't just y'all. All the different big evil ones all got horses in this race too."

"Is Asag one of these?"

"Oh, hell no. He ain't no horse, more like an evil horse farmer, with a field full of his own evil murder horses. He don't want to win the race. He wants to burn the track down."

Elves could really torture an analogy. I would have kept questioning her, but Harbinger's voice came over the radio. "The ruins crew is assembling at the west side of the circle. Form up with your team. We leave in five minutes."

I was out of time. "This conversation isn't over." I rushed Tanya through the details of my vision while she listened intently, smacking her lips while chewing gum and blowing the occasional bubble. After a couple of minutes I asked, "Any of that help?"

"Nope." Tanya twirled some of her hair around her finger and shrugged. "But at least it reminds me to tell Mama's trackers to try and not accidently run off the good ghosts hanging 'round you."

It was a weird thing to wish for, but right now I would have loved to have been able to see the world the way an elf did. "Are there many friendly ghosts here?"

"The evil pushes most away, but there's a few of the strongest watchin'. Real stubborn-like."

I could guess who those were, and I was glad to hear it, because I needed all the help I could get. "Thanks, Princess." I began walking away.

Tanya waved goodbye. Nate had returned carrying a rocket launcher and looking forlorn. He mouthed the words, _Take me with you._ Edward had already disappeared. Contrary to our princess's wishes for a bodyguard, Ed would inevitably wander to wherever the action was. If you ordered Ed to do something, and he actually did it, that was probably just a happy coincidence. He was more of a force of nature than an employee.

Tanya called after me. "Don't worry. Those ghosts got your back!"

_They always do._

# CHAPTER 18

There were over a thousand Hunters on this operation, but it wasn't like we were all in one place at one time. Logistics are unforgiving, so there were Hunters staying at the harbor. There were more at the airfield. Our little air force wouldn't fly itself. The biggest group remained guarding the camp around the *Bride*, because if we lost our forward operating base, we were screwed. Then we had our giant convoy, but not all of us could go beneath the ruins. Half would be staying outside with the vehicles, because losing our transportation and walking back would be a great way to get picked apart or freeze. Every part of the operation had to be manned and secured at all times, and lots of us would be serving as mechanics and ordnance handlers rather than trigger pullers.

All that meant only a few hundred of us would be going underground on this first attempt, but that many heavily armed and prepared Hunters was nothing to sneeze at. Especially when we were worried about things like giants, so we were packing hardware like AT4s and bunker busters.

The interior of the ruins were unnervingly *off*. The haphazard blocks were subtly wrong, like the geometry was skewed somehow. I'd gotten a glimpse of this place before it had been nuked, and it had been even weirder then. The original builders—my gut told me that wasn't the Asakku—had been sufficiently alien that their rubble couldn't even lie in a heap right.

Everything was blackened by a clinging, moist, ashen dirt, but when you struck that off, the blocks were a silvery gray beneath, and it wasn't any material that I could recognize. It looked like a smooth, slightly reflective concrete, yet soft enough you could leave a little dent when you accidentally struck it with something hard like the barrel of a gun. Cody and the big brains were probably taking samples. I hoped they were wise enough to not bring any of this cursed shit home.

The whole area left me with a vague sense of unease. It was like I'd told Nate: places like this had a way of getting into your head. It would wear down your will to live if you let it, leaving you raw and vulnerable. It didn't help that the rubble was the same color as the strange creatures we'd shooed off. Those obsidian monkeys would be practically invisible here, and the constant threat of ambush weighs on your nerves.

For today's objectives I was on Kiratowa's squad. We had a very important job, so we were holding back at the base of the pyramid while the others searched for a way down. One of the nearby Hunters found some old carvings that were relatively undisturbed and went to dust it off with his glove. "Hey. Check this out. There's writing on here."

Milo was walking by on his way to join up with the lead team and grabbed that Hunter hard by the wrist.

He glared at the man over his little round glasses. "Don't . . . Just don't." It wasn't very often that you got to see Milo be threatening. Normally Milo would be the one fascinated by all of the nifty new stuff to discover, but when even somebody that intensely curious was getting the vibe that things were best left undisturbed, it was best to listen. "That's not for us. Got it?" Milo waited for the young man to nod in understanding before letting go of his wrist.

My friend was right. I'd seen a vision of what was beneath that grime. I hadn't gone crazy—yet—but it certainly couldn't be good for my long-term mental health. "Trust him. You don't want that in your brain."

As Milo walked past, he whispered. "I've got a really bad feeling about this place."

"Good luck down there."

"You too." Milo was still a little disappointed that Earl had shot him down about going through the portal, but the expedition would get the most use out of its mechanical genius if he stayed on this plane of existence. "Good luck *out* there."

It only took ten minutes for our scouts to find the first entrance. The path underground was so well camouflaged—just some deeper shadows beneath an overhanging rock—that it would have taken us hours to find it. Except our orcs could follow the traffic by scent and knew right where to go.

Earl's team blazed a trail. After a few minutes, we got the call to move out. It was time to descend into the dark.

The ruins raiders had been broken into squads of various size, depending on our responsibilities. Team Harbinger was the biggest, and their job, provided

Nikolai's maps were still even sort of accurate, was to find and secure the portal. Kiratowa's squad would then enter the portal and find our missing Hunters.

There were twelve of us. There had been a lot of debate between the companies who would get this dubious honor. It made more tactical sense to send a group that had been working together for a long time, but that meant only one company would be represented, and since MHI was footing the bill—through Management—it would be one of ours. Except everybody else pitched a bitch fit and threatened to bail. In the end it was decided that every company who had someone missing from the Last Dragon would send a man. It takes guts to volunteer to go into the City of Monsters. It takes suicidal bravado to volunteer to go into another dimension. Yet even then, there had still been over a hundred volunteers before we'd whittled it down to something manageable.

Assuming we could capture the portal, through it would go a dozen men, the best of the best, and we'd find our missing or die trying. Unless, of course, Rothman's theory was right, because then I'd be on my own. I tried not to dwell too much on that. If the time came, I'd do what I had to do.

The way beneath was a blacker hole into black rock. I had to duck to get through the entrance. Beyond that, it opened into a wider tunnel, really more of a hall, and wide enough that we could probably get a four-wheeler through it. The path was already well-lit. One squad had set up a generator just outside, and the lead team was unspooling electrical cord and placing compact radio relays and emergency lamps as they went.

The relays were to boost and bounce signals so we could maintain comms underground. Besides the construction lights, we all had night-vision devices, weapon-mounted lights, flashlights, little personal LEDs, glow sticks, and worst-case scenario, we'd use lighters and rags to make torches. We weren't screwing around on being able to see. MHI had learned its lesson fighting Martin Hood, and we were in this for the long haul. In addition to our radiation sensors, we also had monitors for the oxygen level and poison gas. Besides fuel and bullets, we were shipping batteries up here by the pallet. We'd tried to think of everything and could only pray that something we hadn't thought of wouldn't come along to bite us in the ass.

The tunnel angled sharply downward. It was enough of an incline that it made your shins hurt, and like everything else around here, just enough off that it made you feel dizzy. Within a hundred feet, the blackened rubble turned into that weird silver-gray. The unnatural stones were so well-fitted that you couldn't fit a knife blade between them. We were out of the wind, but it was still too cold. Really cold air should feel dry. It should bite. This air felt *moist, squishy.* I hated it.

The lead team kept giving status updates as they went, noting every side tunnel and branch for future exploration. Already they'd found variations from Nikolai's maps. That was a bad sign. Earl had said his old foe was crazy, but not that kind of crazy. It was more likely that the KGB agent's theory was correct, and the ruins were somehow changing.

Kiratowa signaled for us to stop. The team ahead of us had entered a large chamber. We weren't supposed to crowd up on them. If they needed to fall back, it would be going past us while we covered them. In exchange for his company joining the expedition, Kiratowa had demanded a personal spot on the portal squad. Since he was the most experienced, Earl had put him in charge. He took the chance to go down the line, inspecting each of us lunatic idiots dumb enough to step through a portal to the Nightmare Realm willingly.

Everybody had a partner. They checked in with their squad every few minutes. Each squad checked in with the others every ten minutes. The guard convoy was doing the same, and the radioman on the *Bride* was correlating everything. If anybody went missing, we'd know about it fast. In addition we all had GPS trackers on our armor, so at least the others would be able to recover our bodies, provided the signal wasn't lost underground.

Kiratowa stopped in front of me. I was nearly a foot taller so he had to look way up. "How are you doing, Pitt?"

"Why does everybody keep asking me that?"

"Because your father just died and I want to be certain it does not cause you to become a liability. I intend no offense, but you have a reputation. You are a man of strong passions, very good at what you do, but can become foolish when angered."

That was actually a fair assessment. "I'm okay."

"Warriors have emotions too. There is no shame in needing time to regain our focus. I must know if you are still up for this?"

I laughed. "If you'd known my dad, you'd know how stupid that question is." He kept staring at me.

It was hard to see his eyes beneath the shadows of his helmet, but Kiratowa struck me as an extremely focused and humorless individual. I gave the most honest answer I could. "Yes. I'm ready."

"Excellent." He continued down the line without another word.

Since the twelve of us had all come from different companies, and we'd only had a little while to train together in Alaska, I'd partnered up with David Gerecht. We had at least worked together briefly once before. He leaned over toward me. "Don't worry. Kiratowa's got no room to talk about emotions. I heard the reason he insisted on leading the portal team is he's never lost a Hunter under his command before Las Vegas. He took that as a personal insult."

"Not one?"

"Never. Well, his company has, but his personal team? Not one in ten years of him being in charge, until the Last Dragon."

I whistled. The Japanese Monster Hunters were busy too. That was a pretty badass record. Hopefully he carried that lucky ratio with him. "What about you?"

"Ari is a friend. Someone from Maccabeus had to step up. We may be smaller than MHI, but we have a reputation to maintain."

"Don't worry about your rep. The elves are already writing songs about us."

"Good . . . maybe. And you have the ring?"

I held up my right hand. The Ring of Bassus was hidden beneath my glove, but he'd get the picture. It had barely fit over my pinky, and even then it was too tight. The Romans must have had tiny hands. "I just hope it works."

"That ghost stabbed one of my men, so it had better. I'm worried though. Rothman's right far more often than he is wrong, and he's afraid it'll turn back everyone but you. You'll be on your own."

"I know." It was kind of nice that it was just assumed that I'd still go through with the mission by myself, but everybody here would do the same. None of us were quitters. "If that's the case, what'll you do then?"

"Hold that gate until you bring back our friends, of course." He was dead serious about that. "You have my word."

It wasn't just ghosts who had my back. "Good. I really don't want to spend the rest of my life floating around limbo."

Gunfire echoed up the hall.

"This is Harbinger," I heard over the radio. "We've made contact."

The Petrov Report had said that the portal was in a vast cavern directly beneath the pyramid. That much hadn't changed. He had also said it was swarming with hostiles. Unfortunately, that part was also accurate.

The next twenty minutes were the longest of my life, as Earl called down other squads to help clear out the big room and we had to stay in place. Kiratowa's team had to squeeze to the side and watch other Hunters run into danger, while we sat there, useless.

The battle raged on. They were expending a lot of ammo on something. I knew we were being held back for a specific purpose, but it still sucked. We were antsy. When you know it's your people in danger, it's hard not to run toward the sound of the guns. Kiratowa kept telling us to prepare to move, but then something else would happen and Earl would flag us off.

Twice, Hunters ran back past us, returning to the surface, carrying injured. We couldn't even ask them what was going on because they couldn't spare the time. All the Hunters could do was warn us to make room, and they had to shout to be heard over the screaming of the wounded.

"Those were claw marks on them," Gerecht whispered to me after the second group went by. "Bad ones."

The wounded had been shredded, skin rent, muscles exposed. I had recognized both men, but didn't really know either well. I stared, fixated at the trail of blood splatter they'd left on the floor. The radio chatter had said the enemies had white skin and fought like suicidal lunatics. "It's the Asakku."

"That's right," Kiratowa said as he walked back down the line. He paused where a bloody bandage had been dropped on the floor. He poked it with the toe of his boot. "Below us they are fighting the Children of the Mountain, the very army of Asag . . . Yet they are not *our* problem." He looked up at us. "Focus on your mission, gentleman. These men are bleeding so that we can do our job. Will we allow them to bleed for nothing?"

There was some head shaking and muttering.

"Will we avenge our fallen?" He got a chorus of *yeahs* and *sures*. "What? Are you not angry?"

Our response turned to shouts. "Damned right!"

"That's better," Kiratowa snapped, finally raising his voice. "When Harbinger calls for us, we will slaughter without hesitation every vile creature between us and our men! Then we will bring them back and plant the flag of mankind on the bloated corpse of the demon Asag!"

That got a bunch of motivated responses. I was starting to see why this guy's company was so successful. He must have seen how the delay and the helplessness had been eating at us.

"For the Last Dragon!"

*"For the Last Dragon!"* Now I really wanted to kick some ass.

All of our radios popped. "This is Harbinger. Come in, portal team."

"This is Kiratowa. We read you."

"The gate is secured. The enemy has fallen back, but I can't say for how long. We met heavy resistance and they might just be regrouping. You can go through now if you want, but I can't promise we'll still be holding it when you get back."

We exchanged glances. The mood ranged from determined to excited. Nobody shirked. If anyone was scared, he didn't show it.

Kiratowa spoke for all of us when he transmitted. "Portal team is on the way...Move out."

We started running down the hall in a single-file line. It wasn't a really fast run, because in addition to our armor and weapons, every one of us was carrying a heavy pack. We didn't know how long we were going to be on the other side, and there would be no resupply, so if we wanted it, we had to carry it in ourselves. Face-planting was the last thing you wanted to do when you're boogying down a steep slope carrying half your body weight.

The string of emergency lights guided our way.

Hunters had been left to guard each intersection to make sure our main force didn't get flanked. When they saw us approaching, they shouted encouragement. Everybody knew what this team was here to do. There was still gunfire coming from below, but it was more sporadic now. We didn't enter the chamber so much as the hall got bigger and bigger, until our lights could no longer reach the ceiling, and you got hit with the realization that the space was vast. It was bigger than Management's cave and DeSoya Caverns put together. It just kept on going for what seemed like forever. I couldn't see the roof, but everything below us was built—grown?—out of that same gray material. The little bit of light the Hunters had brought into the darkness was reflected and bounced back, and it still left the details of most of the space a mystery.

Kiratowa signaled for us to slow down. We needed to get our bearings. There were glistening white bodies scattered everywhere. The Hunters who'd come ahead of us had gone through one hell of a fight.

"Harbinger, this is Kiratowa. We've reached the chamber, but need to get a bearing."

"Yeah, it's bigger than expected. Keep going straight on from the hall. And watch your step! There's holes and plenty of gaps big enough to fall down. We threw down a strobe. Look for the blue blinking light."

"There's the beacon." I knew exactly what kind of light they were using, and from how small it seemed from here, this space was even bigger than I'd first thought. There was room sufficient to land a 747 in here. Not fit...*land*.

Kiratowa was awestruck too. "I do not care for who built this, but it is very impressive. Now, double-time."

We began running again. The giant packs made us look like a bunch of lumbering gastropods, but I wasn't even breathing hard yet and my muscles were fine. I was really glad I'd spent all those days running up and down Moose Mountain.

Though the floor was relatively flat, it wasn't solid. Like Earl had warned, there were gaps. When I glanced over those edges, I could barely make out more openings below. They looked suspiciously like alcoves . . . doorways and windows maybe. Further down were what appeared to be suspended walkways and stairs to who knew where. The open spaces went on further than our lights would pierce, but I got the impression that there were whole ravines full of honeycombed structures below.

"We aren't running across the floor of the cavern, we're on their roof," Gerecht said.

There were dead Asakku everywhere, riddled with bullets, blown apart by shrapnel, or burned to a crisp by flamethrowers. We couldn't spare the time to examine the dead, but they seemed to come in all shapes and sizes, from dwarflike to seven feet tall. From what I saw, they were humanoid, mostly, but I saw some with two sets of arms and all manner of deformities. Some were naked, others clad in loincloths or scuzzy brown robes. The only thing they all had in common was the eerie, nearly translucent skin, which reminded me of the wrapper on a spring roll. We passed piles of leaking bodies. It was a little unnerving, how the solid floor seemed to be so readily absorbing the puddles of blood.

"That's the portal team coming in. Hold your fire," Earl said over the radio.

The blue strobe was on top of a raised dais. A bunch of Hunters had taken up defensive positions all around it, waiting for the next wave of attackers. We started climbing. The stairs were too small, and like everything else in this godforsaken place, constructed with just enough awkward angles to make you uncomfortable.

My boss was waiting for us at the top. Earl was splattered in blood, and he'd been firing his Thompson so much that I could smell the scorched wooden hand guard from ten feet away. Holly was with him, and she was looking a little harried. I knew from personal experience that when your assignment was to follow the indestructible Earl Harbinger into a fight, you became his gopher and ammo caddy. It was exciting, but not what I'd call fun.

"I've got a feeling the Children will be coming back in force. My gut's telling me there's a lot more of them down here and I don't think we've got much time."

"What do you wish for us to do?" Kiratowa asked.

"It's your asses that are going to be hanging in the wind if they force us to retreat."

"Then you had best come back stronger by the time we return, Harbinger. Point us toward the gate."

"Damn, that's what I like to hear." Earl had a savage grin. "Come on. The big brains are checking it out."

The portal was made out of a similar material to the rest of the city, only smooth and round, like a pipe. It must have once been a freestanding structure big enough to drive a car through, but it had collapsed during the bombing, so now it was more of a hole than a gate. When I got closer, I realized that the pipe material had *melted* through the floor. It hadn't fallen over flat, but was instead lying at an odd angle, sloping downward. I couldn't see what was inside the circle, since it was entirely covered in the same unnatural, heavy mist that had engulfed Las Vegas.

The hole was giving off a nasty vibe. It was cold, malevolent, and *awake*.

"I've seen some weird things, but I'll admit that thing is creeping me the hell out," Holly said as I stopped next to her.

She was right. Every instinct was screaming *stay away*. "Don't worry. We got this."

"You'd better." She leaned in close and whispered. "I'll be honest, I cried a little after you asked me to make sure your kid gets Abomination if you don't come back. I don't like it when people make me cry, Z."

"I don't believe that." I forced myself to give her a confident smile. "Everybody knows Holly Newcastle is too tough to cry."

"You ever make me do it again, I'll kick your ass. Now go be heroic."

Ben Cody was kneeling next to the gate, poking it with some sort of instrument that looked like an old-fashioned TV antenna. Paxton was a few feet away reading numbers off a tablet. She looked up as we approached. "Don't touch the round part. It doesn't look it, and it doesn't radiate, but touching it is like touching a stove. You'll leave skin. As for the inside... I'll spare you the mystical mumbo jumbo, but basically, the other side of this reads a lot like what we recorded at the Last Dragon."

"I concur," Cody said. "This is it."

*Good.* Because we could be stepping into some sort of cosmic garbage disposal for all I knew. Now that would be one hell of a trick: get us to come all this way to voluntarily blend ourselves into mush. Only my instincts were telling me this was a door.

Elmo the Elf was along for the ride. "I also concur. I can feel it. This here is a *hynlyfdraws*."

"I assume that's fancy elf talk for nightmare hole," Cody said.

"Yup. Through that fog's a land of de-spair. This here is some right scary old-time witchcraft, likes of which I ain't never seen before. It takes a mighty power to crack the world open."

Cody stood up with a groan. He was way past retirement age. "Well, there you have it, Earl. As near as my instruments and hill folk Gandalf here can tell, this leads to the same place we saw before. That cyclops was telling the truth."

"Are you absolutely sure?"

"We're dealing with the mysteries of the universe here. We don't get absolutes. Everything on the other side laughs at our laws of physics. However, I'm certain enough that if you hadn't shot me down for being too old and broken down, I'd be going through with them."

Earl nodded. That was as good as he was going to get. "All right. It's your show now, Kiratowa."

The Japanese Hunter didn't mess around. He stepped carefully over the hot edge and began walking down into the unnatural mist. After Rothman's warnings that I'd probably be on my own, I had to admit I breathed a sigh of relief when Kiratowa didn't just bounce off the portal. He watched the unnatural fog curl around his legs, but when nothing horrible happened, Kiratowa resumed walking downward. "Let's go."

The rest of us followed.

"You boys hurry back. We'll be waiting."

"We will return as swiftly as possible, Harbinger."

We were leaving a bad place to enter one that would probably be far worse. The mist crawled up my legs. It was thick, and squishy, like being bathed in evil Jell-O. I watched it rise up over my teammates, and then I could barely see my rifle in front of my face. The rest of my team was just dark shapes, walking cautiously onward, but then it got even harder to see. I could hear the others around me, the creak of ballistic nylon, the thrum of boots against stone, the nervous breathing. Then the feel of the ground beneath me changed. I was no longer walking on rock, but on soft dirt.

And then I stepped into a forest.

Confused, I looked around. This was completely different than last time. I was in a clearing, surrounded by pine trees. It was cloudy, but nothing like the fog-choked nightmare world in Vegas. There was plenty of light to see by. A chill rain was falling, and judging by the puddle I was standing in, had been for a while.

Glancing back, the unnatural fog bank was directly behind me, the oily surface still rippling from my passage.

I took a few nervous steps away from the fog. "Hello?" Nobody answered. The rest hadn't made it through. I walked around the fog, which was easy, since it was only about ten feet across and holding way too still. "Gerecht? Kiratowa? Anybody?"

If this was the Nightmare Realm, then everything here would be conspiring to kill me. I scanned my surroundings for threats, but other than the rain, nothing moved. I readied Cazador anyway. The branches were soggy and drooping, great for hiding all sorts of nasty beasts.

I was getting something in my earpiece. It was weak and filled with static, but some signal must have been able to pass through the portal. The voice on the other side sounded like it might be Earl. He was saying something about the team. They'd walked across the portal, come out of the fog, and still been on Earth.

I transmitted back. "This is Pitt. I'm through. Can you read me?"

All I got back were a bunch of hisses, pops, and a few things that might be words. I tried a few more times in vain. Then I decided to try the main command channel. It probably wouldn't work, but the *Bride* had a much stronger radio, so it was worth a shot. "This is Pitt. I'm on the other side of the portal. Can anybody hear me?"

When I got nothing from the main line, I flipped back to my squad's channel. There was a lot of static, but I think Kiratowa was doing a head count, and he sounded furious that they'd gotten turned around.

*Damn it. Professor Rothman had called it.* The gate wasn't for them. It was only for people like me.

"This is Pitt. I'm on the other side. Do you copy?"

I glanced around nervously. It looked just like the Pacific Northwest. There wasn't anything particularly alien or terrifying about my surroundings. I looked back at the fog bank, hoping for some sign of movement, of some other Hunter making it through, but it just lay there, unnatural and thick, taunting me.

I could still turn back. A few steps and I'd be back on Earth. Nobody would blame me for giving up. I even thought about going back *briefly* . . . To check in, to reassess our plans now that we knew I was on my own, but I didn't, because what if it wouldn't let me back through a second time?

I had already given this a lot of thought.

"Harbinger, if you can hear me I'm going to proceed with the rescue mission on my own."

The voice that answered over my radio was deep and creepy. "The Chosen who destroyed our king has returned. Heed our words, trespasser. We shall feast upon your fears until your mind breaks. When nothing remains of you but a gutted husk, we shall take your power, and use it to rain death upon your world."

*Good old Nightmare Realm.* Well, at least that told me I was in the right place and hadn't been magically whisked off to Seattle. "Listen up, alps. Your biggest badass couldn't take me last time. You've got nothing. Come after me and I'll destroy you."

"You will suffer for your transgressions."

The Nachtmar had been made incredibly deadly because of the Mark Thirteen project, able to take our worst fears out of our heads and shape them into reality, but regular alps only had a fraction of its power...hopefully. "Whatever. Stay off my radio, you little shits."

The nightmare feeder didn't respond. Frankly, I was more worried about other beings who had gotten stuck in this realm than some invisible soul-sucking parasites.

I waited in vain for someone else to make it through the fog. At one point I got the impression that another body had tried to make it through. The fog grew turbulent. It seemed to make the whole world buzz and left my ears ringing. I had a sneaky feeling that particular presence had been Earl Harbinger trying to force his way through. He was supposed to stay there and run things, but had probably decided in the heat of the moment that he'd make a bigger difference on the rescue than on the siege. But this wasn't Earl's destiny, so it wasn't meant to be. I bet that really made him mad.

So it looked like I was it.

It was not the most impressive start, but it would have to do. But then something fell out of the fog and landed with a splash in a rain puddle. At first I thought it was a person, since it was big enough, but it was only another backpack. The living were being turned away, but apparently nothing was stopping gear from getting through. I went into the fog to get the pack, but then had to duck out of the way as another heavy bag seemed to fall out of the sky. It almost nailed me in the head. Now that would have been a really ignominious way to die. Brained by luggage, and nobody would ever know.

"This is Pitt, packages received," I transmitted, just in case. "Thanks."

I waited, but there weren't any more presents. So I grabbed the bags and dragged them out of the mud. There was no way I could carry that much extra weight for long, but I could cache these. It never hurt to have some extra goodies stashed. I checked the bags. They were the same as mine: food, water, medical supplies, batteries, and other assorted useful stuff. Somebody had even given up their rifle so I could have a spare. Everybody on the rescue squad had standardized on weapons using the same magazines, so I had a ton of extra .308 loaded in Magpul PMAGs.

Alert for threats the whole time, I found some good hiding places for the other packs. There was a fallen tree not too far from the portal. One bag got stashed beneath it. Then I followed a gully about two hundred yards to a rocky overhang and hid the second bag beneath it. As I was burying the bag beneath rotting leaves and pine needles, I realized that this might be an entirely pointless exercise. The place was supposed to be malleable by the whims of the strongest will present. The dirt on my hands, was it even real? Or did this forest exist only because somebody had wished it into existence, creating some small bit of order out of the swirling chaos? It felt like I was kneeling on a rock, something that to a human mind equaled permanence, but would any of this still be here when I got back?

If it was the strongest mind that shaped the land, what would happen when that mind was gone? Would it degenerate back to what it was before, or would it stay until a new mind came along to twist it into something else? And what would happen to things from the "real" world that were here when that happened?

It beat the hell out of me. The sooner I got out of here the better.

I went back and checked on the gate one last time. The fog was still floating there, being scary, mysterious, but also promising an escape. This was it. Last chance. Return to the relative safety of my friends, or venture into the unknown.

I set out alone into the Nightmare Realm.

# CHAPTER 19

Dr. Rothman was probably right about the treacherous, perpetually shifting nature of this place, but in case he was wrong, I kept track of my path. I hoped all of that land nav training in Alaska would come in handy, except I was limited to matching terrain features and counting my steps. The needle on my compass spun wildly, probably since there was no magnetic poles here. If there was a sun, I couldn't see it through the perpetual gloom.

The sky was nothing but thick storm clouds. The cold rain never let up. I was still dressed for the Arctic Circle, so it wasn't too bad, but the moisture was beginning to leech in everywhere. I'd nearly gone hypothermic yesterday, so I really couldn't afford to get chilled again.

I kept walking, but I didn't know toward what. It wasn't like I had clear directions, beyond *believe extra hard*. I hoped that by keeping the mission at the front of my mind, I could make this awful place show me the way, even if I had to beat it into submission. Laboring under all this gear, downhill would have been easier, but I went up, in the hopes that I could find a good vantage point and maybe spot something. And because up was the direction I went, I told myself it was right, and if it wasn't, too damned bad. I was going to make it *right*. Because screw you, Nightmare Realm, you're not the boss of me.

And shortly after making that decision, I stumbled across a game trail going in the direction I was headed anyway. Was this the answer to my prayers? Or was this the Nightmare Realm screwing with my head and leading me toward disaster? Either way, it beat crashing through the brush, so I took the trail. And then I got to thinking maybe the trail wasn't anything mystical at all. We knew all sorts of weird creatures from various worlds got stuck here just like we had, so what had cut this trail, and how hungry was it?

*Head up, gun out. One foot in front of the other. Find our guys. Go home.*

The dirt was soft, but I didn't see any tracks. I couldn't help but leave boot prints myself. Maybe I would get lucky and one of our survivors would stumble across my obviously-from-Earth tread pattern and investigate. On the downside, whatever predators lived here would have no problem following me.

My watch stopped. I guess you can't tell time in a place that doesn't believe in time. My watch also had an altimeter, but it alternately told me that I was either five thousand feet below sea level or a mile high. That digital display of nonsense was all sorts of helpful.

Hiking through dense forest while waiting for something to ambush you is nerve-wracking. A normal march, you can put your head down, lose yourself in the labor, and plod on forever, but for this I had to stay alert. The rain would mask the noise of anything sneaking up on me, so I kept my head on a swivel, constantly scanning.

Being switched on for hours is tiring.

I had been training hard, but between the clinging mud, slick rocks, moist chill, and stupid pack, I was starting to feel the burn. It was tempting to lighten the load, but I didn't know what I would need. Our guys had survived here for months, so there had to be something to subsist off of. Since I was drenched, the water part was obvious, but there had to be food too.

The trees occasionally thinned out enough that I could see a little further, but in every direction were other thickly wooded slopes. It seemed like I was in a mountain valley, but the tops always remained hidden in the clouds. I felt like I was tantalizingly close to seeing something. Once in a while I got a good look down, and I was pretty certain that I could still find the portal if I needed to. At least the realm hadn't screwed me over yet.

It was endless green below and gray above. It never got dark. The light remained diffuse through the clouds. The rain kept up. Sometimes it would get heavier, then it would die off to a drizzle, but then it would turn back up.

*Why the hell did I decide* up *was the right direction?*

After what my sore feet and back suggested was a whole day of marching, it still looked exactly like Earth. If I got to the top of this endless friggin' mountain and I saw Portland on the other side, I was going to be ticked off, because nothing would be more annoying than fighting your way through the City of Monsters to get teleported to *Portland*.

I spotted a cave and decided to take a rest. It was more of a depression beneath some rocks than a proper cave, barely deep enough to fit me and my pack, but it was nice to get out of the stupid rain for the minute. At first the lack of continual thumping noise against my helmet made me feel like I'd gone deaf. I thought about making a fire, but everything here was too moist to burn, and I wasn't going to waste any of my C4. That stuff burned like crazy. I didn't know how much time had passed, but I was burning a lot of calories and was starving. I broke out a freeze-dried meal pack and took stock of my situation.

We had been expecting something to try and murder the rescue squad as soon as we came through, so we'd been prepared for a fight and kitted up accordingly. Armor is nice when something's actively trying to murder you, but the rest of the time it is heavy and miserably hot. Since it had been me on my lonesome the whole time, and it looked like I was going to be in this for a long haul, I could probably ditch some gear. If I considered this little cave a third cache, I could even convince myself that I wasn't just being a wuss.

I ditched my helmet. I had a skullcap that would keep my head warm, and it weighed a lot less. Trip had given me the big cool-guy Suunto watch for my birthday, but since it was now useless, it could go too. When I got back I'd lie and tell him I'd lost it in a dramatic manner. It was more exciting that way. I hated leaving my armor because with my luck, ten minutes later something would come along and stab, shoot, or bite me . . . But pounds are pounds. I'd be able to move faster this way. Anything that I could eat stayed in the pack. Anything that shot, stabbed, exploded, or made fire, I kept too.

As I went through my pack, I came across the Ziploc bag of oddball items I'd collected while traveling around prepping for this mission. It was a weird mix. I had old dog tags, a class ring, a cigarette lighter, a nice ink pen, a crumpled photograph of someone's wife and kids, and other assorted odds and ends. I had gotten ahold of a personal effect for every single missing Hunter that I could. These were all things that had been important to them, something that they'd held close and carried with them at times. I didn't know if having these knickknacks would make a lick of difference when it came to finding them, but it couldn't hurt. I opened the bag and shook it over my hand, and the first thing that fell out was a glass eye.

It was one of Lococo's spares. It had been in the compound's barracks, where he'd been rooming while going through Newbie training. It's tough to get a closer personal object than one you actually carried in your eye socket. I wasn't good at the magic or mysticism stuff, but I concentrated on that glass ball, hoping that it would show me the way.

Earl swore to me that Lococo was a good man. He had come from a shoddy company, but risen to the occasion, and saved a lot of lives in Copper Lake. He was an ex-con, and had served time for manslaughter, but Earl had seen a lot of potential in him. Lococo had a bright future with MHI. He'd been invited to the Last Dragon because of how far ahead of the other Newbies he'd been. The experienced Hunters teaching his class had thought it would be a *good learning experience.*

And then I'd abandoned him on a roof, surrounded by monsters.

I rolled the eye across my clammy palm. "If you're still alive, Jason, hang on. I'm on the way." It had landed iris up, so it was like it was staring at me accusingly. Talking to myself was weird enough, but I still felt like I needed to explain. "I'm sorry I screwed up your life. You getting stuck here. That's on me. I can't ever make up for what I've done to you, what I've taken from you, but I'm going to bring you back so you can see your daughter again. I'm going to find you and bring you home."

The eye kept staring at me, but I didn't get any big insight on what to do next. I just felt guilty for giving him the glass eye to begin with, and stupid for talking to it now. I made a fist. It was a cold lump in the middle. "I promise."

I put the eye back in the bag, sealed it, and stuck it in my pack. That bag would never be dead weight. That bag was why I was here. I rubbed my hands together for friction and blew on them for warmth. It was time to get back on the trail.

"You've got to be kidding me," I muttered as I reached the top of the mountain and looked out over the weirdest damned thing I'd ever seen.

It took me several seconds—maybe minutes, who could tell anymore?—of uncomprehending staring before my poor mortal brain began to process what my eyes were seeing.

Below me was the evergreen forest I'd been marching through forever. Beyond that, however, was a land of patches, stitched together with protean fog. In the distance was a desert. Beyond that was a jungle made of orange vines. I turned. There was a land of snow next to a land made of fire. To the right was an ocean, to the left, a never-ending waterfall where the ocean fell off the world. All of them lumped together, discordant, right on top of each other, borders crossing and blurring in that chaotic angry fog we had seen before.

The place we'd entered through Las Vegas had been a borderland. The actual Nightmare Realm was like a patchwork quilt of never-ending weirdness. All of these things, they were copies of somewhere else, somewhere real sucked out of a traveler's memories. The fakes were all crammed in together, competing for precious reality, shaped by thousands of minds, some of which were obviously insane.

Then I realized the horizon curved *up*. I craned my head back. The world kept going and going, more petty kingdoms climbing as far as the eye could see. This world could never be represented on a map, because we were *inside* the globe. The clouds I'd been climbing toward weren't clouds at all, just another border, with competing territories intruding from above.

I needed to sit down.

At first I thought I was delusional. I'd hiked through miles of clouds to get this far, and maybe this was oxygen deprivation, or somebody had put a hallucinogenic mushroom in my meal packet or something, because this? This was some psychedelic, weird-ass, mind-blowing, acid trip experience, and I'd seen the Dread Overlord in person.

*Holy shit. There are sky islands.*

Smaller chunks of disintegrating worlds had broken off and were floating like icebergs, colliding with other realities. I had to put my hands on my knees, bow my head, and take a bunch of deep breaths. I focused on the ground beneath my feet. It still looked like Oregon. I could focus on the ground. Ground was okay. Ground was understandable.

When I thought I was ready, I looked up again, saw the skylands, said screw it, and looked back down at my boots again. I really wanted to puke. This was kind of overwhelming.

Those Hunters could be anywhere. I know I was supposed to bring us together by the power of my will, but come on . . . how could I exert my will over *that?* This was insane. I don't give up easy, but right at that moment, looking at just how ridiculously vast this place was, I wanted nothing more than to admit defeat and walk back to the portal.

On the bright side, it had stopped raining.

It turned out that when I was alone for a while, I talked to myself a lot. "Okay. I can do this. I'm feeling a little in over my head is all. Mordechai, Bubba, Sam, if any of you dead guys can hear me, I could really use some guidance right about now. You got away with helping in Vegas because you said the rules were fuzzy. This here is a whole new level of fuzzy, so if you're listening—"

A twig cracked.

I spun around, Cazador flying to my shoulder. Something had moved in the trees behind me. I hadn't imagined it. That was the direction I'd come from. It was the first sound I'd heard from something other than myself or the rain in a long time.

I'd been asking my ghosts for help, but ghosts didn't step on branches. My pulse was pounding, but I wasn't afraid of whatever had made the sound. The elevated heartbeat was a natural side effect from seeing the world broken into puzzle pieces and dumped into a chaotic pile. I was actually thankful for something to take my mind off the weirdness.

Keeping the rifle at the ready, I walked slowly to the side. There was no cover for me to use. I'd walked out into the open of a rocky clearing to get a better view and had let myself get distracted. That had been stupid. Less than fifty yards away, some low-hanging branches swayed as something brushed against them. I saw a flash of white, startling after all the hours of brown and green, and then it was gone.

It wasn't one of my people, and it had seen me. I had nothing to gain by getting into a fight. I needed to get the hell out of here. Having no idea which way to go, I picked a direction and started walking away.

Something slammed into my pack. I slipped on the damp rocks and fell on my side. The noise of the gunshot registered as the sound continued to echo off the mountainside.

There was only a split second of shocked disbelief as I hit the ground. *Who's shooting at me?* But then I was trying to figure out where it had come from. There was black powder smoke rising from the leaves near where I'd seen the movement. A stark white figure rose from the brush, a long pole in its arms. Its head seemed too big for its body as it leaned forward to see if it had killed me.

Lying on my side, I lined up Cazador's side sights on its center of mass, flipped the safety off, and pulled the trigger. *WHUMP.* The .308 bullet hit it square.

By the time it dropped, I was up and running. It's amazing how light a big pack is when the adrenaline hits. I ran toward the threat. There might be more of them in there, but that was the closest cover, and being behind trees was better than being in the open when they had guns.

The thing was on its back, arms thrown wide, a red hole in the center of its white chest. Dead.

_Oh, hell._ It was an Asakku.

I'd not been able to get a good look at the ones in the under city, but this was obviously the same species. This one was short, maybe four and a half feet tall, and skeletally thin. I could see vague dark outlines of its internal organs through its weird stretchy skin. The eyes were solid black and way too big for its face, like they were designed to soak up every bit of light available in a place where there was none. Its teeth were bared in a final death grimace. That hadn't lasted long since I'd blown a hole through its heart, but those teeth were jagged, crooked, and stained yellow. It had one too few fingers, and the digits that it did have were too long, and ended in thick dirty nails which were more like claws. It was wearing nothing but rags and a rough leather strap with some pouches around its waist.

The nearest comparison I could make for the Asakku's appearance was what they used in sci-fi movies for gray aliens. Imagine one of those, but a caveman version . . . on meth.

This wasn't some memory plucked out of my mind and given form by an alp. I'd never fought these before. Some of the Asag's soldiers had found a way through the portal. There could be more. I took a knee next to a tree and listened. The forest was quiet again. My gunshot was suppressed, but the creature's hadn't been. That sound would have carried a long way. If there were more of these here, then they would have heard it.

But thinking about that gunshot, monsters didn't use guns very often. That was bad news. Its weapon had landed a few feet away. I moved over to inspect it and got another surprise. It was a flintlock. My pack had been shot with friggin' *musket*. Only then I realized this was no antique. The proportions of the stock were all wrong. The design was one I'd never seen before, and I'm a huge gun nut. Heck, even the aesthetic was wrong. Look at old firearms in a museum, and no matter how odd, or how much of an evolutionary dead end the design may have been, they still looked like they'd been built by humans for humans.

The Asakku hadn't scavenged this gun. They had built it.

I went back to the body and pulled one of the pouches off its belt. The leather was soft and made out of some mystery animal, but I recognized the contents. Black powder. And in another, lead balls, approximately seventy caliber. Old-school, heavy and slow, like a Brown Bess, which meant it would probably hit like a freight train.

This was bad, *very bad*. The Asakku the lead teams had fought through in the under city had been armed with tooth and claw, not guns. The Petrov Report hadn't mentioned guns either. If there was some monster gunsmith down there now cranking even this low-level technology out, that changed the equation dramatically. I remembered the confusing mess of the City of Monsters, with all of those unknown tunnels like an ant's nest below us . . . If they could make black powder, they could make bombs.

My growing dread was interrupted by another sound. It was a shout, a deep, reverberating bellow that echoed through the forest. That call was answered, repeated several times, and magnified when it was answered by a set of lungs that were nearby. So that was what the Asakku sounded like. I ducked down and waited, but they'd gone silent again. Probably waiting for an answering cry from the one I'd killed. When no answer came, they'd be on the hunt. I didn't know if they were a patrol from the city, or if they were settled here, or what. All I did know was that it sounded like there were a lot of them, they'd heard the gunshot, and they were on the way to investigate.

I picked the direction opposite the calls and started running.

*Could they track me?* The ground was so soft it was almost impossible not to leave prints, but I tried to steer for where there was an undercoat of leaves and needles instead of bare dirt. But could they track by smell? I had no idea. How good was their hearing? I was a big guy and nobody had ever accused me of being stealthy. I'd taped down everything that might rattle and make noise, but I was noisy just by existing. The Asakku had small vestigial ears, but they'd have to be deaf to not hear me crashing through the branches.

After running for a bit, I glanced back over my shoulder and saw white shapes drawing near where I'd left the corpse. Movement attracts the eye. There was a fallen tree to the side, so I got behind it and hunkered down. I waited several seconds, hoping that none of them had been looking in this direction. There were no shouts when they reached the body, but they could be communicating by hand signals.

I needed to be able to see what they were doing, so I shrugged out of my pack in order to low-crawl around the side of the log without it sticking over the top. Mud leaked into everything that was unzipped as I slid around the rotting bark. There was a spot where I could hide beneath a pine bough and still see out. I had only managed to put about three hundred yards between us, but there were a lot of trees in the way. Since they lived underground, maybe I'd be lucky and they'd have terrible vision.

There were snatches of white flesh visible as the Asakku milled around the dead one. I brought Cazador around to get a better look. I didn't care about coating my body in mud, but I tried to keep my rifle out of it. I braced it over the top of the log and took a peek. The scope was turned all the way down, so I cranked it all the way up to twenty-five power to try and see what they were doing through the trees.

They were ripping the body apart and eating it.

Oh, it wasn't enough for them to be freaky underground mutants, but they had to be cannibals too. *Lovely.*

I couldn't get a very clear picture through the pine trees, but it seemed there wasn't much ceremony involved. They just ripped the little guy limb from limb and started cramming meat in their mouths. There were at least four or five of them feasting. It was savage. Within seconds, the white skin was stained red, and their guts were bulging with fresh meat. They couldn't possibly consume it all that fast, but they'd probably pack out the rest to use as a picnic later. I thought about lighting them up. I could probably kill most of the visible ones before they even knew I was here, only I didn't know if they had brought friends.

Then a *really* big one ran up to the bloody crowd. It had to be a good seven feet tall. The other little ones cowered, subservient, as it began barking orders at them. The abnormally deep voice matched the first call I'd heard. That had to be the patrol's leader. Blowing his brains out was super tempting.

Then my scope blacked out as something moved right in front of it.

Instinct told me to hold perfectly still. There were more Asakku dead ahead, less than twenty feet away. I hadn't seen them because they'd come from below and were moving right past me to converge on the others. These were keeping really silent. Not all of them had called out an answer to their summons. If I'd kept running, I would have blundered straight into them.

They were creeping along, slow and predatory. There were three visible, all armed with similar rough muskets. Their physical features varied wildly, with misshapen heads or uneven limbs. Their see-through skin was decorated with chains and bone piercings. I lay there in the mud, ready to shoot, but praying that they'd keep moving.

The last one in line froze.

*Shit.*

I hadn't made a sound. It slowly turned in my direction, giant eyes heavy-lidded, as it raised its crooked nose. Nostrils flared as it inhaled. My scent had been caught.

*Shit. Shit.*

That Asakku let out a low growl. The other two

stopped where they were. One of them drew back the hammer on its musket with a metallic *click*. The one who had smelled me took a step in my direction.

I shot all three of them.

They never even saw what was coming. I was so close I just tilted Cazador, aimed down the side sights, and *thump, thump, thump*. Less than a second elapsed from first to last. Two dropped clean, the middle one wobbled, so I shifted back, *thump*, and put a hole through its forehead. It twitched and jerked the trigger. The flintlock discharged into the ground.

Throughout the forest around me, Asakku roared. It was on now, might as well even up the odds. It wasn't very far for this setup, and there was no wind to throw me off. I went back to the scope, saw the white skin stained red, and interrupted their feast. The big one had moved out of sight, so I aimed at another little one who had just looked up from the arm it had been gnawing on, and fired. It tumbled from view. The rest scattered like roaches.

*Time to go.* I resisted the urge to stand up and bolt. Making myself a big obvious target would draw their attention for sure. Hopefully, my suppressor was keeping them from zeroing in on my position. I rolled over and slid on my butt down the slope, toward where I'd left my pack.

There was a flash of white as more Asakku charged from the trees.

Still on my back, I shot one, but before I could swing my rifle over to the next, it was on me. It shrieked and clawed at my eyes. I got one hand up and grabbed it around the throat, keeping its gnarly snapping teeth away from my face. It was shockingly strong and stank of rotting meat. I squeezed hard, crushing the creature's windpipe. Then I jerked its face down into the log. When it bounced off, teeth were still embedded in the bark.

Black powder roared as another creature fired. The log next to my head exploded in a cloud of splinters. That one immediately lifted its empty weapon, roared a battle cry, and charged. I barely rolled out of the way just as the musket's stock bounced off the ground where I'd been lying. I kicked out, sweeping that Asakku's legs out from under it.

It hit the ground and instantly scrambled toward me, pulling a wickedly curved knife from its belt. There wasn't room to maneuver my rifle, so I yanked my pistol from its holster and started firing before I could even line up the sights. It jerked as a .45 bullet pierced its shoulder, then stopped as I found the front sight and put the next round through the top of its skull.

The one I'd knocked the teeth out of was still twitching and straining for air, so I shot it too, right through the temple. The coast was clear, so I holstered my STI, got to my feet, hoisted up my pack, and started running. I managed to get the straps over my shoulders without tripping and breaking my neck.

Shots rang out. Giant bullets whizzed through the trees. Luckily the Asakku's smooth bores weren't that accurate or they really were blind in the light. Only there were a surprising number of them shooting at me, and volume can make up for inaccuracy. A puff of white smoke erupted through the bushes ahead. I didn't even slow down as I cranked off several rounds from Cazador. A creature fell through the leaves and crashed into the dirt.

After all that climbing, *now* I was heading downhill. It wasn't a conscious decision so much as that was the direction opposite the bellowing and gunshots. Big dudes can make excellent time downhill, provided you don't headbutt a tree trunk or fall off a cliff. It was taking everything I had to keep my footing. If I tripped, by the time I stopped rolling, the monsters would be on me.

I risked a look back. There were a lot of white bodies coming down the mountain. I hadn't blundered into a little patrol. This was more like a war party—and they were gaining on me.

There were too many to stand and fight, but it was time to put some fear into these things. Hopefully they felt fear. I skidded to a stop, searching for a target. I was hoping to drop the leader, but there was no sign of the tall one. Instead, I picked a creature in the open about a hundred and seventy yards away and gaining rapidly. I wanted the others to see this one die.

My pounding heart was making the rifle shake, but at this distance I might as well be shooting a laser beam. The trigger was damned near telepathic. The bullet hit that Asakku in the abdomen. Momentum carried it forward as it spilled down the rocks.

Many of them must have seen my demonstration, because they veered off behind deeper cover or dropped prone. Good. That ought to slow them down a bit. A few snapped off quick shots in retaliation as I started running again.

I was making great time, but had no idea towards where. The further I went down the hill, the more I lost sight of the weird patchwork universe above. I was glad when that view was hidden by the clouds again. But then, because this dimension blows, it started raining again. Hopefully it would get my pursuers' gunpowder wet enough to cause misfires. The underbrush was getting thicker. Branches tore at my face as I lowered my head and plowed through.

The forest here was darker. It was getting hard to see. The perpetual light above hadn't changed, there was just less getting through. Everything was covered in moss, which I quickly discovered was slicker than snot, when I jumped down on a patch and my feet flew out from under me. I hit hard, then slid and rolled about twenty feet down a muddy slope. I tried to protect my scope and my head, in that order. The impact sucked, but nothing broken, I struggled back up and carried on.

My boots splashed through a stream. Desperation grew as I realized I'd run into a ravine. It would take too long to climb out. I couldn't backtrack. There was only one way I could go, but with only one route to choose from, the Asakku could figure out where I was heading and get there first. All I could do was run my ass off in the hopes I found a way out of this fatal funnel before they got there.

A leg-burning half a mile later, I was still following that damned stream. If anything, the sides had gotten even higher and steeper. I wondered if the Nightmare Realm was just messing with me now. I hadn't seen an Asakku for a few minutes, but I could still hear them behind and above me. There was no noise ahead of me, and that was too convenient. It was like I was being herded, but toward what, I didn't know. There's that old saying about when the hunter becomes the hunted, but let me tell you firsthand, it sucks ass.

Ahead, the slopes leveled out. It appeared to be

a grassy clearing. It was one of the few open spaces I'd seen in this claustrophobic forest. If the creatures were clever, they'd be waiting there.

Winded and nervous, I shouldered Cazador and slowed to a cautious walk. My boots were sodden and heavy. I was simultaneously overheated and freezing. This was it. I could feel it. There wasn't much cover along the stream, but I stuck close to one side so as to not expose myself to the whole clearing at once.

Sure enough, some Asakku were waiting for me. One of them jumped the gun and fired its musket. There was a flash and shower of sparks through the trees on the other side. I cringed and waited for more shots, but that one had been firing in the *opposite* direction.

Suddenly, one of the white creatures broke from the tree line, running for its life. Before I could fire, another musket roared and the Asakku was flung forward as a massive bullet punched through its back. *What the hell?* But I wasn't going to complain about the distraction. More of the creatures rose up from where they'd been waiting to ambush me, to turn and meet their new threat.

I came out shooting. If it looked like a methed-out space alien, I put a bullet in it. I emptied my mag, dropped the spent one in the stream, and slammed in another without thinking about it.

"Come on!" someone shouted from inside the tree line. I'd never been happier to hear another human voice before. He was even speaking English, so either I'd found my Hunters or the Nightmare Realm was really screwing with my head.

The Asakku ambushers were pulling back, so I ran toward the voice.

"Over here!" I couldn't make out the speaker at first, since he was so camouflaged he looked like a bush, with leaves and twigs tied through his clothing and his face covered in mud. He was running a ramrod down a bore, reloading one of the monster muskets. "Which one of you got out—Pitt?" It took me a moment to recognize the big man. He had lost a ton of weight and had grown a huge beard and had a strip of cloth for an eye patch. Jason Lococo just stared at me stunned; then he blinked his good eye a few times in disbelief. "Are you really here?"

"Yeah, Lococo. It's me." I'd found them. I'd done it. I'd actually pulled off the impossible. "I'm here to rescue you."

A bullet flew past me and thudded into a nearby tree. I looked over my shoulder and saw a mess of Asakku swarming out of the ravine.

"Some rescue."

"It's what you get! Run!"

# CHAPTER 20

The two of us took off. Lococo was in the lead, home-made ghillie suit bouncing. Judging from how grace-fully he maneuvered his bulk between the trees, he'd gotten a lot of practice fleeing from things. "I know a spot we can lose them. Hopefully it's still there."

"Hopefully it's still there? I hate this dimension!"

"Try surviving here a couple months!" he shouted back.

*A couple?* I had some bad news to give him, if we lived that long.

"Down here." He gestured with the musket. The path was so covered that I wouldn't have seen it without help. We moved quickly. The path turned into a ravine, which turned into a rocky, moss-covered crevasse. It kept getting narrower and narrower. The only light was a thin strip directly above. Water was cascading down the interior. The water would mask our smell. The trickling would dampen the noise. Lococo must have learned some hard lessons about how to stay alive here.

He kept glancing back to make sure I was there,

like he was expecting me to vanish, a figment of his imagination. At one point I started to say something, but he shook his head in the negative, then pointed at the sky. There could be Asakku directly overhead.

The water level got higher, until we were wading in it, hip deep. It was freezing cold. I was soaked. The gap above got smaller until the sky was nothing but a tantalizing sliver of light streaming in. It was so dark Lococo was just a hulking shape ahead of me, laboring through the water. I felt that the Nightmare Realm's disembodied denizens were in there with us, plucking away at our sanity. They did their best work in the dark. I really wanted to turn on a flashlight to chase them away, but that would just bring the physical monsters down on our heads.

I don't know how long we continued on in silence, through that crack in the rock, when a gray light began to grow ahead of us. There was a growing roar. The stream we were wading through ended with a waterfall.

It was a great feeling, getting out into the light, even this half-assed, not real, perpetual pseudo sunlight. We came out on a flat rocky shelf. Ahead of us was a steep drop-off, behind us was a moss cliff face. Somewhere up above were the monsters.

"I think we lost them," Lococo said. "We should be safe for now."

I walked to the edge and looked over. The water fell for hundreds of feet, terminating in a misty valley far below. There was forest on the other side, but that mist almost felt more like another hole in the fabric of this world than a river. If we needed to bail out again, it was also the only exit I could see. "Where's that go?"

"Don't know. None of that was down there the last time I was here... You said rescue. Where's everybody else?"

"I'm it," I said, exhausted and shivering.

"How? Never mind." He took that pathetic revelation surprisingly well. When you've been in a hopeless situation so long, anything was a big step up. "Okay. It don't matter as long as you got a way back to the real world. You have a way out, right?"

"Probably."

"Home..." Lococo was even bigger and uglier than me, but when that idea finally sank in, he looked like he was about to cry. It was as if he'd been so focused on just existing he'd forgotten there was anything after that. Even after being alone all this time, the man was still hard as nails. He turned away before openly displaying any emotion.

"It's going to be okay, man."

His shoulders were shaking like he was trying not to sob. His voice cracked as he spoke. "I never thought I'd make it home."

I couldn't begin to imagine what he'd gone through to survive here, but I'm not good at comforting people. "I've got a way out. There's a whole army of Hunters waiting for us."

"Sorry. I... it's been a while since I've had anybody to talk to. The quiet eats at you." He wiped his face with the back of his filthy hand, turned around, gritted his teeth, and gave me a determined nod. It was hard to judge someone's emotional state when you could barely see their face through the mud, but I think he was on the hysterical border between relieved and stunned. "I'll be fine."

"I can still find my way back to the portal I came through, and if not, I've got an artifact that is supposed to show the way. I can take you there now."

That seemed to surprise him. "No! I mean, I can't leave yet. I didn't get here alone, I don't want to leave that way. I know where some others are being held captive. I'll need help to get them out."

Earl had been right about the guy. Lococo was hardcore. Even after everything he'd been through, he was still putting others first. "That's fine. I'm all in. I'm not leaving anybody." I regretted saying that as soon as the words left my mouth. I'd already left him behind once. "Not again. We're bringing them all home."

Lococo could have let me have it then, and I would have deserved it, but he only nodded slowly. "Good. Okay, I'll have to get you up to speed first. Come on, Pitt. I've got another hiding spot nearby where we can make a fire. You got a lighter?"

"Yeah. I carried one of everything up this friggin' mountain."

"Thank God. I'm so tired of rubbing sticks on each other."

The hiding spot wasn't what I had expected at all. "How'd a school bus end up here?"

It was an old, rusty hulk now, sunken into the ground, wedged between two giant redwoods, with only the front end sticking out. There was moss growing over much of the metal, but there were still spots where I could clearly see the faded yellow paint. The bus was an antique, but I didn't know enough about cars to guess an age. 1960s maybe? It had been here a really long time.

"I don't know." Lococo said as he climbed up the bus steps. The door had fallen off a long time ago. "This place is messed up. I once saw what I think was an old German U-boat wrecked way up on the side of a mountain."

I followed him in. Both of us had to duck not to hit our heads. All the windows were long since broken. Most of the seats were still here. I didn't know what I'd been expecting, but I was really glad there were no little-kid skeletons sitting in them. The floor was rusted, but still solid enough that even two really big dudes didn't fall through it. Lococo leaned his musket against a wall and began gathering some kindling that had been previously piled out of the rain to dry out. He went to the back, to the hole where the emergency exit had been, and hopped down. There was a sunken spot between the trunks of the great trees with a fire pit of stacked stones.

Lococo began arranging the kindling. "It's dry and warm air gets trapped in the bus. Smoke goes up between the branches, so you can't see it from very far off. This place is like a palace. Give me that lighter," he said.

It felt so good to drop my pack. I had the backache from hell. I found one of the lighters and tossed it to him.

Lococo caught it and went to work. "I never could find a path to that submarine. I tried. The mountain wouldn't let me. Paths kept disappearing. It'll mess with your sense of direction if you let it. I kept imagining that there would be some old German guns inside of it. Better than that smoke pole I stole off a dead skinny. I've been running around with that thing like

I'm the last of the Mohicans. My guns didn't last too
long. By the time I learned how to live here, I'd either
lost them or run out of ammo. I figured at least an
old Nazi gun would shoot straight. That skinny piece
of trash can't hit the broad side of a barn, but the
Assaku are half blind anyway, so they don't care. They
just toss a bunch of lead your way and hope for the
best." It took him several fumbling tries to get the
lighter struck with his shaking fingers.

"I don't remember you being this talkative."

"I didn't like you. Why would we talk? I still don't
like you, I've just been...lonely."

"No offense taken."

"Screw you." Lococo leaned down and blew on
the flame, coaxing it to burn. "Prison, there's at least
conversation. You're not in your head. This is like
solitary confinement, but forever."

"Whatever you need to do to get by...So what
happened to everybody else?"

He wasn't ready to answer that yet. "Look at all
that fire already. You have no idea how happy that
makes me. Nothing is ever that easy here. Pass me
some sticks."

I did. "I've got some food. You want some?"

"Food?" He looked up from the fire, seeming a
little confused by the offer. "Food...Yeah. Sure. It's
been so long I've forgotten about food. I don't know
if I can eat or not. I can try."

Now it was my turn to be confused. "What do
you mean? There's got to be something. You've been
living off the land."

"Heh...Literally." Lococo shook his shaggy head,
seemingly amused at the idea. "Man, living in the

real world spoils you. You don't know yet, do you? No. You haven't been here long enough. When we ran out of supplies, I was starving, but we couldn't quit moving or we'd die. I just kept going and going, until one day I realized I was still alive but I couldn't remember the last time I'd eaten. There's no food in this place. The land, it keeps you alive. You're always hungry, always shaky and weak, but it won't let you waste away. Oh no . . . dying is too easy."

I didn't know what to say. That was awful.

"When we first got lost, it didn't take us long to figure out the things that live here eat our fear; the rest of you were still around for that."

"The alps, the nightmare feeders, you mean."

"Yeah, sure. The little invisible bastards, always there, always watching and sucking your life away. It's like they shove a straw in your mind and slurp out whatever it is they live on. Oh, yeah, the fear ones you met in Vegas? We found out they aren't alone. In this place there's other things that eat your loneliness, your doubt, sadness, regret . . . and some of them just want you to be hungry. Always hungry. It's a win-win. All those alps get fed, you're miserable in a hundred different ways, but you get to stay alive a little longer. I think they call that a symbiotic relationship."

"I'm sorry."

"You should be. It's your fault I'm here."

*Ouch.*

"You ever starve, Pitt? I don't mean skip a meal and get a tummy ache. I mean, get to where you can feel your own body eating itself?"

"No."

"Didn't think so. It's shit. At least normally, you'd

die after a while, but I just keep on going. I don't know. I think I got so used to it and kind of accept it, the monsters can't be getting much suffering from me anymore ... I think when you're all wrung out, that's when this place lets you die."

Maybe the Asakku weren't normally cannibals. They might have just been here long enough that they'd become that desperate. I reached into my pack and found a rubber meal pack. I extended it toward him. "Have some rebellion."

He studied the pack suspiciously. "Beef stroganoff."

"It's better than it sounds."

He took it. "I got so hungry I tried eating dirt for a while. It didn't work." He ripped the corner off the pack and squeezed a little bit of food directly into his mouth. "Oh man ..." It was like he'd forgotten how to chew. He held it there for a long time, grimacing like the unfamiliar sensation was hurting his taste buds. "That's way better than dirt." He squirted a little more in.

"Yeah, well, take it easy." I remembered reading about starving concentration camp victims dying because having food again was too much of a shock to the system. He wasn't nearly that emaciated—this place had to keep you fit enough to keep running for your life, after all—but it still couldn't be good for him to overdo it. "You haven't eaten real food in like six months. It would suck to survive the Nightmare Realm to die from a stroganoff overdose."

Lococo gave me an incredulous look. "I've been gone half a year, huh? Way to break it to me easy."

"Sorry." I sat down on one of the bus seats. The cushion was long gone. The metal creaked under my weight, but it didn't break. "It is what it is."

"How come you're by yourself anyway?"

"The gate wouldn't let anybody else through. We had a whole squad wander through the mist, but I'm it."

"What makes you special?"

"I drew the short straw. It's a long story."

Lococo snorted. "I'd hate for it to cut into my busy social calendar."

"This is going to sound nuts, but some powerful entities pick certain people to be their champions, fight the forces of evil, save the world, that sort of thing. I'm one of them. I guess it's got some perks."

He lay down on his back next to the fire and just kept slowly chewing on the MRE, lost in thought. I was sure he'd talk about the others when he was ready. The man had been through enough that I wasn't going to start pushing him now. Lococo seemed relatively sane, all things considered, but that could be a façade that would crack under pressure. I took my boots off so I could dry my socks by the fire. There might be alps who fed off of suffering, but the ones who lived off of blisters and foot pain were going to be out of luck.

Lococo was staring up, watching the smoke curl around the branches. "The last time I saw the other Hunters was when we got attacked by a bunch of weird creatures. I didn't recognize them—we must not have gotten to that part in training yet—but VanZant said they were Fey."

That was a really broad category of monsters. They may have shared a similar origin now lost to the mists of time, but Fey were a diverse bunch. We grouped everything in there from crafty Baba Yaga to slimy *Vodyanoy*, to the super powerful royal courts which wielded magic as complacently as we used electricity. MHI had dealt with a lot of Fey over the years, and with only a couple of notable exceptions, most of those dealings hadn't gone well.

"Did VanZant say what kind of Fey they were?"

"No time. They came out of the sky riding these big horse-bug monster things. They ran us down...fast. We never had a chance. We were low on ammo. They were wearing armor, like old-time knights, only pitch-black, hideous like nothing you've ever seen. They could have killed us easy, but they didn't. They wanted us alive. They beat us down or threw nets over us. I got away...hid...Not my proudest moment, but there wasn't nothing I could do but watch. They tied everybody up and dragged them off."

Unlike Lococo, I'd gone through all of MHI's monster familiarization training and then some. I knew exactly what that description sounded like, and it was bad news. "You know where they were taken?"

"A fortress made of bone on an island in the sky."

I sighed.

"Don't worry. There's stairs."

I was too tired to dwell on it now. Stupid tired. The alps who feasted on weariness were going to be stuffed. I couldn't even begin to estimate how long I'd been here, and I had been marching or running the entire time. It was sleep soon or crash. Going off of my condition and memory, I felt like I'd been up for at least thirty hours, probably more, but with no outside stimuli to peg, it was really hard to tell. No wonder Lococo had lost track of the days.

It was easy to feel overwhelmed, but I'd made it this far. In the morning—or whatever passed for that here—I'd have a better idea how to accomplish the impossible: to get the rest of our men back from a Wild Hunt.

Lococo had been quiet so long that I thought he'd fallen asleep, but then he spoke up. "Man, I've been here a really long time."

"I imagine it's hard to tell how much time has passed when there's no night."

He chuckled. "You've got a lot to learn, Pitt. There may not be night, but there's darkness. There's darkness here plenty, just waiting. Eventually, darkness always falls. You ain't seen nothing yet."

As befitted a land where bad dreams came from, I had the worst nightmares, but I couldn't tell you what any of them were about. The whole night was just a bizarre fever dream of disjointed imagery.

When there's no sunrise and everything sounds the same, you just kind of wake up when you wake up. The fire was out. The ashes weren't even warm anymore. I'd been out for a while. At least my socks were dry. Lococo hadn't gone insane and slit my throat in my sleep in revenge for me getting him stuck here, so that was nice too.

Every muscle was stiff, and I would never shake this chill, but besides that I was actually feeling about as well rested as I could hope. Lococo was sitting in the driver's seat. That same food pack was on the mossy dash, now half empty, but I hadn't woken to the sound of violent vomiting, so apparently that was working out for him. He was studying something metallic in the palm of his hand.

"What's that?"

Lococo turned around, then held it up to show me the familiar Happy Face company logo. It was one of the MHI challenge coins Earl had made. "Harbinger gave it to me. I had it on me when I got stuck here.... Metal. Solid. Good reminder of the real world." He stuck the small treasure back into his coat. At some point he'd scrubbed the mud off his face, and other than resembling a crazed 1700s fur trapper, was looking like he was doing alright. "How'd you sleep, Pitt?"

"Other than crammed into a rusty bus while invisible demons torment my dreams? Awesome."

"Good. You're doing better than most. Keep that attitude. The nightmares wrecked everyone else when we first got here. Sleep is when they get your best fear. They like to keep you rattled. Some of the guys really fell apart."

"How about you?"

Lococo didn't answer.

I stretched my aching back. I suspected I knew why I'd been fine. The elves called me a Dreamer, but I think that just meant the whole weird psychic Chosen thing worked better when I was in that state. In fact, my biggest disappointment on this trip was that I'd not heard anything from any of my regular ghostly advisors yet. Mordechai Byreika would have probably given me some helpful, if cryptic, advice. Bubba Shackleford the same, only he'd probably tell me to toughen up in the process. And Sam Haven? He'd probably just go fight the Fey himself.

Normally, the closer I was to death, the better the reception. Or another way to look at it, the further I was from regular human reality, the more likely I was to hear from the dead, and I'd left good-old-normal Earth way back in the rearview mirror this time. Sam had told me in Vegas that the rules were blurry here, so even our dead could join in and actively participate in the fight. But so far, nothing.

And that was really concerning me.

I started putting my boots on. "How far is this fortress from here?"

"Distance is kind of hard to—"

"Yeah, I know. Everything is all weird and immeasurable."

"Well, it don't help that I don't have depth perception, on account of only having the one eye . . ."

"Never mind."

Lococo shrugged. "You asked."

"Which way?"

He pointed up—the opposite direction of where I'd come from.

"I've got a cache with some extra equipment and weapons, but it's way down in the valley by the portal."

"Bad move. That's skinny territory. It's a miracle they didn't run into you sooner. We go all the way down to the deep mists, then back up to the broken sky, we're bound to be seen. From here it's better to go straight across the fog fence to the death swamp and the skeleton tower."

"You couldn't name any of the landmarks anything happy, could you?"

"I'm a literal kind of guy."

I began gathering my gear so we could head out. I noticed the other Hunter had his hand on the steering wheel and it was shaking badly. Mentally and physically, Lococo was in bad shape. I honestly didn't know how he'd made it this far. "You know, I could take you to the exit. You go home, then I'd head back up here to get the rest. You've been through enough."

The driver's seat creaked as Lococo leaned back, thinking my offer over. "You really want to die that badly?"

"That's not plan A."

Lococo snarled at me, insulted. "You're a fool, Pitt. You've got access to a guide who's learned how to survive here, and you'd give up that advantage for what? Pity? Guilt?" For the first time the big man seemed truly disgusted. "That's pathetic."

"I was just making the offer. Take it or leave it."

Only Lococo had gotten angry. I must have really offended him. "This is war. You have a resource. You use it."

The attitude was pissing me off. "I was trying to show some sympathy. I didn't know you needed to learn Sun Tzu to get your prison GED."

"Prison is a better teacher than any you've ever had. You said *they* chose you to be their champion, but how do they expect you to put up a worthwhile fight if you make decisions based on weakness? You talk about the 'forces of evil,' like you have a clue what that means, but then you go and underestimate them. You *disrespect* them. Do you really think your enemy is going to allow you the luxury of being soft?"

I had no logical response to that. It was the same kind of thing Dad had tried to beat into me back when he was trying to train for the end of the world. "Mercy doesn't make you weak."

"If you believe bullshit platitudes like that, they chose poorly. You're destined to lose. If you expect to win, you'd better be willing to step up and make sacrifices."

Maybe it was the aches and pains, the bad sleep, or just this rotten world, but I lost my temper. "I was willing to sacrifice you once already!" It was horrible, but true, and I was simultaneously glad and regretful that I'd said it. "I got the job done. I always get the job done. I gave up a few to save hundreds. And I'd do it again in a heartbeat if I had to."

Lococo just stared at me, stone-faced, but slowly a smile formed. It turned into a malicious grin. He began to laugh. "That's more like it. Maybe you weren't such a bad choice after all."

I picked up my rifle and my pack. If my arms were full, I'd be less tempted to punch him in the mouth. "Up yours, then. Let's go kill some Fey."

# CHAPTER 21

We hiked for what felt like hours, first down a different slope, and then up a much steeper mountain trail. The grade was killing my legs, but Lococo was confident that he knew the way, and there wouldn't be any Asakku in this region. Apparently the Fey and Asag's Children didn't get along. Twice, Lococo had seen them run into each other, and both times had resulted in the Asakku getting slaughtered.

Occasionally I would play with my ancient Roman pinky ring. It didn't feel particularly magical or awe-inspiring for an artifact, but I could have sworn that I could feel the tiniest of pressures, almost imperceptible, but pushing in the direction of the portal home. Either that or it was all in my imagination.

Lococo took the lead, his hulking shape looking like a mobile bush. His clothing was tattered rags, and he had laced foliage through all the holes in his jacket. His hood was wreathed in leaves. When he went prone, he was pretty much invisible. I'd offered him some of my dry clothes, but he'd turned me down. He had a system that worked. Why mess with it?

It was quiet except for the rain. All I could smell was damp. This land was actually beautiful. Any of the occasional sweeping vistas would make a nice painting. But that was just to taunt you, because the reality of being here was nothing but perpetual discomfort. We were both breathing hard from the exertion, and when we came across some leaning rocks that would temporarily shelter us from the rain, we took a rest.

He'd polished off the stroganoff without puking his guts up, so I tossed him another meal pack. "So, of you guys, which mind came up with this awful place?"

"Pork patties in sauce. Great," Lococo stated as he read the package. "This place is on me, I think."

"I always wanted to die grim and soggy. Thanks for that. But the woods . . . I thought you were a city boy?"

"I am. But when I was a kid I spent some time at a juvenile detention center up in Northern California. I heard it wasn't normally that bad, but I lucked out and got there the one year it rained all the time." He ripped the rubberized pack open and smelled the contents. "This one might be close to dirt."

"You can go back to starving. It's no skin off my nose." But if he ate it, I didn't have to carry it anymore. I'd probably regret that eventually. I got out another pack for my lunch.

"In rain just like this, the guards had us clear brush all day. They said it was to build character. It was a bunch of hood rats and delinquents whining in the mud, moving sticks with their soft, little, no-callus hands."

"Sounds fun."

"I hated that place so much. All I could remember was trees forever and always being cold and damp.

So here we go again. Of course it isn't going to pick our favorite place and make the world into that. That broken sky would be all tropical islands and alien strip clubs. Naw, it picks the worst thing you remember and blows it all out of proportion."

If his theory was correct, we really needed to get out of here before the realm switched over to the worst places from my memory, because I really didn't want to see their take on the Dread Overlord's endless dimension of madness and suck.

"My real juvenile facility at least had the sun shine once in a while, but not here. You've almost got to admire the alps' ability to accentuate the bad. They're like artists who paint with suffering. On the bright side, the skinnies have a hard time keeping their powder dry in the rain, so when they try to shoot you, they get a lot of misfires. They could have used my old neighborhood; that was pretty nasty too, but I wouldn't mind that so much. My pops was in prison and my mom was a druggie, so I learned to get by young. You get to be okay with crime and violence, especially when you're good at it." Apparently Lococo was back to rambling because he hadn't had anyone to talk to for so long. "So this is a glimpse of my youth. What about you, Pitt? You were a killer in the ring, so I'm guessing your life wasn't too squishy."

I had to smile and shake my head at the question. By his standards my formative years had been downright comfy. "Military brat. Lots of moving around until my dad retired. Never rich, but not too poor. It was okay."

"Bullshit. I fought a lot of tough guys and made a lot of money doing it. When I put a beating on

somebody, they usually had the good sense to quit."
He held up one fist. The knuckles were misshapen
and crisscrossed with scars. "Men don't fight like you
do unless they got a chip on their shoulder, trying to
prove something to someone."

He was a lot more perceptive than I gave him credit
for. I was used to being the big ugly one, constantly
underestimated because I was smarter than I looked.
But Lococo was bigger and uglier than me, and an
ex-con to boot, so I'd fallen into the same silly trap
that some people did with me. "Yeah. I guess so...
My dad was a warrior. I'm not talking philosophically
or metaphorically. Literal warrior. He was a Green
Beret and got the Medal of Honor."

"No kidding? He won the Medal of Honor?"

"He'd correct you if he heard you say that. There's
no *winning* involved. He just did things when nobody
else could, with no concern for himself, bona fide
hero with zero fucks to give. His dad was a GI from
the States, but he grew up in the Islands, dirt poor.
You look at pics of him when he was just a kid, even
then he was like this block of muscle and grumpiness.
I never saw a single photo where he was smiling. He
always looked determined, you know? So tough, even
as an old man he makes both of us look like wimps.
My whole life he pushed me hard to be like him.
He taught me how to fight, how to shoot, and when
his lessons didn't always sink in, he'd take me to old
friends he respected and have them teach me instead.
Judging by the frequency, I think his favorite words
were *try harder.*"

"That actually sounds kind of badass."

"Yeah...now. Paranoid survivalist sounds great.

Back then? It was harsh. Dad was stern. We had to be the best at everything. 'A Pitt never does anything half ass.'" When I tried to sound like him, it made me smile, but then that just made me sad. "Man, we fought a lot. It wasn't just the physical toughness, but the mental too. He wanted us to be smart; he always said to be smart like Mom's side of the family—they were the doctors and the engineers—but actually Dad was really good at crunching numbers in his head. I guess I inherited that from him. Math and a mean streak..."

Lococo was just listening. With everything going on during the invasion, I'd been too busy to think about my father. I guess it was my turn to ramble. "He was harder on my brother: good kid, friggin' brilliant, turned out to be a musical prodigy, but he wasn't naturally combative like me and Dad. Mosh wants people to like him. Me? I'm inclined to piss people off. Can't help it. After we grew up, Mosh could hold a grudge like nobody's business. I think Dad knew he was too hard on us all those years, but by then it was too late. As grown-ups we barely talked, and he didn't see Mosh at all. For a long time we drifted apart. Though I think Dad actually liked the break. For a few years he got to live a regular life; we weren't his problem anymore. Hell, he even took up *golf.* He could be a normal man, without worrying every minute about some prophecy about getting his sons ready for the apocalypse."

"Huh?"

I gestured angrily at the stupid evil forest. "He knew this was coming. You know there's that stereotype about how somebody who has seen war won't talk about it? Not my dad. There was no problem talking about all the gory details. That was just how he was wired. So I never realized just how many secrets he'd kept. I think he never told us about the supernatural things he'd seen because he was holding out hope that we'd dodge a bullet. It wasn't until a few years ago I learned why he was the way he was. All this? *They* showed him. He was like me—Chosen. Only his job was to get the next generation ready. Looking back, Dad took his charge real serious, and he was kind of an ass about it, but if he hadn't been so damned good at it, I'd be dead a dozen times over already." My throat was getting tight. My eyes were starting to water. "And I love him for it."

"He sounds like a hell of a guy. You get us all out of here, I'll personally shake his hand and tell him thanks for raising you not to punk out."

I sucked on my teeth, then spit on the ground. "You can't. He passed away a few days ago...Hell, I'm here missing his funeral."

"Oh..." For once Lococo didn't seem to know what to say. "How'd he die?"

"His job was done. He was supposed to get me ready. And here I am. So they—the ones who picked us—they let him die. I was on the path they wanted. He wasn't of any use to them anymore...so they... they just let him go. Let him waste away in a hospital bed." I had to stop talking.

"I'm sorry to hear that, Pitt. My condolences."

I just nodded.

We were quiet for a long time, chewing on our rations in awkward silence. I couldn't even taste what my MRE was. It might as well have been ashes.

"Hmmm..." Lococo was staring off into the rain. "What?"

"A death like that, for that kind of man, hardly seems fair. It sounds like they used him up and threw him away. You talked about how these things chose you to fight the forces of evil, but are you certain which side is which?"

I wasn't hungry anymore. "Let's go."

There was a flash of lightning, followed shortly by a rumble of thunder.

I froze. Normally in a rainstorm, thunder and lightning wouldn't be so disconcerting, but in this perpetual rain of never-ending dreariness, that was different. And anything different was scary.

We were making our way up a narrow rocky path on the side of the mountain. Below us was a sea of green, and above that was nothing but roiling clouds for miles. Lococo turned around. "It's the Fey. We've got to hide!" The nearest cover was a hundred yards ahead. "Run."

The path was only a few feet wide, barely enough to fit either of us, and it was slippery. We'd been creeping along with one hand against the rock face, because it was a *long* way down. Going over the side meant, at minimum, a bunch of broken bones. Falling was a bad way to die, but the Wild Hunt was worse. Heedless of danger, Lococo sprinted up the trail. I was right behind him.

Lightning struck again. It cast gigantic shadows of alien horsemen against the clouds, horns and antlers, banners whipping, spears lifted high. The thunder nearly shook me from my feet. Off balance a bit, I looked over the side as gravel fell *forever*, but I kept going.

The riders in the sky were barely visible, just black shapes, but they were getting bigger. They weren't flying. They were galloping. These things did not give a crap about the laws of physics.

Ahead, the trail widened out a bit and there were a few bushes and scraggly, crooked trees. Lococo got there first, crouched down, and made sure his leaf-covered hood was up. I was almost there.

*Crack!*

Three feet of trail broke right off the mountainside . . . while I was running across it.

The world tilted as I slid toward my doom. Desperate, I reached out. My fingers struck, grinding across the stone, tearing the skin from my fingertips. I ripped off a fingernail as I hooked a rock. My shoulder popped as all my weight hit.

By a miracle, I held on.

Fall interrupted, I was left dangling by my right hand from a jagged lip of rock, hanging in space.

*Don't look down. Don't look down.*

I looked down just as the broken piece of trail shattered against a boulder far below. My teeth were clenched too tight to scream. As I looked up, dust fell in my eyes. I'd dropped several feet. I couldn't see anything else to grab onto.

My fingers were burning. There was nothing to get my feet on. I swung my other hand up, searching for something, anything, to hold. That hand scraped uselessly across cracks and gashes too narrow to cling to. *Nothing.*

Water and blood were running down my palm. My handhold was beginning to slip.

Maybe there was something I could latch onto a

little higher. Grimacing, bicep straining, I pulled myself up with one arm. Back home on a comfy pull-up bar, I could do that no problem. With the weight of my weapons, ammo, and gear it was really hard, but I was *super motivated*.

Still nothing to grab onto.

The Wild Hunt was getting closer.

My fingers were slipping. Skin was tearing.

The Fey would see me. Then we were both dead. If I let go, they might not see Lococo. He'd still have a chance . . .

"Pitt!" I looked up just as Lococo appeared over the edge. He extended his hand, but I'd fallen further than I'd realized. He was too far to reach. "Hang on."

Funny, I couldn't think of a snappy comeback right then.

Then he stuck the musket over the side. I reached up with my free hand and got hold of the stock. I was careful to avoid the trigger, because if I'd accidentally shot him right then, that would have been *really* bad.

Thankfully, Lococo was still one *strong* son of a bitch. He hauled me up. I found another handhold. Then a foothold. And then Lococo tumbled back, and I flopped over the edge.

A hunting horn blew.

After nearly falling to your death, your natural inclination is to catch your breath. That was not an option. Both of us crawled toward the bushes. Cazador was bouncing against my chest. If it hadn't been slung to my body, I would've lost it. We took cover. I crawled beneath the wet leaves and lay there, gasping, trying to become one with the ground as the Fey passed by.

For the next few painful minutes, I huddled there,

still as I could be, while the Wild Hunt roared past. I don't know how hooves could hammer air, but these did, with a vibration that I could feel in my teeth.

They were terrifying. Black armor gleamed, slick with rain, popping with static electricity. Their steeds were monstrous creatures, an unholy combination of horse and insect. The riders were jagged steel, melded with flesh, white teeth shining beneath their helmets. Some carried a standard, black and ragged, flapping in the wind, with words written in alien runes that burned my eyes but wouldn't let me look away.

From the way they rode, they were proud and looking for a fight. Every instinct told me these things were absolutely deadly. The parade went on, terrible and awe-inspiring. Monstrous hounds snapped and barked as they ran between the mighty hooves.

Visors turned our way, but thankfully, didn't linger.

And then they were past.

I lay there for a long time after that, quivering, in a puddle of rain and sweat, glad to be alive. After I was positive they were gone, I waited a little bit longer to be sure, then I said, "You saved my life. Thank you."

"I probably didn't do you a favor. Falling would have been a much quicker way to die."

"You doing okay, Lococo?"

"Considering we're chasing *that* . . . What do you think?"

I was feeling a little overwhelmed myself.

The march to the tower took days. Or at least I think it did. It was pretty much impossible to tell here. It turns out time gets even fuzzier at the edges of a world.

We'd walk until we were so tired we were in danger of sleepwalking off a cliff, then we'd try to find someplace semidry to crash. The nightmares were continuous but impossible to remember. The only reason we slept at all was because physical exhaustion is the best sleeping pill ever. Split between the two of us, my food had run out fast. Now it was nearly gone, and you can only ration it so much when you're burning this many calories. There was plenty of water. Lococo swore that it tasted fine, but I didn't trust it that much, so mine all tasted like iodine and my portable water filter.

Since all he had for weapons was a dead skinny's musket and a knife, I'd given my .45 STI to Lococo. I'd made him promise to give it back. My wife had made those custom pistols as a gift, one long slide and a matching compact, originally meant for her brother Ray, but after he'd died, she'd given them to me. I'd killed a lot of things with that big pistol over the years, so I was rather fond of it. I felt naked without a handgun on my hip, but I'll be honest: walking this damned far I wasn't missing the weight.

The rain turned to mist, then a thick fog which reminded me of the gelatinous stuff at the gate. The forest grew deeper, darker, and weirder. It changed from the Pacific Northwest to something out of Grimms' fairy tales. The trees were all old and gnarled. The bark formed too many convenient face shapes, and those faces always seemed to be afraid. The leaking sap looked like congealed blood. It smelled like something had died. The soil was black as a fertilized battlefield. Everything here was twisted.

We had entered a Fey kingdom.

If I'd thought the nightmares had been bad in the

place constructed out of Lococo's memories, this place was *awful*. It was flashes of weird beasts, crying children, loved ones being carried off during the night, villages with straw roofs burning, hooves thundering across a field, and refugees fleeing. I dreamed about my dad, dying in his bed, only this time he was desperately trying to warn me of something. I saw Julie, sobbing over an empty crib.

And I woke up in the "morning" pissed off and ready to show this awful place who was boss.

Lococo was already up, sitting on a log. "Wakey wakey, Pitt. It shouldn't be too far now."

"Define far."

"Before the next sleep . . . Man, that sounds odd. I miss sunrise. Okay, I've been thinking. The last time I saw this place, the Fey had a fortress. Like a literal need-a-big-ass-ladder-to-get-over-the-wall fortress, and I got no idea how to get inside."

I groaned and stretched. I never thought I'd miss the comfort of the warm, constantly seasick rocking of my cot on the *Bride of Krasnov*. "I figured we'd wing it," I said sarcastically.

"Since we're going to go storm a castle full of them, what do you know about Fey?"

I rolled out from beneath my comfy rock. "That's like asking what I know about *mammals*. Fey is a really broad category." I wandered off to relieve myself, but not too far. The fog was much nicer than the rain, but I always suspected that there was something hiding in it waiting to kill us.

When I got back, Lococo said, "Tell me what you know about Fey anyway. Imagine you're teaching a Newbie."

"Technically, I am." I grinned. Lococo just smiled and shook his head. Sure, we'd beaten the shit out of each other twice, but you march through hell with a guy, eventually you start to become friends. "What do you want to know?"

"How the legendary Owen Zastava Pitt plans to do the impossible. So dazzle me with your brilliance, asshole."

Monster lore wasn't really my area of expertise. Somebody like Lee or Rigby would be able to rattle off all sorts of myths and legends, and even tell you the page number of whatever old book it was in. I'd always been more pragmatic: where's the bad thing at and how do I kill it? Half the time, the stuff Hunters thought we knew about the supernatural turned out to be wrong anyway. Anybody who thought they knew everything there was to know about a particular monster was either lying or in for a nasty surprise.

"Some Fey are evil, some are . . . I wouldn't say good, but not outright hostile. These things kidnapped our guys, so I'll assume the worst. Some are really intelligent, others just want to eat your face. Some are organized and legalistic. They even have a type of government made out of rival courts, and those have heavy duty Fey knights like we saw. But other Fey have a reputation for being tricksters, and they just like the chaos."

"Every wannabe thinks they're good at spreading chaos." Lococo snorted. "So basically, you don't know shit about the Fey."

"I never claimed to be an expert. We lump all sorts of things in that category. They all originate from the same world, and there used to be a lot more of them on

Earth. Most of the old fairy-tale creatures were probably Fey. Nobody knows why most of them left. Orcs, elves, ogres, probably even gnomes, they're all leftover servant races from when the Fey were a big deal. From the description, I think these things are what the old legends called a Wild Hunt, as in a bunch of badass Fey knights get together, and ride across the sky to hunt the living shit out of whatever they feel like. Supposedly each court has one, it gives them something to do when they're not at war, and the creature in charge of a hunt is always super dangerous."

"So you got a plan for these?"

I'd been thinking about it for a while, but so far, I didn't have anything I'd call good. I went to my pack and got out some of my dwindling food stores. I'd brainstorm better with something in my belly.

"Plan? Hell, I don't even know if bullets work on them. But I've got two possibilities. There are still powerful Fey who visit Earth, and we've got reliable accounts of those making deals with mankind. Back in the Eighties, MHI's Seattle team made an arrangement with one of their courts, a kind of peace treaty. To satisfy that court, a Hunter had to take this thing called the Harper's Challenge and play a violin to amuse them for three days. If he won, they got a treaty. If he lost, they'd eat him or something. Fey are *whimsical* like that."

"So go talk to them and see if they give you some challenge? That's not a rescue plan. That's a sideshow. You play an instrument? Because I don't."

"No, but I used to be able to win Guitar Hero on *hard*." He didn't find that funny. I shrugged apologetically. Too bad Mosh wasn't here. Even with his reattached fingers he could play the hell out of anything. "I'm not saying we can play a lullaby and get them to take a nap or anything like that, but if they're willing to deal at all, that gives us a chance to get inside their walls and close to our guys."

"Then what?"

"I'd hate to carry this C4 all this way and not blow something up with it."

"How much you got?"

I thought about the monstrous hunt we'd seen. Used intelligently, five pounds of plastic explosive went a long way, but there were limits to my creativity. "Not nearly enough."

"And your other plan?"

I finished another bite of processed meat noodle in beige sauce, then handed Lococo the rest of the pack. "We get as close as we can without being seen, wait for them to go off on another hunt like we saw, then we strike. I don't know how many Fey they leave behind, but fighting X minus that scary bunch is better than fighting X."

Lococo pondered on those options for a bit as he chewed. "So basically both of your plans are garbage."

"Heh." His optimism made me laugh. "The suggestion box is always open and MHI's corporate staff loves employee feedback."

"There's a third option . . . Realize we're hopelessly outmatched, tuck tail, and go home. But we both know that's not an option."

"Of course not," I said automatically.

"Why isn't it?"

"Huh?" I looked up from my food. I didn't get the feeling he was fishing to quit. Lococo didn't seem like the kind of give up, but everybody had their limits. Maybe he'd finally had enough. "I don't know. It just isn't. What're you getting at?"

Lococo just sat there, unreadable. "When I first ran into you, and I said I didn't want to leave without the others, you agreed. But I figured after you got to see just how bad this place was, or just how dangerous the Fey were, you'd change your mind. A reasonable man would look at the risks and say, 'screw it, I'm going home. I'm going to go back and comfort my mom the grieving widow, and be with my smoking hot wife, and be there to see my baby get born.' But not you, Pitt. I don't think that stuff ever even crosses your mind."

I thought about how to answer that. Of course I thought of that stuff all the time. Whenever I was too tired to take one more step, I thought of Julie waiting for me, and I went a little further. "Sure, I'd rather be there. But this needed to be done, and apparently those of us who can do it are few and far between. My dad used to say when something's coming at you, pick a direction and run. The ones who hesitate are the ones who get run over."

"Your dad was a smart man. I'm not sure you are, but, hey, that's the direction you picked, you're going to run right at this Asag. What was it you said...a demon so scary he boils the fish in the rivers? He who ends all things, just run right at him and say, 'Come at me, bro.' That's it?"

"Someone has to."

"Provided you ever make it back."

"Then the rest of the Hunters will have to handle him without me. I'm just one guy."

Lococo shook his head and laughed. "With all the bullshit you've told me over the last little while about Chosen and prophecies and cosmic forces steering your whole life to back before you were ever born, and you're going to look at me with a straight face and tell me *you're just one guy*. My ass. One guy. Asag's a god—"

"Wannabe poser god. Man has beaten him before."

"Whatever. Close to a god then. And something out there, some big cosmic fruit loop, has pinned all their hopes and dreams on *you* beating a *god*. And that don't strike you as weird?"

"Well, I did do it once before." Technically, it had been me and Franks—and Isaac Newton—but close enough.

"Oh yeah." Lococo chuckled. "I forgot, you're the *God Slayer*. This Asag had better watch out. We got us a certified badass up in here. The world is saved!"

I had to laugh. Earl had told me about working with Lococo, but they must not have been together long enough for Earl to learn he had a smartass streak. Either that, or living in the Nightmare Realm forced you to develop a dark sense of humor. "Look, man, serious answer. I don't care how scary he's supposed to be. I don't know what he wants, but he's building an army of monsters, and arranging all these little attacks for no discernible reason—"

"I'm sure he's got a reason."

"He's killing innocent people all over the world in the process."

Lococo shrugged. "Maybe that's reason enough."

"I can't let that stand. We'll find a way to beat Asag, because we have to."

"That, I'll have to see that with my own eye to believe."

"Well, yeah. I didn't come here to rescue you guys because I'm nice. I figured at the end of the world I'm going to need all the bodies to hide behind I can get. You're like the tallest guy I know. You'd make an awesome meat shield."

"Don't worry, Pitt. It's the end of the world, I promise I'll be there. I wouldn't miss it."

Since we didn't know if there were any predators in the area, or if the Hunt had scouts, we buried our garbage and tried to disguise any sign that we'd camped here. Equipment checked, we moved out.

We'd only gone about half a mile through the fog and sickly trees when Lococo turned around with a very malicious look on his ugly mug. He'd had an idea. "We need to cause maximum disruption and confuse the Fey as much as possible. You've got two plans."

"Yeah. So?"

"How about we do *both*?"

# CHAPTER 22

We had found the fortress and spent the last two "days" observing it.

Lococo hadn't been joking when he'd said he was literal with the landmark names. From our vantage point, the structure really did look like it was built out of bones. And it was, no kidding, on an island in the sky. Sadly, Lococo just wasn't imaginative enough to have made that part up.

If I thought this place had been messing with my head before, it had really started screwing with me once we got to the Fey lands. The swamp was like a messed-up Tim Burton movie on acid. There were streams through the forest, but made out of congealed fog goo rather than water. Poke one with a stick, and it didn't seem to have a bottom. Fall through one of those and you were probably gone forever. I was either going insane, or the trees kept whispering to me. You can only say out loud 'Shut up, stupid trees,' so many times before you really begin to doubt your grasp on reality.

The worst part was the chunks of land floating above

us. I had no explanation for what was keeping them there. It's like gravity just didn't give a damn. From beneath one, all I could see was black dirt and hanging roots, like the whole thing had just been violently yanked out of the ground, and then tacked to the sky. Every now and then, the angle was right and I could see a bit of what was on top of one, and it looked like exactly the same kind of terrain we were walking through. Even the smallest chunks were still big enough you could build a house on top, provided you didn't mind living in the shittiest neighborhood ever.

Some of the islands were way up there, barely visible in the perpetual twilight. Others were right above the ground, and if I had been brave enough to climb the whisper trees, I probably could have climbed onboard. Most seemed frozen in place, but others floated along peacefully at a few miles an hour. I really didn't like walking beneath those, because I was certain that was when gravity would start giving a damn again and I'd get buried beneath thousands of tons of dirt. My corpse would get digested by the roots of a whisper tree, and it would probably be my screaming face etched in the bark.

Unlike the pine forest dredged from Lococo's mind, there were sounds here besides rain. We were treated to the constant croaking of frogs, insects chirping, and weird things crying. There seemed to be the occasional word mixed in there too, which was fun. I only ever saw one of the croakers. The "frog" turned out to be a six-inch-tall biped waddling along on two legs, like a tiny baby *Vodyanoy*, but it had leapt into one of the fog streams when it saw me, probably worried I was going to eat it.

Occasionally, something screamed. It sounded like a woman in distress. It probably wasn't.

Bigger things tailed us in the fog, but none of them ever showed themselves. I caught glimpses of gleaming eyes a few times, but when they became aware I was watching, they would drift away. Pale lights would occasionally appear in the woods, sometimes white, sometimes blue, but I was never stupid enough to go chasing after them.

Lococo had only been here once before, but I had to hand it to him, because he managed to find the place again. That was a pretty remarkable achievement. When I'd remarked on that, he said it was just luck. Either that or everything in this particular reality was drawn to the fortress eventually.

We camped on the same hill that he'd used to spy on the Fey last time. It was about six hundred yards away, but there was no cover anywhere closer, just low grass and mud. The island was floating just off the ground, but since the fortress was built—or imagined into existence—on a hill, we could see most of it. The last time Lococo had been here, he had watched for a while, but couldn't see much and couldn't figure out a viable way in. Not even knowing if his compatriots were still alive and not feeling like committing suicide, eventually he had given up and gone back to the slightly less evil realm, where all he had to worry about was rain and cannibal mutants. Once I got a look at the place, I couldn't say I blamed him.

However, Lococo hadn't had Poly the Cyclops to let him know his guys were still alive, or a powerful scope to spy with. I was able to observe a lot more than he could, and I spent every waking minute glassing the place and making notes. While I had tunnel vision, Lococo kept a lookout to make sure the trees, frogs, or glowy things didn't come from behind to devour us.

The Fey's fortification was smaller than I'd expected. I was no expert on castles, but if it had been built for humans, you could maybe house two hundred people in there, tops. And that would be really crowded. It had been hard to tell hiding in the bushes while they had flown by, but the Fey knights I'd seen had looked a bit bigger than humans, and their mounts had been way bigger than horses. I didn't see any pastures around here, though those things had looked more like meat eaters than grazers, but they had to live somewhere, which meant there was probably a stable in there taking up a bunch of space too. If they were in the habit of taking prisoners, that would take up even more area. So at most there could only be about a hundred Fey living here.

Of course, that was assuming the interior of that place didn't laugh at the laws of physics and my concept of space, which considering they rode horse things across the friggin' *sky* probably wasn't that farfetched. But hopefully we were *only* outnumbered fifty to one.

However, making up for that cheery news, the walls did appear to be made out of stacked bones, like the catacombs of Paris, only from creatures that had to have been the size of whales. It didn't look like they were cemented together so much as slightly melted and then solidified. *Magic weirds me out.*

Something told me that this wasn't actual Fey architecture, as much as it was from one of their memories. It just didn't look that solid or sensible as a fortification. All those big scary-ass walls, but the doors weren't impressive enough to stop a battering ram. When the doors were occasionally opened, I could see right into the interior. There was no secondary defense. No portcullis. No murder holes. This fortress was for show.

There were four walls, about thirty feet tall, surrounding one central tower. Because of the jagged, haphazard nature of the building materials, they looked climbable. And probably would have been easy to get over, except I could always see guards patrolling along the top.

The guards looked like the Fey knights I'd seen before. They were vaguely man-shaped, but the proportions were off somehow. They were far too lean and spindly. I never saw one without armor, and for that, I was thankful. For a group of creatures who were lousy with shapeshifters and illusion makers, who throughout history had often appeared as creatures of ethereal beauty, word was that the royal Fey in their natural guise were *hideous*.

I learned these Fey liked to play a musical instrument that sounded like a cross between bagpipes and a tortured goat. It made me miss the croaking and mysterious screaming, but I learned that the guards changed at every shriek of the bagpipe goat. Like Lococo had said, there was a wide stair leading to the swamp floor. At the top was a great big wooden double door, wide enough to drive a pair of their superhorses through. On the wall above that gate a guard was always posted.

Were they here by choice, or were they trapped? Were they a conquering force or was this a criminal hideout? I didn't know what this small contingent of

Fey were doing out here in the Nightmare Realm all by themselves, outpost or outcasts, but they seemed wary. The guards' movements were crisp and alert. If Fey took smoke breaks or snuck naps on the job, I never caught one. Every so often they would open the gate and a pair of them would patrol the exterior, but they never ventured past the base of the stairs. Either they didn't want to get their boots muddy, or there was something dangerous out here in the swamp. And I don't mean us.

The weapons I saw seemed to consist of swords and weirdly designed spears, but for how little I knew about these things, those spears might shoot fireballs. And their black metal armor might or might not stop a round from my .308. We were dealing with too many unknowns. There's the old saying about a sufficiently advanced technology being indistinguishable from magic, but Fey had a laugh about that, used magic to grow walls out of whale bone, and rode sky horses, so screw your science.

So for two of the long periods that I'd come to think of as days, we watched. We ate the last of our food and waited for the magic hunger to set in. I prayed the Fey would go hunting soon, because we were only going to grow weaker. We went over our plan repeatedly, and then we whispered about everything else, because that's what you do when you're killing time, waiting for the signal to go do something stupidly dangerous.

I awoke from my nightmares, still lying behind my rifle, to the sound of a horn. Through my scope, the castle was a flurry of activity. Drums beat. Hounds howled. Black banners unfurled down the walls. The gates opened and the Fey paraded out. Each monster horse had a steel-clad killer saddled on its back. Their beasts ran to the edge of the island and kept on running right into the sky. I counted as they went by, tapping out a rhythm on the cold metal forearm of my rifle. Eighty alien killers were embarking on a quest to go put the hurt on somebody. This was our chance.

The hunt was on.

Once I was sure the Wild Hunt was far away, I took the long, lonely walk across the muck to the base of the stairs. They were sunken into the muck, and up close appeared to be made of the same yellowed bones as the fort. Aggressive vines were growing all over them, spiraling upward for a few stories. With everything to lose, but no better choice, I started climbing.

Of course the Fey saw me walking up their stairs. There was really no way to avoid that. I could hear the warning shouts high atop the wall. Their language was surprisingly melodic. If I could hear them, then they were close enough to hear me, so I shouted at the top of my lungs, "I've come to talk. I demand that you release your prisoners!"

I wasn't expecting these guys to speak English, but in previous dealings with Hunters, the more powerful Fey were always able to transcend language barriers and communicate somehow. Either they understood me, or they were curious enough to see what a lone human was doing way out here, because they didn't immediately roll a boulder down the stairs.

A black helmet appeared over the wall. The visor was shaped into an eagle's beak. That Fey said something incomprehensible, then hoisted a spear and prepared to hurl it down at me.

*Okay, that kind of communication worked too.*

I lifted Cazador and snapped a shot into the wall directly below him. Bone chunks flew off as he ducked. I hoped that got my point across. I could have brained him if I'd felt like it, and I hoped the Fey was smart enough to realize it.

As their emissary pulled back behind cover, I bellowed, "I've come to parley, but if you screw with me I'll blow your head off!" We'd put a lot of thought into the plan itself, but I hadn't really considered what I was going to say when I got here. "I demand to speak with your supervisor!"

While the Fey were probably deciding what was the most amusing way to murder me, I kept going up the stairs. Each step was carved from a single rib. They made an almost musical *thunk* when my boots struck them. Fey were supposed to take the verbal contest thing seriously, so just in case they were about to drop a cauldron of boiling oil on me, I doubled down.

"Come out and face me. Warrior against warrior! Man versus Fey! Come on. Do Fey only fight humans when we're lost and starving and you outnumber us? Your best warrior against me. I win, you set my friends free! Let's go! Show me you aren't cowards!"

If I was lucky, there were only a handful of them inside, and they'd be stupid enough to let me get close. That's all we needed, because I was merely the distraction.

Through my scope, I'd spotted thick roots that hung clear to the valley floor. We'd never be able to scale those without being seen by the guards, but if

I could get all eyes on me, Lococo could climb up the other side, get over the wall, free our guys, and get out before the Wild Hunt got back. It was a really shitty plan, but considering what we had to work with, it would have to do.

Fey have a very scary laugh, like a hyena. The noise made the hair on my arms stand up. There was suddenly a strange warmth in the air. It might not have been noticeable except I'd been chilled for so long. I figured they were channeling magic of some sort. The voice that came over the wall was deep, yet almost musical, vaguely Irish sounding, and obnoxiously confident. "Can your weak mind understand my words now, human?"

I reached the end of the stairs. The ground was packed black dirt with nothing between me and the gate. "Yes, I understand. Did you understand my demands?"

"You are in no position to make demands of the *churt deh'ung.*"

I guess there were limits to his translation software. "Come out and meet my challenge. Or are you chicken?"

I didn't even know if they knew what a chicken was, or if being one would be culturally significant, but it seemed to do the trick. Several more black helmets rose over the wall above me. The Fey were curious, and I hadn't even needed to make chicken noises. They didn't belong here either. The Nightmare Realm was probably as dreary and soul-sucking for them as it was for us. At least I was something new and interesting.

There was that awful laugh again. The eagle-beaked

one was the talker. "A filthy vagabond stumbles in from the mist yet expects courtesy." The other Fey on the wall laughed too. It was a chorus of deep, cruel, yet oddly musical noises. "Yes, we have taken human prisoners. You will soon be joining them. An inferior cannot force a challenge upon his betters. You lack the station to challenge and you have nothing of interest to trade. Luckily, you amuse me. Rather than disembowel you and throw you down for the swamp *taibhs* to feast on, we shall take you as a slave."

They were probably getting out a big net to toss down on me, but I was too weary to be frightened, and when faced with smug monsters I have a tendency to be a flippant dick back to them.

"I'll forgive your ignorance, Fey, because you must not realize who you're addressing. I'm Owen Zastava Pitt, Monster Hunter International, United States of America, planet *Earth!*"

It was hard to read their body language, but the helmets swiveled back and forth to look at other, confused. Apparently they didn't keep up on Earth's current events. "So?"

Lococo needed more time. *What the hell, might as well run with it.*

"So? *So?* I am the man who destroyed Lord Machado and turned back the Old Ones' invasion. I stabbed Martin Hood in the heart and put the Arbmunep back to sleep. I defeated the Nachtmar, king of this Nightmare Realm. I once killed a werewolf with office furniture. But most of all, I traveled across space and time to obliterate the Dread Overlord in his own living room with the mighty wrath of Sir Isaac Newton!" I was laying it on a little thick, but I was going for the gold. "My queen is the most beautiful warrior woman on my planet and I ride around in a flying murder ship driven by the Skull-Crushing Battle Hand of Fury himself! Son of the Destroyer, brother of the Great War Chief, they call me the God Slayer. Whoever crosses me dies poorly, and if you don't give back my men, so will you! After I kick your ass, I will take that fancy helmet and use it as a bowl to eat my Lucky Charms for breakfast, because they're magically delicious. So the real question is: who the hell are you to tell me that I lack station, jackass?"

Julie would be so proud of my diplomacy right now. Being Earl's XO had been a real learning experience for me.

But the Fey weren't buying it. "I am Riochedare of the *churt deh'ung*. Our hunt was banished to this foul realm to endure a century of punishment by decree of our queen, because our savagery on the field of battle was deemed *too* merciless."

"Uh-huh. Sure you were." I had been hoping one of them would come out and fight me, because that would put on the best distraction, but since that didn't seem to be working, it was time to get drastic. As I walked up to the doors, I pulled out my bomb and stripped the cover off the sticky tape. My assessment had been right. These doors weren't that sturdy. Whoever had imagined this castle into existence hadn't bothered giving them a proper door, so these guys had improvised one out of swamp wood. "That's nice."

"My amusement has worn thin. You are deranged, human. I first thought to cage you with the others, but your insolence suggests you would annoy me far too much."

"You're probably right about that." The gap between

the doors was just wide enough to see through. There were Fey on the other side. I could see exactly where a big crossbar was holding the doors closed. The sticky tape probably wouldn't reliably hold this much weight against damp wood, but there was a rusty metal handle on my side, so I squished the blocks of plastic explosives right on top of it. The fuse Cooper had put together was a relatively foolproof sleeve of black powder attached to an igniter. I removed the safety pin, gave the ring a quarter turn, and pulled. It made a *pop*. I waved at the Fey knight through the crack, then hurried off to the side.

"I grow bored of this foolishness. Spear the human."

"Whoa! Whoa! You're forgetting one very important thing!"

The Fey knight laughed at me again. "What is it now, pest? Do you intend to beg the *churt deh'ung* for your life?"

"Not really. I just needed to run down a thirty-second fuse," I said as I lay down and covered my ears.

"Behold, the human cowers before—"

*BOOM!*

If all eyes in the fort hadn't been looking my way before, they sure would be now.

I leapt up and ran into the spreading smoke. It was still raining splinters. Four pound-and-a-quarter blocks of C4 had done a real number on their doors. A circle in the middle had been rendered into pulp, leaving a hole big enough to climb through, but since the crossbar had been into a secondary projectile and nearly decapitated the Fey who'd been standing behind it, I just shoved the whole smoking wreck open. It was more dramatic that way.

The blast had taken them completely by surprise. There were several of them just standing there, flat-footed. They must have spent way too many years running down helpless survivors lost in the Nightmare Realm to be ready for someone to actually bring the fight to their house.

The Fey I'd been talking to had tumbled off the wall and landed in a mud puddle in the courtyard. He saw me coming through the smoke, pointed, and shouted, "Warlock!" These Fey must not have been from any of the branches which had visited Earth, because they seemed to have no concept of *bomb*.

Other than the one with the crossbar embedded halfway through his helmet, I counted seven more in the courtyard. Eagle Face seemed dazed and was struggling to sit up. I covered him with Cazador, but since I didn't know how tough these things were, I held my fire. If they turned out to be bulletproof I was going to have a whole lot of explaining to do.

"I gave you a warning. Now I'm pissed. *Let my people go!*"

Either he didn't know what guns did, or he didn't care. "Kill the human," the grounded Fey ordered. I could see his pointy chin wagging beneath his helmet. There was blood on his jagged teeth from the fall. "Kill him now."

The creatures drew their swords and began walking slowly toward me. Despite being clad in a lot of metal, they made no noise. Instinct told me they could move a lot faster, but the explosion had rattled them. They were being cautious now, but their blades still rose.

"I'll take you with me." I put a bullet into the mud puddle right next to the Fey leader's hand. Cazador was suppressed, so it wasn't that loud, but that close, a .308 hits with a pretty impressive impact. The resulting water geyser got my point across. The Fey flinched at the hit, and just that tiny, nearly human reaction, told me I had a chance. "Call them off."

The swordsmen had paused when they saw the bullet hit, probably wondering if that was the same kind of magic I'd used on their door, but then they started walking toward me again.

"Call them off or the next one is in your head."

I couldn't read a metal mask, but I could tell this one was doing the math and factoring in the belligerent door-exploding warlock pointing some sort of bronze murder rod at his head. "Hold."

The Fey immediately froze.

"You wanted standing. I just demonstrated my standing. Now I'll tear this place down bone by bone until you give me back my men."

The haughty laughter was gone. It's amazing how polite some of these stuck-up supernatural assholes got when you knock them off a big wall and shove a gun in their face. "I am afraid I cannot do that."

"Look, I can tell you're stuck in this shithole too, and neither of us wants to die today. Just turn over your prisoners, and we're out of here."

"You do not understand, human. They are not my prize to give away." His chin was visible beneath his visor as he spoke. It was shriveled, green, and pointy. Up close, his eyes were red dots through the visor. "The trophies belong to the hunters."

"What do you mean? You're not the Hunt?"

"Nay. These are but the squires. Too young to ride. They have not yet earned that honor."

I glanced nervously between the otherworldly terrors. Each one was spindly, but taller than me. Their strange swords were nearly four feet long and looked sharp enough to behead an ox. They were holding perfectly still, but it was a coiled, deadly stillness. Like a spring ready to pop. One wrong move and they'd all charge. Any strike with a blade like that and I was a dead man.

And these weren't even their warriors...

"I am but a retainer, too old to ride," Riochedare said. "I have been commanded to watch over this humble court in our lord's absence."

"You were sure talking a lot of shit up on that wall about how important you were a minute ago."

"My cohort was banished from the greatest of all kingdoms, condemned to barely scrape out a poor existence in this dismal land. One must take joy in the small things. I would gladly release your kin, but alas, it is not my decision to make. You will have to wait for the return of our Huntsman. Their hunt was to be a short one. They should be back soon. You will have to petition him, O mighty warlock."

Fey could be tricksters, so either he was lying, and I was screwed, or he was telling the truth, and I was screwed. "Fat chance of that. I've got a very full calendar and need to be on my way. So, prisoners now, or else."

"I am sorry. My lord would execute me if I gave up his trophies."

"He might kill you, but I will for sure." To accentuate that, I nodded toward the dead Fey with the bar through his skull. White brains and green blood were leaking from the crushed helmet. A bullet didn't have a fraction of the energy of five pounds of C4, but they didn't know that. "Here's the deal. You're going to send one of your Fey to release all your human prisoners. Bring them here where I can see them. Then they're going to walk out the gate and down the stairs. I'm going to keep my weapon on you the entire time. When I am certain they are free, I will leave you in peace. If you try anything, I will kill you all."

Riochedare mulled that over. My gut told me this was one crafty Fey. If there was a way for me to get screwed here, he would find it. Why couldn't I have wound up with the Fey equivalent of Kevin, the high-powered Las Vegas attorney?

"What if I do not agree to these terms, human?"

"My counteroffer involves a lot of murder."

"You could try, but even our youth are supremely skilled."

From the look of them, I didn't doubt that at all. "You die first either way. That part's not up for discussion . . . But here's a thought: your boss likes to hunt people. Tell him some crazy human came in here throwing his weight around, but you were smart and decided to let us all go, knowing he'd enjoy chasing us. All you did was give us a sporting head start. This realm sucks. You were just looking out for him so you could all have a little fun."

"Intriguing . . ." The metal eagle's beak tilted to the side. "You are truly deranged, human, and I will enjoy watching you be skinned alive, but we have reached an agreement. I accept and grant you custody of the slaves." He began saying something in their singsong language to one of the other Fey.

"English, you tricky bastard." I didn't want them to

deliver all of my friends' heads minus their bodies, or some nonsense like that. "Keep it simple."

"Of course...Oga, free the humans from their cages. Bring them here for inspection." The visor swiveled over to look directly at me. "Unharmed, of course."

"Of course," I said.

The Fey named Oga sheathed his sword and rushed toward the tower. Fey had an awkward-looking, but extremely quick run. The rest of them waited in silence, but they never lowered their swords. Their arms had to be getting tired.

The lead Fey stated, "This is shameful. I am sitting in the mud."

"You should have thought about that before you were a prick."

"We do not get many guests. You are only the second in a century. May I at least have the dignity of standing up?"

"Sure. After I leave. Now shut up."

A minute later the tower door opened again, and thank goodness, human beings came out. I couldn't help it. I began to grin. It must have been really dark where they were being held, because they were holding up their hands to shield their eyes from the murky cloudlight. They were all bearded, filthy, and skinny. Their clothing was filthy and tattered. The sight of their miserable state filled me with cold anger.

"Did you torture them?"

"There was nothing to gain by putting forth the effort. They were tortured no more than this land tortures all of us."

No, the Fey had just kept them in cages, like pets. Like friggin' hamsters. It was a sad commentary on the things that we dealt with, that overall that was far better treatment than I could have hoped for. They wouldn't starve here, but they looked weak, and it was a long walk back to the portal. "Addendum to our deal. We're taking some of your clothes too, blankets, supplies, that kind of thing."

"That was not our agree—"

I fired another round into the dirt right between his legs. I didn't know if Fey had genitals, but if they did, I guarantee his sucked up into his abdomen right then. "Not open for debate. Tell your Huntsman it was so we'd be a better challenge." I could have stolen some of their steeds too. The stables were on the other side of the tower, but from the weird noises coming from there, the things inside were more likely to eat us than let us ride on them.

I almost didn't recognize John VanZant. He was short, but normally easy to pick out of a crowd because he was an extremely solid, square-jawed guy. Only he was damned near gaunt now, and above his scraggly beard his eyes were sunken into his face. He was obviously suspicious as to why they were all being herded outside, but he lit up when he saw me. "Monster Hunter!"

All of the survivors looked my way. There was a moment of shocked disbelief, and then they began to cheer. At that moment, they looked like they were about to jump the Fey, steal their swords, massacre everything, and loot the place. The transformation was so sudden, the hope so fierce, that I realized my earlier concerns were for nothing. These guys still had heart. They had never given up hope. They would fight for every inch to get back home.

There were six of them ... but Poly had said there were six survivors left, but with Lococo that made seven. They were all too battered and disheveled to match the pictures I'd seen, so I didn't know who was who. I'd figure out the discrepancy once we weren't surrounded by Fey. "Hey, you guys ready to go home or what?"

"Pitt?" VanZant stumbled over. It was obvious they hadn't had a chance to stretch their legs for a while because they were all having a hell of a time walking. "It's really you? Where's everybody else?"

I didn't want to say in front of the Fey that there were only two of us. "I'll explain later. Grab whatever supplies you need for a long walk. Then head down the stairs, across the mudflat, and straight toward the tallest hill. I'll cover you until you're all there."

"Got it." No matter what he'd been through, his head was still in the game. That was why VanZant had been a team lead, and from the way the other survivors snapped to when he started yelling at them, it was obvious he'd been picked to be these Hunters' leader too. "You heard him, boys. Let's get out of here!"

Their ragged, defiant cheer brought a tear to my eye. They began ripping through the Fey's belongings. It was really tense, because though the young knights kept their distance, they were still poised to attack. The Hunters were wary, but there was obviously a lot of resentment there, and when a Hunter resented something, our knee-jerk reaction was to kill it dead.

"John, as tempting as it might be for you guys to hack these assholes down, I just cut a deal with them so we can get the hell out of Dodge."

"Yeah . . . I feel you. Yo, Rothman. You're getting eyeballed." VanZant shouted at one of the Hunters. "If you pick up that sword, I think that one is going to have a problem with you."

That Hunter slowly let go of the weapon he'd been touching. The Fey who had been ready to slash him remained still.

I'd been too busy to notice, but the fort was in even worse shape than I'd thought. Most of the Fey slept out under the sky on mats made of grass. The exterior bones looked solid, the interior was crumbling and covered in moss. They had been given these really impressive walls so that everything else in this crappy realm would be afraid of the Fey, but everything inside was garbage. Our meager thefts would actually hurt. I bet that their queen was probably the really spiteful type.

"Okay, we're loaded. Everybody out!" VanZant ordered. The Hunters hurried through the ruined door and toward the stairs. He stayed by me. In true MHI fashion, he planned on being the last out of danger. Which was great and all, and I really did appreciate the sentiment, except I was the one with the rifle.

"Go, John."

"I know what you're doing, but I'm going to watch your back. Don't ever trust these things. They're shifty, tricky, lying bastards."

The lead Fey sighed. "Oh, human, I was unfailingly polite to our guests."

"Polite?" VanZant reached inside the remains of his shirt and pulled out a thin piece of metal he had sharpened into a shiv. "You're lucky Pitt showed up when he did, Riochedare, because I was saving this for you in particular."

I didn't know if my partner in crime had ever made it over the walls or not. I raised my voice and shouted. "Lococo! Are you here?"

"Jason's not here, Z," VanZant said sadly. "The six of us, we're it."

VanZant thought I meant as a prisoner, not a rescuer. I'd catch him up later. Lococo must not have been able to scale up the side of the island after all. But we'd planned for that too, so he'd be falling back to our staging point on the hill. "Okay. Get out of here. I'm right behind you."

"Thanks. We owe you."

"Damned right you do." As the last of the Hunters left, I kept my rifle on Riochedare. The Fey watched us go. They were unreadable beneath those helmets, but they had to be fuming. "Listen up, chuckleheads. I can kill you with this thing further than you can see. If you follow us, I will drop you."

"Go then, human. We will not trouble you, but make haste. For when my lord returns, he will be outraged at this slight. You have made a grave mistake, for nothing escapes a Wild Hunt."

There was nothing else for me to say. I kept my rifle on the Fey as I retreated through the doorway, just waiting for the youngsters to try something. I walked backwards all the way to the stairs, rifle shouldered, continually moving the muzzle from the door to the top of the wall, but no helmets appeared.

The other survivors were slogging through the mud toward my hill. VanZant and I hurried down the stairs after them. He was having a hell of a time just walking. VanZant was a martial artist and an athlete, seeing him in this state just pissed me off.

But he was beaming anyway. "Sorry. Not a lot of room to stretch the old leg muscles when you're suspended in what's basically a birdcage."

"No-bullshit assessment time: can your guys survive the journey back to where you were captured?"

VanZant must have seen how grim I looked. "Why? Oh hell. You're it, aren't you? Okay, don't worry about us. If it means getting out of here, we can do anything. They may look weak, but they are mighty. Their spirits are high, and in this place, that's what matters most."

"Good."

"Besides, we'd all rather die fighting than rot away in a birdcage."

"How long are the Hunts usually gone for?"

"It's hard to tell time here, but I imagine you've gathered that by now . . . They're usually out of the fort for what feels like two, three days tops."

That meant we only had a couple days' head start. We needed to run until we collapsed.

# CHAPTER 23

Lococo wasn't at the agreed-upon rally point. There was no sign of my friend. It was like he'd been swallowed up by the swamp.

By the time I got to our hilltop hide, the Hunters had found my pack and were using my knives to cut holes in Fey blankets to make ponchos. Luckily they all still had shoes, because trying to cross this terrain barefoot would be a death sentence. We'd be moving out in a minute. Hopefully, Lococo was on his way back. I just prayed that some swamp predator hadn't picked him off after we had separated.

They were hurrying. I don't think I've ever seen so much determination expended over such a simple task. These men were dead set on getting away. But when they saw me climbing up the hill, they dropped what they were doing and rushed over.

I got handshakes, pats on the back, even tearful hugs. I didn't know what to say to a bunch of dudes with lice-encrusted beards weeping on me. "It's okay." I represented the most hope they'd had in months. I knew each of them, but mostly through stories told to me by their friends and teammates in Alaska, or by their trinkets I'd collected in a Ziploc bag. It was hard to believe they were here in the flesh. "Everything is going to be okay."

Now we just had to get away.

"Listen up. There's not much time. I'm Owen Pitt, with MHI. Bad news. I'm the only one who was able to come through to get you." There was some obvious disappointment at that. Couldn't say I blamed them. "Good news. There is a portal back to Earth, and there are Hunters waiting on the other side for us. Only it's a long ways off. If we want to make it home, we need to get there before the Wild Hunt catches us. So we're going to have to haul ass."

"How will we keep from getting lost?" someone asked. "Last time the terrain kept changing around us. We couldn't find anything."

I held up my glove. "On this pinky I've got a magic ring from an undead Roman—I shit you not—and it's supposed to point the way home. If I get killed, take the ring and keep going. It's really on there so you'll probably have to cut my finger off. I won't be offended. Any questions?" I was sure there were plenty of questions, like *how the hell were we going to pull this off?* but nobody wasted time asking the obvious. "No? Good."

"What're we waiting for?" one of the men exclaimed. "We get out of this shithole, the first round's on me!" It wasn't that funny, but everybody had a laugh. Hunters were an obnoxiously optimistic bunch, and we'd just pulled off an interdimensional jailbreak, so an ultramarathon across nightmare land running from killer Fey was no biggie.

I glanced around the swamp. There was still no

sign of Lococo. "Somebody else was supposed to meet us here."

"Who?" VanZant asked, perplexed.

"Jason Lococo."

All of the smiles died.

"What's wrong with you guys?"

"I'm sorry to tell you, but Jason's dead," VanZant explained.

That didn't make any sense. "No. He was just here. He was supposed to sneak in the back to free you guys. He was the first one of you I found."

VanZant exchanged a confused glance with the other survivors. "I don't know what to tell you, Z. Lococo died fighting the Wild Hunt."

Now wasn't the time for jokes, but it was obvious they weren't pulling my leg. "You're wrong. He survived somehow. I was just talking to him."

One of the Hunters was shaking his head. "No mistake, friend. He saved all of our lives, but got wounded on the way out. I tried to stop the bleeding, but couldn't do anything for him without any proper medical supplies. He bled out."

"We buried him on the mountain," said another. "We dug a shallow grave with our bare hands. It was all we could do, at least spared him the indignity of the skinnies eating his body."

This made no sense. I couldn't even process what they were telling me.

"Are you okay, Z?" VanZant asked.

He'd been in a dungeon for months, and here he was asking me if I was okay? But I wasn't okay. I took a deep breath. "It's just that we walked all the way here together. He showed me where to find you."

The Hunters exchanged nervous glances. Now they were worried this place had already driven their rescuer insane.

*Had it?*

Poly had seen one of the lights go out. That must have been him. *Had Lococo been a ghost all along? Had all that been in my imagination?* Only he had saved me from certain death and hauled me up a cliff. The missing fingernail and aches and pains told me I hadn't imagined that. There was no time to make sense of this now. I could ponder on it when the Wild Hunt wasn't on our trail.

"Whoever I saw, it doesn't matter. We've got to move."

It was far faster leaving the swamp than going in. There was a big difference between searching for something without getting spotted, as opposed to getting the hell out as quick as you can. Since I was the only one who'd been living off of real food instead of nightmare fuel, I was in the best shape by far, so I got in front and blazed a trail. Surprisingly, I didn't have to stop and wait for the single-file line of Hunters to catch up very often.

The Ring of Bassus seemed to be working. Whenever I paid attention to it, I could feel just a bit of heat and pressure. When I went in the indicated direction, it was like it was guiding me toward trails and clearings that I didn't even realize where there until I was right on top of them. I had to have faith. The Roman had said that it would guide me back to what I loved most.

*Julie, here I come.*

The little frog people, swampy lights, and mysterious howlers all avoided us, which was lucky for them, because anything that got between this bunch and home would have gotten promptly beaten or stabbed to death. I'd passed out my spare knives, but we only had the one firearm between all of us.

Which was another head scratcher. Had I loaned my sidearm to a ghost? How the hell did that work? The idea of ghosts hanging around me wasn't odd. Only it was exceedingly rare for a ghost to physically manifest, and those instances had been brief. Sam had joined in the fight in Vegas, and Mordechai had once been so angry at a particular vampire that I'd been able to use his cane as a stake, but that kind of thing was odd and brief.

This was different. I'd hung out with Lococo for what had to have been close to two weeks, and he had given me zero indication of being dead. Did he even know he was dead? I had run into that kind of denial before. Had the Nightmare Realm brought Lococo back as some kind of cursed revenant? Our foggy death march didn't give me much time to dwell on it. We were moving quickly, so I needed to concentrate on my surroundings. A sprained ankle now meant doom.

We walked and walked, and whenever the terrain allowed it, ran. When we got to the point that men started falling down constantly, we stopped to rest. Before we could sleep, we had to tend to the split blisters and sloughed-off patches of constantly wet skin.

It was in those brief moments when we stopped that I understood why these men had all started looking to VanZant as their leader, because he checked on each one, making conversation the whole time, trying to check their state of mind and lift their spirits. It was obvious he cared more about their well-being than his own. At this point, their shoes were held together with rags, and it is a humble leader who personally checks the soles of his men's feet.

When VanZant limped over to me last, I asked if everyone was going to be okay. My biggest concern was illness, especially since we'd spent the day covered in rancid mud, but he assured me that in all their time here, none of the survivors had ever gotten sick or shown any sign of infection. They figured if you succumbed to disease, the Nightmare Realm could no longer feed on your suffering, so nobody got off that easy.

That "night" I passed out my most important possessions—my extra pairs of Danner socks. For the lucky survivors, it was like Christmas. Unable to make a fire, we huddled together for warmth. Surprisingly, my nightmares were almost hopeful. It's amazing what you can get used to. A few hours later, we dragged our exhausted carcasses up and started running again.

The moist clingy fog was slowly replaced with rain, and the trees went from twisted Fey nightmares back to regular old pine trees. I never thought I'd be so happy to see the miserable pseudo-Pacific Northwest again. We had reached the border faster than expected. Either the ring was leading me on a more direct route than Lococo had, or maybe our hope was actually transforming the landscape in our favor.

I kept checking the sky and listening for thunder. The threat of the Wild Hunt was gnawing at my mind.

We were making good time, but if they caught us, we were toast. At one point, VanZant saw me watching the clouds and warned me that they might not come from above at all. Last time they had been on the ground so that their hounds could follow the scent.

It was like a never-ending endurance race. After an unknown amount of time spent in painful exertion, VanZant came up to me, drenched and exhausted, and told me that if we didn't stop to sleep again soon, we were going to start losing people. None of them had complained to me. I may have been their rescuer, but after what they'd been through together, I was an outsider. They weren't going to tell me if they were about to drop. But VanZant they would confide in, trusting that he'd know when to call it. I had never been this tired before; I couldn't even begin to imagine how they were feeling.

We found a small cave that was out of the rain and crashed. There were even enough dry sticks inside to start a fire. That small mercy filled my heart with joy. As we huddled around the flames, sharing body heat, I could hear their stomachs growling. Mine was too, but not as bad yet. Before they started passing out, I realized that I had something belonging to each of them. So I got out the Ziploc and passed it around.

A Hunter began to cry when he found the photo of his wife.

I vowed that I was going to get these poor bastards home, no matter what.

There were several unclaimed items left in the bag. We'd never known which of the missing had been among the survivors Poly could sense, versus those who had died and we'd just never recovered their bodies. Seeing those forgotten bits made me sad. The small good luck charm from Kiratowa's man was still in there, so he was dead after all. Kiratowa was going to be pissed that his streak was actually over.

On first watch, I passed the time staring off into the rain, listening to the snores, too exhausted to think. My eyes burned with the effort of keeping them open.

When VanZant took over for me at the mouth of the cave, he whispered so as to not disturb the others. "I've got the rest of this, Pitt. Get a few hours for yourself."

I just nodded, but I didn't move. I figured I'd probably just close my eyes and pass out right there. When every muscle was this sore, it didn't really matter what position you put them in. Something was still going to hurt.

VanZant looked back at the sleeping Hunters. Half his face was covered in shadow, the other half in firelight. He was wearing his old dog tags that I had brought from Earth, because at least those were a tangible connection to memories of a place other than here.

"You know, Z, I did the best I could to keep us together, to keep them all focused and fighting. You give up here, you're gone . . . Your soul rots. This place sucks you dry and leaves a husk. We ran into a few of those . . . the lost, wandering. They're like these lonely, crazy wraiths. I just have to tell you. I was close to giving up. I don't think I could have lasted much longer. As soon as I had the chance I was going to shiv a Fey. I had no delusions of escaping, but I hoped they'd get angry enough to execute me for it."

"Sounds reasonable." Getting killed by a monster was a far better way to go than giving up and turning

into one. If you're going to die, might as well be
defiant about it.

"I'm trying to say thanks. Better to die fighting
than wither away captive. Even if we don't make it,
this way is better."

"Naw. You've kept them alive this long, John, it's
just a little further. If the Wild Hunt finds us, you've
got to take them the rest of the way. These guys love
you. You're the only one who can keep them moving
and I'm the only one in condition to buy much time.
So if that situation arises, let's not waste time having
a debate over it."

VanZant obviously didn't like where I was going
with that line of thought. "Nobody else is getting
sacrificed. You've already done enough finding us."

"Sorry, John, but I'm really not the one who found
you."

"Get some sleep, Z."

I closed my eyes. "Tell me where you buried him."

"You're going to laugh, because this sounds farfetched, but it's true. I don't know how one wound
up here, but we buried Jason's body next to an old
school bus."

I was asleep in seconds.

A horn echoed through the mountains.

The Wild Hunt was closing in.

That haunting sound turned my blood to ice water.
Every one of us had frozen in place and was staring
back in the direction we'd come from. All I could
see was endless trees, concealing our doom. We had
been moving single file along a ridgeline, drawn this
direction by the now constant warmth of the ring.

There was a river below us, and somewhere past it was the gateway home.

*Not now. We're so close.*

"They've caught our scent. This is what happened last time!" one of the Hunters cried. "There's no getting away!"

"Might as well die here. I can't walk anymore."

These men were hard as nails, but you can only push someone so far beyond exhaustion before they start to give up. Several of them were leaving bloody footprints, so it wasn't like we could hide. We'd been moving nonstop for what felt like several days. I could see it in their eyes. When that horn blew, it signaled the end. It had sucked their will to live.

Not all of them however. "Shut up," VanZant ordered. "None of that talk. We're not giving up." Ari Rothman had started to sit down, but VanZant grabbed him by the arm and pulled him up. "Stand your ass up." VanZant shoved him along. "After everything we've been through, you can't stop now. Move, Hunter!"

But they were dejected, beaten. The portal was probably still miles away.

"This is it . . ." someone whispered.

"Not yet," I muttered as I started walking back down the line of bearded, quivering, near-skeletal survivors. They were all out of breath, obviously in pain, and I'd be damned if I let them go down like this. I stopped by their leader, who was too annoyed to be scared. "John, how far do you think that horn was?"

"A few miles at most. At the speed they ride, unless they stop for a leisurely lunch, they'll catch up to us before we can cross that river."

"Not if I make them pay for every inch." I chamber-checked Cazador. My rifle was loaded and ready. *Good.* It should have been, but when you spend this much time in a delirious haze you shouldn't take anything for granted. "Remember that talk we had the other night?"

"I remember."

"Good." No need to waste time arguing then. I bit my glove and pulled it off. Getting the Ring of Bassus off my pinky was a lot easier than expected. I'd shed a lot of weight recently. "Here, take this."

VanZant knew exactly what I was doing, but it hadn't sunk in for the sleep-deprived, starved others. They were all looking back nervously, waiting for the Wild Hunt to appear and ride us down, but their leader knew what was happening. VanZant just gave me a grim nod as he slipped the ring on one of his fingers. Having been through a lot together, that one look said everything that needed to be said.

"You feel that?"

"Yeah . . ." VanZant clenched his fist. "There's an unnatural energy to it."

"Good." I hadn't known if the Roman's magic would work for others like it had for me. "Follow that. My gut tells me it shouldn't be too much further."

"Thank you for everything, Z. I'll tell Julie about this."

"No need. I'll tell her myself after I kill all these assholes and catch up."

I could tell there was more he wanted to say about me volunteering to die here, but there wasn't a lot of time to spare for emotional partings. VanZant raised his voice. "All right! We've come too damned far together to give up now. I can't carry any of you bastards, but by God you know I'll try! So if you give up, you're killing me too. You're killing all of us! So quit moping and start moving!"

If any of them had been on their own, they probably would have curled up and surrendered, but a Hunter will push through anything for his team. Determination registered on their emaciated faces. Even stopping for that short of a time had given them a chance to catch their breath and refocus. They would carry on.

As they began moving down the ridgeline, I started walking in the direction of the horn, looking for a good spot to set up an ambush. The survivors didn't even realize they'd lost me. Knowing VanZant, he would probably use my covering for them as a motivator when they next had to stop and catch their breath. *He's buying us time, so let's not waste it.* That sort of thing. It's what I would have done.

This ridgeline had a nice field of view. We had just passed a rock pile with scraggly bushes growing from the cracks. I headed straight for that spot. It would provide a little bit of extra elevation, excellent concealment, and the terrain would slow down any Fey who tried to climb up it to stab me. Assuming they had senses similar to a human, I could probably get off a bunch of shots before they spotted me. The trees immediately below that position were relatively sparse, so my attackers wouldn't have much cover. I picked a good boulder to die on and began setting up shop.

I'll be honest. Even though the odds sucked, it felt good to stop running. My feet hurt and I was sick of being chased. I wanted to show these Fey who the real Hunter was.

I had long since gotten rid of every bit of excess weight. After I'd handed out my gear to the survivors, I'd ditched my pack. However, I'd never left behind a single round of ammunition. Minus what I'd shot at the Asakku and at the bone fort, I still had most of my full load-out. Odds were they'd overwhelm me before I could burn through all of it, but I'd try. After that, I had my kukri, which was a big, friggin' scary knife, but not that useful against things wearing suits of armor and carrying swords longer than my legs. I would have loved access to heavier weapons, but emphasis there is on the word *heavy*, and after hiking up and down this stupid dimension for weeks, even this much stuff had kicked my butt.

I pulled out a couple of mags and laid them on the stone beside me; that way I wouldn't have to wrestle my reloads out of a pouch while lying on them. Flipping open Cazador's bipod, I went prone, got as comfortable as possible, and started estimating the ranges to various terrain features. Assuming the Fey would be directly following our trail, my first clear glimpse of them would be approximately nine hundred yards away.

That was something that my wife would have been able to pull off in her sleep, but it would be a challenging shot for me. I had memorized the ballistic tables Milo had given me for this load. At this range I would be lobbing bullets in with a trajectory like a rainbow. It was safe to assume the Wild Hunt would close fast, so I'd have to remember to keep adjusting for range. At least there was no wind to compensate for, just the ever-present drizzle. But at this distance, even the cumulative effect of striking raindrops could alter a bullet's trajectory.

Lightning burned across the sky. Thunder rocked the mountain.

It was strange, but I was too weary to get freaked out about what I was about to do. In the back of my mind I was thinking about my family, and my child who I would never meet, but the front of my mind was focused entirely on the here and now. My only purpose in life now was to bleed these Fey as much as possible. There was no use getting worked up, that would only increase my heart rate, which would make me shake, which would make me less accurate, which would spare more Fey. If I made the cost of this hunt too high, they would have no choice but to back off, and my guys could still escape.

But no matter what, nobody was coming to save me. *So be it.*

I saw the first flicker of movement, something black rushing through the green. Sure enough, they were on the exact same trail we had used. It would have been nice to leave some Claymore mines behind us, but I might as well wish for a pony while I was at it. I got my head down and peered through the scope. With the US Optics magnification turned all the way up, I could see that it was one of the Fey's hound creatures, misshapen head swinging back and forth as it followed our muddy footsteps. It had to be two hundred pounds of muscle, with protruding jaws that could bite right through a man's leg.

The horn blew again, much closer now. I could almost picture one of the Fey lifting some weird, curling, ram's horn to his ugly lips. They knew we were close and were trying to scare us. Banished to this awful land, the thrill of the hunt was the only thing that kept these creatures entertained.

At the call of the horn, the hound thing stopped, waiting obediently.

Safety off. Range estimated. Scope dialed in. I put the reticle on the target. The dumb beast was standing there, looking eagerly back toward its masters, forked tongue lolling out of its open mouth. *Inhale.* My finger moved to the trigger. *Exhale.* I squeezed on the respiratory pause.

Cazador barely moved, so I never lost sight of my target. It took about a third of a second for the bullet to get there. Mud flew up from an obvious hit just low and to the left of the creature's paws. My estimation had been slightly off. *Inhale.* I adjusted my aim using the scope's Horus grid. *Exhale.*

The dog thing was still staring, confused, at the odd new hole in the mud when my second bullet nailed it in the ribs. Startled, it leapt back, landed, spun, and managed to run a few feet before falling over. I must have pierced something vital. I watched it twitch through the scope.

Then I could feel the thunder. Only this wasn't from the clouds, it was from hundreds of powerful hooves slamming into the ground.

*Here we go.*

The Wild Hunt burst through the trees, terrifying and ferocious. They were approaching the dead hound. I picked one of the creatures in front. *Inhale.* They were moving with shocking speed, but directly toward me at that point of the trail, so no need to lead them. Plus their steeds were gigantic targets. *Exhale.* Black banners were whipping in my scope. *Squeeze.*

Cazador gently thumped my shoulder. A massive horselike beast twisted to the side as the bullet struck.

Its front legs collapsed. Its head hit the ground, and momentum took it end over end, crashing violently through the brush with the Fey still on its back.

I still didn't know what my bullets would do to a Fey knight's armor, but they worked fine on their pets and livestock.

Most of the Wild Hunt was still charging forward, though some had seen the crash or the dead hound, realized something was wrong, and were pulling back on their reins. Good. Slow-moving targets were easier to hit than fast-bouncing ones. I picked another knight and fired. I must have hit the mount, because it reared back on its hind legs, front limbs kicking. The knight on its back was thrown from the saddle.

More and more black shapes were appearing, roaring down the trail. They were so bunched up that it would be hard to miss. I kept firing so fast it became a blur. Target. Fire. Target. Fire. Only their animals were incredibly tough. Some I was certain I hit, but they didn't show much reaction at all. I could still put bullet holes in them, try to hit something vital, and just pray that Fey critters had blood pressure like ours did.

One of the knights who had been launched from the saddle stood up, right in the open. He seemed stunned. I shot him dead center, so clean that I actually saw a strange green flash as the bullet impacted his breastplate. The knight staggered back a couple of steps, but didn't fall. It hadn't penetrated. Their armor was enchanted after all.

*Not good.*

A .308 bullet loses a ton of velocity across that distance, so hopefully I would have more luck as they got closer. But until then I went back to wounding their unarmored steeds. If enough Fey were walking, they'd have to give up on catching my friends. Cazador's bolt locked back empty. I leaned it to the side, ejected the mag, shoved in another, slapped the release, and dropped the bolt. I got back to shooting as soon as the bipod was flat on the stone. Hot brass went rolling over the side of the boulder.

Some of the Fey were milling around, confused, as their horse things got shot out from under them, but others were still charging past them down the trail, heading my way. They were nearing the white rock I had estimated at seven hundred. *Damn they're fast.* Riding hard, they were bouncing erratically over the uneven terrain, and since they were no longer heading straight at me, I had to lead my targets. If I fired directly at them, by the time the bullet got there they would already be gone. So I needed to shoot ahead of them for bullet and target to intersect. Travel time of the bullet and travel time of the animal made for a much more difficult shot.

There was another green flash as I hit a Fey's leg armor, but he jerked back on the reins so hard it caused his mount to skid sideways into another creature. Both of them crashed into the mud, limbs flailing and banners snapping.

I made it through a second twenty-round magazine, picking targets and firing as fast as I could. The suppressor was getting hot enough to boil the collected raindrops off of it. There were so many Fey they must have cleared out the whole fort. *Riders nearing five hundred. Adjust.* I started burning through my third twenty-round mag, and the Fey still didn't know where their attacker was.

But then my scope landed on one Fey in particular. This one was *huge*. He appeared to have a ghostly green halo. His black helmet was decorated with flared bat wings and he was on a horse thing the size of a rhinoceros. Big flags—*his* flags—hung from spear shafts jutting from both sides of his beast's saddle. This was clearly their leader, a being of pure terror, but worst of all, somehow he was staring right at me.

I aimed just ahead of his galloping steed's head as he pointed toward me with one gauntlet. I pulled the trigger. The world exploded around me.

There was a blinding blue flash as I was hurled violently down the rock pile. I landed on my back. I lay there in pain as rock and dirt rained down around me.

*That fucker is using magic.* He was some kind of Fey Huntsman, of course he was using magic. *Cheating son of a bitch.*

It took a few seconds before I could see again. The boulder I'd been lying on had been cracked in half. I reflexively struggled back to my feet before I realized my sleeve was on fire. I hastily beat it out. Good thing my clothes were perpetually soaked here. Cazador had landed a few feet away. Luckily the blast hadn't knocked the glass out of the optic, so I scooped it up and went back to the fight.

I stumbled around the rock pile as the rain beat down the dust. The Wild Hunt was still charging up the ridge. It was going to take more than some boulder-splitting bolts to make me quit. Luckily, I had managed to brain their leader's mount, because it had crashed. I couldn't see the Huntsman behind its bulk, but hopefully he'd broken his neck on landing.

They were charging up the ridge now. *Adjust to three hundred.* Now this was a range that I was actually good at. I cozied up to another rock, set Cazador's bipod down, and picked my next target.

Since they were climbing at a steep angle, this time when I shot a horse thing through its neck, it made for a spectacular tumble back down the hill, right into the legs of another creature. One knight bounced off a rock so hard that it raised green sparks. I picked the next closest Fey and started working my way back down the line. Target. Fire. Target. Fire. They were close enough now that I could hear the screams of their wounded steeds.

I was reloading when the next spell hit. My only warning was when the rocks I was hiding behind began to vibrate ominously. My first thought was *earthquake* except then the whole world rushed up to smack me in the face. I dove to the side as the ground beneath me erupted upwards, dodging most of it. The majority of what hit me was soft wet dirt, but there were enough hard bits in there to really hurt.

Only this time the dust didn't settle. It continued to whip and circle around me. Grit stung my eyes. Rocks cut my skin. The Huntsman was blinding me so his warriors could get closer. I closed my eyes tight and headed for the edge of the storm. Since I couldn't shoot at anything for a moment, I adjusted my range to *too close for comfort* and cranked the magnification on my scope all the way down so I could engage them faster.

Stumbling out of that cloud, bleeding, coughing, half blind, I didn't bother taking a rest to shoot. They'd just blow it up with magic. The Wild Hunt was right below me, crashing through the brush. I shot at everything that moved. Green sparks flew whenever one of my bullets hit their strange armor. They were unbelievably quick and closing fast. Every fiber of my being was screaming for me to run, but if I turned and fled, they'd just cut me down. So I stood my ground and kept shooting, wounding animals and sending them tumbling down the rocks.

The next spell was in the form of a gust of wind. It came screaming out of nowhere. The raindrops went horizontal right before the air hit me like a truck. It flung me against a tree. Which hurt, but worse, it had thrown off my aim and I'd wasted a bullet. I tried to push my way free, but the wind kept howling, shoving me back. I could feel it tearing at my skin. It was like sticking your head out the window of an airplane.

The magical wind died off and I could move again. That was fire, earth, air . . . so if the pattern held the Huntsman would probably hit me with a tsunami next.

Only he wouldn't need to. The Fey were on top of the ridge with me.

An arrow embedded itself in the tree by my head. Then I had to duck as a Fey rode by, swinging an axe. It caught nothing but bark. I used the side sights as he went past, shooting his horse thing in the ass several times. It crashed haphazardly through the forest.

They were trying to ride me down. It was pure chaos as I was engulfed in a black-armored wave. A sword swung, leaving a shallow cut across my shoulder. Then the mount clipped me, hurling me into the dirt.

I looked up just as another beast was going to ride me down. I barely had time to raise my rifle, firing wildly. Green blood burst from the creature's snout as it reared back. Magic sparks flew as the Fey knight was struck. The hooves descended.

By a miracle, it didn't stomp me to death. It bruised my shoulder and cut a gash on my leg, but I scrambled out from beneath it as it kicked and thrashed. The rider was trying to control it, reins in one hand, spiked mace in the other. His visor turned toward me as the mace descended.

I shoved Cazador right into his eye slit.

The bullet blew a hole clean through the Fey's skull, but when it hit the enchanted armor on the other side, it must have fragmented into a million pieces because his head simply *popped*. Blood and sparks squirted out the visor. The wounded beast went snorting away, the dead rider flopping around on its back.

I was struck hard in the side of the head by something. I landed face first in the mud. Cazador went bouncing away.

Lying there, dazed, I waited for the killing blow. They could have speared me, or trampled me ... I could feel the hooves striking the dirt only a few feet away, but they were waiting for something. Blood was running from my scalp into my eye. Groaning, I got to my hands and knees. Half a dozen Fey were riding around me in a circle, laughing and taunting in their bizarre language as their beasts licked their sharp teeth and bayed for my blood. One of the warriors was swinging some knotted ropes in a circle so fast they made a whistling noise. They probably worked like bolos. The Hunt intended to capture me.

*Screw that.* I wasn't getting skinned alive or spending eternity in some birdcage to amuse these jerkoffs.

I didn't see where my rifle had landed. Instinctively,

I reached for my belt, temporarily forgetting that I'd loaned my pistol to Lococo. *Stupid.* But then I saw the mace the knight I had killed had dropped, and it was only a few feet away.

The Fey swung his arm, the ropes flew. I ducked, rolling, as the bolos bounced through the bushes. I snatched up the mace.

The weapon was really heavy, made out of the same dense black-green metal as their armor. It was nearly long as my arm, with a cluster of thick spikes on the end. It would be like swinging an iron baseball bat. I stood up, and with a roar, took a shot at the nearest passing horse beast.

The impact reverberated up my arm. The animal's leg shattered. The beast screamed. The rider screamed as it reared back. I screamed as I smashed its back leg. Beast and rider went down. I got on top of them, and before he could do anything about it, I brought the mace down on top of his helmet. Green sparks flew as magic absorbed much of the energy. I clubbed him hard again, and from the sickening *crack* that came from beneath the metal, I'd just split his skull.

The riders stopped circling.

Apparently fun time was over.

Panting and bleeding, I stepped away from the dead Fey. The horse thing was still thrashing about. There were a lot of spears pointed my way. This realm had made the Fey soft. They weren't used to their prey showing this much stubborn resistance. I'd stung them, and for that, I was going to suffer...

Only my guys still needed more time. I was as good as dead, but I started shouting to be heard over the screaming of wounded horse things. "Come on, you pussies! I've only killed two of you for sure! I've still got a bunch left to go! Come on! I don't got all day. You Fey are supposed to want a challenge, prove it!"

This time there wasn't any bullshit about station. They accepted the challenge because one of the knights dismounted and started walking confidently toward me. His helmet was shaped like a lion's face, and his red eyes gleamed from between the lion's teeth. The metal armor only made a whisper. The ones back at the fort had been babies compared to this monster. He was built like an NBA center and when he drew his sword, it hissed with green fire.

The Fey said something. All the other Fey laughed at me. That really pissed me off. I didn't speak their language but it had to be something like "Dance for my amusement, monkey."

I hoisted the clumsy mace. "Bring it, then."

He swung the sword gracefully, spinning, twirling, showing off for his friends, the blade leaping from hand to hand faster than my eye could follow. This guy could sword fight like Edward the Orc.

I didn't even see him strike. The sword just came out of nowhere. He hit me in the leg. Then it swung up and cracked me in the neck. The monster pulled back. It stung, but I should have been squirting blood everywhere. He'd only hit me with the flat. The knight was toying with me. He would mock me first, then kill me. The Wild Hunt were dicks.

I threw the mace at him.

The knight easily blocked it with his sword, but he hadn't been expecting me to follow it by tackling him around the waist. We hit the ground hard. Air shot out from his lungs. Fey were tall, but they were lithe, graceful. I was a lot of dense angry human, and four feet of sword didn't mean shit once I was on top of him.

The Fey struck me with his fist, but I trapped his sword with my knee, spied a flat rock about a foot across, picked it up in both hands, and went to town on his helmet with it. Green sparks flew with every hit, magic absorbing some of the impact, but I was still ringing his bell. His gauntlets scratched down my face, but I just kept hammering away.

The other Fey could have easily stepped in and stopped me, but it turned out they really did respect a one-on-one challenge, because they stood there while I beat their companion's face in. My fingers were bleeding around the rock as calluses tore. The green sparks ran dry, and then the helmet deformed like regular metal. At some point the Fey had passed out or died, because he quit trying to choke me. I beat him until the lion's face was a deformed mess and they would have to cut the helmet off with a can opener.

I staggered up and tossed the bloody, cracked rock at the feet of the nearest creature. The monster horse snorted and pawed nervously at it. That knight on top poked at the rock with his spear.

I was breathing so hard it was difficult to talk. "That's three . . ." I groaned as I bent over and picked up the mace again. "Who's next?"

Say what you will about Fey knights, they weren't cowardly. Four of them dismounted at the same time and promptly got into an argument over which one would get the honor of taking my head. *Good.* I needed a moment to catch my breath. I was scared to death and trying not to show it. I was totally surrounded.

Fey were lining up to take a shot at the title. Dirty tricks weren't going to work again. These things were proud, but they weren't stupid. The next one wasn't going to show off. He was going to cut me down.

The argument was interrupted when their Huntsman walked purposefully into their midst. When they saw him, they immediately quit their jabbering and began to bow and scrape. He must have been outraged, because with a swipe of his hand a gust of tornado wind knocked the four Fey sprawling. Their beasts let out fearful whines.

The Huntsman strode toward me, red eyes glowing like Christmas lights beneath his bat mask. Well over seven feet tall, he was walking destruction cloaked in a crackling green halo. The raindrops flashed into steam when they hit him. The plants he brushed past immediately wilted and turned brown. His voice was a terrible growl. My ears rang as he twisted magic to make his words understood.

*"I am next."*

# CHAPTER 24

The Huntsman loomed over me, a being of pure malevolent Fey magic. There was a sword sheathed at his waist, but he hadn't bothered to draw it yet. I probably wasn't worth the effort. The batwing helmet tilted as he studied the corpses littering the ground. The horse thing I had crippled was still screaming. The Huntsman must have been tired of listening to it, because he pointed at it, and the creature simply died.

I was so screwed...

He studied me for a time. I tried to look intimidating. It probably didn't work.

"I have been misled. This is no mere human..." His voice was low and dangerous.

Another Fey had followed their leader. From the eagle beak visor it was Riochedare, the one I'd threatened at their fort, and he'd gone from haughty to sniveling and obsequious. "As I said, my lord, he is a powerful warlock, worthy of your—"

"Fool. Can you not see the chains upon him? This one has been claimed by another. He was not our prey to chase."

"Forgive me! I did not—" But then Riochedare's head departed from his neck in a rather spectacularly violent manner.

I jumped back. I hadn't even seen the Huntsman draw his sword. "Whoa!" The head went bouncing down the ridge, helmet magically sparking against every rock it hit. The blow had cleaved through his neck so cleanly that it took the body a moment to realize it was dead before it fell over.

"Mistakes have been made." The rest of the Fey had gathered around, but none of them seemed very surprised at their leader randomly decapitating one of them. "Though my Hunt has been banished, I wish to someday be allowed to return to my court. I would not further displease our queen by starting a war with another faction."

"Okay." I looked at the headless Fey, then at the absurdly dangerous sword the Huntsman had swung as if it weighed nothing. "Shit happens. Let's just chalk this one up to a cross-cultural failure to communicate and go our separate ways with no hard feelings."

"You are amusing." The Huntsman had a cruel laugh. All the other Fey joined in. The laughter went on for a bit. I even gave them a nervous smile. His laughter stopped abruptly. "No."

I shouldn't have gotten my hopes up.

"Perhaps if we had come to this understanding before you stole my property, human..."

"That property happened to be friends of mine. We frown on that kind of thing where I'm from."

"We are clearly not *where you are from.*"

"This isn't your home either. We're both stuck here."

"Do not pretend that you are in any way my equal.

I have been banished here longer than you have been alive. By your pathetic standards, I am an immortal. I am astonished any faction would be so foolish as to pick such a worm to be their champion."

I was desperate, but really doubted I was going to be able to talk my way out of this. "We can still make some sort of deal."

He didn't need to think it over for very long. "Once a hunt has begun, honor demands that it be seen through to the end. The horn has been sounded. This prey has shed our blood and stolen our goods. You've killed several of my knights and it will take a long time to grow enough *falairdirs* to replace the ones you crippled. Some of us will have to *walk* home. To return empty-handed now would bring unforgivable shame upon my Hunt. My queen will understand."

"Let's be reasonable." That was an ironic thing to say, standing in the middle of a mass murder of my creation. "My people have made arrangements with Fey before."

"I was told about that event. That was another kingdom with a far different court, possessing a queen far more forgiving of humans than mine. Besides, that princess was a twit. They were glad to be rid of her... For us, this insult can only be rectified through the shedding of blood."

"You might be surprised whose blood gets shed today, Fey."

"Do not be confused. I specifically meant your blood."

"Damn, you things are literal."

The Huntsman lifted his sword and touched it against his helmet in salute. Green sparks leapt between the two. "You have made this hunt a challenge, our first real struggle in a very long time. There is beauty in the hard chase. For this, I thank you."

For once I didn't really know what to say. "You're welcome?"

"The greatest part of the chase is the end, that moment when the prey reaches their final understanding, the enlightenment that can only be achieved by passing from one world into another. This is my gift to you. Do not worry, human. I would not dishonor you by offering a quick or painless death. I would not rob you of the experience . . . Let us begin."

The weird mace was way too big and balanced all wrong. The handle was too fat, made for long, spindly Fey fingers. Plus, I had absolutely no idea what I was doing and was up against a monster who clearly did. I lifted the mace anyway, because, damn it, I wasn't going down without a fight. We began to circle.

I lunged for him, but by the Huntsman's standards, I was slow and clumsy.

*Clang.*

With a lightning-fast flick of the wrist, the Huntsman struck. My stolen weapon went flying off so hard the spikes were embedded in a tree. He had moved so smoothly that I was left staring at my stinging fingers, dumbfounded.

The Fey all laughed at my misfortune.

"I see that it begins to dawn upon you just how insignificant you really are." The Huntsman smoothly sheathed his sword, then raised his massive metal gauntlets, fists high and knuckles toward me like an old-fashioned gentleman boxer. "Since you are now disarmed, let us keep this sporting."

Since he was covered in magic metal, he either didn't understand how delicate human hands really are, or Fey had a drastically different definition of *sporting*. The rest of the knights had dismounted and were clustered around us, excited to watch their leader bludgeon me to death. They began chanting something, probably their Huntsman's name.

The Fey wasn't nearly as smooth with his bare hands as he was with a sword, but he was still faster than me and had arms like a gorilla. I barely moved back in time as the gauntlet whistled past my ear. He surged up. The next shot came from below, hit me in the abdomen, lifted me off the ground, and sent me skidding back.

*Ooof.* The Huntsman hit as hard as Franks. I staggered into some of the other knights, and they roughly shoved me back into the circle.

The ground was covered in slick rocks and mud, but his footing was sure. He was a foot taller than I was, with corresponding reach. I couldn't find anything to use to my advantage. One of the Fey must have kicked Cazador off to the side because I couldn't see it. The bolo rope they'd tossed at me was hanging from a bush, but I didn't know what to do with that. I still had my knife, but drawing it would probably just give him an excuse to go back to his sword, and then I was toast.

I was able to stay ahead of his next few casual attacks, but then he caught me with a backhand that sent me rolling through the mud. Only a few fingertips had clipped me, but made of metal and moving that fast, they had still split my face open. By the time I got up, my left eye was starting to swell shut.

Head aching, abs burning, I got up and kept circling away. If I tried to run, the other Fey would just
push me back in. He kept following, almost leisurely.
I couldn't see his hideous face under the mask, but
I bet he was smiling. The Fey were having a grand
time of this. When they got bored, he'd finish me.
My only consolation was that this circus was giving
my people time to get away.

But stalling wasn't good enough. I really wanted
to kill this asshole.

He swung an almost comical haymaker at me. I
ducked because otherwise it would have been like getting hit by a car, but then I came up inside and went
on the offensive. I kicked his knee, but might as well
have kicked a brick wall because my boot bounded off
in a shower of green sparks. I searched for something
I could punch without breaking my hand, but had to
settle for shoving hard against his breastplate. All that
did was move me back and sting my palms.

I retreated past his retaliatory swing, but I wasn't
running, I was analyzing. Everything had a vulnerability. Like Earl said, all sorts of things were supposed
to be immortal, until you figured out a way to kill
them. Rifle bullets bounced off his magical plate, but
there had to be a gap, something that I could exploit.
Only I saw no exposed skin or cloth. He was sealed
up like a space suit.

The Huntsman was cocky, but he wasn't stupid.
He'd felt that kick and, if he wasn't magically invul-
nerable, would have been crippled. He kept following,
but his manner had changed slightly. This was still
just a game to him, but a potentially dangerous one,
and he was a bit more wary. His helmet turned as

he looked over his men, probably checking to see if they had noticed his momentary hesitation, because no leader wanted to look chicken about squishing one little human.

Only, when he turned his head, he showed me a way to kill him.

I went over to the bush and picked up the rope. It was actually three cords stuck together, each about three feet long, with a big knot on each end.

"What's it going to do with that? Lead my steed?" one of the Fey knights shouted. The others laughed.

But the Huntsman knew I was up to something. He intended to end this. The red eyes behind that helmet were burning hot as the glowing monstrosity charged.

*Good.*

At the last instant I flicked the rope toward his eyes.

I didn't expect it to actually hurt him, I only needed to make him blink. My bullets had already proven that Fey knights instinctively flinched just like us.

It worked. Involuntary reaction meant closed eyes. I ducked beneath his outstretched arms as they shot past. The fancy helmet must have cost him some peripheral vision, because it took him a split second to realize I'd gotten behind him.

Turning his head earlier had shown me that there was a gap in the magical armor at the neck. The Fey knights shouted warnings as I reached way up and grabbed the bat wings on his helmet. I yanked back as hard as I could. I don't care how friggin' tough you are, when somebody's cranking back on your vertebrae with the big stupid levers you provided on top of your head, you go down.

I didn't want him to fall all the way. As he toppled,

I went for my knife. His helmet landed on my shoulder, and the instant it tilted back far enough to reveal his wrinkly gray-green throat, I dropped the curved edge of my kukri on it. Skin instantly parted.

I stopped.

So did the Huntsman. He was precariously off balance, leaning back, knees bent, with a heavy, razor-sharp blade resting on his throat. The only thing holding him up was me, and the only thing keeping his head attached was my rapidly dwindling patience. Green blood began oozing around the wound. He knew I had him.

I was breathing so hard it took me a second to form the words. "Who's laughing now, bitch?"

Outraged, the Fey knights surged forward.

"Stop!" the Huntsman bellowed.

I could have sliced him wide open. We both knew it.

Those red eyes were right next to mine. A metal bat wing was smashed against my ear. We were so close I could hear his breathing and the rain pinging off his armor.

"I thought we agreed to be honorable, human. I sheathed my blade."

"You ride flying dinosaurs to chase down unarmed starving men. Shove your honor up your ass. I didn't agree to anything. Now you're going to listen and do exactly what I tell you. I sharpen this thing so religiously I don't even need to push. I let go and gravity will cut you. If I so much as feel the slightest twinkle of Fey magic or fairy dust or whatever the hell you dickbags use, I take your head. Got it?"

The Huntsman couldn't even nod without risk. "Your threat is understood."

I eyed the assembled Fey. There were a ton of them, and they were all supremely ticked and ready to make a move. "You wanted to know why some faction chose me? Because I'm really good at killing things like you. Your boys try anything, I'll give them a demonstration."

"Very well..." The Huntsman seemed relatively calm. "How do you wish to proceed, human?"

I wasn't exactly sure. It wasn't like I could walk my giant deadly hostage the rest of the way. "First, we're all going to stand here like this until I'm sure my friends are safely back on Earth."

"How will you know when this occurs?"

"I don't know yet. So you'd better pray to whatever Fey pray to that my arm doesn't get tired before then. After that we're going to revisit our earlier discussion about how I'm going to walk away and we forget we ever met."

There was a new sound, so out of place that it took me a second to figure out what it was. Somebody had begun slow clapping. I glanced in that direction. "What the hell?"

Somehow, Jason Lococo had appeared in the circle of Fey. His hood was up and still wreathed in foliage; he looked like some primeval forest creature. I could barely see his face, but there was no mistaking that hulking figure. "Well done. That was impressive." He stopped the ironic clapping and put one foot casually up on the dead horse thing's side. He folded his arms and leaned on his knee. "As many as you've destroyed, you'd think monsters would have learned not to underestimate you by now."

The Fey knights seemed more surprised to see

Lococo standing there than I was. Swords which had been intended for me were quickly shifted in his direction. The Huntsman hissed a warning in his language. That really seemed to scare them, as every one of the Fey knights assembled took a nervous step away from the overwhelmingly outnumbered Lococo.

Ghost or Fey trick, I didn't know what he was, but I kept tension on my knife. "VanZant told me how Jason died. Who are you?" Nervous, I shifted my attention back to my prisoner. "Who is he?"

But the terrifying Huntsman didn't respond to me, instead he addressed Lococo. Even though I was ready to cut his throat, it was like the new interloper was the far greater threat. There was genuine fear in his voice. "Forgive us. We meant no insult. Please. I beg. We did not know it was you who had laid claim upon this human's life."

"Well, you sure screwed up then," Lococo growled.

Something was terribly wrong. The knights were shifting, trying to decide between fight or flight. Their hound beasts had lowered their heads and were whining.

But worst of all, out of nowhere, the rain stopped. The silence was deafening.

"Please . . ." The Huntsman actually sounded terrified now. "Spare us, great one."

"Who is he?" I demanded again. *"Who!"*

The Huntsman never got to answer, because an invisible weight fell on top of my kukri. It chopped through his neck like a guillotine. The Huntsman thrashed, trying desperately to get away, but it was as if we were both locked in place. "No!" I tried to pull the blade away, but the downward force increased. I couldn't let go, like a vise had clamped around my fingers. I was hit in the eyes with arterial spray. The force let up once the arteries and trachea were severed. I gasped and stepped away, covered in green blood. The Huntsman dropped in the mud, reaching for his ruined throat, legs kicking spasmodically.

The Fey screamed as they saw their leader dying. Several of them charged, some at me, some at Lococo.

"Come on, Pitt." Lococo casually stretched his hand toward the mace embedded in the tree trunk, then he swept his arm toward the charging Fey. The mace ripped free in an explosion of splinters, flew through the circle at an incredible velocity, blasted a Fey in a shower of green fire, and sent him hurtling into the others, scattering them like bowling pins. "You know who I am."

*I did now.*

All I could do was duck as a Fey attempted to slice my head off, but suddenly that Fey was completely engulfed in flames. The heat was so intense that I had to raise my arms to keep from scalding my eyes. The Fey shrieked as his armor melted to his bones. Within seconds he had turned into a molten puddle burning a hole through the rock.

I ran for my life.

The demon who was wearing Lococo's face walked after me. He waved his hand dismissively toward the other Fey rushing him. They were instantly hoisted a few feet into the air, and held there, kicking futilely, until he made a fist and the knights' armor suddenly crumpled inward, crushing them as easily as an empty soda can. Bones shattered, organs popped, blood squirted. It was horrifying. They died there in the air, and as he strolled past, they dropped, forgotten.

I kept running. I didn't look back. From the screams and crunching coming from behind me, all the Fey were being slaughtered.

Then Lococo appeared directly in front of me. "Where are you going?"

I crashed right into him, but he effortlessly caught me by the shirt, spun me around, and hurled me back. I hit the ground hard, bouncing and skidding across the rocks.

All around, the Fey were dying. The world was shaking. Pillars of earth erupted into the sky, flinging screaming knights to their deaths. Lightning struck from the clouds, blowing Fey to pieces. For the first time since I had been in this awful place, it went dark, but I was surrounded by so many burning puddles of armor that there was still plenty of flickering light to see by.

While I was trying to breathe, a pair of worn-out boots crunched to a stop right in front of my face. "We're not done yet." He kicked me hard and flipped me onto my back. "Know who I am now?"

I lay there, dazed and bleeding, looking up at the demon that was wearing what was left of Jason Lococo like a suit. "You're Asag."

"One name of the hundreds your kind has thought up for me, but it'll do as well as any of the others." The demon squatted down by my side. The hood had fallen back revealing that through his empty eye socket was a darkness that stretched forever. "You know, I feel like we've really gotten to know each other. I've enjoyed our talks. I think we need to have one more." He cocked back one fist and knocked me the hell out.

# CHAPTER 25

I woke up looking down at my feet. They were dangling a few feet off the ground.

One eye was so swollen that I could barely see out of it. I had a splitting headache. Groaning, I raised my head. I was upright, but not sure how. There was a pressure on my chest, so tight I could barely inhale, let alone move. I had been bound to a tree with rope.

I tried not to panic.

The Nightmare Realm was still oddly dark. But I could tell that I was still on the same ridgeline because the metal puddles that had once been armor were still on fire. Only now instead of Fey, the area was swarming with the thin, clammy white bodies of Asakku.

There had to be dozens of them. Actually *singing* while they worked, they seemed to be in an almost festive mood. Their music was like the choir at an insane asylum, but with less harmony. It took me a moment to understand what the creatures were doing, and then I gagged.

They were butchering the dead Fey.

Using simple tools to crack open the armor to get at the meat, the Asakku were working frantically. It was like watching starving people breaking open lobsters. It was the first time I'd seen the Fey knights out of their armor, and they were truly hideous, simultaneously elven and lizard. But right then, rather than disgust, I just felt pity. Once peeled from their shells, other Asakku cut off the Fey's underclothing and then hacked the corpses into manageable pieces. They weren't just devouring them right away . . . no, this was a victory feast. Though from the blood-stained mouths, some of them couldn't resist snacking.

They were throwing the body parts in a big pile. The Asakku had built a bonfire, and on top of it rested a giant metal pot. Where the hell had they gotten a friggin' *cauldron?* A gnarly, four-armed Asakku tossed a Fey knight's foot into the bubbling mix. The chef was making stew.

I was close enough to smell the cooking meat and feel the warmth of the fire. I had a bad feeling I was going to be getting a lot closer to that fire soon.

My mind was still reeling. Asag wasn't supposed to be in the Nightmare Realm, he was supposed to be in the tomb beneath the City of Monsters. He'd tricked us all. I was screwed, but what did this mean for the mission? Had the Hunters walked into a trap? I had to get back and warn them. I tried to shift my weight, looking for a weakness in the ropes, or maybe a protruding piece of bark I could rub the rope against to try and cut it with friction. It felt hopeless, but doing something beat waiting to go in the soup.

There was a whisper of wind, and Asag appeared before me, still wearing Lococo's form.

"Son of a bitch." My first instinct was to kick him, but the ropes had absolutely no give.

"You're finally awake. This body I claimed has a great deal of strength. I thought maybe I'd put you in a coma." He reached up for my face. I tried to flinch away, but had nowhere to go. He poked roughly around my battered eye, then let go. "That's just a cut. I thought you might have lost your eye in that duel. Now that would've been an ironic twist."

"What do you care I ruined his eye? You're not really him."

"Of course I'm not, but I am telepathic. Jason was a very honest, straightforward type. Not at all like me. However, before the Fey killed him, I watched and learned. That's what I've been doing ever since you woke me up: watching and learning, observing humanity, and trying to understand what you've become. But having some of you here was a great opportunity to study you up close. Jason was the strongest of them. All his memories, his emotions, his bitterness . . . I took them, used them. It made for a far more convincing act than just wearing his skin as a mask." Asag sat on the ground in front of me, cross-legged. "The hard part was trying not to be too talkative. My performance wasn't perfect by any means; it wouldn't have fooled his friends, but you two had never exactly been close."

My mind was reeling. I'd talked with him, confided in him, trusted him . . . "Pretending to be a dead Hunter is a dick move."

"What part of 'I'm a god of chaos' confuses you? I know what they say about me back in your world. Asag, the great demon so hideous that he boils the fish in the rivers. You knew we would meet someday.

Did you think I was going to look like the old graven images, and I'd be sixty feet tall, with the head of a man, the body of a bull, and eagle's wings? How's that supposed to work? The humans who carved those exercised some artistic license once I was gone."

To be honest, he had me there. "He Who Ends All Things" was not at all what I'd expected.

"You probably thought I was going to conquer the Earth, all *rawr giant monster smash,* like those careless blundering Great Old Ones you've fought. But I'm not at all like that. Most Old Ones are ambivalent. Life is inconsequential to them, either in their way or not. Me? I *care* about each and every one of you." The demon surveyed the burning ridgeline and the slaughtered Fey. "What you see here is an anomaly. Contrary to what you think you know about me, I don't like using brute force. I'm more of a facilitator. However, in this realm where there are so few rules that I can twist matter on a whim, how could I resist?"

We had been expecting Fenrir and had gotten Loki instead. "What do you want, Asag?"

"To get to know you better, Pitt. After all, they picked you to defeat me. I merely wanted to understand why. That's why I allowed you alone to make it through the gate. Don't look surprised. After all, I'm the one who built it. Extra humans would just have complicated matters. The only reason your associates survived here so long was because I allowed them to. The parasites that dwell in this realm—the things you call alps—I kept their hunger in check, only allowing them a taste. Just a little bit of torment." He held up his thumb and forefinger close together. "I've been gone so long, I wanted to learn how my adversaries had evolved while I was away. The best way to do that was to observe them under stress."

I said nothing. If Asag had killed the others, he would surely be gloating about it. He probably would have left their bodies displayed for my benefit before tossing them in the soup. I could only hope that they'd been able to get out.

"I can read most human minds, but not yours, Pitt. Which is interesting, because in my research I learned that in the past other powerful beings have been able to crack you, but not anymore. I can only get little bits and pieces. Everything else is obscured. Either you've unconsciously learned to harness some of the gifts you've been granted, or it's a defensive mechanism provided by your benefactors. . . . Regardless, I don't need to read your mind when your face so clearly betrays your thoughts. Yes. Your friends got away. I allowed them to. You are welcome." He made a theatrical bow.

I didn't understand Asag's motivations, but I was no stranger to dealing with powerful otherworldly entities. If they let anything good happen, there was always a catch. "Why after all this would you just let them go?"

"It's never been about them. It's always been about you, the man chosen to defeat me." Asag seemed genuinely amused. It was weird, because I don't think Lococo's real face had ever actually worn that big of a smile. He even had a twinkle in his eye. The other one remained a black hole through the universe. "I learned everything I could about modern Hunters from them. Now they'll return and tell the others that the last they saw of Owen Zastava Pitt, he was preparing to lay down his life against an army of Fey.

Hiding the spark of your life from the MCB's remote viewer is a simple task for me. Yes, I know about their cyclops as well. And the other Chosen? Harbinger and Kerkonen for the Beasts; Franks on behalf of the God of Light—now *that* pick was unexpected; and eventually the Guardian's draftee, your own wife? They will all accept you are dead. No one will ever risk a search."

Asag seemed so sure of himself, but eventually Mordechai or one of the others would find me.

"You try to conceal it, but I can smell your hope. I know about your ghosts. In this realm, I can hide you so well that even your allied dead can't sense you. Face it. No one loves you *that* much."

The demon could just kill me now and get it over with. He'd had plenty of opportunities to murder me in my sleep on our journey across the Nightmare Realm. Hell, Asag had even saved me from falling off a cliff. "You don't want me dead at all. You want me imprisoned. You want me stuck here. Why?"

"Because at this point, if I just kill their appointed champion, they might still have a chance to prepare another. Like when your faction fell back to you after Raymond Shackleford was corrupted."

*What was he talking about?* But I held my tongue, trying not to give away my surprise.

Only Asag could read my battered face like an open book. "It's true. You weren't their first choice. Not even their second or third. However, I would like for you to be the last, because I've been playing their game for forty thousand years now, and frankly, I am tired of their shit."

"Untie me and I'll put you out of your misery."

Asag laughed. "That defiant spirit illustrates why

they picked you. A rational man would look at his circumstances and give into despair."

I sure wasn't feeling optimistic, but I'd always remain an oppositional sort just on general principles. "Up yours."

"You had a different destiny plotted for you, but after you survived Lord Machado's ordeal, you demonstrated you had the potential to stop me. The last human they picked to defeat me became so powerful and consumed with pride that afterwards he thought he could rise up and challenge his creators, and they had to cast him down. They probably thought you have more flaws and humility than the last, so you'd be easier to control. Plus, since in your battle against Machado you inadvertently shattered time and woke me, passing the mantle onto you was poetic justice. Your faction is big on that karmic silliness."

I didn't know how much of this was true and how much of it was Asag yanking my chain. I was unprepared for this. Exhausted, beat up, and starved was hardly the right state to play mind games with a trickster god. "Bullshit. My dad was warned about you before I was ever even born."

"Just because I've been playing against them, doesn't mean I get to see which cards my opponents still have in their hands. There are many of us seated around the table. You were a backup plan for a backup plan. Plots within plots, contingencies built on top of conspiracies, uncaring invisible hands steering fate in order to prepare their pawns—"

"You're mixing up chess and poker analogies."

"I've been indisposed for a bit. I'm rusty."

*Screw it.* If he was going to poke and prod at me,

I was going to poke back. "You lost hard. I saw it through the eyes of one of your Children. You were so certain victory was yours, but at the last minute they pulled the rug out from under you. You got put in the ground for a long time." That wiped the smirk off his stolen face. "Yeah. I thought so. You don't like losing."

"Only losers like losing, Pitt. That was a temporary setback."

"What is it you expect to win then? What're you fighting for, Asag?"

Asag chuckled. "So you expect me to grant you my vision for your world? Martin Hood was stupid enough to. Would you like me to explain all my plans to you, in the off chance that you find a way home, so you can stop me? You must take me for a fool."

"I was thinking you're more of a dick—"

A wave of telekinetic force knocked the snot out of me. My skull rebounded off the bark. It had been like getting hit in the face with a two by four. My lip had split open and blood came running out of my nose.

The demon was still smiling. "I enjoy this dimension. On Earth that would have taken effort."

I spit out a gob of blood. "That the best you got?"

"I had the opportunity to understand you, so I suppose no harm will come from you understanding me. Besides, it will give you something to dwell on during your stay." Asag raised one hand and snapped his fingers.

The mountain faded. Suddenly, I was somewhere else. Glass and steel skyscrapers rose all around me. It was as if I was standing on a busy street, only the vision was erratic, jerky, like watching a film on fast forward. The sidewalks were thronged with colorful pedestrians. Traffic lights flashed a rapid cascade of green, yellow, red, as thousands of cars jerked to a stop then leapt out of view.

Asag's voice was a whisper in my ear. "Look at them. They are computers made of meat and electrical impulses. Each has a tiny shred of eternal potential, and for that, I despise them. They incorrectly assume they mean something. They mean nothing."

I could smell the city stink, humanity, exhaust, and garbage. I could hear millions of voices, sirens, horns honking. Only all of the senses were sped up, so that it was a jackhammer of stimuli as days flashed by with each heartbeat.

"Your world is based on rules. For actions, there are consequences. For a stimulus, a response. For each sin, a punishment. How very stifling. It is because you obey that I loathe you."

Day turned to night. Night turned to day. Only a deeper darkness slowly descended over the city. It was insidious. The flashing crowd couldn't see what was coming. The ambivalent face of humanity slowly turned suspicious, angry, and hateful.

"As I said, I do not enjoy brute force. I merely show others a different way. I am a guide, a teacher, a guru, a prophet. There are hundreds of supernatural creatures and millions of your fellow humans with schemes to destroy everything. Occasionally, one of them finds their way to me, and for one glorious moment, they become truly free. Only the rest of you blind cowards rush to stifle them. I would free all from their bonds. I let them spread their wings and fly."

The lights went out. Garbage began piling up in the streets. Graffiti appeared. Windows broke. The pedestrians began attacking each other. A car flashed by on the sidewalk, tossing bodies. Stores were looted. Fires broke out. Somebody picked up a baby stroller and hurled it in front of a bus.

"I am the randomness in your system."

The violence grew in frequency and intensity. Bombs exploded. Bodies were flung through the glass.

"I am Disorder."

Monsters roamed free. Horrible things were summoned and released. War bands roamed through the wreckage. It was a million scenes of rape and murder.

I couldn't close my eyes. "That's madness!"

"That's nothing. That's a *start*. Life is a symptom, nothing more. The universe desires entropy. Rules disgust me, down to the molecular level. I would undo them all. Even the gods must die. In time I would disband all cohesion. What has been created can be undone."

Then I saw the world *disintegrate*.

My brain couldn't even process what happened. Everything was rent apart. Reality was unorganized. It was the end of all things.

"Isn't it beautiful?"

I vomited down my shirt. Since my stomach was empty it was mostly retching and bile.

We were back on the mountain.

"Don't worry, that last part is still a while off. It took billions of years to make all of this, it will take time to reverse the process, but time is the one thing I have. I may despise order, but I understand the necessary evil of sticking to a schedule. Now that you know what I'm fighting for, what do you think?"

I was having a hard time thinking at all. Trying to understand the last part of that vision had completely unnerved me. It was like my brain had tried to shift gears and had broken the transmission. "What're you going to do after that, just float around nothing forever?"

"That would be ideal. Sadly, your masters keep creating worlds faster than my kind can unmake the ones that are already there. Only that's big picture, far beyond the scope of our current conflict. Focusing on the here and now, first I'll bring about the utter ruin of your world. I've done it to others before, and in comparison yours is already off to a fine start without me."

My head hurt and speaking only made it worse. "You'll fail."

"I forget sometimes just how difficult it is for you mortals to truly comprehend things. It's like trying to explain calculus to a dog." Asag was still sitting cross-legged in front of the tree, only now, the hole over his missing eye had spread to cover the whole socket, and there were black veins visible beneath his skin. I swear that on the other side I could see stars. "The factions trying to stop me falsely believe there is a balance, as if they can control the pendulum that swings between order and chaos, between agency and destiny. The Great Old Ones desire total control, to shape everything in their unknowable image. I merely want to set the pendulum free."

"More like break the pendulum off and beat us with it."

"Humans have a way with words. I will have to remember that."

"We're going to stop you."

"Possibly, but that is what makes it so interesting! Speaking of which, I have a proposition for you."

"Fat chance."

"Don't be hasty. Let me tell you what is at stake before I make my offer. After I leave you here to rot for eternity, I will return to the City of Monsters, beneath which a hundred thousand of my Children and monstrous allies have gathered. I shall lead my great army, and in one fell swoop, eradicate many of the heroes who would stand in my way, since you gathered them in one place for my convenience."

"Lies."

"Let me drive your bleak situation home. Your child has already been born. Congratulations. You have a healthy baby boy. So I have dispatched an exceedingly foul, yet capable, creature to collect him."

I roared something incoherent and struggled against the ropes.

"Now that you understand what is immediately at stake, time for my offer..." He reached inside his coat and pulled out the .45 I had loaned him. "I've been curious about you since you first woke me up. I've watched from afar, but that wasn't good enough. In our time journeying together, I believe I've truly come to understand you, Owen. May I call you Owen? You have become the closest thing I have to a friend."

Breathing hard, dizzy, I was almost inarticulate with rage. "I'll kill you if it's the last thing I do!"

It was hard to tell how much of it was an act, or if that had really hurt the demon's feelings. "It is lonely being a force of nature." Asag thumbed the release and dropped the magazine into his hand. Then he tossed the pistol at my feet. It landed with a *clunk*. "In a moment I will release you. I will only allow you a brief freedom, because after that I am going to bury you so deep in this realm that no one will ever find you. If you are the man I suspect you to be, you will take the opportunity to kill yourself."

"You're insane."

"No. I'm Disorder. For the sake of your world, of your family and friends, think carefully about what I'm saying, Owen. Escape is impossible. You've seen what I can do here. Yet, if your life was severed now, your faction would still have the chance to pick a new champion. Who knows what other contingencies they might have put in place? How will the game unfold with you removed from play? You can't stop me now, but maybe the next Chosen will. Plus, if you're dead, I have no motivation to steal your child. Harming your family does me no benefit. I will call off my minion."

I glanced down at my pistol. It had to be a trick.

"This is merely me granting you mercy, which is more than I can say for your masters who used you foolishly and abandoned you here. I am the one taking all the risks here, Owen. I like you. I'm making this offer because I truly do not wish for you to suffer . . . Believe what you will. Selfishly hold onto vain hope, or save your child and possibly let someone else save your world. It is your choice."

The ropes suddenly released. Freed of the restraints I fell. My legs were numb, so when I hit the ground I collapsed face first into the mud.

"Decide quickly. I've got a lot of Hunters to kill."

The pistol was right in front of me. The ridgeline was quiet except for the crackling of flames and the bubbling of the cauldron. The Asakku had stopped working and were all watching me, curious to see what I would do. Asag was waiting, giving me a patronizing smile.

I picked up my .45. There was mud all over the

steel. The textured grip felt familiar and comforting in my hand. I couldn't separate the truth from the lies, but *this* was real.

"There is only one bullet in the gun. I would suggest putting it in your mouth angled to destroy the base of your brain. It's better to be certain. Trust me. This world has ways of making you linger."

I was confused, weary, but I still had a choice. I could believe a king of lies, or do what I knew every good Hunter who'd come before me would have done.

I aimed the pistol at Asag's forehead and pulled the trigger. It went off.

*WHAP!*

The bullet struck something invisible between us. A gigantic red hand appeared directly before Asag's face, the bullet embedded in its palm. The clawed fingers immediately closed into a fist. Then the air shimmered as the rest of the creature revealed itself. The thing was a muscle-bound humanoid, large enough to make Lococo's body look small in comparison. Leathery wings stretched from its back. The legs were covered in coarse black fur, and instead of feet it had cloven hooves. Horns grew from its misshapen head. It was staring right through me with glowing eyes, including the third one in the center of its forehead.

"Disappointing, but not surprising," Asag said with a sigh. "It is easier to die for your child, than it is to fight to stay alive for them. Since I can't read your mind or see your fate, I actually didn't know what you were going to do there. I suppose that uncertainty is why I enjoy your company so much."

The demonic bodyguard must have been waiting there the whole time. How many times in the forest or the swamp, when I'd felt unseen eyes on me, had it been Asag's errand boy watching us? From the description, this was the beast that had killed Management's lawyer. The red-skinned monstrosity casually tossed the deformed hollowpoint back to me. The bullet had mushroomed uselessly against his skin.

The monster spoke, its voice low and powerful. "It is time. We must leave, master."

"Thank you, Prince," Asag nodded at the monster. It bowed and moved aside.

"You had this big red bastard watching over you the whole time," I snarled, "because you're scared. He was ready to step in the whole time in case I ever figured out who you really were. If you were as powerful as you make yourself out to be, you wouldn't need a bodyguard around to protect you from me. You're no god. You're a fraud. You're vulnerable."

"On the contrary. This body I've claimed may be fragile, but I am eternal. I'd explain, except your time is done. I'm afraid our conversation is over, Owen."

The dirt shifted beneath my knees. Roots burst from the ground, moving like snakes, crawling over my legs, then up my chest, and over my arms. I pulled against them. Some roots snapped, but others quickly took their place. No matter how hard I fought, more kept wrapping around me. I was encircled in seconds. Then all the roots tightened violently.

I was being pulled into the soft ground.

"I swear I'll kill you, Asag!"

"You broke time to wake me, and for that, I will never forget you." As my legs sank beneath the dirt, the demon stood up. He actually twisted Lococo's face to appear saddened. "Goodbye, my friend."

As dirt rose over my chest, Asag and the red devil vanished. I kept up my futile struggle as cold mud reached my neck. The Asakku watched, curious, as the roots dragged me under, but then they went back to their feast. I held my breath as dirt covered my mouth and nose. I was deafened as it covered my ears. Dirt spilled over my eyes. Everything went black but the roots still kept pulling me down.

The Nightmare Realm swallowed me whole.

Lungs burning, heart pounding, I held my breath as long as I could. Blind, deaf, encircled by hundreds of roots that cut like steel cables, panic began to set in. I strained as hard as I could, but the roots wouldn't give. Suddenly the dirt that had turned soft enough to sink through seemed to harden around me.

Frozen, I couldn't move. Pain was growing in my chest. I was going to suffocate and die.

Don't panic. *Concentrate. Think.* No oxygen. I'd be unconscious soon, dead shortly after.

I'd nearly drowned once. This was like that, but worse. A ghost had saved me that time. Only in this place, I was alone.

The pain got worse. I had to exhale, but there was nowhere for it to go, lips and nostrils buried. Lights were popping in my head. The pain was excruciating. I couldn't scream. I couldn't thrash.

I should have shot myself when I had the chance. At least that would have been fast. I was terrified. My heart was beating so hard that it was going to burst. My air ran out and nothing happened.

I focused on counting the explosive beats. Each time my heart pumped it was like being electrocuted.

Thirty. Forty. Fifty. I should have passed out by now. Seventy. Eighty. How was I alive?

*Calm down.* Asag put me here. He didn't want me dead, just removed. My thoughts weren't fading. They were a panicked jumble, but clear.

*This place has ways of making you linger.*

It wouldn't let you starve. It wouldn't let your wounds become infected. It wouldn't let you die of exposure. So of course it wouldn't let you asphyxiate.

*Son of a bitch . . .*

An unknown amount of time passed. It still hurt unbelievably bad, but if I wasn't dead by now, I wasn't dying any time soon. Something weird was going on, and I forced myself to be analytical about it. My heart was slowing now, but for those few minutes the alps must have feasted on all the terror I'd provided. Those little bastards had probably thrown as big a party as the Asakku eating the Fey.

There had to be a way out. I tried moving every muscle in my body. If they were going to give me eternity, I'd scratch my way out with my fingernails if I had to. Only there was no give at all. I was so trapped I couldn't even flex a muscle or bend a joint. I didn't know if that was because the ground was hard as concrete now, or it just felt that way because I'd been weakened so much. This had to be some sort of weird magical stasis. It was like everything was shutting down except for my brain. I was utterly trapped and would be completely aware of it the whole time.

Oh, this would be a miserable way to spend eternity.

# CHAPTER 26

It was a living hell.

At first the pain made it so that I couldn't think. It probably would have driven me insane, if I'd not somehow disconnected myself from it.

I don't know how much time passed after that, but I spent all of it angry. Assuming that lying bastard was actually telling the truth, Asag was sending something horrible to steal my kid. It would still have to get through Julie, but the thought of them in danger filled me with dread. All of the Hunters on Severny Island were going to get attacked, yet I couldn't warn anybody about it, stuck here inside my head.

I had to think of it that way, because it turns out that when you're artificially kept alive, laws of physics and biology be damned, it hurts so damned much that eventually you tune out the physical world and retreat totally inside your thoughts.

It was sort of like being disembodied, but without the perks. My spirit had left my body before, so I was probably better prepared for this than most. It was a little bit like being dead, and I'd done that before too.

Only this time I couldn't leave my body and go for a stroll. My consciousness was anchored to my flesh, and my flesh was being utterly useless.

I tried concentrating, praying, wishing extra hard, you name it. My limited understanding of magic had demonstrated it was all about focus and desire, but I wasn't getting anything. I tried to think about nothing, but meditating never worked for me. I couldn't even manage to clear my head when I was buried alive with nothing else to do, and this Chosen gifts thing had always been a crapshoot.

Supposedly a strong enough will could twist the Nightmare Realm to suit them, but I'd been here long enough to grow out my beard and I still hadn't even been able to do anything about the obnoxious weather. Meanwhile, Asag could just twist reality and microwave Fey by thinking about it. Head to head, Asag would kick my ass, but I hoped that once he left the realm, maybe I would be the strongest will around and I'd be able to finally get something done. It was a small hope, but it was all I had, so I clung to it.

I wondered if the story about Lococo's childhood and the juvenile detention center was stolen from the real man, or if the demon had just made that up too. It felt real. Lococo's past had formed this one corner of the realm, and Asag had seen fit to leave it as a memorial. I was furious. After all we'd been through, I had felt like I had really gotten to know him. Hell, we'd spent so much time together on the road that I'd talked to him about my *feelings*.

I was such a sucker.

We had even talked about my father's passing. I hadn't even really talked about that with Julie yet.

She'd been too far away, but Trip, Holly, Earl, Milo...
all my closest friends had all been there for me, but
no, I had to be a stoic to them and, instead, then
go and confide in an ancient chaos demon about how
Dad's death had affected me.

Dad would never have gotten played like I had. Dad
didn't trust anybody. He knew the end was coming.
He would've seen the con a mile away. If it had been
him instead of me, he would've figured a different way
out, and Asag would be the one buried. *What would
you have done differently, Dad?*

Of course, I didn't get an answer. Nobody else
could hear me, so why would he?

But he'd taught me for years, so I didn't need him
to answer. I already knew exactly what he would've
told me and exactly how he would've said it. *You
screwed up, son. You can either be a useless baby
crying about it, or you can get your shit together
and fix what you screwed up.*

Damned right.

So I spent a long time thinking, concentrating,
spinning in my head, and occasionally ignoring the
agony long enough to go back into my body to see if
I could move something. Asag had taken everything
else from me, but from Auhangamea Pitt I'd inherited
a stupid amount of determination.

There had to be a way to use it to get out of here.
I tried imagining the roots falling away. I visualized
myself bursting from the dirt.

It was pointless. You can only imagine something
*so hard.*

*Improvise. Adapt. Survive.*

I'm trying, Dad.

*A strong man knows to ask for help when he needs it.*

I'd been doing that for a long damned time now, but nobody was getting the message.

Once in a while I'd drift off to sleep, only it turned out that Asag had been telling the truth about keeping the alps at bay, because during that, the nightmares pulled out all the stops. Everything I'd experienced before was nothing compared to the awful images they inflicted on me while I was buried.

They'd done this to Mark Thirteen, trapped in never-ending nightmares, until his sanity had broken like a dropped egg. They'd been forced to put him into a medically induced coma. Nobody was going to do me that favor here.

When I came to, all I could remember was vague terror and trying to scream for help. Either I was forgetting on purpose, or worse, maybe the alps just wiped the slate clean that way so that when I fell asleep again they could recycle the same torments they'd cooked up and they would seem fresh. Alps struck me as lazy and spiteful like that. I'd been planted in the ground and now they were going to farm me like a potato.

In some ways, awake was worse than the dreaming because my imagination was worse than anything an alp could come up with. What if Asag was gone, and my mind had finally succeeded in subverting this realm? Only not in a good way, and the forest had been burned away and above was a facsimile of the sanity-rending awfulness of the Old Ones' universe.

I needed to get out of this sensory-deprivation hole soon, or I was going to lose my mind.

Maybe it came to me during a tortured dream, or maybe it was a long-forgotten memory resurfacing—because with crushing despair I knew nothing could reach me here—yet I heard a voice in my head. It sounded like a little girl, only she didn't speak like a kid.

*Heed my words, Owen. You must stay alive. You must fight. This is not the end.*

Where had I heard that voice before? It was so familiar, but beyond my grasp. A doppelganger had once taken the form of a child I hadn't recognized, and it had sounded exactly like that. The creature had seemed surprised when its disguise had failed to confuse me. I'd had no recollection of who it had been pretending to be, so at the time I'd dismissed it as a trick, only this was definitely the same little girl.

*Understand, the opposite of disorder is not order. It is messy, beautiful, creation.*

I drifted back into oblivion.

The next time I woke up, I actually *felt* something.

I paid attention to my body and was immediately consumed in agony, but I stuck around, because any change was good. Even if an Old One was about to dig me up with its tentacles and eat me as a snack, that was an improvement.

*Vibrations?* The ground was shifting. Was it an earthquake? Was I dreaming awake? Or had so much time passed that Asag had ruined Earth, and he was coming back to rub it in my face? Feet were stamping the ground. I could feel it in my dirt-filled inner ear. Either something was happening above me or my mind had finally broken.

I tried to force my limbs to move. Nothing happened. Muscle tremors at best, and I probably imagined those. I had no air, no energy, *Help!* I couldn't make a sound, and this might sound desperate and stupid, but I *thought* it as hard as I could. *Help! Down here!*

The vibrations continued. There was a rhythm to them. *Thunk. Scrape. Thunk. Scrape.* Someone was *digging.*

The sound continued. It wasn't a shovel, stab and lift. It was like they were using a flat rock. Drive it in, scrape it out. Was I being rescued? Or had the Asakku decided that they were still hungry, and since their master was away, they might as well eat me too? The vibrations were getting stronger. It felt like they were getting closer.

The digging stopped for a bit. *No!* Had they given up? I tried as hard as I could to move, to give them some indication that they were working in the right spot. Even if it was a disobedient and hungry Asakku, that was better than this hole.

Thankfully, the digging started again. I felt something. *Moisture?* Water must have been pooling in the hole and seeping through my dirt. Then something touched me. It actually scraped hard across the top of my scalp. It hurt, but it was a new and different kind of hurt, so that was the best thing ever. Then I felt desperate fingers feeling around my head as dead roots were stripped away by hand.

I felt the patter of raindrops on my head. The fingers reached my eyes, roughly brushing the dirt away. An errant fingernail knocked my eye open the tiniest crack. By the time I could see anything at all, the mystery digger had freed one ear too.

My vision was so encrusted and blurred that all I could see was a darker spot in the night. The mud was like earplugs so I could barely hear, but the rainwater was running in and rinsing some of it out. "Almost there," the shadow whispered.

It was a man and I didn't think it was Asag. This was the happiest moment of my life.

I still couldn't move—I suspected I needed to breathe for that—but he scooped a few handfuls of wet dirt away from my nose and mouth. My lungs should have long since collapsed, but it was like they caught on fire when the first air molecule hit. I reflexively inhaled as my body broke free of the magical stasis.

"Shhhh. Quiet," the shadow hissed. But a white shape appeared behind the man. Something had heard my gasp. "Hang on." He pulled away and disappeared.

*No! Come back!* I cried out in my mind, but I didn't make any more sounds. My body was coming back to life, but with an awful, tingly sensation, like a million hot needles being stabbed into every nerve and vein.

The white thing got closer, revealing that it was a curious Asakku. The awkward creature got closer, peering down at me, surely wondering why my face was suddenly exposed to the elements.

The shadow rose behind it. One hand covered the Asakku's misshapen mouth. Then there was a flood of red as the creature's throat was slashed. It struggled soundlessly for a moment, then it stopped, and the shadow lowered it gently to the ground.

He appeared over me again, and now I could see the whites of his eyes, gleaming in a face that had been blacked out with greasepaint. He immediately went back to digging. He kept his voice down. "Try to move now."

I did. It hurt unbelievably bad, but I was able to shift my body a little. The soil had never been that hard, I had just been that weak. The magic that had animated the roots had long since died off, because I was able to tug against them and there was some give. I tried to tell my rescuer that I could move now, only breathing was fire. Talking was impossible. Deprived of air, thirst had been so far down my list of problems that I hadn't even realized how dry my mouth was. As soon as I could use my hands again, the first thing I was going to do was pry a bunch of dirt out of my mouth.

He kept working, glancing around constantly, watching for more Asakku. I could sense some movement, and I thought I heard snoring. There were a couple of small campfires nearby. The big cooking bonfire was out. My nose was too plugged to smell anything, but I was guessing the Fey stew had been gone for a long time. The burning armor piles had probably cooled into solid metal blobs by now. The stranger got one of my hands free, and then with surprising strength, began pulling me out. Some of the roots made an audible *snap* as they broke.

The stranger froze. I was halfway out of the ground now, and realizing that the Asakku had made camp only fifty feet away. A snoring Asakku grunted, but then rolled over and went back to sleep. The man watched for another moment to make sure we weren't spotted, then pulled me the rest of the way out of the hole . . . slowly, to avoid loudly snapping any more roots.

The stranger went prone next to me. I could barely make out his features in the dark, especially since his face was painted. He was wearing an old-fashioned boonie hat and tiger-stripe camouflage fatigues. He was younger than me, a little smaller, but solid as a rock. "Just breathe slow. Don't cough. You cough, they'll hear. Gather your strength. Wait for the curse to fade. It'll take a minute for your muscles to work again. I'll carry you until then."

I lay there, quivering and hurting. My limbs felt like boiled noodles. Though he was whispering, his voice sounded familiar, but it couldn't be...

*Dad?*

Was this whole thing a hallucination? Even if it was, I'd run with it because it was better than the hole.

Beneath the brim of his hat, his eyes were tracking an Asakku that was wandering in our direction. Those eyes narrowed, and though this man was only in his twenties, I'd seen that same look a multitude of times. The look told me he was analyzing a problem and figuring out a plan to take care of it. Didn't matter if it was repairing the roof, mowing the lawn, or killing a sentry, it was the same expression. There was a creak as his fist tightened around something. I now saw that the bloody thing in his hand was my kukri. Without a word he began low-crawling through the brush toward his target, moving like a ghost. Within seconds I lost sight of him.

Was this another trick? Had I been found by Dad's ghost, or had Asag taken another form to fool me again? What would he have to gain? Had the demon dug me up to give me hope, only to snatch it away? Even in this messed-up place I was pretty sure I wasn't dreaming. This seemed real.

There wasn't just one Asakku, but two, and these were actively patrolling, with muskets over their shoulders.

Then the one in back dropped. Its death was so clean and quiet that the one in the lead hadn't even noticed. A few seconds later that one got pulled behind a tree. There was a brief gurgle, and then silence.

It was brutally efficient. I hadn't just been dug up by my dad, but I'd been rescued by the Vietnam-era, snake-eating, jungle-commando version.

He didn't come back for what felt like forever. By the time he crawled up, scary quiet, I felt like my arms and legs might actually respond to my commands. Dad had been busy. He was covered in blood. Just like the bedtime stories he'd told us as kids, he had been *taking scalps*.

"You gonna walk, son, or do I have to carry you?"

We made it all the way to the river with me leaning on his shoulder before the Asakku realized a bunch of them had just gotten murdered, and they raised the alarm.

They were sure to track us. Running was out of the question. My legs weren't working very well at all. My balance was so shot that I couldn't stand on my own without falling over. No running meant fighting. Dad had my kukri. I had been surprised to learn I still had my pistol, because the roots had tethered my fingers to it, so I'd had it in my hand the whole time. Only it was empty. So I stuck it into a mud-filled cargo pocket, and hoped that this magical stasis bullshit would wear off before the Children got here to eat us, so I could at least go down fighting.

When the Asakku began shrieking, my dad stopped and looked back that way. "They'll catch up, but we've got a few minutes." He gently set me down on the grass. The river was a few feet away, wide and fast. "Can you talk yet?"

I tried, but failed miserably. I'd been coughing up dirt the whole way, so at least my airway was clear.

"Hang on." He went over to the river, then came back with his cupped hands full of water. He held the water to my lips and I choked some down. I never knew water could burn your throat. I tried to give him a thumbs-up.

He knelt next to me, looking exactly like the old photo Mom had given me in the hospital: confident, competent, and mean as hell. "You're still feeling the side effects of being imprisoned. It should wear off rapidly, but you're gonna be hurting for a while. Keeping you at the ragged edge between life and death is a hell of a strain."

My dad came back for me. If I could have cried, I probably would have. I tried to tell him thanks.

"You were right, son. Asag was top dog here, but as soon as he left, your mind started changing things. You've got more power than he thought. He thought you'd go insane or catatonic. You might not feel like it right now, but you're stronger than anything else here. You're dragging the exit closer and closer. Just follow the river and you'll get home."

I managed to gasp something that sounded like, *"How?"*

"How do I know? Or how am I here?" He grinned. His teeth were really white compared to his painted face. I think he was enjoying himself. "That's all on you. Listen, I know you're all emotional and shit right now, but here's the ugly truth that you already know deep down inside. I'm not going to pussyfoot around about it, because you know the real Auhangamea Pitt never would. The demon wasn't lying when he said he'd blocked ghosts from finding you. When you needed to survive, you thought back to the man who taught you how to survive."

I didn't understand, or maybe I did, though I really didn't want to.

"I'm not really here. I'm not your dad. You needed a way out, so you created one."

And when I left, he'd cease to exist. Again. I'd be killing him all over again.

"I know what you're thinking, but don't. You're wrong. The real me is just fine. Auhangamea Pitt got one hell of a life out of all that borrowed time. He loved one woman—a wonderful woman. He had two boys . . . and they grew up strong. You'll never understand how proud he was until you watch your own grow up. *If* you get to, because you know Asag wasn't lying about that either."

I nodded.

He tilted his head to the side and listened. "They're closing faster than I thought." He got up, walked over to a chunk of log, and picked it up. "Should be buoyant." He dragged it over and dropped it on my legs. "Hold onto this. Hold on like your life depends on it. No matter what, don't let go."

Coming out of my imagination or not, I tried to tell him thanks.

"You're welcome." He squatted down next to me again. "Now let me tell you something you don't know. Your real dad would have kept that promise to wait, but lying there in that hospital bed, he got offered a choice. He was given one last chance to help. They knew ghosts couldn't get through, sure, but maybe, just maybe, if it came from a ghost that cared hard enough, a little piece of one could reach you. Given that choice, Auhangamea Pitt didn't even hesitate. What snuck through, what you've got right here is just one small aspect of a great man. He sent the part that scared even him, the part that he kept locked up until it was needed. He wouldn't need it anymore where he was going."

My equilibrium was still too screwed up to walk carrying the log, so he stuck the tip of the kukri in the dirt, then dragged me down into the cold water. It was another shock to my already shocked system. He let go of me and went back to retrieve the knife. I began floating downstream.

"When you needed me, I was ready, and you gave me form. You asked for help. You got the Destroyer. So now I'm gonna go do what I was made to do."

I managed to croak the word, *"Kill."*

"Naw. My mission's always been to get everybody home that I could. The killing is just a happy bonus."

As I was carried away on the current, a horde of Asakku came rushing out of the trees. Muskets roared. Heavy bullets smacked into the river. The Destroyer nodded goodbye, and then went to work.

I watched him cut down a monster, shoot another with its musket, and then flip it around to use as a club to beat a third one's head in before the river took me out of sight.

The waters were very fast. I held on for dear life as the log careened off of rocks. My face was drenched in freezing spray. I kept getting sucked under, and then I'd pop back out, gasping, a moment later. I couldn't steer. All I could do was try to hit the oncoming rocks with something other than my head.

I think the cold violence of the river snapped me out of the magical lethargy. Either that, or it was the insane terror of body surfing rapids. My log was cracking and splintering from the impacts. I interlaced my fingers and hugged that thing like it was the most important relic in the history of the world. I would have married it if I could.

With every fiber of my being, all I wanted to do was get out. It was a good thing nobody could read my mind anymore, because right then I internally sounded like Dorothy. *There's no place like home. There's no place like home.* If I was really capable of warping this reality now, then I wished for this river's course to change so that it flowed directly into the portal. If I couldn't steer my log, I'd steer the whole damned river. I would have kept my fingers crossed, but that would have slightly loosened my grip on my log, so screw that.

The speed and intensity of the river continued to get worse. I kept getting sucked under. Logically, I'd learned this place would keep you alive even without air, but instinct is instinct. Each time my head was above water, the roar got louder. Or maybe the river had cleaned all the mud out of my ear canals. After one bounce, I came up sputtering and choking, but this time facing in the direction that I could see where I was going.

At first I cringed, thinking I was heading straight for a waterfall, but then I recognized the weirdly glowing fog around it and realized that the river was flowing directly into the portal.

I'd gotten my wish.

It wasn't a fall. It was a swirling drain. There wasn't even any time to dread what was going to happen next. It all went too fast. One second I was being dragged along, and then I was falling through a weird world of waves and purple mist. Directions quit making sense. And then I hit something really hard. My fingers popped and I lost hold of the log.

Submerged, still being pulled, I spiraled through the darkness.

And then I was rolling down a flight of stone stairs covered in a few feet of rushing water. It was the worst water slide ever. I hit every stair on the way down and then slid across the floor. I crashed into a cable, then struck a toppled construction light. The light was still working, casting bizarre shadows as every horrible thing that had been living in the Nightmare river swam by. I caught a metal bar and held on tight. I managed to get my head up to gasp in a lungful of air. Which was when it sank in that I was holding onto something real, made of steel, screws, and rubber-wrapped copper wire, which had been made by humans . . . On Earth!

A powerful light blinded me. "Over there! I got something." I could barely hear them over the water rushing by my face.

There were other lights pointing my way. I couldn't see a damned thing. I couldn't lift a hand to shield my eyes because I was worried I'd get swept away. One of the lights bobbed closer. From the way it was bouncing, it was coming from a headlamp. Somebody was fighting toward me through the deluge, probably attached to a safety line so he wouldn't get swept away to plummet over the edge into the City of Monsters.

"I think it's one of ours!" the closest one shouted. "It's Z!"

*Trip!*

"Tie that down. I'm going after him," he told some-one else. "Hold on, Z! I'm on the way." He made his way through the rushing water, repeatedly getting knocked off his feet, but always getting back up and fighting on. "Hang in there, buddy. I've got you." He landed next to me. I could hear the creak and twang of a cable attached to his armor. That was the only thing keeping him safe. He was risking his life for me. He fumbled with a D-ring, got a cord over my head and one arm, made sure it was snug before shouting, "Pull us back!"

Compared to my river run, getting dragged through this little bit of the City of Monsters was a piece of cake. Once the lights weren't shining directly in my eyes, I could see what was going on. The portal was still there, only it had turned into a massive fountain and a whole river's worth of water was exploding through, geysering high into the air before spilling in every direction. I couldn't even guess how many thousands of gallons were pumping through by the minute.

Come to think of it, if Asag really had assembled an army below the City of Monsters, I might have just drowned them. *Sweet.*

"I was starting to give up hope you were ever coming back!" Trip shouted in my ear.

"Me too."

There was a group of four Hunters gathered at the highest spot of the dais around the portal. It was the only thing that wasn't currently submerged. Judging by the flooded equipment sticking out of the water, they had set up a base camp right next to the portal. Tents were being washed away. Pieces of equipment had been turned over. When we got closer, a couple of other Hunters splashed down the steps, got hold of me and Trip, and helped us the rest of the way.

There was a diesel generator on the dais, so the lights up here were still on. I recognized most of the faces, but Trip was the only other American and member of MHI.

"Ha!" One of them was the Israeli, David Gerecht. "I told you I'd still be holding this place when you got back."

I sat on the stone, shivering. Somebody immediately dropped a dry blanket over my shoulders. Trip gave some orders, and the other three Hunters sprang into action, anchoring ropes so we could get out of here safely.

"This crazy flood started a few minutes ago." Trip had to shout to be heard over the super fountain. "We took cover up here."

"Sorry." My teeth were chattering. "Flood's my fault."

He laughed. "I kind of figured."

"Where's everybody else?"

"Outside. Last few days we've only been leaving one skeleton crew to monitor the gate, just in case. One of your team has been here around the clock always. We never gave up on you, man. Never. You cut it close, though. Once these guys clear a path, we can wade over to the main tunnel. I can't believe this. You're the last one. We can go home!" Trip looked triumphant. Apparently they had been eagerly awaiting this moment. Too bad I was about to ruin the mood.

"You got a radio? I need to talk to Earl fast."

"Zero comms since the storm started. It's causing some sort of interference."

I didn't know what storm he was talking about. "Have you seen Jason Lococo come through?" Trip shook his head in the negative. "Good. If you see him, *shoot him.*"

"VanZant said he was dead."

"He is. That's why you need to shoot him. VanZant made it?"

"Him and five others. That was about seventy hours ago."

No wonder I felt like crap. I'd been in the ground for nearly three days.

"They thought you had bought it. The expedition was already worn out. The tomb below was empty. We held out as long as we could, but once the survivors got back, Earl had to make a call. The siege is over, Z. Most of us have already left. The rest are breaking camp."

"Already? The plan was to hold this place for a month!"

Trip put one hand on my shoulder. "Z, buddy, I hate to be the one to break it to you, but you've been gone for six."

# CHAPTER 27

When Trip had mentioned a storm, he hadn't specified that it was a blizzard from hell.

The convoy out was a lot slower than the one I'd ridden in on because our trucks had been replaced with fat, lumbering, snow crawlers. They were basically big boxy cabins on tracks. There was no way our armored trucks could cross this place in the winter without getting stuck, but we weren't supposed to still be here in the thick of winter.

Outside the snow crawler's windows, it was a compete whiteout. Howling winds were driving the snow sideways. Everybody who'd been drenched at the portal had dried off and changed clothes before going outside, otherwise we would've frozen to death in the time it took to make it to the vehicles.

"How the shit is it winter already?" I asked through chattering teeth.

"It's been winter for months. Just be glad this piece of crap has a good heater." Trip tried the radio again. "Come in, *Bride*. This is Skeleton Crew. We've retrieved the last MIA and we are all returning to base. The site is abandoned. Over." He waited, frowning, but got nothing but static in return.

There were five Hunters in the crawler. Most of them had their guns ready and were watching out the windows for threats except for Dr. Boris, who had been waiting at the crawlers, and who'd been poking, prodding, and shining lights in my eyes ever since. He was currently checking my blood pressure. He'd not said hardly a word to me, but then when he got done reading the gauge on the cuff around my arm, he turned to Trip. "He's in awful shape, but he's human all right. Not another doppelganger."

When he said that, the Hunters who'd had their weapons ready relaxed a bit. They hadn't just been worried about monsters out in the snow, but rather monsters hiding among them. "Guessing you guys have had a problem with those?"

"You have no idea," Boris muttered as he removed the Velcro cuff. He handed me a protein bar. "Now eat something before you die. Slowly. Doctor's orders."

I put my borrowed parka back on, then started cramming what tasted like compressed plywood dust into my mouth. It was the best meal ever. "Oh, thank you, thank you." I was going to eat this thing and then pass out.

"If you start to puke like the others, at least have the decency to hang your head out the window first. Those men will all be fine by the way. They're recovering at the *Bride*. Gretchen made them soup."

I would commit all sorts of terrible acts for a bowl of Gretchen's foul-tasting healing soup right now. "How's Julie? Have you guys heard anything from Julie?"

"Not for a few days...Oh man, you don't know." Trip grinned. "Congratulations, Dad."

It was a lot to take in, and I had a million questions, but only one thing really mattered right then. "Are they safe? Did anybody try to kidnap the baby?"

"What? No. Last I heard they're just fine. Your little dude is adorable. And since you weren't around to argue over the name, it's Raymond Auhangamea Pitt. You know how the Shacklefords are about tradition and all their Raymonds. Julie won't let Earl call him Little Bubba."

I closed my eyes and breathed a sigh of relief. *That lying trickster bastard had been screwing with my head.* Everything was going to be okay. We just had to make it home. There were only two other crawlers behind us. It was a far cry from the impressive convoy I'd ridden in on, and we didn't have any air support either. "Are we safe to make it across with just this?"

"You missed a lot, man. We've been busy," Trip explained. "There's nothing left to fight. We killed pretty much everything."

"It was epic," Boris added helpfully.

"Except once Krasnov ran out of bodies to turn in, there was no payments to skim, so the authorities started getting anxious." Gerecht said. Somehow the guy from a country in the desert had wound up driving a snow crawler, but he seemed to be doing okay at it. "Krasnov just went back to Moscow to beg for more time. Good thing you showed up when you did because they're probably going to evict us soon."

"Evict or bomb. That part's up in the air still, but either way, we've gotta go."

*We won.* I couldn't believe it. We hadn't killed Asag, but we had beaten the City of Monsters, and pulled off the wildest rescue mission ever. *We had won.*

Then the earth split open beneath us and our snow crawler tumbled into the dark.

There was blood and snow on my face. The crawler was on its side. The other Hunters were lying still, covered in broken glass. It smelled like gasoline and dust. My ears were ringing from the impact. There was a body across my knees, pinning me down. I was too dizzy to move. The white storm was above us. Everything around us was black. We'd crashed into a tunnel. Slowly sound began coming back. I heard groans and coughing, the creaking of metal, and the crunch of glass beneath boots.

Whoever was walking around stopped right in front of me. It took a moment for my eyes to adjust to the shadows.

"I didn't expect to see you here," Asag said, still using Lococo's voice, still wearing his face. "I truly don't know how you managed to escape. An unexpected turn. Uncertainty used against me? It's a thing of beauty."

Someone's rifle had landed nearby. I reached for it, but an invisible hoof stepped on my hand. I shouted as Asag's demonic bodyguard ground my fingers against the metal.

"Stop, just stop, Owen. We don't have much time. These will wake soon, or the ones above will come down to rescue you, and then I'll have to slaughter them all. You should have stayed buried. Now I either have to kill you—and have to learn about an all-new champion before the final battle—or break you once and for all."

"You're supposed to be this big force of uncertainty; flip a coin, asshole."

"Leaving the fate of millions up to pure chance?" An

evil smile split his face. *"I love it."* He was still wearing the tattered jacket, covered in now-frozen leaves, and from an interior pocket he produced his MHI challenge coin. "They buried Jason with this. Harbinger gave it to him. It meant a lot to him, a symbol of a fresh start."

The Hunter on top of my legs was still breathing. Out of the corner of my eye I saw that his coat had fallen open, revealing a holstered pistol.

Asag held up the coin and showed me the Happy Face. "Heads you live. Tails you die."

"Do it."

He tossed the coin into the air, tracking it upwards with his one eye.

I hoped even the invisible demon prince would be momentarily curious enough to watch the result, so I went for the holstered gun with my left hand. I ripped the Sig P320 from the holster, lined up the sights on Asag's chest—hoping this unknown Hunter didn't do something stupid like carry chamber empty—and pulled the trigger.

*CRACK CRACK*. Two to the body. *CRACK*. One to the head.

The coin landed.

"Master!" The red demon became visible as he violently swatted the pistol from my hand.

But he was too late. Lococo's head was thrown back. He stayed that way for a few seconds, shuddering, as if he was staring up at the storm. Slowly, Asag took a halting step toward me, revealing a splatter of bloody brain chunks stuck to the wall of the crawler. He faced me and dropped to his knees. There were two red holes over his heart and the last bullet had disappeared into the black hole consuming half his face.

Asag twitched as he struggled to hold on just a bit longer. Blood spilled from his mouth. "I liked possessing this body. Now it's ruined. I'll have to find another."

I'd failed Jason, but at least I could make sure he was finally laid to rest. "You didn't deserve this one."

The red demon lifted his claws to rip my throat out, but Asag shouted, "Wait!" The creature stopped. Asag pointed one shaking hand at the coin.

It had come up heads.

*I win.*

"Let him live. He'll wish for death soon enough."

The monstrous prince didn't like it, but he obeyed his master. Claws retracted back into his fingers. The weighty hoof lifted from my fingers. Cringing, I brought my injured hand to my chest.

"I promised to see you at the end of the world, Owen. I'm looking forward to it very much." Asag's stolen body was obviously dying, but he crawled toward me, over the unconscious Hunter, until he leaned in close and whispered into my ear, "And when we meet there, just remember that I am the one who stole your child."

The body collapsed on top of me as the ancient spirit fled. The back of his skull had been split wide open. Snowflakes fell in the hole.

Only the red devil remained. "It's your lucky day, human."

I suspected that Asag had been telling the truth about my son. I didn't feel lucky.

The prince leaned over and picked up the coin. There was blood all over it. "Monster Hunter International . . . If only I had known what a thorn you would eventually become." He looked with disgust at the unconscious

Hunters around him. "My greatest regret is that when I killed Bubba Shackleford, I did not eradicate his entire bloodline when I had the chance." Then he vanished, leaving behind smoke and the stink of sulfur.

Twenty hours later, a hundred Hunters from a dozen companies and three species stood on the rocking deck of the *Bride,* beneath the northern lights, watching the distant shadow that was Severny Island.

The sky was made up of brilliant green and purple streaks. My dad had stared up at these same lights when he'd died the first time. I could only hope that he was up there, watching over us now. I needed to be as strong as he had tried to make me for what was coming next.

Earl Harbinger walked up and stopped at the railing beside me.

"Any word from home?"

"Nothing yet. They're still trying."

I could only nod. The expedition had been cut off from the outside world for several days. First it had been the super storm, and then, once it passed, the Russian Navy had been jamming our signals. Last we'd heard from the other teams, the army had escorted everybody else to the airfield at gunpoint and forced them on flights out of the country. After our crashed snow crawler had gotten dug out, all the remaining Hunters on the island had been evacuated to the *Bride.* The military had let an icebreaker get us off the beach and cut a path to open sea, but other than a brief warning about what was about to happen, nobody would talk to us, the radios were still blocked, and we couldn't even get a satellite signal. Apparently we had worn out our welcome.

"I should be there for them, Earl."

"But you aren't, because you were saving the lives of six good men."

"I couldn't save them all."

"You never can, kid. You never can . . . We lost people, but we derailed a plot to destroy the world. We broke a super monster's stronghold and set his plans back years."

"Will that be enough, though?"

"You never know, until it's not."

I was just so weary. "This enemy isn't what we expected, Earl. Not at all. He's a force of nature, but this is all a game to him. The more things break down, the more they fall apart, the more he wins. Even fighting him feeds him. I'm not sure how we survive this one."

"We'll figure it out because that's all we can do. First things first. The minute I'm sure they won't shoot him down, Skippy can get you to the mainland. Then you're going to hop on a jet back to Alabama." He reached over and rested one hand on my shoulder. "Don't worry. I'm sure they're fine. Because come on, can you imagine what Julie would do to anybody stupid enough to mess with her family?"

Night briefly turned to day as a nuclear bomb detonated inside the City of Monsters.

"Good riddance," I whispered.

Our expedition had cleaned the place out, but the city would rebuild. More monsters would move in. Until it was excised, it would remain a perpetual, festering source of evil. Supposedly, this time they'd dropped a ground-penetrating bunker buster directly on top of the gate to close it once and for all.

"Well, now that the world knows about their *weapons test*, maybe they'll quit blocking our calls." Earl paused to light his cigarette. "Bunch of ingrates."

The Hunters watched in silence as the shadow of the mushroom cloud rose. Then most of them began to cheer, because to hell with that place.

*Hang on, Julie. I'm on the way home.*

# EPILOGUE

A card table and two folding chairs had been set in the center of the warehouse. Two men sat across from each other, one mustached and fat, the other unnaturally pale and thin. Their respective bodyguards hung back a polite distance.

"Did you get it?" Stricken asked.

"Do you have my money?"

Stricken hoisted a duffle bag off the floor. He made a show of it being heavy and dropped it on the table so it would make a satisfying thump. It was all about the presentation. Then he unzipped it so the Russian could see all the cash inside. "I'm a man of my word. Now it's your turn, Mr. Krasnov."

The Hunter looked to the side and nodded. One of his men approached carrying a plain cardboard box, about three feet long, six inches wide, and six inches tall.

"You stuck an ancient unholy relic of absolute destruction in a cardboard box. That's like carrying the Mona Lisa around in a shit-encrusted wheelbarrow."

Krasnov shrugged. "Had to put it in something."

The thug placed the box in front of his boss, then hurried off like Stricken was a ghost. So they still told scary stories about him here ... *Good*.

Stricken was almost giddy with excitement. His plans were coming together. Only Krasnov didn't immediately open the box to show Stricken the prize, nor did he reach for the money. He hoped the mobster hadn't gotten cold feet, because slaughtering all of these Russians would be a pain in his ass and he was still hoping to catch the symphony tonight. Moscow had a pretty good one.

"We had a deal, Krasnov."

"Some of my men died getting this. They would be ashamed to know who for. Unicorn has done much evil. I would not like it if this thing was used against people ... most especially other Hunters."

Krasnov had been a lot more amenable to the idea of stealing this when Stricken had first approached him, so he must have become fond of his rivals during their long expedition. Fighting side by side did that to most. Loyalty was a far more complicated motivator to deal with than simple greed, so Stricken cut to the chase. "Spare me the sanctimonious bullshit, Ivan. I do what needs to be done. Period. Nobody else on your little expedition knows I held back one page of the Petrov Report from everybody but you. Your men were the only ones who could access the secret chamber in Gorod Chudovish. None of the others ever has to know, and if they ever hear a legend about the existence of this thing, they'll assume it just got melted in a nuclear fire. I've already paid you a significant advance to retrieve that item for me. So hand it over before things get complicated."

"That does not answer me. What will you do with it?"

"Whatever I damned well feel like." Stricken just stared at him through his oddly tinted glasses, daring him to argue. Krasnov was beginning to sweat. "You didn't try to use it, did you?"

"I'm not a fool, Stricken. A device of such nature is not for man. It corrupts all it touches."

"That's loser talk. Beneath that city you got a little glimpse of what's coming. You can't beat that with bullets or bombs. It's time to fight fire with fire . . . But look, if it makes you feel any better, I only intend to use that thing to succeed where all of you Hunters failed. I'm gunning up for big game."

"Take that foulness and get it out of my country." Krasnov snatched the bag of money off the table and stomped away. The bodyguards followed.

Stricken waited until they had left the warehouse before opening the box to examine his prize. It was beautiful. "Now *I* am become death . . . Oppenheimer ain't got nothing on me."

He began to giggle.

# THE FORGOTTEN WARRIOR SAGA

***Son of the Black Sword***
9781476781570 • $9.99 US/$12.99 CAN

***House of Assassins***
9781982124458 • $8.99 US/$11.99 CAN

***Destroyer of Worlds***
9781982125462 • $8.99 US/$11.99 CAN

# THE GRIMNOIR CHRONICLES

***Hard Magic***
9781451638240 • $8.99 US/$11.99 CAN.

***Spellbound***
9781451638592 • $8.99 US/$11.99 CAN.

***Warbound***
9781476736525 • $7.99 US/$9.99 CAN

# MILITARY ADVENTURE
with Mike Kupari

***Dead Six***
9781451637588 • $7.99 US/$9.99 CAN

***Alliance of Shadows***
9781481482912 • $7.99 US/$10.99 CAN

***Invisible Wars***
9781481484336 • $18.00 US/$25.00 CAN

**BEOWULF'S CHILDREN** (with Larry Niven & Steven Barnes)
TPB: 978-1-9821-2442-7 • $16.00 US / $22.00 CAN

**STARBORN & GODSONS** (with Larry Niven & Steven Barnes)
HC: 978-1-9821-2448-9 • $25.00 US / $34.00 CAN

---

## THE JANISSARIES SERIES

Some days it just didn't pay to be a soldier. Captain Rick Galloway and his men had been talked into volunteering for a dangerous mission only to be ruthlessly abandoned when faceless CIA higher-ups pulled the plug on the operation. They were cut off in hostile teritory, with local troops and their Cuban "advisors" rapidly closing in. And then the alien spaceship landed . . .

### LORD OF JANISSARIES
(with Roland J. Green)
TPB: 978-1-4767-8079-5 • $15.00 US / $20.00 CAN

### MAMELUKES
(with contributions by David Weber & Phillip Pournelle)
The long-awaited culmination of the Janissaries series!
HC: 978-1-9821-2462-5 • $25.00 US / $34.00 CAN

---

## AND DON'T MISS

### EXILE—AND GLORY
HC: 978-1-4165-5563-6 • $23.00 US / $26.99 CAN
PB: 978-1-4391-3293-7 • $7.99 US / $9.50 CAN

### FIRES OF FREEDOM
PB: 978-1-4391-3374-3 • $7.99 US / $9.99 CAN

A NEW URBAN FANTASY FROM

# A.C. HASKINS

### The Most Dangerous Weapon Is a Past Scorned . . .

Thomas Quinn, a former Sorcerer of the Arcanum, is haunted by the deeds he's done to defend the human world from djinns, demigods, and dragons. Now retired, he wants nothing more than to run his occult shop and find solace in his books and his whiskey. But when a ritual murder rocks his city, he re-joins the Arcanum in hopes of making peace between the human world and the magical world. He's prepared to combat rogue sorcerers and magical monsters—but is he prepared to face his own demons?

# BLOOD AND WHISPERS

PB: 978-1-9821-2523-3
$16.00 US/$22.00 CAN

# TIM POWERS

"Other writers tell tales of magic in the twentieth century, but no one does it like Powers."
—*The Orlando Sentinel*

## FORCED PERSPECTIVES
HC: 978-1-9821-2440-3 • $25.00 US / $34.00 CAN
PB: 978-1-9821-2525-7 • $8.99 US / $11.99 CAN
*Sebastian Vickery and Ingrid Castine are chased by ghosts and gurus as they rush to save Los Angeles from a god-birthing ritual.*

## DOWN AND OUT IN PURGATORY
PB: 978-1-4814-8374-2 • $7.99 US / $10.99 CAN
*Tales of science fiction and metaphysics from master of the trade Tim Powers, with an introduction by David Drake.*

## EXPIRATION DATE
TPB: 978-1-4814-8330-8 • $16.00 US / $22.00 CAN
PB: 978-1-4814-8408-4 • $7.99 US / $10.99 CAN
*When young Kootie comes to possess the ghost of Thomas Edison, every faction in Los Angeles' supernatural underbelly rushes to capture—or kill—boy and ghost.*

## EARTHQUAKE WEATHER
TPB: 978-1-4814-8351-3 • $16.00 US / $22.00 CAN
PB: 978-1-9821-2439-7 • $8.99 US / $11.99 CAN
*Amongst ghosts and beside a man chased by a god, Janis Plumtree and the many personalities sharing her mind must resurrect the King of the West.*